Advance Praise for *Adam Unrehearsed*

"*Adam Unrehearsed* will shake your soul. It's comical. It's lyrical. It's menacing. It's gritty. It's tender. And it rings true. Futterman's novel returns us to that moment in our lives when we begin to try to grasp the seemingly ungraspable adult world. It brilliantly captures the shifting sands of boyhood friendships, sibling adulation, and the confusion that marks even the best intentions of mentors and students. This is a sure-handed debut, compassionate and propulsive. It nudges up against today and reaches back to the past where our betrayals and alliances infinitely lie."

–**Colum McCann**, author of *Let the Great World Spin* (National Book Award for Fiction), *TransAtlantic,* and *Apeirogon* (National Jewish Book Award for Fiction, longlisted for the Booker Prize)

"Don Futterman has written a classic. This hilarious, deeply moving, beautifully written novel brilliantly captures the atmosphere and the angst of Jewish New York of the early 1970s. *Adam Unrehearsed* is an American Jewish coming of age story, whose twelve-year-old protagonist struggles to understand his relationship to the Holocaust, the Soviet Jewry protest movement and black-Jewish tensions, while navigating the torments of junior high school and his impending bar mitzvah. The portrayal of young Adam's inner life, and his emerging Jewish identity, is one of the best I've read in contemporary American Jewish fiction."

–**Yossi Klein Halevi**, senior fellow at the Shalom Hartman Institute and author of *Like Dreamers* (winner of the Jewish Book Council's Everett Family Foundation Book of the Year award)

"Don Futterman is a master storyteller. In this gripping, moving, coming-of-age novel, Futterman bravely explores the often-unspoken boundaries children growing up in multicultural environments learn to navigate instinctively. With a sharp eye and a pitch-perfect ear, Futterman deftly brings those of us who grew up in Queens right back to that rich, complex, world—without forgetting those who would find that time and place unfamiliar. Most important of all, this must-read is a fun-read."

–**Professor Gil Troy**, author of
The Age of Clinton and *The Zionist Ideas*

ADAM
UNRE
HEAR
SED

ADAM UNRE HEAR SED

A Novel

DON FUTTERMAN

WICKED SON

A WICKED SON BOOK
An Imprint of Post Hill Press
ISBN: 978-1-63758-901-4
ISBN (eBook): 978-1-63758-902-1

Adam Unrehearsed
© 2023 by Don Futterman
All Rights Reserved

Cover Design by Jim Villaflores

Post Hill Press
New York • Nashville
WickedSonBooks.com

Published in the United States of America
1 2 3 4 5 6 7 8 9 10

For Shira, my first reader, first in my heart.

CHAPTER 1

M
r. Beck informed the seventh-grade Two-Year SP class that they would no longer be coddled. Elementary school was behind them, and he was going to make their brains burst. Like his classmates, Adam had never had a male teacher before, and Mr. Beck was fierce.

Adam's new school was on triple shift, squeezing 1,800 junior high students into a building built for less than half that number—the result of citywide budget cuts and miserable district planning. The school song for JHS 189 touted the number of the school rather than its actual name—the bureaucratic mentality made verse.

Adam skittered through the crowds in the endless dimly lit halls to find his next class during the three-minute breaks. These strangers had no idea that Adam Miller had been student organization president of PS 24 less than nine weeks before, that he had made a speech at graduation, or that his family had moved over the summer while he was away at camp, where, much to his own astonishment, he had a girlfriend.

"Listen, you SP brainiacs. You are goddamned lucky to be born in this part of the twentieth century, because we are going to conquer space in your lifetime. That's if we can convince those fools in Washington not to cut NASA's budget so they can help the poor, as if the poor would ever see a dime from that money. You with me? Dammit, you're not."

Mr. Beck wiped the sweat from his rubbery features, transferring his perspiration in one swipe to his pants leg. Adam Miller was thrilled to overhear the thoughts of an adult, of a teacher, but most of the class had no idea what Mr. Beck was talking about, instantly wrong-footed by their own—apparently inexcusable—ignorance.

Mr. Beck turned to the blackboard, chalk held high, poised to begin, but then stopped to face them again.

"You'll be here only two years, but listen up: this is the opposite of a free ride. You're going to work harder than anyone else in this building. Science is politics, science is life. Science is the future!" Mr. Beck roared. "Here we go."

Adam was revved up, ready to love science and head into space.

But this momentum quickly dissipated during the rest of the day. Size-placing had positioned Adam in the first row throughout elementary school, but seating was random in junior high. The teachers used charts, with student names inscribed in boxes representing their assigned places. Adam had to make his own chart to remember where to sit from one class to the next. He was learning the teachers, but they weren't learning him. They never heard his voice.

Outside class, Adam felt lost in time and space as he tried to grasp the layout of this new maze. The main building was a long and rectangular box of red bricks, together forming a single colossal brick. The brick had two centers—the lunchroom and the auditorium—but there was no center to his day. One forty-two-minute lesson followed another in a dozen different subjects and just as many rooms, as chaotic as Adam's loose-leaf binder struggling to contain it all, the lick-on reinforcements clinging to the pages to keep them between the subject dividers.

The gymnasium was in a separate space-age capsule, bathroom-tiled in bright teal and with metal latticework around the windows that suggested prison bars, designed to keep thieves out, and in general, to ward off invasion. There was a massive schoolyard outside, but no basketball courts, no handball walls, no fountains, no benches, no monkey bars, nothing that invited any sort of organized fun. And nothing separated the yard from the streets of Flushing except an eight-foot-high chain-link fence. The ninth-grade boys had beards and smoked; the ninth-grade girls wore makeup and smoked.

In the third week, Mr. Beck was teaching about energy, and Adam decided to open his mouth no matter what.

"Name the different forms of energy."

Adam had no clue.

"Electricity," volunteered the tall Korean girl, Elizabeth Kim.

"Excellent answer!" boomed Mr. Beck. He wrote it on the board in a sloppy cursive that sloped precipitously downhill and that could not have been more different than the rounded letters and ruler-straight lines of Adam's elementary schoolmarms.

"Magnetism," offered Peter Hahn, the smartest kid in the class.

"Magnetism is cor-*rect*!" Mr. Beck announced, scribbling the word below electricity.

"Heat," jumped in Valerie Caruso, an Italian girl whose purple eyes made Adam twitch.

"Absolutely right!"

Aha! Adam's hand shot up.

"Adam Miller," Mr. Beck called, matching his location with his box chart.

"Cold," Adam offered, breathless already, his eardrums pounding.

"Wrong!" Mr. Beck accused. "Cold is not a form of energy. Cold is the absence of heat."

Stupid stupid stupid stupid! How could I say something that I wasn't absolutely sure was correct?

"Class, remember that!" Mr. Beck went on. "Energy is electricity and heat is energy, but…"

Stupid stupid stupid.

"Cold is the absence of energy! And energy is everything."

Stupid cold. Not everything. Absence of everything…smart.

"The stuff we are made of, the mass of our bodies, us—that stuff can be converted into energy. Energy is stuff times the speed of light times the speed of light. Einstein figured that out, and we made the atomic bomb and won goddamned World War Two. And Einstein wasn't in the Two-Year SP."

Stupid cold stupid Einstein stupid Two-Year SP. Cold equals absence of energy.

"Listen to me good. You are the best and the brightest in this school. Science must be your vocation because science is our future!"

The best and the brightest! They were gifted and also kept separate from the rest of the school, except for gym, where they were most vulnerable. Their accelerated program would clear space in New York's overcrowded schools while sparing them the superfluous eighth-grade curriculum.

"We cured polio because of science! We landed on the moon because of science!"

Yes. Adam had talked about the moon landing on the PA system as GO president at PS 24 before he was cold and stupid.

"You don't want to end up as a garbageman."

No, Adam didn't, but didn't Mr. Beck know that Ryan's father *was* a garbageman? Ryan's face zapped down to his desk.

Of course Mr. Beck didn't know. Ryan was a name in a box. And now he was the stupid kid crying in science class sitting in front of the stupid kid who thought cold was a form of energy who would never be a scientist.

"What the hell's the matter with him?"

Adam was desperate to explain, but he had spoken enough for one day. Everybody from PS 24 knew exactly why Ryan was sobbing, but nobody was going to say it.

"You're going to have to toughen up if you're going to survive here," Mr. Beck warned them.

Toughen up?

Mr. Beck was right about that.

There was a war going on in the corridors between a black gang and rival white gangs. Busloads of students arrived from the South Bronx every day, most of them black, supposedly to be integrated into the school. But in practice, they were shunted into the Opportunity Classes—the OC—to mingle with a few local underachievers.

The Italians called the blacks the N-word, a word outlawed in Adam's house on pain of a literal mouthwash with bar soap. The blacks called the Italians the G-word and the W-word, insults Adam had never heard before, either separately or together.

On the same floor as the lunchroom, there was a black bathroom and an Italian bathroom—the *hitters'* bathroom—each one off-limits to anybody else without an escort, except during the occasional hiatus when Mr. Vogel would clear the smokers out of the bathrooms and the toilets would be up for grabs for twenty minutes. There was no Jewish bathroom or Japanese bathroom or Chinese bathroom or Korean bathroom. In desperation, Adam sometimes waded through the smoke into the Italian bathroom, preferably with Ryan—Ryan was Italian despite his Irish moniker—or, in an emergency, on his own. At worst he'd get bumped into a wall or sink. The black bathroom absolutely required Curtis or Derek, but they were not in the SP and Adam only saw them in gym class. Kevin Mathis was in the SP, but he was not from PS 24 and Adam had only just met him.

The kids from the Bronx panhandled during lunch, usually asking for "a dime, spare change for me," but sometimes reaching for your pockets, which made the first weeks hair-raising. Adam got smart fast—*sorry, man, no money*—pivoting to the brown paper bag holding his daily salami sandwich wrapped in aluminum foil, and his perennial dessert, a Red Delicious apple (never a McIntosh). Adam pitied Dennis, who forked over change day after day under no greater threat than a glower. He'd seen boys like Dennis have their lunch money taken by force in the hallway.

Time to toughen up indeed.

"Oh for crying out loud," Mr. Beck said to Ryan in front of the class, after Takashi Moto whispered the truth to him. "Don't take it personally, kid. It was only a goddamned metaphor."

Except it wasn't. Adam's parents were teachers, and his father had been a principal for a year before the teachers' strike and his voluntary demotion, and that was still better than being a garbageman. They all knew that.

CHAPTER 2

They were at Yankee Stadium on Bat Day, on their own, all the way from Flushing.

It was summer. Transistor radios were blasting, hot dogs boiling, the heat so ferociously thick and humid that Adam hummed the melody of "Raindrops Keep Fallin' on My Head" to keep himself cool until it was his turn at the ticket window.

"No grown-up, no bats," the man mumbled from his cage, answering a question Adam hadn't asked. His sideburns ran so far down, his face was behind bars. He pointed to a huge sign: *Bats given to the first 10,000 guests 14 and under, accompanied by an adult.* He slid the ticket envelope across the counter.

"Them's the rules. Next."

It was the first foray of Adam's bar mitzvah year, and he was about to strike out.

Why had he insisted on going to the Yankees game on his own? "I'm a Yankee fan," he'd declared, rejecting his father's plea that they watch the Mets at Shea instead of taking on the wilds of the Bronx. "Nothing will happen."

Adam had to fix this and quickly. He needed an adult, any adult. He stepped back from the booth, examined the entrance line, trying to locate a man who could pass for his father, their father, the father of any one of the four boys.

"What are you doing?" asked Jason Boyer, Adam's best friend.

Adam pointed at the sign.

"Holy shit!" Jason said.

"This sucks," agreed Stu.

"Yeah," said Dennis, attempting to be agreeable with no idea what he was agreeing to.

Stu was Jason's buddy, a second-string friend whom Adam rarely met on his own. Poor Dennis was nobody's pal. He had asked to join the pilgrimage to Yankee Stadium at the bar mitzvah orientation. Adam had been standing next to his mother at the time—since she'd joined the Sisterhood, she practically lived at Temple Gates of Hope—and her maternal glare made it clear Adam could not say no. Jason had not forgiven Adam for tainting their trip with an interloper, especially one Jason had dubbed "a weaselly chickenshit."

Adam spotted a family of blond humans, twins and dad with sun-bleached hair and Sinclair dinosaur hats leftover from the 1964–65 World's Fair. But when the twins noticed Adam giving them the once-over, they slinked away.

Behind them was a Puerto Rican family, taking pictures of themselves holding a Mickey Mantle bobblehead with their Polaroid camera. Also. Not. Them.

A man with a leisure suit. Maybe. But a leisure suit at a baseball game?

"You kids need tickets?"

The scalper looked like two spherical blobs, beach-ball head and medicine-ball belly, both drooping, dripping insanely with sweat. He wore a Yankee hat that was far too small for his head.

"Twelve bucks," he said. "Field box."

"No, thank you," Adam replied curtly. He clutched his own field-level tickets inside a fist buried as deeply in his pocket as it was possible to dig. Four dollars each.

"You selling?" he asked. "I'll give ya two bucks apiece."

"Not selling," Adam snarled, calculating the scalper's profit margin, but then Adam turned nice. "Hey, how about if you take us in?"

Adam pointed at the sign.

"Deal," he said. "Ten bucks."

"Two," Adam offered.

The scalper laughed.

"I'll take you in," said a voice behind the boys. Old, gaunt, red-faced, stubbled-cheekbones threatening to emerge through the skin, beer breath—but he was offering.

"All right, five bucks," the scalper countered.

"For free," said Grizzle. "Come on, boys."

"Thanks," Adam said. "Deal's off," he told the scalper.

There were two crewcuts behind the turnstile, chewing toothpicks, one taking tickets, the other dragging bats out of long cardboard boxes stacked on their sides. Adam could feel in the rectitude of his middle-class bones that they were not going to hand over their lumber.

Grizzle said, "Give me your tickets."

Adam hesitated. *Grizzle didn't look fast, but suppose he wanted to steal their tickets and run away, or claim they were his, or work some scam Adam couldn't imagine?*

Adam's father would palm a five-dollar bill and shake hands with Mr. Bats, but Adam dared not risk such an adult move. Of course, if his father had been there, they wouldn't be having this problem. The tickets were handed over and handed over again.

The bat man counted out four bats. The ticket-taker grouped the tickets together to rip off the stubs, when he noticed that Grizzle had a bleacher seat. Mr. Turnstile put his hand up. "How come you're not sitting together?"

Grizzle worked his mouth several different ways, but no words came out. The bat man shifted the bats away from the boys.

"You're embarrassing my grandfather," Jason rallied.

"That's not your grandfather," Dennis said. Stu punched him so hard, Dennis moaned.

Grizzle found his voice. "They're good kids."

Looks were exchanged among the three men, and the decision was made silently at altitude. They handed over the bats.

"No trouble, boys."

They were practiced in reassuring authority, and all four *Yessir'ed* with vigor. They had no plans to take a swing at anybody.

"How about a drink, lads?" Grizzle asked, once inside.

"Sure," Adam answered, not knowing exactly what Grizzle meant.

"A beer costs a dollar fifty," Stu explained, privy to knowledge that eluded the others. They fished in their pockets, but Dennis didn't move, so Adam put in enough to cover Dennis. They were relieved when Grizzle left them.

Emerging from the gray concrete tunnel, they saw the field—the endless green, the giant, leaping blue sky. The air was different inside Yankee Stadium, crisp and electric and clear. Adam felt like jumping but settled for going up on his toes a few times, and then sang "The Star-Spangled Banner" with such vigor Jason and Stu laughed at him.

At last, the game began. When a Yankee made contact, all four boys popped out of their seats like the morning toast, and whenever the ball dropped in safely, their voices joined the transcendent roar. They stopped every concessionaire. Adam, Jason, and Stu downed two hot dogs each, along with Cracker Jacks, Coca-Cola and ice cream. Not until they finished the ice cream did Adam ask Dennis why he wasn't eating.

"My stomach hurts," Dennis mumbled.

Not likely, Adam thought, cursing himself for not having noticed sooner. Adam drew on the emergency fiver his father had stuck in his bus pass case and bought two bags of peanuts. Dennis devoured his like a starving man.

But the Yankees went comatose, striking out on awkward swings and falling one run behind. Dennis insisted the Yankees would be eliminated from Series contention by mid-September. He was right, of course, the numbers proved it, *but why was he talking?*

Jason gave Dennis a murderous look, then expanded the glower to include Adam, just as Thurman Munson hit a foul ball two inches over Dennis's head, as if Munson could also hear and wanted to silence Dennis for good. Adam wished he had brought his glove. A Munson memento—*wow!* That would have been something.

To shut him up, Adam offered to teach Dennis how to keep score, which Dennis took to compulsively. Stu proclaimed that "scoring is a total waste of time," since it had no impact on the game. Adam decided to avoid an argument and focused instead on supervising Dennis filling in his scorecard, a detailed record that would allow them to relive the game in detail at home. (Adam kept his small stack in his closet, although he never looked at the scorecards again.)

That's when Adam discovered that Dennis had never been to a baseball game, that his parents were Holocaust survivors and knew nothing of baseball. *No wonder no extra money. How would they know they sell food at a baseball game?* This terrible deprivation made Adam soften toward Dennis while also seeming to confirm Jason's worst suspicions.

As the bottom of the ninth loomed, the majestic voice of Bob Sheppard ordered them to "Stand up and cheer for your 1970 New York Yankees! Let's see those bats!" The boys waved theirs wildly at the TV cameras, flaunting their weapons like cavemen. This revived them and must have also revived the team, because Horace Clarke walked—*"a walk's as good as hit..."*—passing the bat to Bobby Murcer. When Murcer smacked a two-run home run to win the game, forty thousand people flew out of their seats and raised their cheers to the heavens.

"Did you see that?" Adam screamed.

"Did you see that?" his friends echoed.

Adam had seen it all right, tracking the ball cleanly from the loud crack until it landed in the left-field bleachers. The boys bounced up and down as the stands emptied around them, slapping each other five, reliving the home run again and again, glorying in the astonishing fact of their presence to witness this comeback.

The boys headed to Flushing with chests as full as their stomachs. Adam's heart was beating against his ribs, his body thrumming inside and out. Every passenger was adorned with pinstripes or caps with the entwined *N* and *Y*, flying high from the victory. Adam whispered to Dennis that he would give him the scorecard as a present—they had each completed half—when Jason and Stu were not looking.

At Grand Central, they switched to the Flushing-bound 7 train, snagging the last seats as they downshifted from raucous Yankees boosters to weekenders completing their Manhattan Sunday on the local. The subway screech reached a crescendo, metallic yelps became shrieks as the train ground to a noisy stop between stations. The very slight breeze from the open windows vanished. A raspy delay announcement made the obvious official, and a groan rose as engines were shut down and their car became a sweatbox.

Exhilaration gave way to exhaustion as their voices dried up. Cigarette smoke choked their throats, as if drifting out of the ads for Lucky Strikes in the fitted glass cases. Adam tried to distract himself by deciphering the brush strokes of graffiti swirling over the walls, benches, ceiling, and windows. The train finally jerked into motion, and the boys stared silently at the route line, counting down the twenty stops until Main Street Flushing.

And then Jason told a joke that made Dennis laugh so hard snot flew out of his nostrils, hitting a man standing near them on his left buttock, where it stuck. They boys could not look at the snot, the buttock, or each other, in pain from trying to suppress the laughter. The cramps in Adam's cheek muscles exploded just as the 7 stopped at Queensborough Plaza.

Twenty teenagers rushed into the car at once, taking it over, commandeering the standing space, knocking into each other with wild joy.

"Check this out!" one of them yelled, grabbing the silver pole with one hand and flinging his body around at high speed. Another did pull-ups from the leather straps, banging into seated passengers, puncturing their newspaper shields, daring them to complain. A child dropped the *Daily News* comics section on the floor but was afraid to retrieve it. One of the teenagers snatched it up and read two panels of *Dondi* out loud before losing interest. He crumpled it up and dropped the wad on the kid's lap.

The last gasps of Adam's laughter attracted their attention, and when they moved in a pack toward Adam and his friends, they squeezed out their joy like a dying tube of toothpaste. They were older, years older, giants, black. They acted friendly, a pose, obvious even to Dennis, or perhaps most obvious to Dennis, his fear sensors so finely attuned. Adam was already afraid, wished his father had come, or his brother, wished his black friends had joined them—Curtis and Derek were both tall, and if they had been with them, Adam thought, they would have somehow, magically, redirected this gang away. He had seen such threats diverted before—on buses, in Kissena Park—but he didn't understand how it worked, couldn't do it without them.

The gang forced the boys to make room so they could sit between them, separating Adam from Jason, Adam from Dennis. Adam tried to make eye contact with the adults seated nearby, trusting them instinctively, but the grown-ups hid behind their tabloids, fished for objects in their shopping bags.

Stu played it cool: "Yeah, we went to the game, no big deal, Yankees won." Dennis prattled that we were in a bar mitzvah group together. *Idiot*, Adam thought, advertising that they were Jewish. Jason's thin lips disappeared.

"Lemme see that," one of them ordered, motioning toward Adam's bat. Adam hesitated, imagined comic book heroics—*SMACK! KRAK!*—but there were so many of them, and how could he hit a person?

Adam handed his bat over, Jason and Stu followed, Dennis conceding last, as if he'd also had some thought of protecting himself but didn't know how.

The bats were passed from one teenager to another. Adam hoped that cooperation would appease them, encourage them to turn their attention elsewhere. But having sized up their victims and relieved them of their weapons, the friendly flirting ended.

A jumpy youth put his face up to Adam's. Adam's black friends were growing Afros, but this boy's hair was shaved close to his head, so Adam guessed he must have crazy strict parents. The bags under his eyes were deep-set creases, crevices. Adam felt his breath, heard his mumbling. It took a while until Adam could make out the words, words he was repeating over and over.

"Jew-ball bastard," he muttered, "Jew-ball bastard."

Adam wasn't sure he'd heard it right. Adam concentrated on the boy's mouth. There it was, coming at him, "*Jew-ball bastard*," the volume increasing as he moved his head closer. Adam knew anti-Semitic slurs like Hymie and kike, but he'd never heard one spoken aloud and never this odd version.

"What'd you say?" Adam asked, shock exceeding his fear.

"Jew-ball bastard," he said a little louder, as if those were the only words he knew in the English language. It wasn't clear if this was in answer to Adam's question or simply the next beat of his steady hum. Adam couldn't know that the words meant little to the youth, they were simply a melody to him, a refrain triggered by Dennis, by "synagogue." Just another word connected to Jews that he knew little about.

The gang's leader had cutoff sleeves. He grabbed Adam's scorecard, plucked out the insert—nine innings of careful documentation on two pages of card stock. Adam peeped "Hey!" at the same time as Dennis, already sharing ownership and mourning their loss. The leader ripped the scorecard into small pieces while his two friends placed their arms across Adam's chest to keep him from lunging for it.

Their Yankee victory swept the subway floor.

Sleeveless signaled Adam to stand while Jew-ball breathed his mantra into Adam's ear. They led Adam out of the car, two more joining the escort, through the cowering riders and across the gangplank, a rush of hot wind, putrid outside air, and into the next car. The car was empty, the last car always left empty now, as passengers sought safety in numbers.

Adam braced himself. He had wrestled frequently with his brother but knew nothing about street fighting. It didn't take long. Jew-ball struck Adam in the mouth. Adam tasted blood.

"Shut the fuck up," Jew-ball said. It was so startling that Adam swallowed his objection that he hadn't said a thing. Jew-ball seemed angry that Adam was thinking.

"*Jew-ball bastard*," the teen hummed as he went through Adam's pockets. Adam had been drilled from age zero to give muggers whatever money he had, a standard survival tactic in New York City. *Money can be replaced. All that matters is that you don't get hurt.*

Jew-ball took out Adam's bus pass, as Adam watched him remove each of the four dollars left from his emergency reserves. They escorted Adam back across the bridge in the clattering outdoor heat. The sun, the blood, the fear, the shock. They weaved through the standing passengers and returned Adam to his seat between two jeering goons.

Adam was dazed. The grown-up world had abandoned him. Mortified and furious, he felt irreparably severed from the rules he knew.

He watched his friends disappear one by one for the shakedown in the next car. He couldn't help seeing the tears on Jason's cheeks when he returned, and when Jason turned away from Adam, Adam turned away as well.

They would be rougher with Dennis. He wore glasses, radiated vulnerability, anxiety loss, tragedy. *Hit me*, Dennis's very being seemed to say.

"I can't get hurt," Dennis hissed.

Adam imagined Dennis's parents with their refugee clothing and thick accents, not knowing what a baseball game was, teaching Dennis to be scared of everything and everyone. They would probably never let Dennis leave the house again. Maybe they were right to be afraid.

Adam stood up. "Leave him alone!"

Jew-ball pulled Adam down harshly, angry at himself for having relaxed his guard. He pressed something into Adam's side. *A switchblade? Maybe.* Adam knew nothing about knives. Adam wanted to punch Jew-ball in the face. He wouldn't have minded just then if someone had killed him.

And then someone did step forward. A man pushed two of the teens aside and took their spot in the middle of the car. He was thickset, a wide face with a prominent, square chin, dressed in a black suit, a white shirt but no tie. He had a black hat, pushed back, the antithesis of debonair.

"What you are doing to those kids?!!" he yelled in a thick accent.

Yelled? His voice was a sonic boom, like he had a bullhorn in his throat. The man pulled Dennis free, shoving him back to his seat as Dennis yelped in fear.

The gang laughed at him. The man turned to the other passengers, but they found their Sunday sections and purses, searched the floor for gum.

The gang leader told the man to "Get the fuck off this train." But at the next stop, the man positioned himself in the doorway, letting the doors bang into him and rebound open.

"POLICE!" his grand voice rang out, tolling over the hisses and creaks of the subway. "COME NOW!"

Grating gutturals from the subway speakers: "Stand clear glahglahglahglah."

The doors did an impotent stutter step, the rubber bumpers striking the man, sliding open again. The doors could not close, and the train could not move.

A standoff.

The passengers grumbled, irritated. Adam hated these appallingly passive adults, but who would want to take on the gang? Or the man in black?

A transit policeman appeared at last in the car. Their defender stepped inside, and the doors snapped shut in satisfaction. The train started moving.

"What you are waiting for?" the avenger blared. "Arrest the hooligan robbers!"

The transit cop considered his options, studying the man, glancing at Adam and the boys or out the window, but not at the gang. Finally, the officer turned to the leader of the gang, and said, "Are you bothering these kids?"

"Got no business with you."

"They take them in the next car, first one, then another one," screamed the man. "They take money. They tear up book! That book belong to that boy."

He pointed at Adam. Scraps of scorecard were dispersed across half the car, the cover sucked against the crack in the door opposite.

The officer looked at Adam too.

"That your book?"

"Yes, sir," Adam said. "It was."

The officer's cheek was pulsing.

"You ought to clean that up before you get off the train."

What?

Adam felt his stomach shrivel into his groin.

The redeemer became irate. "Why you do nothing? You man or chicken?"

The other passengers abandoned their pose of indifference at last, watched the transit cop chewing his lips, waiting to see what he would do. Just as the doors began to close, the transit cop jumped backward onto the platform, brushing the door edge, but not enough to trigger the open mechanism. The subway rumbled on without him.

"Chickenshit!" Sleeveless howled, his pals jeered him on, the gang a single organism, rippling with mockery and bravado.

Adam couldn't move, couldn't breathe.

"Police not do nothing but I WILL NOT ALLOW!" roared their protector. The snickering stopped. This man had crossed a threshold of crazy, all veins and popping eyeballs. He made the gang members nervous, made Sleeveless nervous. He made *Adam* nervous.

"What they take? Tell me!"

Jason, Stu, Adam stayed silent. Dennis chomped the words in his mouth like gum, but never blew a bubble. He cleaned his glasses, cleaned them again. Adam wanted to hit Dennis himself.

"They take your book?" the avenger said to Adam.

"Yes," Adam said. He felt pressure from his side.

"Money?"

Money can be replaced. Give them your money.

"We didn't take no money."

"That's a lie." It was out of Adam's mouth before his brain could calculate the odds.

"You give back money."

"Fuck you, old man!"

Three of them came closer, emboldened by the F-word. Adam had a feeling he didn't recognize—that he no longer cared what would happen to him. He wouldn't be back at Yankee Stadium for a long time anyway, and he knew what he wanted now.

"Those are our bats," Adam said.

It was as if the man grew in size, in volume. His legs spread and his voiced filled the entire car.

"GIVE BATS BACK NOW!"

With that blast, every cowardly tiny shivering shriveling soul in the subway car lifted their faces to the guardian. Adam stopped breathing. The train turned a corner, threw everyone sideways, screeched so awfully Adam felt it in his teeth.

Instead of closing in to smash the man, to shatter his black suit into blood and bone, they meekly handed over the bats. The four boys said thanks, politeness bred into their bones, and didn't try to smash their skulls.

"Stay back!" the man ordered the gang. "Back! We getting off. You stand there!"

The train pulled into 111th Street. The doors opened with a deep sigh, as if the 7 had also had enough.

Adam squeezed the handle of his bat with all his strength as he pulled away from Jew-ball, slipped under their protector's arm, making him his shield. Stu, Dennis, and Jason moved to Adam's side.

"Good," the man said, once they were standing on the platform and the train rumbled on. "You get bats." He put his arm on Adam's shoulder.

"We should have fought them," Stu said. "If my brothers were here…"

If our brothers, our tall friends, our black friends, our fathers…

"Our money…" Jason blurted out.

"I knew it!" the man exploded, "they do steal your money!"

Adam pretended he was not in tears. He wished their guardian angel would take him to his parents, would disappear, would make it not real.

On the next train, they rode in silence to Willets Point-Shea Stadium, where Mets fans filled the car. Adam scanned the new passengers for their assailants, but they didn't appear. They'd probably hopped the return train to Queensborough Plaza to find new victims. The man rode to the end of line with the boys, followed them up the stairs to Main Street.

"Which one be Roosevelt Avenue?"

He said it Roosie-velt, which made Stu crack up, but Adam was not able to laugh yet, nor were Jason or Dennis.

"You're on it," Adam said, and pointed. He knew the street well. Temple Gates of Hope was three blocks away.

"You are safe," the man declared. "They not coming back. Goodbye. Good luck." He headed off, a bull strapped into a black suit.

Dennis rushed for a pay phone, called his parents, reported his entire disastrous day, making his anxious parents terrified. As soon as he hung up, he started running home without another word. Stu and Jason headed off to Carlyle Towers, the apartment complex across from Adam's old house.

Stupid Dennis going off like that, they could have taken the bus together. Adam's stomach flipped each time he saw a black teenager. Not him. Not them. Revenge fantasies abounded.

He was ashamed to tell his parents what had happened, but Adam was strangely silent for a post-Yankees victory and eventually the story came out. His parents briefly considered calling the police but concluded that would be a meaningless exercise. Adam's father said they were right to have moved to a safer neighborhood, a side comment meant for Mrs. Miller, which made Adam jerk.

This had nothing to do with where we live. This happened on the subway in the city.

His parents moved off the sore subject, both extolling the stranger.

"Did you ask his name?"

"No." *But that man was crazy*, Adam thought. And then, finally, he told them he had lost his four dollars. Even with the stranger's help, he couldn't get it back. Adam began to cry.

"It's just money. We can replace it. We can replace it right now. You didn't get hurt, that's what's important."

Why? Why is that what's important?

Mr. Miller handed Adam a fresh five-dollar bill.

"It was only four dollars," Adam mumbled.

"Take it. Keep it with your bus pass."

Adam's mouth didn't sting, but hadn't he been hurt? It wasn't the money that caused the hole inside him.

Adam didn't tell them about *Jew-ball bastard*. The phrase echoed in his mind long into the night. Bastard was clear enough—but what was a *Jew-ball*? A ball made out of Jews? A ball Jews played with?

Adam didn't know that for Jew-ball, whom Adam would never see again, taking Adam's pocket money and dignity was the least dangerous thing he would do all week, that belowground crime was exploding, that the city had given up on keeping subways clean or safe, that nothing and no one could untangle the weird dance of solidarity and resentment and condescension and anger between blacks and Jews and whites in New York City in 1970, and that for Jew-ball, it was just a melody.

CHAPTER 3

Hebrew School was Adam's alternate universe. Adam was the Hebrew School Hebrew expert thanks to his summers in Camp Ramah, where the rule was *No Hebrew—no potatoes.* His Hebrew School teachers adored him, but it was hard to rally much enthusiasm. Each year was like the last, as they relearned Jewish holiday basics and the letters of the Hebrew alphabet and were taught fascinating expressions like "I walk," "I sit," "I talk," stuck in a perpetual loop of *Introduction to What You Forgot Since Last Year.* Some of Adam's classmates, like his best friend Jason, couldn't master Hebrew's vowel notation—a single dot or line, a triangle of three dots, or a tiny *T* tucked under or over the letters—showing how to pronounce the string of Hebrew consonants that could otherwise go any which way. Adam was the master speed-reader of the *siddur*, able to rapidly declaim pages of prayers from the prayerbook without making a mistake (or understanding a thing).

But the gritty classrooms, warped chalkboards with eraser-resistant streaks, the ancient wood and metal flip-top desks, the chiseled horizontal creases for writing implements and the holes for ink jars, long since distant anachronisms, all proved one thing: *Hebrew School didn't count.* So Adam's stardom had little currency and none among the kids.

Saturday morning services completed the task of eviscerating the weekend, and few of his public school friends took part. Still, Adam enjoyed being a junior cantor at Junior Congregation. He had a high voice and an extremely limited musical range, but he knew exactly when to start and finish each prayer, and he loved being on the sanctuary stage, making evenly spaced rows of boys and girls launch into song in unison. He adored the old synagogue, its cavernous high-church sanctuary, long mahogany pews, massively tiered chandelier, and perpetually locked balcony of mystery. It was Old Europe in Flushing, a sense reinforced by the Junior Congregation maestro, Mr. Rockowitz, who carried his Yiddish accent from Poland and wore the same loose-fitting, dark brown, and increasingly shiny suit every Shabbat morning.

Adults had their own services in the new Temple Gates of Hope building around the corner, an airy glass and steel complex with spring-loaded cushioned seats, softened only by its floor-to-ceiling panels of modernist stained-glass windows. Adam preferred the antique and mysterious edifice to that airport of tomorrow.

For five years, Adam and Jason had walked to Hebrew School together three times a week: Monday and Wednesday afternoons after PS 24 and Sunday mornings. On weekdays, they would stop at the Cove Luncheonette for egg creams on the spinning stools at the counter, invariably dawdle too long, and have to run the last four blocks to arrive on time.

Now they lived miles apart and came to Temple Gates of Hope from opposite directions. In an effort to revive their chit-chat, Adam offered to walk the extra distance past Hebrew School to meet Jason at the Cove for egg creams—Adam's treat. Their Bat Day disaster nipped at Adam like an irritating dog, but he didn't bring it up. If anything, Adam worried that his permanent relocation to the farthest end of Flushing might tip their friendship off its axis, institutionalizing Adam's annual disappearance to summer camp. Adam could not find the right segue to his bigger revelation—his summer camp fumble with Sharon on the bus to Bear Mountain—before Jason burst in with news of his own.

"I'm going to be a brother again," the excitement or the anxiety making Jason's voice flutter. At first Adam thought Jason meant that their friendship had not been smashed by Adam moving away or by Bat Day, but then he understood Jason was telling him his mother was pregnant. Most kids missed Jason's sweet side altogether because of his cutting jokes, and Adam was touched Jason had shared the news with him. Adam had neither the desire nor the option of becoming a big brother—his mom was older, already in her forties. He would pass on this update to her and then forget about it. The two moms were phone friendly if not exactly friends.

Adam had always liked Mrs. Boyer. Jason's mother was not glamorous like Peter's, nor a nagging chimney like Buddy's mother, a cigarette glued into the corner of her mouth, but glossy and clean like a shampoo commercial, with a Laura Petrie flip to her hair that defied gravity. She always sent Adam home with care packages—large plastic bags of home-baked cookies, which Adam would partake of as he went down in the elevator and crossed the street to his house—*"no more than two or three!"*—his mom's strict rule, so *three* it was. She would deposit the remainder in the freezer, where they'd languish forgotten until they were randomly rediscovered.

Unlike Adam's mother, Mrs. Boyer did not work, but Mr. Boyer had the best job in the world: he printed DC Comics. Each month, weeks before they went on sale, he brought Jason two sets of the latest editions—one for Jason, another for Adam. Adam's older brother Seth was addicted to Marvel, a sign of his "greater maturity," and dismissed Mr. Boyer's magical supply line, but Adam loved *The Flash*—Adam ran fast and imagined himself to be like mercury.

Jason took five comics from inside his notebook and handed them to Adam.

"The *Justice League* is the best one. Check it out, 'Millennium.' I'll wait."

Adam read the entire issue while Jason watched, until Adam gave his verdict.

"'Earth-Two' is fantastic. I wish they drew today's Flash with his silver helmet like in the Golden Age."

"Imagine, Mills, if there was another version of you."

"That would be so cool. A good you and a super you."

"A good you and an evil you."

This reignited their old argument about whether *Invasion of the Body Snatchers* or *Invaders from Mars* was the best sci-fi movie ever. In *Body Snatchers*, Kevin McCarthy and his girlfriend are the last ones to realize that giant pods growing in the fields are forming robotic repli-cants who replace the townspeople while they sleep. The only defense is to remain perpetually awake, leading to the moment when Kevin McCarthy's girlfriend encourages him to take a nap, and he realizes a) she's been podified, and b) he's alone!

Jason lobbied for *Invaders from Mars* with its similar plot: A boy sees a flying saucer land in his backyard, sends dad to investigate, dad comes back talking in a lobotomized monotone. The takeover contin-ues until the army is called in. Jason loved the soldiers blasting alien creatures to bits, but Adam found the cardboard characters and lack of moralizing irredeemably inferior.

Adam always played the same ace. "At the end of *Invaders from Mars*, you find out it's all a dream! That sucks!"

"It *does* suck," Jason agreed, and laughed his little nasal screech, which made Adam happy.

"Imagine if our parents weren't really our parents," Adam hypoth-esized.

"You'd know in a minute if your real parents were gone."

"Oh shit, it's four o'clock."

They were fifteen minutes late for Hebrew School. To evade their prowling principal, Mr. Beiner, they used their secret entrance—a ground-floor window that did not lock properly from the inside and led behind the Junior Congregation sanctuary stage. A passageway connected the old synagogue to the Hebrew School building next door.

But today they didn't have to jimmy the window open because it had been smashed. *A baseball from kids playing in the parking lot*, Adam thought at first, but the windows on either side had also been broken. The boys were careful to dislodge the jagged shards still embedded in the wooden frame as they climbed through. Adam's foot landed on something, which made him topple over. When his hand hit the ground, it was cut by the glass lying on the floor.

"Damn!"

Adam wiped the blood on his shirt. He had tripped on a brick. The boys found three red bricks lying on the floor, surrounded by splinters and slivers of glass of various sizes.

"Wow! This was on purpose," Adam declared. "We have to tell Mr. Beiner,"

"'Beinerbrain will think we broke the windows to sneak in.'"

Adam laughed. Jason had nicknames for everyone, and his fertile mind would generate new ones in every conversation.

"You go ahead," Adam suggested. Adam knew Jason was irritated by all things Temple. "I'll wait a couple of minutes and then I'll tell Beiner I saw something suspicious. I'll meet you in class."

"You sure?" Jason asked.

"He likes me."

"Milleria, they all do."

Mr. Beiner seemed to know about the secret entrance, which surprised Adam, and did not interrogate Adam about what he'd been doing at the rear of the old building. He surveyed the crime scene for several minutes, his face contorting as he debated what to do. At last, he handed Adam one of the bricks and sent him to show it to the rabbi. "But don't say a word to anyone else. Especially not the Greens. Do you understand?"

The Greens were the office secretaries, Mrs. Greene and Miss Greenberg, devoted to the rabbi's uninterrupted tranquility. Adam had to skulk with his brick for a long time until they both looked away in tandem.

Rabbi Arthur Ellenbaum was intimidating, with his stentorian, scholarly way of speaking, his gaze both distant and penetrating, his thick hair with a touch of silver that glinted off his steel glasses with authority. Unlike Mr. Rockowitz, he didn't look religious except for his small knitted kippah. His private study was in the corridor of the new building, across from the glass-walled office of his gatekeepers.

Adam knocked rapid-fire on Rabbi Ellenbaum's oak door, hoping he wouldn't hear, wouldn't be there, that he wouldn't have to face him, that the secretaries wouldn't spot him. The door opened just as Miss Greenberg rose behind the glass to intercept Adam.

"You're holding a brick and you're covered in blood. Are you building a bookshelf or starting an insurrection?"

"Umm…"

"Come in, come in. Take this." He handed Adam the handkerchief from his jacket pocket. "Apply continuous pressure, and after you tell me what's what, you'll go to the restroom and wash it thoroughly in the sink."

"Yes, sir. I'm Adam Miller."

"I know who you are, Adam. Your parents are old friends."

They are?

Adam sputtered out his report.

"More bad news." Rabbi Ellenbaum let out a pained sigh. "Let me walk you back to class, but first the bathroom."

After Adam rinsed his wound, they went to inspect the broken windows. The rabbi poked his head with care through the shattered glass, laid the brick down outside, then led Adam around to the front entrance. "Let me handle this, Adam, and I'm going to have to ask you not to say anything about this to your friends."

"Jason was with me. We found it together."

"Jason?"

"Boyer."

"Boyer? All right. Thank you. Not a word to anyone else, though."

"Right."

The rabbi rarely entered the old Hebrew School building, so the class was rattled when he strolled in with Adam.

"Where were you?" mouthed Jason, as the others snapped to attention, secreting comic books and spitballs inside their desks, the teacher leaping out of his seat so fast his kippah fell on the floor. He picked it up, kissed the yarmulke, decided he need not have kissed it, dropped it again, picked it up again without kissing it, and clipped it to the hairs covering his bald spot. Adam expected Rabbi Ellenbaum to explain about the broken windows, warn them to report suspicious strangers, and wondered if he was going to give Adam credit for reporting the incident. But he was wrong on all counts.

The rabbi's news was that Mr. Rockowitz, the head of Junior Congregation, would be out sick for several months and could not prepare them for their bar mitzvahs. The new cantor would take over training the bar mitzvah boys immediately. He would teach them to sing the haftarah, the extra passage from the biblical books of the prophets that they would perform on their big day. The bar mitzvah boys were ordered to accompany Rabbi Ellenbaum around the corner to the new synagogue. Adam remembered his brother Seth's bar mitzvah as the grand event of his childhood and was eager to equal him.

Rabbi Ellenbaum quietly asked Adam to walk with him, ahead of the small pack. He looked straight ahead but gave Adam his charge.

"The bricks you found today could be nothing—vandalism, most likely. But some people don't like the fact that we have taken over Parsons Boulevard with our new synagogue. It's too early to tell if they are run-of-the-mill anti-Semites or something more ominous. Please remember. Don't talk about this incident to anyone but your parents. We don't want to cause a panic. Can I count on you?"

Adam gulped twice.

There are run-of-the-mill anti-Semites in Flushing?

"Yes, sir."

"Very good. And pass the word on to your friend…Joseph?"

"Jason Boyer?"

"Right. Boyer. Tell him to keep mum."

"I will."

"Good. Go back to your friends."

His classmates grilled Adam for information. "What'd he say? Are you in trouble?"

"Nothing," Adam insisted. "Nothing important."

Rabbi Ellenbaum left the entourage on their own to wait for the cantor in the banquet hall, a refurbished all-purpose room outfitted with a soundproof folding door hidden by velvet curtains and newly installed ceiling molding in inexplicable swirling patterns designed to suggest elegance. Adam had never seen this vast empty space naked, lit only by fluorescents, absent banquet tables, food, frills, music, or lighting. The bar mitzvah group hugged the walls and marked time making jokes quietly.

"Boys!" a voice boomed, as a bullish figure strode to the center of the room directly under the chandelier. "Why you are standing there? Chairs! Now!"

It was him! *The crazy man from the train!*

He didn't recognize Adam, or if he did, he gave no sign. But Adam was sure he was the avenger of justice who had faced down the gang, saved his bat, and exposed their helplessness. Adam wanted to share his astonishment with Jason, but Jason—his hopes that there would be no bar mitzvah lesson crushed—had fallen into a sulk.

Could it be a different man with the same wardrobe—white shirt, black suit, and hat, but with a tie?

"We will start already," the Cantor ordered. "I not going to stay all night. Boys. I have to go home to Brooklyn, a long trip."

How far was Brooklyn?

They dragged a stack of all-purpose chairs to the center of the ballroom and formed a tight circle, so close they could not hide behind their books or pretend they couldn't hear. There was so much air between them and the grand ballroom ceiling that their voices receded before they took a breath.

Don't you remember us?

The words jostled in Adam's mouth but wouldn't come out.

They droned together, chanting the blessings Mr. Rockowitz had taught them.

"This sound terrible," the Cantor told them. "We will do it again till you sound like alive people and not sickening dogs that got ran over already by a truck."

Adam laughed, but Jason snickered, having determined the Cantor was a fool. *Was he a fool? Perhaps Jason had seen through him, or worse, maybe the Cantor was not trying to be funny.*

The Cantor led the way, as each boy lagged a quarter-note further behind, scheming to hide his voice in the blend. But the Cantor caught on. They sang again, then one more time, and again.

"Now we sing solo."

Every boy fell apart in his own way.

Adam's Hebrew pronunciation was perfect, but lacking confidence, comprehension, and breath, he went flat at the end of each line. Jamie Karsh—legendary for lighting a Hebrew School teacher's hair on fire while singing the Hanukkah blessings—was incapable of not mangling any Hebrew word he read. Adam had recruited Karsh to his football team because he was built like an offensive tackle (he played on both sides of the ball), and the Cantor instantly liked him, brothers in body type.

Albert Feigenbaum was an excessively tall redhead, whose inability to hide in a crowd was matched only by his timidity. Albert could not get his voice out of his mouth.

"Ho-ho! Up there!" the Cantor chided. "I don't hear no sound."

Albert cleared his throat until a high-pitched flute peeped out.

"Oh. Nice bird. You will sing pretty. Next."

Robbie Roif started off-key, stayed off-key, and croaked more or less like a frog.

Martin Kohn brayed.

"A Co-hen who can't sing," the Cantor stated flatly.

"It's Kohn," Martin corrected, emphasizing the single syllable.

"Kohn, Cohen, same thing, boychik. You don't hide from me."

Jason couldn't do it, couldn't get started.

"What's wrong?" the Cantor barked. "You nervous? You got to sing anyhow."

Jason glared. He closed his prayer book.

"You don't close *siddur* on me!" roared the Cantor, a quick temper. "This is bar mitzvah class."

Jason reopened his *siddur* and searched for the page, held his face close to hide his red anger, almost kissing the print.

"You got nothing to be nervous from, boychik," the Cantor softened. "You can't sing no worse than Roif or read no worse than Karsh." He'd caught their names fast.

Adam was girding himself to launch the question that would save the day, *Remember us from the train?* But before he risked it, Jason said, "I don't want to sing."

"I don't want to teach you. But I got to, and you got to."

Jason made noises, clearing his throat. He took some breaths, but he couldn't get any sound to come out.

"You sing with me this time," the Cantor said. "Next time by yourself. One, two, three…"

And the Cantor sang, with his full-bodied operatic tenor, and Jason hummed along, barely a whisper, until they finished the blessing together.

"That stink," the Cantor said, "but no worse than nobody else. Listen, boys, next week you do better—or else."

Or else what?

The minute they were outside the building, Adam grabbed Jason. "It's him! The guy from the train! We got a crazy man teaching us bar mitzvah lessons!"

"No way."

"Didn't you recognize him?"

"I hate this guy. And it's not him."

Jason's insistence made Adam doubt himself. Although there wasn't really any question.

"He's all right," Adam disagreed, just to be disagreeable. Jason's confidence could be exasperating.

"Look how he talks," Jason proclaimed. "And the way he dresses."

Adam took strange accents and obsolete clothing as a given inside the Temple but agreed that they were embarrassing out in the real world. Adam didn't like fighting with Jason—*Was his memory broken? Was he ashamed of having cried? It wasn't his fault, any of their faults. And why hadn't the Cantor mentioned the incident on the train? Was it possible he hadn't recognized the boys, that he'd forgotten already? Or might the Cantor have been embarrassed about his own reckless, insanely courageous loss of control?*

Adam diverted Jason to the even more disagreeable topic of their bar mitzvah parties.

Jason's party would be at Leonard's, the bar mitzvah factory in Great Neck. Mr. Miller would someday be synagogue president, so it was understood that Adam's reception would take place in the shul's banquet hall right after services, with the full Sabbath restrictions—no Las Vegas razzmatazz, no music, no candle-lighting, no photography. The Millers were against ostentation by nature and principle, and Adam would have been happy if his party was over in a blink. No band meant no dancing, and no dancing meant summer camp Sharon would not discover Adam couldn't dance. In lieu of the music, Adam's parents had booked a ventriloquist. Jason and Adam wound themselves into hysterics inventing titles for his act, their favorite being "Stanley Grabber and his dummy, Dick the Shmuck (*not their real names*)."

Jason turned sour again. "My mother wants me to have a bar mitzvah, but I hate this place." Jason had no choice, of course, as the Cantor had said, just as Adam had no choice.

But unlike Jason, Adam wanted to sing the haftarah perfectly. As a junior cantor, he'd learned he was the community's messenger, and this one time in his life, Adam would be standing in front of the adults, representing them, leading them, his parents, his brother, all his relatives, his friends from school, Hebrew School and summer camp, the rabbi, the Cantor, the community. Rabbi Ellenbaum would say what he was supposed to say about reaching manhood, and nothing would be different in Adam's life the day after the bar mitzvah, but Adam was determined to be a perfect messenger and to put on a great show.

CHAPTER 4

Jeremy Miller's stomach flipped each time he thought of Bat Day. *How could have I let him go* to *Yankee Stadium? Suppose he'd been killed?*

The police needed to set the limits when it came to real violence, but the cops had evaporated, *pop! pop! pop!* abandoning subway riders to fend for themselves. The city was out of control.

The boy got scared. That's all.

Helen wasn't home, but she didn't need to be in the room for Jeremy to hear her measured rebuke.

He got hit, Jeremy!

He didn't die.

That's not nothing.

I didn't say it was nothing.

Sometimes their lines were reversed, because clearly, the argument could go either way.

What Jeremy wouldn't admit to his wife was that he wanted to punch his son's attackers in the face, break their bones, watch their blood pour out, and throw them under the train.

No, that was too much.

Jeremy had spent his career in inner-city schools in the Bronx, then Queens. Jeremy was known for wrangling appearances from authors at his high school so his charges would understand there were human beings behind the books they were asked to grapple with. But he worked his real magic below the radar, in the early morning hours. When he figured out that so many of his students were failing because they couldn't read at grade level, he started showing up at 7 a.m. to tutor them before classes began, ostensibly to jumpstart their understanding of the textbook, but really to help them stop reading one word at a time. Reading in stutter-step was so exasperating—and embarrassing—they'd lose the meaning before they reached the end of the sentence.

Jeremy had finished one year as principal back in the Bronx when things went to hell and the strike tore the city apart. He stepped down in what proved a pointless gesture of goodwill—*of futility!* Helen would correct, *you sacrificed yourself for nothing!*—to try to help resolve the strike.

Jeremy could picture former students who might very well be terrorizing subway commuters for sport, which was inexcusable, but… but…but…*goddammit,* no one believed in those kids, no one told them things would be all right and replaced the four dollars in their wallets. And they *were* kids, despite their knives and hoodlum posturing. Jeremy knew their stories, knew their *parents'* stories, and they could break your heart. The families evicted, the brother doing drugs, dealing drugs, the homeless kids, fathers in prison, the drinking, car thefts, gangs of course, heart attacks, diabetes getting no care, the dead children, so much preventable misery, and then all those beleaguered single mothers and four-square families trying to blow a bubble of safety around their kids, which offered just about as much protection as a bubble. Expectations always rock-bottom. "They're all like that… At least in school, they're safe…"

But we're not safe, his wife chided, in absentia.

Jeremy had been a wrestling champion in high school. He could protect himself, but yes, Jeremy had gotten stitches after being attacked by three students in the hallway of his own school. Jeremy was warned to let it blow over by district officials, bigger problems brewing, the union wouldn't be in his corner. Jeremy didn't call in the cops, wouldn't have considered it unless there was a repeated pattern of wrongdoing, because he knew what kind of justice the system offered these kids. But he wanted his faculty—and himself—protected by clear boundaries, consistent policy consistently imposed, formal school probation. A second chance—which was crucial—could only work if coupled with setting limits. But goddammit, almost nobody wanted to hear a nuanced argument, preferring instead to scream and slam their phones down and throw tables over.

Jeremy operated under a triage system. If there was at least *one* caring parent in the picture who showed up for parent-teacher conferences and parents' assemblies, who pulled their kids away from petty crime and gangs—the student's chances of success were increased by 100 percent.

Parents, after all, had organized the *protected zone* for Jeremy's car, for all the faculty cars arriving from Queens, Long Island, Westchester, and Manhattan, a single block of vehicles untouched at the end of each school day. Those parents knew—and Jeremy Miller knew—his team of teachers was their kids' single best hope to break out of ghetto gangs and nowhere futures.

Would the other teachers have been more forgiving; would they have recognized themselves—or perhaps their thick-skinned fight-all-comers immigrant parents—if these kids had been white? Or were they too worn down, too frightened to locate the youthful spark in these teens, the spark that had made them teachers? (Even Helen was teetering.)

But then again, when somebody attacked Adam, his own kid, Jeremy Miller was ready to go to war.

CHAPTER 5

Mr. Selenko told the SP students not to take their seats because they could not stay in the classroom to do the work required. They paraded haphazardly after their drama teacher down the empty corridor of 189, hushing their own rowdiness in the eerie class-time quiet. Mr. Selenko stopped suddenly, withdrew a large ring of keys from his pocket, and unlocked the metal entrance to what looked like a supply closet, the door battleship gray, drips and blobs of paint solidified along its edges.

"Enter."

They stepped into the shadows to find a large room, cluttered with ladders, rolls of brown paper, corrugated aluminum garbage pails. Alan Silver came last, and as the door shut behind him with a crash, they lost the hallway light, all at once inside the anti-urban true darkness never achieved in windowed classrooms. It was like the nighttime inky black of the backyard of Adam's new private house, blocked from the streetlights by the high hedges and the house itself, and so unlike his old, much smaller row house. The students bumped together. Pushing, grumbling, giggling.

Mr. Selenko flicked a lighter, the flame reflecting off his face, jumping with his features. Tall and angular, his features geometric, Mr. Selenko's puppet head perched atop his high black turtleneck. The only male teacher to have abandoned jackets and ties, Mr. Selenko radiated cool.

"Light," Mr. Selenko said.

Was he going to smoke a cigarette in front of them? Their voices receded, all eyes drawn to him. He didn't say anything more for a long time. Adam watched the flame, a tiny campfire around Selenko's nose and thick eyebrows and brush mustache, black lines rearranging themselves in quick cuts.

The lighter flicked off.

"Darkness."

Silence. No shoving, breathing paused.

"Follow me, quietly."

They stuttered forward in the blackness.

"Gracie," Selenko said.

Gracie took the lighter from his hand and they set off after the flicker as it retreated into the distance. "No," Mr. Selenko corrected. "Follow me," leading them away from Gracie's little flame.

One spotlight went on.

They were on a stage.

Adam felt himself shrink in the vastness of the dark auditorium. Mr. Selenko moved them down to center stage, took a knee, as if he were their football coach.

"Please face me," he said softly. "You're all actors now."

"We're kids," countered Buddy.

Chuckles and snorts followed. Adam recognized Jason's rat-tat-tat laugh.

Adam caught Mr. Selenko's slight twitch, sensed him calculating quickly, deciding to head off another derisive joke.

"And some of our finest started acting as kids. Mickey Rooney, Shirley Temple, Elizabeth Taylor—"

The Partridge Family, Adam thought, cranking up his nerve to speak.

"The Partridge Family," said Naoko.

"Yes, the Partridge Family too."

But the Partridge Family is made up.

"That's made up," said Jason, thinking in sync with Adam, "not a real family, right?"

"Right," Adam said with confidence, to echo Jason. He wasn't sure, but a sit-com family in which no one spoke like an actual human being must be fictional.

"Shirley Jones was a well-known actress and singer," Selenko explained, "long before she was cast in this show."

"And she's not named Partridge," Adam said, surprised both that he had spoken and that he had clarified the point Jason had failed to make.

"Who's Shirley Jones?" Ryan asked.

"The mother, dummkopf!" Buddy barked.

Why does Jason like jerks? Adam wondered.

"We will do without the insults," Mr. Selenko said. "The point I'm making—"

"How about the Brady Bunch?"

It was Gracie. The pause was brief, then:

"Made up!"

"They're married!"

"They're not real."

"They're two families!"

"I don't believe you."

Mr. Selenko's face opened, his smile shone, and Adam could glimpse the bright demons of his imagination through the gap between his two front teeth.

"This discussion is perfect," Mr. Selenko declared. "As actors, pretending is what we do. We devote ourselves to convincing our audience that our characters are real."

Mr. Selenko's dark eyebrows and mustache danced when he spoke, restless smears of black. Adam considered that Mr. Selenko's head would look the same upside down.

"More than the script, the story, the plot, the lighting, the music— the actors make us believe, convince us their story is real."

"Buddy's not real," Valerie quipped.

Laughter.

"We'll see if that's true," Mr. Selenko smiled, agreeing to call Buddy's existence into question. He tapped his foot on the hardwood floor.

"We call these *the boards*. You'll get used to strutting the boards. In a few short months you will face the most magical gathering of human beings known to man. I want you to slowly turn around. Gracie! Now!"

Lights went on at once, and they were facing eight hundred empty, pale brown wooden folding seats.

"An audience."

A ripple of understanding, a "duh" from Buddy.

"You are now actors. You will convince the audience sitting down there that the world we are creating up here on this stage is real—more real, more vivid than life. As actors, you possess remarkable power."

"I feel stronger already," said Buddy.

"You'll see what I mean," Mr. Selenko went on. Adam watched him, transfixed, his bright eyes flashing quickly—excitement, anger, annoyance, Adam couldn't tell.

And there was the other magic element—Mr. Selenko's voice—the slight burr when he spoke softly, the crystal clarity when he projected, shifting volume and tone seemingly without effort.

"Let's start working."

Mr. Selenko told them to each find a space of their own on stage with enough room to move around a bit without bumping into a neighbor. Next, he instructed them to express a very strong feeling, any powerful, distinct emotion, but to do so without speaking. Once they had found a physical expression they were satisfied with, they were to freeze. He would then try to decipher their emotions by reading their bodies.

They were embarrassed. They were the SP, used to delivering the right answer on cue, scoring points for thinking fast or spitting back what they had been told. Many of the boys, including Adam, loved sports, but when it came to performing, it had always been their brains that mattered.

"Ignore each other. No laughing now, that's nerves, that's normal, let it out and be done with it. You can do this."

They started as Mr. Selenko commanded, seeking and settling into emotion-laden poses. Mr. Selenko strolled through the forest of statues, stopping here and there, releasing each student with a tap once he had enunciated their emotion, "fear," "sadness," "happiness…"

He told Adam not to break his pose, then asked the class to relax and look at him.

"Most of you made wonderfully expressive faces, but look at… what's your name?"

"Adam Miller," he hissed through gritted teeth, afraid to move his jaw.

"You can see Adam Miller is angry, but look at how much his body talks to us. Look at Adam's arms and fists. They are poised to protect him from attack, but at the very same moment, his legs are getting ready to run. There is real anger and hatred radiating from Adam's body. That's important because most of the audience can't see an actor's facial expressions if they're not sitting in the first two rows. Keep holding."

Mr. Selenko took a breath as he circled around Adam. Adam could hear his classmates shifting their bodies slightly to get a better view. All eyes were on him, seeing him radiate power. Adam felt himself becoming larger. More solid, almost…dangerous.

"I don't know what you are thinking about, Adam Miller, but I wouldn't want to meet you in a dark alley. Some applause, please. You may break your position."

This was Adam's first happy moment in junior high school.

CHAPTER 6

While Adam's father ruminated silently, Adam's brother Seth offered retroactive subway counsel.

"You do not enter an empty car. Not ever."

"They forced me into the empty car."

"You go to the two cars right in the middle, those are the conductor's cars, but the conductors are not always in them. If there's no conductor, you go to the most crowded car you can find."

"Our car was pretty full."

Seth was five years older than Adam, had transferred to Stuyvesant High School in Manhattan before the summer, commuted by subway, had girlfriends, and lived much of his life beyond their parents' surveillance. They shared a room and Seth dictated the rules.

"Never, ever, under any circumstances, make eye contact with anyone on the subway. Not even on the platform—especially not on the platform. Between the pervs and the muggers, you're asking for trouble. When you're getting off the train, you position yourself near the door, and you don't get off the train until the very last second."

"How do I know when's the last second?"

"*Stand Clear of the Closing Doors*—when you hear that, that's when you jump off the train. You know why?"

"If I wait any longer, I won't be able to get off?"

"No, genius, so if a mugger has picked you out, he won't have time to follow you."

Seth went back to his book, but only for a second.

"I'm sorry for what happened to you. I wish I'd been there."

"Me too."

Adam reproached himself—*We were holding bats. How could we not have stood up to them?*—he forgave himself, reproached himself.

But that wasn't the question Adam asked Seth.

"Why did that kid keep saying, 'Jew-ball bastard,' over and over, like a song stuck in his head?"

Jew-ball bastard...Jew-ball bastard...

"Maybe he was crazy."

Adam's stomach clenched, his scalp itched, he wanted to rip the sound out of his skull.

"No, I mean, why would a *black* kid say something like that? Jews and blacks are on the same side."

"We're on their side. They're not on our side."

Seth always had things all figured out, no room for dispute, with confidence and turn of phrase Adam profoundly envied.

"Anyway," Seth summed up, "a lot of them hate us."

"Connie doesn't hate us."

"She's our maid."

"Mom doesn't like that word."

"Our *cleaning lady*."

"Her daughter doesn't hate us."

"We sent Ellie to college."

"We did?"

"Dad wanted to give her an *equal opportunity* since Connie couldn't afford it."

Adam thought about this. "Wasn't that a good thing?"

"Ellie wrote to Mom returning half the tuition, saying she didn't want to be in debt to the White Man who oppressed her people. I guess it's okay to be half-oppressed."

"Maybe she didn't have the money anymore."

"Mom cried she was so upset." Adam pictured his mother crying, which made him choke up.

"Gracie doesn't hate me. And neither does Kevin."

"Who the hell are Gracie and Kevin?"

"Kids in my class."

"I'm not talking about them, nimbus-brain. I mean the Black Power types, the Black Panthers, the Afro-American Students Association."

"Why would *they* hate us?"

"We live in nicer houses. I don't know."

Nicer houses? That couldn't be it. And Adam had never lived in a nicer house than his black friends. Well, until now.

Seth sighed in mock exasperation, secretly relieved to be liberated from the nineteenth-century Zionist tractate he'd been attempting to read. "I'll show you something."

Seth unlocked the black steamer trunk in which he kept his life. (It doubled as a writing desk and a table for board games.) Adam peeked over Seth's shoulder to get a glimpse of Seth's treasures, but he only spotted a *Playboy* stashed under piles of pamphlets. Seth dove into the clutter and pulled out a Converse All-Stars shoebox.

"Your sneakers?"

"Wait, idiot," Seth snapped, tilting the box in Adam's direction. "Ever hear of Julius Lester?" No response. "When Mom says his name, she spits three times. 'Julius Lester *tfoo tfoo tfoo!*'"

"*That's* what she's saying? I thought it was something in Yiddish."

"Mom doesn't speak Yiddish."

"She's always telling me to stop *hockin* her *cheinik*."

"Cause you're a pest. Here."

Adam read where Seth was pointing.

"Looks like a poem."

"A black teacher—a *teacher!*—read this masterpiece written by one of his students on Julius Lester's show."

Adam read the poem:

Hey, Jew boy, with that yamulka on your head
You pale-faced Jew boy—I wish you were dead.

"That was allowed on the radio?"

"Ever heard of free speech?"

Adam gulped. But before he could form words, Seth read more:

Then you came to America, land of the free
And took over the school system to perpetrate white supremacy.

"It doesn't really rhyme."

"That's not the point! We're Jewish, not white. And there's lots of Jewish teachers—"

"Like Mom and Dad—"

"Yes, like Mom and Dad, because those were the best jobs people like Dad could get with a GI Bill college degree."

"What's a GI Bill?"

"That doesn't matter. One of the parents said on Julius Lester, 'Hitler didn't make enough lampshades out of them.' That's a quote. You know how many Jews who live in New York went through the camps?"

Adam felt his blood vessels contract, his muscles vibrate. He'd had nightmares ever since he'd seen the documentary *Night and Fog* at summer camp—dead, naked Jews stacked higher than a building. Every night, he offered God his life in exchange for the Six Million— one jump in time was all it would take—but his bargaining had produced no results.

"You know what pisses me off?" Seth pondered aloud, instructing his younger brother. "I got in all that trouble taking over the principal's office, and I was protesting that six black students had been murdered in Georgia."

"What was the principal supposed to do about it?"

"That's not the point! Jesus!"

It was easy for Adam to get Seth mad, but calming him down was also simple.

"See, you're just like Mom," Adam offered. "You did what you thought was right. And it was right."

"That's true too." Seth paused. "It's complicated. You know they wanted to get rid of the Jewish principals in schools in black neighborhoods. That's what caused the teachers' strike."

"But everybody wanted Dad to be their principal."

"Because they knew Dad really cared, that Dad is the best principal you're gonna find. *Was* the best principal. Now leave me alone. I gotta read."

Seth's patience with his younger brother could dry up in an instant,

Adam didn't quite grasp the politics of his father's career, but he knew Connie said she loved the boys *like her own children*, Gracie had liked him since fourth grade, had been his partner on school projects, or really, he had volunteered to be her partner when no one else would. *Jew-ball* was the only person who had ever said anything disparaging to Adam about his being Jewish.

Was it possible that black people secretly hated Jews? Adam always believed Seth, but this time he wasn't sure.

CHAPTER 7

Two fill lights with red cellophane filters scattered illumination above them on the stage, lighting that signaled a new Mr. Selenko scheme.

"Clichés are the shortcuts the lazy actor takes," Mr. Selenko submitted. "They make everything feel predictable, and predictability is the enemy of drama."

Mr. Selenko's mustache twitched wildly.

"Because we do not in fact pull our hair out when we are worried or look up to the ceiling when we want God's help. Let's take hunger as an example. What do you do when you're hungry? Do we rub our bellies? No? We don't? So how do we act?"

"Sometimes I open the refrigerator like ten times in a row," Adam said.

"Excellent!" Mr. Selenko celebrated. "Could you mime that for us?"

Adam rose, imagined a refrigerator, felt his hand un-suck the door open, let his hand ride the top of the door, rocking it gently forward and back, while he tried to visualize what was inside. He closed the door and started over.

"Watch closely. Adam is staring at the contents, closing the door, and then begins again! A simple, banal act, repeated endlessly, like a loop of film. But thespians, that is authentic human behavior! If you keep opening the fridge on stage, you are showing the audience that you're hungry without saying, 'Hey! Look at me rubbing my stomach! I'm hungry. *Get it?*' And you're showing them that you're restless. Two for one. Think about that for a moment."

They did.

"We are so used to clichés on television, real human behavior can surprise the heck out of an audience. And now," said Mr. Selenko, winding up, "tell me the key. What is the opposite of the predictable?"

"The unpredictable," snorted Buddy, testing the anti-Selenko camp.

"Hmmm," Selenko hedged, neither confirming nor denying.

"Something you didn't expect." "The unexpected." "Something you didn't predict."

Adam listened to his classmates paraphrase the question and one another. The answer was obvious. Instead of waving his hand madly, he spoke under the noise of the class.

"Surprise."

"Correct! You see, thespians, even someone whose photograph is hanging in the post office like Adam Miller has a functioning cerebellum. By the way, Miller, the machine gun doesn't do you justice."

Laughter and snorts, and for Adam, delight, as he flashed on himself clutching a machine gun to his chest, the belt of linked bullets dripping down in two directions, *Wanted!* emblazoned above his head.

"And now, class, your next assignment is to…surprise us! At any time in the next eight weeks, you must surprise the members of this class in some way that catches us off guard so completely and yet so organically, that…. *What* will happen? Will our mouths hang open?"

"No!" Adam yelled, along with all those aboard the Selenko train.

"And why not?"

"That's a cliché!"

"That's right. I am throwing down the gauntlet," Selenko said with glee. "The time and place are up to you. The *Surprise Challenge* is afoot!"

Elementary!

Three girls showed up two days later wearing pink pajamas under their winter coats, which set off an epidemic—fuzzy pajamas, pajamas with feet, Barbie pajamas, inside-out pajamas—until Selenko declared pajamas to be a "cliché." Ryan and Peter rigged up black lights, then Kevin rigged up a strobe. Mr. Selenko was so enchanted by the stutter-step effect that he kept the strobe going throughout the class pantomime exercise. Bernie Silverstein and Susan Levitow met the class at the stage door dressed as butlers, and Amy served homemade blueberry muffins. The scandalous rumor was that they were a couple and had seen each other naked, but Adam had no idea if this was true and wouldn't dare ask.

Adam's need to be original and astonishing grew in inverse proportion to his dribble of ideas. The only thing he was sure of was that his surprise had to be about Selenko. He could not disappoint his favorite teacher.

I could paint everyone with Selenko mustaches, but that will evoke Groucho Marx. No!

Thinking about comedy led Adam to Selenko's endlessly recycled joke-lines, his sarcastic digs that told his students they were part of his secret club. "This is not a library" meant you were speaking too softly on stage to be heard by the audience. If one's acting had the life of a statue, he would say, "Michelangelo would have loved you."

But what could Adam do? Paint Selenko's sayings on the wall?

He was determined to find the most unexpected surprise that had ever been staged. With each class he felt more enthralled with drama, and he was allowing the thought to settle that theater—and not science—was going to be his passion despite Mr. Beck's remarkable drive. Alas. No idea was good enough.

CHAPTER 8

Each lesson with the Cantor was the same. The boys started by singing the trope—the musical notation that appeared just below or above each word indicating how to sing the word. The Cantor pronounced the word "*trup*," so that's what they called it: *singing the trup*. Adam scrambled to put together the vowels and letters of Hebrew words, but the *trup* would not make friends with his brain.

Adam's struggles were nothing compared to Jason's. Jason could not read Hebrew unless he focused his attention with laser discipline, but Jason didn't get far with zero motivation.

"You are not trying!" the Cantor yelled.

Jason readied an answer but kept silent.

"I don't care that you don't sing good, but you don't try. Karsh tries. Miller tries. Kohn sings awful but Kohn tries. Only you not trying."

Jason's face puckered. The Cantor had nailed him, of course.

One winter day, the Cantor arrived so late, the boys transformed the banquet hall into a sock-hockey rink, with two tables as goals and Adam's rolled-up socks as a puck.

The Cantor's call—"What you boys are doing?"—broke up the game before his heavy black shoes reached them.

They tried to invent poses of study, but their sweat and forward motion gave them away. It was understood that Adam would explain to the Cantor, despite being sockless, because he was the star of Hebrew School and his father was on the synagogue board.

"Playing sock hockey," Adam said.

"You got no sticks," the Cantor objected.

"We play with our feet," Adam explained.

"Football!" the Cantor cheered, confusing the boys, who knew nothing of global sports lingo. "First practice. Then we play."

Adam liked the *we*. The *we* saved them, even if the Cantor got soccer's name wrong.

"In America," Adam said, "we play first, and we only sing if you win."

"So you think we are not playing football in Romania?"

Adam had never thought of Romania before this moment.

The Cantor removed his hat, placed it down on the table with delicacy, and laid his long black coat gently over the back of a chair. His shoulders rippled back into the depths of his suit jacket. He reached to his throat, flicked his button open and tugged his tie down in one swift movement.

"We play. I win, you sing." His face soured. "In America."

Adam blanched. Reminding the Cantor he was an immigrant wasn't fair.

"We'll make teams," Adam offered.

"You six against me," the Cantor ordered. "This be almost fair."

The Cantor blocked with his bulk, shedding the boys to the left or the right, thumping Albert and Roif into the wall with a hip check, knocking Dennis to the floor with a butt smash. His jacket heaved up as he crabbed down the ice, a giant black rectangle they couldn't get around, keys and coins jangling in his pocket, his theme music. His hard black shoe hit Adam's shin in a piercing crack, leaving Karsh alone to protect the goal. The Cantor didn't hesitate. He knocked Karsh over and scored easily.

"I win, you sing."

"It takes seven goals to win," Adam said.

"You did not say that."

"We know the rules already."

"All right. Three goals to win."

"Five."

"Compromise. Three."

"How's that a compromise?" Karsh mumbled.

"Play football or we start lesson now."

The Cantor knew how to keep the sock puck skipping between his feet with surprising soccer control. *Feet feet feet*. The boys were used to baseball and American football—all hands.

Adam called a time-out.

"What time-out? Time-out time to sing! Finish game."

"Spread out like a power play!" Adam yelled to his teammates. "He can't cover all of us at once."

But the Cantor had the puck. One more goal and they'd be singing.

"Karsh!" Adam called. "Get in his way. Jason, you and me, under his arms. Dennis and Albert, be goalies!" They would be useless, but out of the way.

Adam's plan worked too well. The Cantor tumbled over Adam, hurtled into Jason and Albert, and smashed into the table, which collapsed in a thunderous crash. Adam kicked out the puck from under the pile but couldn't see what happened next.

"What is this racket?" the rabbi shouted a moment later, furious and godly in the doorway, his arms raised like Moses at the Red Sea. Dennis also had his hands in the air—having kicked the puck in to win the game. While Dennis and the rabbi looked ready to take turns bowing, the collapsed table leaned on one end, a kneeling horse. The other boys were piled on the cherry-faced Cantor.

"I was picking up my pen under the table," Adam said, "and I accidentally knocked the leg of the table out. The Cantor was trying to help me and he tripped."

"Cantor," the rabbi said, with a long exhale. "I didn't see you there. Please come to my office."

Only after Rabbi Ellenbaum left did they notice Jason rubbing his face hard with both hands. Blood was pouring out of his nose, tie-dying his shirt.

"He hates my guts." Jason said, the minute the Cantor left the room. "He knocked me down on purpose."

Adam didn't think the Cantor did anything on purpose.

"He doesn't hate you."

"You don't know what you're talking about."

The boys were soon informed that the Cantor would no longer be teaching the bar mitzvah class. A rabbinical student would take over and meet them around the corner in the old building.

Except for Adam Miller. Adam was going to continue with the Cantor. Adam would be the Cantor's special project.

CHAPTER 9

A dam knew his father was delighted that the Cantor had singled him out. Jeremy Miller admired musical excellence—he'd studied classical violin—worshipped any form of excellence really. He adored both opera and its stepsister, cantorial singing, and treasured his Koussevitsky hazzanut records. Agnostic bordering on atheistic, Jeremy had a tiny crystalline yearning to be pulled back to tradition. Now that he was being groomed for Temple president, Jeremy and Helen had started attending Shabbat morning services, where each week, Jeremy was moved by the Cantor's passion, which Jeremy himself was unable to feel. He judged correctly that the Cantor and his fine tenor voice were on a spiritual mission, not seeking applause.

Helen Miller was quarterbacking the bar mitzvah reception, determined that their Jewish-American values—responsibility, learning, hard work, self-reliance, independence, community, and belonging—would be expressed by Adam's fanatical preparation for his morning performance on the *bimah* and then by the celebration immediately after, to which the entire congregation would be invited, literally next door in the Temple ballroom. Adam agreed with his parents' declaration that the service took priority over the party, but that didn't mean his mother would let the affair be less than perfect.

Part of becoming a man, she insisted, was for Adam to do his share in the organizing. *Job One* was for Adam to figure out the seating at his dais, who would sit by his side in the places of honor and where each friend would be placed in descending order of importance. His mother gave Adam a simple chart to fill out, and repeated her request many times, because "the caterer *has to know!*"

Assigned seating was a kind of torture only adults could invent, and the bar mitzvah was eight months away. Why the caterer had to know *now* was above Adam's pay grade, but Adam did his duty.

MY BAR MITZVAH DAIS

ADAM	Jason	Takashi	Ryan	Peter	Stu	Buddy	School Friend Boy	School Friend Girl	School Friend Boy	School Friend Girl
Cousin Kay	Cousin Harvey	Cousin David	Albert Hebrew School Friend	Dennis Hebrew School Friend	Karsh Hebrew School Friend	Barry Camp Friend	Marla Camp Friend	Eddie Camp Friend	**Sharon Summer Camp Girlfriend!!!**	ADAM

Adam's summer camp girlfriend was his tremendous secret. His summer camp friends, who went to Jewish day schools, would discover Adam lived in a larger world with many friends who were not Jewish. His regular friends would be shocked by Sharon's existence and dazzled by her beauty. He planned to invite other girls so she wouldn't be the only one—but whom?

CHAPTER 10

"Stand up," Seth said.

"I have a test tomorrow."

Adam was kneeling by his bed, his notebooks, worksheets, and textbook spread across his mattress, as he memorized the dates of the Roman Empire. Exams took top priority in the Miller household and was the only arena in which Adam bested Seth.

"So you'll get a ninety-eight instead of a hundred for once."

"I always get ninety-eight. Jason gets ninety-four. Peter gets a hundred."

"This is important."

Adam's memory train wouldn't get back on track until he gave Seth what he wanted. He got up, relocated the blue seltzer bottle with its spritz lever to the flat surface of his desk.

"You can never mention what you're about to see to our parents. Can I trust you?"

"Yes."

Seth exhaled with great drama, gazed up, as if he was about remove his visor and destroy the ceiling with rays shooting out of his eyes. He pulled two sticks out of his knapsack. They were about a foot long, the width of a broomstick, and were connected by a short chain.

"These are nunchucks. I am going to swing this at you, but I have total control. I'm not going to hit you unless you move. Then you'll get hurt badly."

Seth tilted them up, holding the lower end of one of the sticks in his right hand. The second stick dangled from the chain. Seth moved

Adam to the entrance of their bedroom. He exhaled again with a great flourish.

"Stand perfectly still."

"Why?"

"Because I don't want you to get hurt."

Adam threw his shoulders back, held this posture tight. His brother drew himself up to attention, his knee-high boots lending him a military bearing.

"Ready?" he said.

"Can I trust you?" Adam asked.

Seth thought Adam was mimicking him, but Adam had meant his question sincerely. Adam held his breath while Seth held one end of one of the sticks and whipped the nunchucks downward. The second of the two sticks flew at Adam. Adam jerked his head back as the stick came close to his face, but before it could hit him, it was snapped back toward his brother. To Adam's astonishment, Seth caught the flying stick in his left armpit. Seth winced and bit his lip.

"Are you okay?"

"Didn't hurt," Seth reported. "Now stay still. I have to practice."

Adam didn't understand how *practice* and *total control* went together, but he spent the next fifteen minutes summoning his will not to flinch as nunchucks whizzed past his face. After a series of attack thrusts that pummeled Seth's underarm on each return flight, Seth swung his weapon in a figure-eight, a continuous churning of nun-chucks that kept the second stick flying toward Adam in a rapid blur, creating a slight but erratic breeze. Adam tried to follow the motion of the nunchucks, which made him dizzy enough to totter forward. The nunchucks caught the fleshy part of his arm.

Adam howled.

"I told you not to move!"

"I'm not a goddamned statue!"

When Seth saw the impressive welt he had created, his bluster gave way to brotherly concern. He led Adam to the kitchen, loaded a brown paper lunch bag with ice cubes.

"Hold that on it for a few minutes, and make sure you wear a long-sleeved shirt this week. If Mom or Dad ask you what happened, tell them you got hurt playing football."

Seth confided that he never went to Stuyvesant High School unarmed anymore because he was harassed in the city for being a proud Jew.

"Because of your buttons," Adam said. "That's why you get hassled."

Seth's jeans jacket was engorged with buttons pinned on for Jewish causes. *Free Soviet Jews* embossed over a Jewish star trapped behind bars inside a much larger, red Soviet star. *Am Yisrael Chai! The People of Israel Live!* Several buttons showed a raised fist against a Star of David.

The Jewish stars glittering across Seth's knapsack were an invitation to every anti-Semite in New York City to start up with Adam's brother.

"Don't tell Mom and Dad," Seth lowered his voice. "But these are from the JDL."

"Are you in the JDL?"

Adam had heard their father railing against the Jewish Defense League's leader, Meir Kahane, "a fascist madman" who was turning people against Jews in New York.

Seth blushed. "I'm in Betar, but the JDL has better buttons."

Seth described his new Zionist youth movement as "street-wise Jews from Queens, Long Island City, and Brooklyn—all muscle," nothing like the "naïve goodie-goodies" in the synagogue youth group that Seth had quit. Betar was named for a legendary stronghold in the Jewish rebellion against ancient Rome.

If only Seth had come to Bat Day, he could have broken a few bones with his nunchucks, and they wouldn't have had to be rescued.

Seth led Adam down to his Fortress of Zionist Solitude. Unlike their old basement, with its sectioned-off bedroom and dank crawl-space of treasures, this basement was extensive and finished, its green-topped folding ping-pong table, its built-in bar (neglected), Seth's cast-off make-out couch, its bathroom, its second stereo system—inherited from deceased cousins—and Seth's record collection. Posters crowded the walls three rows high—rock bands such as Cream, Led Zeppelin and Jimi Hendrix alternating with psychedelic optical patterns and Peter Max. Tacked to a bulletin board were small photos of the Jewish underground fighters executed at Acre Prison by the British in the 1940s during the British Mandate in Palestine.

"You want a button?"

Adam had already been mugged while carrying a bat, and it seemed more likely Jewish buttons would attract muggers than scare them off, but Adam did not want fear to rule his life.

"Sure."

Seth emptied out the green speckled box that once held their 45s, inviting Adam to pick. Adam considered a Jewish star inside a fist—*Jewish Power!*—apparently from the same designer who turned out Black Power buttons. Adam wanted to radiate strength like every twelve-year-old boy, but a fist was angry, a fist was for smashing. *Ka-Bam! Crash! Smash!*

Adam didn't want to smash anyone, not even Jew-ball, although he wouldn't have objected if someone else did.

Adam chose a button with the face of a man yelling *Speak out for Those who Can't! March for Soviet Jewry!*

Seth was not done with Adam's education. He shoved two books and a pamphlet into Adam's chest.

"You have to read these if you want to understand what's going on."

"Okay."

The books were by Elie Wiesel, who, Seth explained, "lived through it all firsthand. These are the most important books you'll ever read. There's a third book, *Night*, which I'll give you when you're older."

Wiesel was not yet the Nobel Prize–winning prophet of the Holocaust, still known only to a tiny circle of Jews and French anti-fascists. Adam had never heard of him.

"It's a secret that I'm in Betar."

"Mom knows."

"She's happy it's a Jewish group, and they're all the same to her. And don't think about joining. For one thing, you're too young. If Dad thinks I got you into Betar, you'll screw it up for me. Dad can tell the difference. Dad's thinks it's wrong to fight violence with violence."

"It *is* wrong, isn't it?"

"He's living in a fantasy world. People always want to murder Jews. Our grandfather came here in 1905 and spent thirty-five years making money to bring his brothers over, one at a time. But he couldn't convince his sisters, and then it was too late and the Nazis put them in ovens and made them into soap. They murdered more than a million Jewish children."

Adam shuddered.

"But it's 1970," Seth went on. "We have Israel. They attack old Jews in Brooklyn, brother, it's clobbering time!"

Seth's grasp of the politics of laying claim to both banks of the Jordan River, Betar's anthem, was mythically motivated—Seth was vanquishing Nazis in biblical guise or playacting the Six Day War. Adam's knowledge of such matters was nonexistent, but the *Fantastic Four* reference hit home.

Adam returned to the basement later and appropriated *Night* from Seth's shelf. He devoured the memoir in one afternoon when no one else was home, only to be immediately haunted by its horrific images. He moved on to *Dawn*, a brief novel about Elisha, a young survivor in a life-and-death situation during the British Mandate in Palestine before Israel was an independent country. Adam imagined himself Elisha, desperate to avenge the Six Million, to murder Hitler, to strangle a Nazi.

The Jews of Silence was different, detailing Wiesel's visit to Jews behind the Iron Curtain, where Judaism was outlawed by the Russian police state. Three million Russian Jews were second-class citizens, kept out of top positions and universities. Anyone who asked to emigrate to Israel lost his job and was left to starve.

That's happening right now!

Adam was proud to be a Jew and hated getting pushed around. But their father was right too—*wasn't he?*—that you could easily become a thug like *them*. But maybe just to be a little more willing to fight wasn't a bad thing, especially if you had a bat—or nunchucks—in your hands. Adam would wear his Soviet Jewry button, but beyond that, he had no idea what he was supposed to do about any of this.

CHAPTER 11

Dennis and Adam walked home together, a compromise of convenience since they now lived in the same direction. Adam's new house was so much farther that he was zoned for a different school but used his old address to stay with his old pals. Adam felt pity for Dennis because of their Bat Day debacle, an unpleasant feeling to harbor for even a second-string friend.

They walked up Sanford Avenue, fits and starts of conversation—Adam could never get in a rhythm with Dennis—turning on 149th Street toward Northern Boulevard, where, thankfully, they would part and Adam would wait for his bus. Despite his tendency to care for strays, Adam had only seven blocks' patience for Dennis.

Adam didn't pay special attention to the group blocking the sidewalk until somebody seized his arm and someone else ripped the watch off his wrist. It was a diver's watch with an oversized face, glow-in-the-dark numerals, rimmed by a beveled air-tank dial. Three things registered with terrific clarity:

1. Adam had to get the watch back because it was Seth's. He had not asked permission to borrow his brother's watch because he knew the answer would have been no. Adam had his own diver's watch, but it was half the size.
2. Adam was facing a gang again.
3. Dennis was running away, which meant Adam was alone.

To Adam's left were grass patches and trees that reached the gutter. To his right, a rectangular lawn fronting a ten-story apartment building. The lawn was protected by low chains that drooped from one knee-high post to another, warding off dachshunds and keeping pedestrians from stepping in dog poop.

In front of Adam were ten, fifteen teenagers, in small clusters, all of them staring at Adam. Some were black, some were white, an unusual detail to which Adam paid no attention at the time. They were, it seemed, waiting to see what he would do, wondering why he had not fled with Dennis. They didn't know Adam could not face his brother without his watch or that he had just decided that Jews had been pushed around enough and that he was not going to run away from a fight again.

One boy took off up Sanford Avenue, his wavy orange hair and brown ankle-length car coat flapping behind him. Adam was short but he was fast, a sprinter, a wide receiver, and his legs made the decision for him, overcoming his fear, preventing thought. He caught up to the boy at the end of the next block, grabbed him by the coat, the kind of coat Adam's father would wear.

"Give me my watch!" Adam sputtered, both of them bent over and breathing hard.

"Don't have it," the boy insisted, putting hands up to expose the deep pockets on the inside and outside of the coat. He had several inches on Adam, and with his hands raised in the air, seemed about to swoop him up in his arms. "You can check."

Adam slid his hands in, keeping eye contact. Those deep pockets were empty.

"So why'd you make me chase you?" Adam yelled, furious at his failure.

A tiny smile fought his hard stare. "I like to run."

He was a decoy. *Damn them damn them damn them!*

Adam's heart sped up, pounding against his ribs. He raced back to the site of the mugging. He was certain the gang would have scattered, his brother's watch gone forever.

To Adam's surprise, they hadn't left but had shifted onto the lawn, with only a trio still blocking the path, waiting for their next victim.

Adam joined them on the grass, put his best scowl forward, and said, "I want my watch!"

Their chatter abruptly halted. They formed a circle around Adam, with Adam as the nucleus. They began to close in, the last three stepping over the low chain onto the lawn. Adam clenched his muscles, expecting to be hit. Changing tack now, he scanned for a way out.

"You lost something, little man?"

He was black, taller than Adam, with a sparse beard, but not a kid, older than Seth, his Afro accentuating an impression of a triangle. All heads swiveled up toward him in as if connected to the same string. He was the boss.

"You stole my watch."

"I said I got this!" another teen yelled, as he stepped forward into the gladiatorial ring. This opponent was younger and closer to Adam's size, although also taller—they were always taller—his midsized Afro making him seem taller yet. He was skinny like Adam, but tougher, stronger, sinewy where Adam was soft. "What are you still doing here?"

"My watch—"

He got in Adam's face, and Adam, seized by a demon, a cantorial impulse, pushed him in the chest to back him off. That brought whoops from the group. Adam was Elisha—no, Spartacus—but he knew the crowd would give him the thumbs-down.

"I didn't touch you, man," the boy said, but then he did, shoving Adam backward.

If he'd been in his bedroom, swinging a pillow, Adam would have known what to do, but he was on the street.

"It's my brother's diver's watch!"

"I don't have it!"

"Give it back!"

"You deaf? Did you fucking hear what I said?"

They repeated their lines two or three times, taking turns shoving each other.

"Get the hell out of here," the boy ordered, "if you know what's good for you." He pushed Adam in the chest with both hands. Adam stumbled backward, fell down to ground level, completely vulnerable. But instead of piling on, nobody touched him. Adam turned his head in all directions, seeking escape. The metal caught the sunlight, a momentary shimmer, and there they were, under a bush, a pile of watches, Seth's watch on top.

Adam stuffed his bundle of books under his right arm, as if preparing to submit to the gang and depart, moved from his knees to a squat, and at the last second, snatched the watch with his left hand, scrambled to his feet, and bolted out of the circle, knocking a girl sideways—"Hey!"—running as fast as he could, his ears pointed behind him. He put a block between himself and the Watch Gang before daring to look back.

They were still there, an ambling amoebic mass. He couldn't tell if they were watching him, but they were not in pursuit.

Adam mounted his bus with a sense of relief, checking his wrist repeatedly to make sure Seth's watch was there. The bus moved slowly, accepting and discharging passengers at each stop, Adam anxiously scanning for gang members. But no, they hadn't followed him. After a mile, when he remembered Dennis, fear gave way and Adam began to fume.

At home, alone, Adam returned the watch to his brother's desk, determined never to borrow anything from Seth again without explicit permission.

He calmed down, allowed himself a particle of pride. He had stood up for himself and retrieved his stolen property. Lesson learned. He would not tell anyone what had happened. It was all over. End of story.

Just after arriving home from her day at school, Adam's mother got a call from Mrs. Feigenbaum, Albert's mother. A gang outside of school had stolen the watches of more than a dozen kids, including Albert. Mrs. Feigenbaum had organized a core group of parents to bring the matter to the police, to disperse the gang while the stakes were still low, "*to nip this criminal behavior in the bud before it gets out of hand.*" So far, only Dennis's parents had refused; they didn't care that Dennis had lost his watch, they wanted nothing to do with the authorities. Mrs. Feigenbaum had heard from Dennis's mother that Adam had also been robbed.

"The Nazis made them scared of their own shadow," Albert's mother insisted, "but we have no excuse." *Would the Millers join them?*

"I'll call you back."

Adam had gone bike riding to face the world on his two wheels. By the time he returned, Adam's mother had been fuming herself, too anxious and frustrated to wait for a powwow with Jeremy. She informed Adam a police officer was coming to interview him.

"What for?"

The police were investigating the complaints of a gang stealing watches off kids' wrists on Sanford Avenue.

"When were you going to tell us?"

I wasn't going to tell anyone.

"I got my watch back," Adam shrugged, omitting that it was Seth's watch. "Nothing happened." *Except that Dennis abandoned me.*

Soon, a squad car parked outside, siren off, lights twirling. The only policeman who had ever been in Adam's house was their cousin Harry, the first Jewish precinct captain in New York City.

They spoke at the kitchen table. Adam could have given the cop a detailed account of the thoughts that had raced through his mind throughout the incident, leveled serious charges against the traitorous Dennis, but they wanted names and identifying information of the assailants. Adam could only recall a black kid with a medium-sized spongy Afro, the red-haired kid with freckles and a car coat "who I chased down the block and caught. But he didn't have my watch."

"He was white?"

"A bunch of them were white."

"You don't say."

"There was a blonde girl with long hair. And a black man with a goatee and a big Afro. He was like the ringleader."

"A man? How old would you say?"

"My brother's seventeen, and he looked older than him."

"Light-skinned black or dark?"

"What?"

Adam had never thought of such a distinction before, but yes, right, the "man" had darker skin than some of the other black kids. He wasn't sure. And no, he didn't recognize them, didn't know if they went to his school. There were 1,800 students in 189. Adam knew his twenty-nine SP classmates and a handful of other kids who had also come from PS 24.

"Thank you, Adam. You've been a big help."

"I have?"

Adam went back to *F Troop*. Its grating laugh track took the place of wit, but it distracted a tiny part of Adam's brain.

The next morning, Adam was startled to be called up to his homeroom teacher's desk and told by Mrs. Bell to go to Dr. Lefkowitz's office. Adam had never met the principal. He was terrified that someone in his family had died, or that an obscure crime had somehow been discovered: helping Stu cheat on his math test, using his old address to be zoned for 189, cursing his parents for moving, inadvertently abandoning Jason on the football field along with the rest of his teammates when their frustrated opponents started beating them up.

"I'm Detective Riley, and this is Detective Fein."

They were plainclothes officers. Detective Riley had a mustache like Selenko's, but he was bald, had a paunch, and frequently scratched his ear. Detective Fein was younger, fitter, stood tall, shoulders back. He replaced his dark glasses with humanizing, fragile owl glasses halfway through the conversation. They asked Adam to try to identify any gang members involved in the watch thefts.

"Did you catch them?"

"We'll go from class to class."

Adam hesitated, but the officers told Adam they'd be with him every minute, that he wasn't going to be a snitch; he was going to make sure no one else got robbed, to stop things before something more serious happened.

"I got my watch back."

"That's right," Officer Riley said. "But most kids were too scared to stand up to the gang."

I tripped and found the stash of watches, Adam thought. *It was luck. I should have grabbed all the watches and returned them to their owners.*

The cops attracted all the attention when they walked Adam to the front of each classroom. Adam had the teacher's view but felt the police presence made him invisible.

Adam didn't recognize anyone. Not the red-haired boy, the blonde girl, or the black kid with the Afro. Adam wasn't sure he could have identified them if they'd been paraded in front of him.

The most peculiar stop was in the Opportunity Classes for struggling learners and behavioral misfits. Kids were spacing out on bean-bags and a small couch, one shaking his head from side to side as if uncontrollably locked into some private hell of disagreement. A shiver coursed through Adam as if he'd seen something he shouldn't have.

Detective Riley shook Adam's hand when they finished, a muscular handshake that denied the bulge over his belt. "That was a brave thing you just did."

"It was?"

It hadn't occurred to Adam that it required courage to walk around a school with two policemen.

"I want you to take this card."

Detective Alan Riley, 14th Precinct, Flushing, Queens.

The precinct address and phone number were printed below. Adam had never been given a business card before, and the lines of print felt formal, adult, powerful.

"You carry that with you. If you have any problem with these boys or girls again—any problem at all, no matter how small—you call me. I'll make sure you're safe. You never know when you might need it."

"Okay."

Adam put it in his back pocket. It became a kind of charm that Adam moved from one pair of pants to the next.

Now Adam could forget about the watch incident, but not about his unreliable walking partner. Adam made sure not to leave the building with Dennis, pairing up instead with Albert Feigenbaum. Just outside the school gate, Adam saw his father standing next to their double-parked Bonneville. Mr. Miller was never free during school hours and had never picked Adam up before.

"Hi, Dad. What's going on?"

Mr. Miller told the boys he wanted to make sure there was no sequel to the mugging the day before.

Was it a "mugging"?

Adam asked if they could give Albert a ride home, although it was only a few blocks, and opened the side door.

"No, don't get in the car."

Mr. Miller wanted them to walk on their usual route to Adam's bus. He would drive next to them in the street.

Why is everyone making such a big deal out of this?

Thankfully, the gang corner, 149th and Sanford, was empty. They continued toward Northern Boulevard and reached Albert's building.

"I'll keep going with you," Albert said, a friendly gesture even if it made no sense.

It was on Thirty-Eighth Avenue, one block from Northern, that the mob appeared waving sticks and bottles.

"There he is!" one yelled.

They raced toward Adam and Albert.

"Don't run," Adam ordered Albert, eager not to have a second Dennis, his fear neutralized by his father's presence, and fascinated by the gang's reckless approach. Their fastest scout reached Adam first and took a swing at his head. Adam jumped out of the way but took the blow on his shoulder. The rest of the pack was steps away from the boys when they heard a smack. It was Adam's father slamming the lead runner into the side of the Bonneville. The boy bounced off the car, sputtered to the ground, stumbled to his feet, and ran away.

Jeremey Miller was not a big man, but he was strong and fierce with his heavy five-o'clock shadow and three-piece suit. He grabbed the arm of the second boy to arrive, twisted it behind his back in a long-dormant wrestling move, forcing him to drop a broken bed-board slat. He seized the boy's weapon in his left hand and waved it over his head.

Instantly, magically, the gang froze, then scattered.

One adult and they were gone, *snap!*

Adam and Albert were left alone with the boy trying to twist out of Mr. Miller's grasp. Mr. Miller instructed Adam calmly to open the back door, told Albert to get in first, slide across, and make sure the opposite door was locked. Then he forced the kid into the car, nudged Adam in next to him, and told Adam to lock his door as well. He had blond hair cut in a fan, which Adam found odd on a boy, and maybe, Adam thought, this was the one he'd mistaken for a girl.

Bonnevilles were massive beasts, wide enough to fit five kids across so they had to hold on to their captive. Still, Adam felt powerful, protected. His dad was here. Everything would be fine.

But what are we going to do with him?

They drove off.

James—they discovered his name later—expected to be beaten, worrying only that they might kill him, dump his body in a parking lot.

Instead, they drove back to school. Mr. Miller ordered Adam out first, then grabbed James when he stuck his foot out, before he could run. Gripping James by the arm tightly, Mr. Miller pulled him through the main entrance of 189, Adam and Albert following the forced march to the principal's office.

Dr. Lefkowitz seemed delighted by Mr. Miller's vigilante arrest. They were chalkboard brothers, trained to inspire inquiry but expected to control violence. (And Dr. Lefkowitz had read about Mr. Miller's school strike saga.) Albert's mother had called repeatedly since the previous afternoon, one of many parents who had complained, although the thefts had taken place off school grounds. Dr. Lefkowitz took his seat behind his desk, asked Adam and Albert to sit facing him and then to describe the assailants. Adam's father stood behind the boys, watching them, watching James, ready if James made a break for the door. Albert was too agitated to speak, so Adam began, recalling the boy with the freckles and red hair in the car coat, and Dr. Lefkowitz cut in.

"That must be Tommy Lyndon."

James immediately corrected him. "No, that was Bob Tulane. Tommy wasn't there."

Dr. Lefkowitz wrote down Bobby Tulane's name. "Who else was there, James?"

"I'm not talking."

Of the black kids, Adam could summon only the boy with the medium-sized Afro—perhaps he was the one he had fought the day before, but he wasn't certain. The rest of them were a blur, their size—larger, older than Adam—leaving more of an impression than their features. He didn't remember more, but this was enough for the principal to work with.

"You mean Robert Farrar..." Dr. Lefkowitz said.

"That was Michael Mason," James corrected again.

Adam caught on to Dr. Lefkowitz's trick. Adam would give an inadequate description of a vaguely remembered assailant, Dr. Lefkowitz would throw out a random guess, and James would provide the real name.

Dr. Lefkowitz teased out a list of eleven gang members, each time James repeating, "I'm not talking." Adam pitied James because he could be fooled so easily, but any guilt over manipulating a stupid boy was overcome by performing in tandem with his principal.

Dr. Lefkowitz asked them to leave James in his care, promised he would be in touch with the Millers later, and thanked Adam's father profusely, "Good citizen...deteriorating neighborhood..."

They left as Dr. Lefkowitz began dialing the phone.

Back in the car, victorious, heading home to receive their laurels, Jeremy's pride in Adam and in himself flagged as his adrenaline dipped. For a moment, Jeremy Miller considered what he had just taken part in, why Dr. Lefkowitz hadn't followed procedure and called James' parents or the police before the interrogation. Adam was left with one question alone: *How had his father been able to predict the attack?*

But things were not quite done.

That night, the police sent another squad car to Adam's house. This time, Adam was energized to see the boxy blue vehicle, red light rotating in a glass box above its cool white top. He was eager to report how his father had thwarted the attack, how Principal Lefkowitz had discovered the perpetrators' names with his help.

But what if the police were coming to arrest Adam and Mr. Miller for kidnapping? His father would lose his job! They would both go to jail!

The officers only wanted them to prepare a statement, and make sure they would appear at the precinct station the following day at 7:30 a.m. along with the other victims of the Watch Gang. The police said it was imperative to *nip this phenomenon in the bud.* Albert's mother called Mrs. Miller three times that evening to make sure they were going to show up.

"What a nudnik," Mr. Miller said.

"I think she's trying to convince herself," Adam's mother explained.

Would the gang be there?

Yes. The police were talking to their parents as well.

Adam refused to go to the police station. He had not lost his watch. He had been attacked. He had canvassed the entire school with two police officers. He had helped the principal figure out the names of eleven gang members. But he did not want to face the Watch Gang at a police station. He had done enough nipping and budding.

It wasn't his decision.

Mrs. Feigenbaum had rounded up three other victims in addition to Albert and Adam. She had given up trying to persuade the Kohns, Dennis's parents, but together the rest of the parents were going to *nip these attacks in the bud.*

When Adam's mother rousted him from his jagged dreams at 6 a.m., his sleep fog gave way to jitters. Mrs. Miller believed in arriving pathologically early for appointments, multiplied geometrically when facing officialdom. Adam insisted that she stay home, arguing that his father—both a witness and a participant in the second assault—was enough. His parents grasped that facing his attackers with his mother by his side would be emasculating without Adam having to explain it.

The Watch Gang—fathers and mothers in tow—was already at the precinct when Adam and Jeremy Miller arrived, milling about the open foyer, fronted by the intake sergeant's high desk adjacent to a buzzer-controlled light brown wooden gate that led to the precinct's inner sanctum. Matching high wooden benches lined one side of the waiting room, but nobody sat down. Some of parents were black, some white, and many were smoking. An ineffectual fan rotated overhead, swirling the smoke in slow circles. A few of the men were dressed like Mr. Miller, on their way to offices, others were in T-shirts or short sleeves, some hovering over their kids, others establishing a distance to prevent an automatic association.

Adam's staccato glances revealed little. In books, a person's image is always being etched in your memory, but it was the opposite in real life. No one seemed familiar. Faces became distorted and confused, conflated with other people, with characters from television. One of them reminded Adam of Jew-ball on the train, but it wasn't him. A couple of others rang muted bells. Except for James, Adam would not have been able to identify a single one for certain.

Mr. Miller parked Adam on the wooden bench closest to the desk sergeant. Adam sat back, realized his feet didn't reach the floor, and inched himself forward to perch on the bench's edge, touching down his toes to avoid feeling—and looking—like a child.

Adam was the only "victim" to have arrived so early. Once Albert arrived, he would have someone to talk to. He didn't know who else was supposed to join them.

Adam had never been inside a police station and was astonished to see *WANTED!* posters hanging on the wall, enlarged mugshots making every criminal appear demented, depressed, and a bit blurry, with a list of their crimes underneath. Some were wanted for robbery, others for bombings!

A WANTED! poster!

That was the answer to Mr. Selenko's Surprise Challenge! Adam would make a *WANTED!* poster with Mr. Selenko's picture on it.

For the only time that morning, Adam smiled.

How weird to find the solution here at the police station.

Adam's attention snapped back to a loud argument between a boy and his mother, only a few feet away. Jets of smoke were exiting the boy's nostrils. Adam hadn't ever seen a kid smoke in front in front of his parent. This alone was fascinating. The boy's mother told him to put out his cigarette and the boy answered in a very loud voice, "Go fuck yourself!"

Couldn't he be arrested for that?

The strangest incident was that one of the gang fathers, a black man in a charcoal gray three-piece suit almost identical to Mr. Miller's, put his hand on Mr. Miller's shoulder. Adam's father blinked into recognition. There was a pause, awkward, as the men considered how they had come to meet at this spot, but their hands grasped in a handshake, which also lasted too long to be perfunctory. Mr. Miller reached into his jacket for a pack of Camels, shook one out, extended the package toward the man, who returned a grimace of thanks before taking one for himself. The fathers lit up, inhaled deeply, blew smoke toward the ceiling, standing next to each other for one cigarette's duration, exchanging a sentence every few minutes, which Adam could not hear.

Mr. Miller finally sat down next to his son. He lit another cigarette. Adam waved the smoke away, the sweet smell suddenly acrid, stinging. By 7:50 a.m., the other complainants were officially late. No Dennis, of course, but also no Albert. No Albert's mother. None of those parents so passionate about *nipping and budding*. At 8 a.m., Detective Fein told Mr. Miller no one else was coming. He squatted in front of Adam.

"If good citizens refuse to step forward, the police are helpless."

Adam tipped himself further forward on the bench, almost standing, conspiring with Detective Fein, and whispered the truth.

"I didn't want to come. I got my watch back. The principal got all the names. Why do you need me?"

"You can make sure that tomorrow one of your classmates won't have his watch stolen, that no one will have to fear walking home. And you'll be doing these gang members a favor, by stopping them before their criminal activity gets more serious and wrecks their future. Are you brave enough, man enough, to help us do our job?"

Adam wanted to be both brave and man enough. He said yes.

After that, Adam didn't have to do much. The gang members had incriminated one another, filling in the details that James had forgotten. Some were brothers. Two of them were not minors—they would be treated as adults. Stealing watches was nickel-and-dime, but it was an unusual combination of white and black kids, and a couple were also involved in more serious activity.

Lucky me, Adam thought, *mugged by an integrated gang.*

They brought Adam and Mr. Miller into a conference room, the gang already crowded around a table, standing, sitting, some smirking or scowling, others humbled. They took Adam and Mr. Miller out of the room. They asked them if these were the assailants from the attempted assault the day before.

Adam's father said yes, he believed they were. Adam nodded. If his father was sure, there was no question.

The police said that some of them went to 189. Aside from James, Adam couldn't say exactly who had done what, but Adam wasn't asked to identify anyone, only to certify that their self-incrimination was accurate.

Detective Riley led them to his private office. He read out a typed description of the watch theft and the thwarted "attempted assault" witnessed and prevented by his father.

They asked Adam to sign.

Adam reminded Detective Riley that he got his watch back, a point of pride. Detective Fein scribbled this in by hand.

Adam signed.

Back home, Helen Miller had it out with Mother Feigenbaum. Albert's mom had been up all night, tortured by second thoughts, third thoughts, fifteenth thoughts: *They were surely underprivileged, and we, who have so much, could certainly overlook the loss of a few watches. A police record would ruin their lives.* Helen had been refuting these same arguments to Jeremy for five years. Mrs. Feigenbaum had called that morning but *didn't want to wake them at an ungodly hour,* and by the time she rang, Helen had told her they'd left for the station. She'd been convinced the other parents would show up.

So much for nipping and budding.

"Kids can't be going to school scared that they're going to be robbed," his father reassured Adam.

As part of their probation, the gang members were not allowed to come within ten feet of Adam, and they could be sent to reform school if they "so much as laid one finger…"

Adam's parents trusted the system. Adam had done the right thing. But what did Adam care about ten feet or one finger? The gang members knew Adam by name and by sight, and he would have to face them every day, scared his arm would be ripped off his body.

CHAPTER 12

Adam's private lessons with the Cantor excused him from some Hebrew School classes, sparing him the sight of Dennis, who had never apologized and had earned permanent residence in Adam's spleen.

Adam received a green stapled practice booklet with a drawing on the cover of a bar mitzvah boy wearing tefillin—black leather straps he was supposed to wind on his arm and head for daily morning prayers once he was thirteen. Adam made decent progress reading the haftarah, the three pages he would have to chant at his bar mitzvah, but *chanting* was a euphemism for singing, and singing was the problem. The Cantor's voice was clear, rich, resounding. Adam's was flat and nasal. The Cantor called Adam's voice "skinny." He promised he would make it "thicker," like gravy. Adam came home crying from every lesson.

"There is tears today, but there be smiles tomorrow," the Cantor told Adam's mother on the phone. "What I teach him, he will remember for his lifetime."

The Cantor was on a personal mission to rouse the congregation of lawyers, doctors, store owners, accountants, insurance agents, and even one assemblyman (although not representing their district) to vigorous prayer. The Cantor was going to roar his way into heaven and take everyone with him. Adam was untapped potential Exhibit A and would prove how much a child could master.

"We going to tap it!

"Can't I just memorize it from a tape like the other kids?"

71

"What tape? What kids?"

"Nothing."

The bar mitzvah tutor hired to replace Mr. Rockowitz had made each student a cassette tape of the section he had to sing, with instructions to go home and memorize it. They weren't bothering with trope symbols.

"You want to be parrot?"

"No."

"No, you not parrot! Parrot don't need the Cantor. You read, and you follow word after word, then comes *trup*, and you will sing!"

I am not parrot. Parrot not have bar mitzvah. Parrot is nobody's special project.

The Cantor taught Adam to tap out the beats of the musical notation, the *trup*, on his fingers. One finger tap for each beat, starting with his thumb, moving in succession to his pinkie, then back to his thumb.

"This way you will not by accident skip. You don't press one beat of the music into the other beat or syllable of a word into different one."

Tapping became Adam's default position. He tapped his fingers on his thigh, on the armrest of a chair, on the bus, in class, during dinner, and in his sleep. For the first time in his life, the chattering voice inside Adam's head was singing. Fortunately, there was no need for rhythm in singing the haftarah because Adam had none.

The Cantor's recognition of Adam's limited musical abilities did not blunt his ambitions for Adam's big day. He told Adam that chanting the twenty-seven biblical verses of the haftarah was the warm-up act. Adam was also going to *sing* the Torah reading, the much longer section from the *Five Books of Moses*.

"No other boy will do this! This will you remember for rest of your life!"

This challenge was of far greater magnitude. Adam would sing directly from the Torah scrolls, not from a book. There were no vowels to tell him how to pronounce the strings of consonants, so every word required decoding. And there was no punctuation—no commas, no periods, no quotation marks, nothing. Adam couldn't tell where a sentence began or ended. It was as if the national anthem had been written like this:

oh sy cn y s b the dwns rly lt wt s prdly w hld by th twlts lst glmng

"What happened to the vowels? The punctuation?"

"They not invented those things three thousand years ago when the Torah is written down."

"Why wasn't it added later?"

"Because it wasn't."

The clincher was that not only did the Torah have its very own musical Torah *trup*, but to produce maximum confusion, the musical notation was the exact same set of squiggles and dots used for the haftarah, now sung differently.

"Why did we need two *trups*?"

"Because they not the same."

"But why?"

"You hear how they are different?"

"*Nyet.*"

"I am not Russian."

"I forgot," Adam said regretfully, recalling Romania.

"I'm American."

Okay, we all are.

The Cantor sang the *trup* in order, beginning to end. Adam could hear they were different, but he couldn't explain why.

"Energy is different. Listen again. Energy goes down in haftarah *trup*, energy goes up in Torah *trup*."

The Cantor sang again, perfectly, effortlessly. They were in different keys, he explained but Adam didn't know what a key was. When he practiced on his own during the week, the two competing sets of tropes—*trups*—blended together.

Adam had an inspiration.

"Can you make me a cassette of you singing the two different sets of *trup*, so I can practice by myself?"

"You have cassette player, your own?"

"I'll ask my parents to get me one. I'll learn faster that way."

The Cantor's smile filled up his cheeks, bright red and full. "Smart boy Adam. We do this little trick on your parents and you will learn *trup* at home. Faster."

"I promise."

When he brought his new Panasonic portable cassette recorder to his next lesson, the Cantor was tilting back on a chair, his feet up on the table, his bare legs sticking straight into his black shoes. His socks were rolled up into a ball and sitting on the table.

"If you read good and sing beautiful, Miller," he said, "then we going to play."

"One-on-one?"

"One-on-one."

Adam hadn't practiced enough, which usually meant he'd go off-key.

"If I don't sing good?"

The Cantor took his rolled-up socks and separated them. "I put these back where they go from."

Adam reverted to finger tapping and silent trope review, his new habit to quiet his worries and get through silences, the gentle rhythm that would steady Adam throughout the year, a background beat, as the Cantor had promised, for the rest of his life.

"I will sing beautiful for you." And he did.

They played sock hockey-soccer, the Cantor barreling past Adam to score time after time. They stopped and the Cantor taught Adam to protect the sock-puck between his feet. Adam was fast, had excellent reflexes, but foot control was new.

"Enough," the Cantor said at last, and it was. They were sprawled on the floor.

Adam told the Cantor he wanted to invite him and his family to his bar mitzvah party. Adam had seen the Cantor's family in the synagogue lobby once, his wife with her wig and his kids with their Hassidic ghetto names, Avrum, Ruchele, and many others. They dressed in black and white, like the Cantor, and hung out with the rabbi's kids, Jewish day school students decked out in normal clothes and situated culturally between the Cantor's old world and Adam's own.

"Thank you. You are good boy."

The Cantor was uncharacteristically quiet.

He couldn't know that the Cantor was following a melody of memory and future, reincarnating himself in Adam. If only he had been born thirty years later, in a free America, in a safe America. *Fine young Adam, loving, athletic, curious, free,* free in a way the Cantor would never be, his own children could never be, under the yoke of his bitter experiences, the weight of Jewish law, of his accent, their traditional Jewish way of being, his ever-present over-there-ness.

"My family not come inside conservative shul when I am davening. But thank you, you are thinking of them."

"You come by yourself. You can sit with my family at the party. My father would love it."

"I will want to rest after services. But thank you, you are thinking of me. Is not for me. Party is for your family and all the little friends."

"And for my girlfriend."

He'd said the word "girlfriend" aloud, to an adult, to someone besides Seth, to the Cantor, without thinking, an impulse to counter that "little friends" remark, perhaps. He hadn't thought it through, the sentence had leapt out of his mouth, not his brain.

"Oho. Adam has a girlfriend? Tell me."

Adam told the Cantor about Sharon, about camp, about snuggling on their bus ride in the dark for more than an hour. Only Seth and the Cantor were privy to his secret.

"A bus ride in dark. A very good place to be with a girl. When do you visit her?"

"She lives in New Rochelle. I think it's far away."

"New Rochelle is not so far."

"My parents would have to drive me. It would be embarrassing."

"That you have girlfriend? This is to be proud."

"I don't know if she'd want me to visit."

"You ask her on the telephone."

"I'm not good at talking on the phone. What would I say?"

"You never will know you don't find out. If you don't see her, don't talk to her all the time from summer camp until now, then, boychik, she is not your girlfriend. Maybe there is another boyfriend."

"You think?"

"You will call her up. How else you know?"

"I don't know."

"Better to know, I think."

Adam wasn't sure. Ignorance allowed him to go back to Bear Mountain at will, to imagine that next summer there would be another bus ride.

CHAPTER 13

Adam had suffered from feeling invisible when he started seventh grade, but now he wanted to disappear, counting on those same crowds of unknown students for his safety. If he missed his bus and had to walk to school, Adam would arrive late to an empty schoolyard, winds whipping through with menace, lofting brown paper lunch bags and candy and cigarette wrappers on test flights, pinning these harpies of detritus to the fence.

For a week, Mr. Miller had driven Adam to school, puttering nearby until Adam went through the gate, a routine repeated at the end of the school day, when he trailed Adam to Northern Boulevard, only then signaling him to enter the car. (Adam couldn't know how many favors his father owed colleagues who covered his classes so he could run this car service.) For weeks after, Adam imagined his father continuing his surveillance in borrowed cars with tinted windows.

A few Watch Gang members—the red-haired boy with the car coat, some others he couldn't identify—went to 189. Adam developed anxiety antennae and knew when they were near. Some would fall in step with Adam in the corridor, matching him stride for stride, or running up to Adam, counting off steps—*the ten-foot gap*—and yelling, "Hey, Miller!"

"Hey," Adam always answered. He would not cower like Dennis.

To make matters worse, there were fire alarms almost every day, false alarms, and somehow, no matter which part of the building his class was in, when his class marched down the corridor toward the stairs and the exits, the boy with the medium-sized Afro—his shoving match opponent—would find Adam. He would sidestep—a kind of dance—parallel to Adam, darting between students passing by Adam to make sure he could be seen, but never looking Adam's way. Not a coincidence; no, Adam had seen him push past other students to reach his position directly within Adam's view.

School became about anxiety, fear alternating with tedium, waiting for the fear to return.

Mr. Vogel, the gym teacher with the grand mustache, the King of the Cafeteria, recruited the SP boys to lunchroom Door Patrol (DP) to keep the inmates inside—"You're smart, reliable, the SP always does DP." Adam, Jason, and their friends, Takashi, Ryan, Stu, and Peter, ate at two tables. Ryan and Peter were physically imposing—both linemen on Adam's football team. Peter was lumbering, all agility in his mind. Only Ryan combined size with speed. The rest shared Adam's dimensions, short, smart, quick, first-row friends from public school. They knew it was their badges that gave them authority as emissaries of Mr. Vogel, amplified by the wake of intimidation that trailed Mr. Vogel wherever he trod.

The tables entirely blocked the double doors of *Exit #1*. They would move the tables aside to allow a student with an exit pass to leave the cafeteria, then quickly restore them. The most common tactic for fugitives was to slide under the tables, slip through the door, and scamper down the hall before the boys could follow. Adam calculated that if the six hundred students in their 10:40 lunchroom shift stampeded to escape a grease fire, the DP would likely be crushed, but life was full of risks.

Serving on the Door Patrol meant Adam and his friends never had to search for a seat, and the panhandlers, fearing their cheap badges, wouldn't hassle them. The downside was that a permanent place meant that the Watch Gang knew where to find Adam, so Adam took the head of the table to ensure his back would not be to the lunchroom, sacrificing foot comfort for security. Adam counted on Mr. Vogel and his regular circuits to check on "his DP boys."

Three weeks after the watch incident, Adam encountered the gang back on their corner. Not as many this time, the older ringleader was gone, but a cluster of them were smoking cigarettes. Albert looked down at his feet. Adam checked the bushes—no stack of watches—and tried to keep his head up. He surveyed passing cars, but there was no sign of his father. They could have crossed the street, but Adam had sworn off evasive action.

Would they trip him? Punch Albert in the neck? Adam checked his wrist, decided it was foolish to call attention to his watch, but once he had started the action, felt compelled to complete it. It was 1:54 p.m.

"Time for rats to go home to mommy," somebody said, and laughed.

The kid with the mid-sized Afro called, "Hey, Adam Miller."

Adam froze, suddenly on the subway again, flashing on the razor-cut part in Jew-ball's closely shaved head, on being taken onto the next car, Jews herded onto trains, history repeating itself, but this kid—*was* he a kid? he was Adam's size, but seemed older—this kid from the corridors dancing in and out of Adam's peripheral vision, his gladiatorial adversary, he knew Adam's name, so he must have been at the precinct, must now be on probation, must have been in on the attempted assault. Had he been carrying a stick? A bottle?

"I'm talking to you, Adam Miller."

"That's me." Adam said.

"I'll be seeing you."

"Me too," Adam answered.

And they were past.

What kind of idiot response was, "Me too?"

As the weeks passed, Car Coat vanished, the others seemed to lose interest, but two or three times every day, Adam's adversary flitted into his line of sight through the crevices in the crowd, to Adam's side, backstepping with an occasional skip, always near, the hair, his Afro. That's what Adam would spot past the throngs, that dancing Afro growing by the inch, by the foot, blocking out the light, casting a shadow that reached to the ceiling.

He's my size, no giant. But he has bigger hair. Or different hair, because my hair is too long, according to my father. Hippie hair, according to my mother. Don't listen to them, according to Seth. He didn't punch me in the face, that was a different kid in a different incident. Now I see him, now I don't. Is he waiting to finish our fight? What does he want?

Adam couldn't imagine a more horrible feeling than uncertainty defaulting to fear, but then he found one.

Adam zipped through the door on the fifth and final chime for Beck's science class, breathing hard, damp collecting in his armpits. A stranger was sitting next to him in Jason's seat. He was tall, seated, a head taller than Adam, taller than Albert, but willowy, fluttery.

"Excuse me," Adam called up, "I think you're in the wrong place."

"That guy switched seats with me," he whispered, becoming ramrod stiff but pointing over the heads of their classmates unmistakably at Jason. Mr. Beck was striding toward his desk to mark the seating chart, and Adam lost focus for the rest of the lesson.

After class, Jason vanished before Adam reached the corridor, and at lunch, Adam found himself alone at the DP Table. He stood on his chair and spotted his friends at Table Three. Adam must have missed a new directive from Vogel. He wanted to go over to them, but he couldn't leave Table One unguarded. He waved furiously and was sure that Peter, then Ryan, saw him, but they made no sign in reply.

In their next class, nobody—not Jason, Ryan, even Takashi— would talk to Adam. It was as if he had become a ghost. They kept up the silent treatment for the rest of the day. The next day, the joke continued, as Stu disappeared from the seat next to Adam in English class and Ryan moved away in Spanish class.

"Very funny," he said to Peter because it was funny how disciplined they were. But Peter walked past him.

It didn't stop and it was not fun. They'd let up for sure at the football game.

Saturday afternoon, Adam raced home from Junior Congregation, changed into his shoulder pads and number 13 football jersey, his football pants with knee pads sewn in, tied his white Converse All Star high-tops, strapped his navy blue Giants helmet with the interlocking NY to his banana seat, and bicycled to the gloriously limed World's Fair Grounds football field, hyped by the knowledge that the prank would now end, since, as team captain, he could hardly be ignored. The fall was giving way to winter, and soon they would need extra layers, but the autumn cold had the perfect bite for a football game. Running would keep him warm. The park grass was effervescent green, not yet withering from the frost, and the hundred yards of white-striped lawn went on almost forever, ending with the most beautiful professional goalposts on any public field in Queens.

It was their first game since the Lefrak City debacle before the summer—a game that infamously ended after halftime when their frustrated opponents started to beat them up. As quarterback, Jason suffered the worst, missing Adam's call to "Run!" while the rest of the team escaped.

Today, the team was already gathered, jumping up and down to get their blood flowing, cheering each other on with back slaps and high-fives. Adam would typically start game prep with his review of their strategy—they had ten set plays they practiced—and a bit of a pep talk, but they hadn't waited for him. Nobody slapped him on the back, and only Takashi gave him a weak high-five. They kept up the silent treatment in the huddle.

Jason called the buttonhook fake, Adam's scoring play. Adam deked the cornerback and broke free, slanting across the middle, already picturing his friends swarming him after he scored a touchdown, laughing about how far they'd taken their practical joke. Jason pumped to Adam, but then flipped the ball to Ryan, who carried it forward for three yards. Adam could easily have gotten fifteen, or a touchdown.

"I was open," Adam muttered.

Jason told Buddy to tell Adam to sit out the next play and wait for a substitution.

Why was Jason talking through Buddy?

"What's going on?"

"It's Takashi's turn," Buddy announced with glee.

And there was Takashi, crouched at the sideline, his glasses glinting behind his helmet mask, ready to run onto the field. Buddy waved Takashi in.

"Just this one down," Takashi said quietly as he passed Adam.

Jason threw a touchdown to Takashi on the buttonhook fake, Adam's play.

Adam's team kicked off, and Adam was so distracted he missed a tackle, costing the team thirty yards. He saw Jason conferring with Buddy.

"Sit down for this next series," Buddy announced so all could hear.

"I'm the captain of the team."

"Were!" Stu said.

"What?"

Jason had convened the team a half hour early, and they voted to replace Adam as captain with Ryan, their best all-around athlete.

But I'm the captain. I set up the games. Why would Ryan agree? Why had they all gone along with it?

Size being a premium, Adam had played Ryan on the line, paired with Karsh, the Hebrew School muscleman, but now Ryan was the running back. For three plays in a row, Jason handed off to Ryan, who followed Karsh up the middle. Adam did not play another down that day, except for kickoffs, when the teams lost count of how many players were on the field.

"Sorry," Takashi said at the end of the game. "They told me it was one down, then one more, then one more. That was really not nice. Sorry."

"How's your stomach?" Karsh asked.

"My stomach? Fine."

"Buddy said you had a stomachache."

"He…lied."

"What gives?"

"I don't know," Adam answered. Nobody else spoke to Adam, until Buddy called Adam over.

"We're playing Saturday mornings from now on."

"I can't play Saturday mornings. Neither can Karsh."

Adam had Junior Congregation. Buddy knew that.

"Karsh says he'll come sometimes, but everyone else's got stuff in the afternoon," Buddy continued. "And no other team wants to play then."

"I always get us games." Fifteen games over two years.

"No, really," Ryan said, his sincerity was matched only by his gull-ibility. "They called them all, and they said they can't play on Saturday afternoons. Or Sunday."

"Who'd they call?" Adam asked, but he lost heart because he knew this was not about scheduling. "You want me off my own team?"

"If that's the way you want it," Buddy exulted. "Hey, everybody, Miller quit!"

"I didn't…"

Jason's mouth was twisted, working hard to keep the laughter down somewhere deep, where it stank. Stu couldn't hold it in anymore. His eyes bulged out when he let loose, and Adam wanted to smash them back into his boney eye sockets.

Why did they think this was funny?

"Hey," Adam called, "this is no joke,"

"You're right," Buddy laughed. "It's not."

Adam rode away, but Curtis and Derek caught up to him on their bikes.

"Hey, Miller," Curtis said.

"What?"

"We quit the team."

"We joined the All Blacks of Corona," Derek explained.

"But you're not from Corona!" *And why would they want to be on a team with only black kids? Our team…*and then Adam remembered he wasn't captain. He wasn't on the team. There was no *our team*.

"Did Buddy make you quit?"

"I wouldn't let that honky push me around."

Honky?

"Black is beautiful!" they said mysteriously, raising their fists in the air, laughing and riding off on their Stingrays.

Usually after a football game, Adam's muscles were so sore and cramped, he could not stand up straight for days, a posture he wore as a badge of honor, but he had been in so few plays there was no after-burn, no strain, no nothing. He felt fine, except he felt awful.

The next day at lunch, Adam sat at Table Three. But his friends were nowhere to be seen.

"Why aren't you at your post?"

It was Mr. Vogel.

"I switched to Table Three."

"And what's with your friends? They quit Door Patrol today, all except Tatushi."

"Takashi."

"You're not quitting, are you?"

"No."

"Good. There's a hole at Table Two. From now on, you're at Table Two."

Table Two. With strangers, unfriendly DP kids from another class who knew each other and had no interest in him beyond his name, and not at the head of the table either, with his back to the lunchroom. He ate by himself, monitoring the doors and talking to no one. In gym class, his former friends picked kids ahead of him who could neither shoot nor defend for their half-court games. With his bank shot and reliable layups, Adam stood out among the non-athletes, but there was no pleasure in these second-rate games.

Adam hoped Hebrew School would be neutral territory, but Jason turned away if Adam spoke to him, and cozied up to Dennis— *Dennis!*—to recruit him to his shunning campaign. Jason was determined to maintain a universe in which Adam did not exist.

When Adam could take it no more and phoned Jason's house after school, Mrs. Boyer asked when he was coming over. She had cookies and brownies waiting. Mrs. Boyer was utterly reliable and practically perfect, so Jason would surely return his call. Adam left the same message every day for seven days.

Adam wanted to know why they were doing this, and he wanted it to stop. It was exasperating and it was exhausting. He tried calling Stu and Pete, but they hung up when they heard his voice. He heard Stu tell his mother it was a wrong number before the click. Nobody would speak to him, not in person, not on his special phone with *Unlimited Local Calling!* What was the point if there was no one to call?

Only Ryan said what they all must have been told: "I am not allowed to talk to you. Jason says…"

"What did Jason say?"

"Look, I just can't talk to you, all right?"

"No. It's not all right."

Adam hated Jason, and he missed him, missed reading *Justice League* and *Green Lantern/Green Arrow* together. Without Jason, his supply line was shut down—and he had to pay for comics at Haben's. For crying out loud, the Knicks were defending their championship, and there was no one to share it with.

Nobody came over, and Adam didn't ride his orange Stingray to anybody's house. He couldn't console himself rereading his old favorite comic books—the series he had collected and stored in plastic bags so diligently had disappeared in the family's summer move. Adam practiced for his bar mitzvah much more than he had planned to, and his mother chalked up his radical new homebody lifestyle to reordered priorities. On Wednesdays, when she didn't work as a reading specialist at any schools, Mrs. Miller made Adam a second lunch, bowls of soup overflowing with noodles and vegetables.

Adam tried running up and down the long hallway of his cursed new house that had taken him away from his friends, slamming himself off the paneling to get some energy, clueless about why'd he become a pariah. His foot got stuck on the carpeting, and he hit the wall so hard without bracing for the collision that he crumpled to the floor, adding injury to insult. Tears came.

"I'm fine," he managed to call out before his mother came to investigate, but he wasn't. Fear and loneliness were twisting Adam's soul. He became suspicious and nervous and sad and angry. He imagined prowlers in the deep darkness of their backyard, mothers abandoning crying babies, and dreamt of stealing his brother's nunchucks to crack open Jason's skull. (Or that dancing Afro. Or Dennis. Or Buddy. Or Jew-ball.) He hated everyone.

CHAPTER 14

Adam's better grades, summer camp, moving away, not hating the Cantor-Hebrew School-shul-bar mitzvah—their long friendship yielded many possible causes for Adam being banished by Jason, but all seemed unlikely. Was Jason embarrassed that Adam had seen him cry when they were mugged on the subway? They had all cried. Their disagreement about comics and science-fiction movies? Verbal sparring to a draw, that was the heart of their friendship. The football game might have been a reason. But the others had fled along with Adam, Buddy included, and it was only when they'd reached a safe resting spot that they'd realized Jason had been left behind. And Adam had spent a week of afternoons with Jason to make up for it. Buddy was egging things on, but Jason didn't take orders from Buddy. It was the other way around. Jason had not been robbed outside school, probably knew nothing about the Watch Gang, but had he seen Adam with the police? Was that this was about? Adam wondered what Dennis had told him, dismissed this because Jason despised Dennis, despite his pretense at Hebrew School.

Adam had always pitied school loners, outsiders. He had befriended a few of them for brief intervals in elementary school and they'd seemed pleased, but it occurred to him now that they must have wished for an ongoing friendship and were probably hurt when Adam got sucked back into his own circle.

Am I one of them now?

Gracie Fells had always been treated differently. Not only had she been the only black girl in their elementary school class, but she'd dressed primly and was terribly shy. Gracie and Adam did several projects together in public school because she'd been kept at a distance by the other girls, and most boys wouldn't partner with girls.

Loners or the Excluded?

Adam appreciated Gracie's smarts; she kept pace with him and did an equal share of the work, so he'd always thought himself the beneficiary of these pairings. (And yes, he thought he was doing a good deed, so a double win.)

Adam was hazy about the girl cliques, couldn't parse out someone else's social status when his own had bottomed out, but noticed that Gracie had giant stylish purple glasses and had smartened up her clothes, seemed to have friends and was no longer the only black girl.

The single exception to Jason's ruthless discipline was Takashi Moto. Three weeks into Adam's expulsion, Takashi decided to be Adam's friend again, dividing his time by alternating days, one day with Adam—the next with Adam's former friends. On Adam's days, Adam clung to Takashi. This continued until Adam made the mistake of playing up their chumminess, laughing too loud, noogying Takashi on the shoulder, a show for Jason.

"Adam Millenium and his great friend, Takashi Traitor!"

Takashi was careful not to drop Adam outright because he thought the ban was wrong, but he did not like being a prop and reduced his time to one day a week with Adam. When Adam apologized to Takashi, Takashi's smile swallowed his entire face. Takashi sat with Adam every day that week, and he confirmed Adam's suspicions about Jason.

"I think he started this as a joke and then everybody followed and then he didn't stop it because why should…I don't know why," Takashi recounted. "They're acting stupid, that's all."

Adam pondered Takashi's words for hours on his bed—*Acting stupid, that's all*—tossing his Spalding up to the ceiling, snatching it before it smacked him in the face. Adam's gloom spread over the both of them at lunch, and by trying to do the right thing, Takashi was subjecting himself to mopey meals.

Adam witnessed Buddy issue the warning. Takashi was so small that it was like a father scolding his little boy. The following week

Takashi went back to alternating days, until Takashi disappeared from school.

Had Adam done something to hurt Takashi? Of course! The most dangerous thing. He'd been his friend. Now Jason was somehow behind Takashi vanishing.

Adam bicycled to Takashi's building, took the elevator to the seventh floor, listened at the door, heard people talking Japanese, and rang the bell. The voices went silent. Takashi's sister poked her head out, and said, "Go way, away, away," brushing Adam out of Takashi's life with tiny sweeps of her hand.

Adam heard soon after that the Motos had moved to Japan. No goodbyes.

Could Jason really do that?

He asked Mrs. Bell in homeroom if she knew why the Motos had left, and she tsked, "Poor dear." He didn't know if she meant Adam or Takashi.

(Much later, Adam discovered that Takashi's mother had died, which made him sad for his absent friend. He never learned why this had been kept secret or why it had sent the Motos across the world, where Takashi's father soon remarried.) Carole King crooned her song "You've Got a friend" from Seth's record player, as he played her *Tapestry* album again and again in their bedroom. Adam knew if he called out anyone's name, he'd hear nothing. (Or get *Jew-balled*, or have a brick thrown at him.) With impeccable timing, Adam's mother ordered him to finalize the dais seating for his friends, because the caterer *could wait no longer!*

Friends!

The word flattened Adam.

Why had he ever thought that Jason was his friend? They both liked egg creams, comics and sci-fi, they were a good pass-catch football tandem, enjoyed watching TV together, doing nothing. Jason made fun of people—which Adam would never do, but which felt daring, the slightest bit criminal. Adam had loved Jason's sense of humor—until.

Isn't loyalty part of friendship?

Are my other so-called friends enjoying my misery? If they could be ordered out of my life by Jason Boyer, were they ever my friends?

Adam's nightmare was that Jason would mock him from his own dais at Temple Gates of Hope, but he knew the mothers were in cahoots and would insist the boys attend each other's bar mitzvahs and confirmations, regardless of "momentary quarrels."

His Camp Ramah friends would save him, and Sharon would be his salvation, but the Cantor had made him anxious. Camp was an alternate universe that went into deep freeze between summers, but suppose this wasn't true, and Sharon had forgotten him. Adam sorted through the mail his mother deposited daily on the kitchen table, searching in vain for the tiny reply envelopes from his camp pals, from Sharon in the mysterious land of New Rochelle.

Adam dared not show his mother his revised seating plan:

MY BAR MITZVAH DAIS (2)

Karsh Hebrew School Friend	Albert School & Hebrew School Friend	Barry Camp Friend	Eddie Camp Friend	Marla Camp Friend	**Sharon Camp Girlfriend!!!**	ADAM	Brother Seth	Cousin David	Cousin Harvey	Cousin Kay

CHAPTER 15

Haben's was a deceptively large stationery store, its five long aisles vanishing into the depths, impossibly far from its Kissena Boulevard entrance. Comic books lived in wooden racks under the math workbooks in the center of Aisle One, a straight shot to the front door.

Cut off from Jason's supply, Adam hungered for the next issues of his favorite series: *Green Lantern/Green Arrow* was thrilling in its gritty political realism. Adam had a sentimental attachment to *The Flash*, and the fictional reality inside a fictional reality of *Justice League of America*'s "Crisis on Earth-Two" seized Adam by the throat—*If only I could transport myself to a parallel universe where Jason was in Japan and Takashi was in Flushing, where evil Jason was podified by good Jason.*

Adam stuffed his favorite comic books under his coat and began his brief life as a criminal in a mad dash out of Haben's. A grip on his shoulder arrested Adam with one foot on the street pavement.

"Stop right there, kiddo!"

It was Mr. Haben. Under the tight helmet of salt-and-pepper hair, disappointment and anger boiled in his black eyes.

"Show me what you're taking," he croaked, his voice perennially hoarse from yelling down to the other end of his very long store.

Adam gave the answer of imbeciles the world over.

"Nothing."

"Come on now," he said, "don't lie to me on top of stealing."

Adam unzipped his jacket and handed him the pile.

"Do you have money to pay for these, or do I have to call your parents?"

How could you make us so ashamed? his mother's voice would crack.

And for comic books! his father would bellow. *That garbage will never be allowed in the house again.*

"I was just going outside to get the money from my brother."

"Then let's go together."

They did, Mr. Haben behind Adam, as lies follow lies.

"I don't see anyone," Mr. Haben said. "What's your phone number? Is your mother home now?"

"My brother was just here," Adam said.

"Your imaginary brother skipped town, is that it?"

And then, Adam did see someone. He saw his shadow, the kid with the dancing Afro, sitting on a fire hydrant smoking a cigarette. Adam had a crazy idea, much crazier than fleeing down Kissena Boulevard.

"There's my…there's my…my cousin," Adam said, pointing at the kid, wishing instantly that he'd just called him his friend, wishing he hadn't said anything.

"You think I was born yesterday?"

"No, really. My…my uncle is…um…Negro…black."

Mr. Haben's eyes narrowed. But Mr. Haben wasn't only checking Adam's face for lying. Adam could tell he was also scanning the street for other black teenagers. He spotted no one else of color, decided he could take both kids if it came to that.

"Your grandparents must be thrilled."

"No.… They're…um…dead. Just now, actually. My grandfather."

Mr. Haben paled. He had not intended such a breach of etiquette. Adam paled for lying again. His grandfather had died two years before.

"Sorry, kid, sorry for your loss," he mumbled switched back to curmudgeon. "What's his name, your cousin?"

"Dance," Adam answered without hesitation, the clarity of his mission blasting the dust from his thinking.

"What?"

"That's what everybody calls him."

"Hey, Dance!" Mr. Haben called. "Yes, you."

Dance considered them for a moment, ground out his cigarette, ambled over. He was wearing a loose army jacket and a skimpy sweatshirt. Without the cigarette in his mouth his face seemed more childish, a kid with tall hair.

"Your cousin says you're gonna pay for his comic books."

Dance's lips puckered as he sized up the situation. Adam's fate was in his hands.

He smiled.

What an idiotic miscalculation! I am stupid stupid, a stupid criminal!

"How much are they?"

"A dollar fifteen."

Dance cackled. "He likes comic books."

"Come to the register to ring these up," Mr. Haben said. "I don't take money in the street."

Dance grinned as they stood at the counter together. He was a bit taller than Adam, but his Afro made him older, bolder.

To keep himself from smiling—*I cannot believe this is going to work*—Adam studied the tips of his Converse All Stars.

"You tell his mother that I'm letting him off this time."

"I'll tell her all right."

"But if I catch him taking anything again, I'll call the cops."

"You should call Detective Alan Riley," Dance said. "He's good with delinquents."

Mr. Haben's world went cockeyed. He squinted at both boys.

"You sassing me?"

"No, sir," Adam was quick to appease.

Outside the store Adam wanted to whoop, to leap in the air.

Adam tried to slap his new partner five.

But Dance jumped away and said, "Ten-foot circle!"

"It's all right," Adam said. And to prove it, he defied the probation rules and stepped right up to him. "Thanks. Really. I'll pay you back tomorrow at school."

Dance strolled away, heading up Kissena Boulevard, forcing Adam to follow him since he had not handed over Adam's comic books. When they reached the huge white steps of the Flushing Post Office, he sat down, sprawled his legs apart, and leaned back, stretching himself across three steps. Adam stood over him. The grand ionic columns stood over them both.

"You owe me ten bucks," Dance said.

"What?"

"One dollar and fifteen cents for the comics, three dollars and eighty-five cents to keep quiet, and five bucks for calling me Dance."

Stupid thieving brain-dead imbecilic me trusting a hardened criminal!

"Ten bucks tomorrow, Adam Miller."

And he knows my name!

"Bring the money or I'll call your mother." He laughed again; his Afro bobbed above his guffaws. "She always loves hearing from me."

"Our number's unlisted."

It was. When they moved, Mr. Miller made sure they'd be hard to track down.

"I'll find you."

Probably true.

"It's 'cause you're always dancing around me…that's why I called you that…. And because I forgot your name." No response. "What *is* your name?"

"Michael Mason."

"That's right," Adam said, defeated.

Michael Mason kicked at the ground. Adam kicked at the ground. Adam took a chance.

"Five bucks, and I won't call you Dance anymore. Ever. I'm sorry I called you that."

Michael Mason took out a pack of L&M's, lit another one. When he offered Adam one, Adam was startled speechless.

Michael Mason put his cigarettes away.

"Okay," he said. "Five bucks."

Why didn't I say four dollars? Why didn't I say two dollars? Where am I going to get five dollars?

Michael Mason held out the bag of comics. "I don't read this crap."

"Okay." Adam had spent his life trying to convince his parents that comic books were not garbage, but he wasn't going to try to persuade Michael Mason.

Michael Mason took off his jacket, his sleeve got caught, and he used his other hand to free it up. He pulled out a copy of *Playboy*. Adam was shocked but enthralled. Was it legal for a kid to look at *Playboy*? And how could Michael Mason have been so composed with Mr. Haben while he was stealing from him?

"Next time, use the sleeves, from your wrist to the elbow. Much harder to see from the outside."

Michael Mason leaned back, spread his legs wider on the wide white steps, and blew smoke in the air. He opened the magazine, shook it, and several pages came loose. He turned it around and held it up.

"You see her?"

There was an astoundingly naked woman covering a single giant three-page photograph. Adam had never seen a naked woman before. She was wearing high-heeled shoes, so she wasn't completely naked, but her breasts thrust forward. Adam couldn't speak, could not redirect his eyes to any place in the world from her nipples.

"That's my sister," Michael Mason said calmly. "She's the centerfold."

His sister was in *Playboy*? This was a centerfold? *She* was a centerfold?

"You think my sister's pretty? Yeah, you do. I can tell."

Was it possible this was his sister? Maybe it was. Why else would he want the *Playboy*?

"She's…white."

"So are you, and we're cousins." Michael Mason cackled again, loudly, Afro bobbing above him.

"Disgusting," a woman muttered as she passed them going up the steps.

"Put it away!" Adam spat between his clenched teeth. Adam checked if he recognized her, if she knew his parents. The columns of the Flushing branch of the post office condemned them both. "People are looking!"

"That's why they sell *Playboy*," Michael Mason answered, and blew a smoke ring.

"At us!" Adam hissed.

"See you later, sis," Michael Mason said, and coolly refolded the photo into the magazine. Adam didn't want the centerfold to disappear but was relieved when his brain was freed from her magnetic field.

His sister? This suddenly seemed ridiculous, but what did Adam know about Michael Mason?

"She's not your sister."

"I'd let you take her home, but..." Michael Mason stood up, stretched his arms to the sky, peeked inside his *Playboy*, sighed, tucked the magazine into his jacket, threw his butt down, ground it out with his heel, the way Adam's father would do. "She doesn't like children with shit for brains."

Michael jumped back to restore the magic circle.

"But we already broke the ten-feet rule."

Adam moved toward Michael Mason too quickly, lost his balance, stumbled down three steps, landing off-kilter and breathless.

"See you with my five bucks," Michael Mason said with a full-body sneer as he strutted down one step, a second step, a third. "You've already been to the OC so you know where to find me."

Adam wanted to know how to strut like that, wanted to want to strut, to think that was strong and fine.

"Okay," Adam said. "See you."

For one second, the sneer was gone from Michael Mason's face, a smile, chipped front tooth, space between the teeth, goofy, then back in pose.

Michael Mason had saved Adam, and Adam owed him money and was going to pay him. They had a contract.

That night Adam emptied his old leather pencil case, borrowed a dollar from his brother's wallet, wrote an IOU that he slipped into one of his rolled-up socks, a reminder to himself, not a confession to Seth. Adam sealed the coins and bills in a blank envelope.

Adam read the latest edition of *Justice League of America* in the bathroom, saving *Green Lantern/Green Arrow*. During the hour of solitude between his bedtime and Seth's, Adam stared into the points of light and blackness that comprise the dark, envisioned the ten-foot probation circle, teasing distance, remembered how Michael Mason had danced backward in front of him for three months.

And now, at any time, for any reason, Michael Mason could tell Adam's parents that he was a thief, caught in the act by Mr. Haben. He could blackmail him for the rest of his life.

Adam made the handoff the next day, taking the bathroom pass but racing instead to reach the Opportunity Class with its poofs and sofa before the period chimes rang. Adam left the envelope on the floor outside the classroom door and motioned toward it maniacally when Michael Mason emerged at last. Instead of counting the money, Michael Mason scribbled something on a scrap of paper, which he left in the same spot.

"It's a receipt," Michael Mason called from down the corridor.

"I don't need a receipt."

Adam retrieved the note, which said only, "SFB." Adam stuffed it into his pocket. He didn't know what that meant.

CHAPTER 16

"There is no practice here in what you're singing today!" the Cantor yelled, starting to unroll his balled-up socks.

Adam tightened and twisted his mouth, tapping out the haftarah trope double-time, triple-time on his thigh.

"Very disappointing."

The tears came.

"I can't do it."

The Cantor's face went dark, an angry Buddha. He didn't comfort Adam or offer him a handkerchief. Adam dabbed his tears with his fingers, wiped them on his shirt.

"You want to be like other boys? They know nothing. They forget everything one day after bar mitzvah. What I teach you, you will learn forever."

"You told me."

"I told you? I tell you a hundred time. A thousand time. Till you sink in."

His English made Adam laugh.

"That's better. Now you tell me why you so giving up today."

He couldn't tell the Cantor about losing his friends, the Watch Gang, Michael Mason. Adam scrambled his brains, invented tragedies—a car crash, a heart attack, a death in the family—then discarded them, fearing the cosmic consequences.

"I still didn't hear from Sharon."

"Sharon? Who is Sharon??"

"My girlfriend. From summer camp."

The Cantor sat down. He pulled a second chair around to face him and put his feet up. The Cantor took pride in his Adam from this sun-shiny land of baseball and bar mitzvah booklets, knowing nothing of his neighbors' potential for murder. Adam had been spared all that, all of them had over here, so lucky, but it's right for children to be spared such things, he wouldn't wish it on anyone. The refugees who knew everything, felt everything in their flesh, but could express it only with a thick accent, were opaque to them, thought slow, backward, stupid, by their fellow Jews—especially by their fellow Jews.

"Oh yes. Girlfriend which we not sure is girlfriend. You call her like we say you call?"

"No."

"You write to her?"

"No."

"She is not your girlfriend."

"No?"

"You don't speak to her all the time from summer until now. Not your girlfriend."

The Cantor leaned back, reclining as best he could on two straight-backed chairs.

"Why not cute girl from Hebrew School?"

"There aren't any."

"You not looking."

There *was* one girl, light brown hair, a pixie cut, her skin so fair it was translucent, her veins visible like internal calligraphy, but she was a year younger than Adam, still in public school. Her oldest sister—there were three—was friends with Seth, so maybe next year when she reached junior high, he'd ask his brother's help.

The Cantor undid his tie, put his hands behind his neck, wiggled his feet to loosen his shoes.

"Boychik. When I am your age, there also is girl that I like.

"Was she pretty?"

"She is beautiful girl. I dream about her. She have older sister, three years older. So then I see sister, I forget this girl and I dream about sister."

"Did you ever speak to her?"

The Cantor sat up suddenly.

"This is story I cannot tell you."

"You can," Adam urged, hoping to use up as much time as possible.

"You're child."

"Did you forget I'm having a bar mitzvah? I'm going to be a man."

"This I am not forgetting for a minute." He exhaled dramatically. "Not to tell parents."

"I never tell them anything."

"The girl, sister I am talking about. She has body like grown up woman, her…you know…up here…makes you want to squeeze. Nope. I cannot tell you story."

"Now you have to. We made a deal."

"Don't remember no making deal, but you are interested, so maybe is time…no…no."

"Yes, yes."

"I not sure this is right."

"My brother tells me plenty. I'm not a little kid."

"All right. What happen is this. I am walking from school and she is on the other side of street. Older sister, not the girl. She ask me, 'Can I walk with you? I don't like alone here. Is not so safe.' I say, 'Yes, of course.' This I am dreaming will happen every night for whole month. She lead me into alley. I am nervous. Maybe hooligans are waiting to hurt me, rob me. They beat up Jews all the time in Romania. But no, she puts her arms around me, and she kiss me."

"She did?"

"I almost faint, it so exciting. Then she puts my hands on her— you know." Adam gulped, so loud he could hear it. "Adam, this story for grown-up. I am sorry I start. Is mistake." The Cantor laughed. "We done."

"You can't stop now! Just tell me what happened next. Please…"

The Cantor did not speak for a long time.

"Okay. For you only. Secret. Man to man. This is what she say to me. 'I see you looking at me all time. At them. This is what you want, yes?' she say. 'Now you touch them.'"

"What did they feel like?

"You, boychik, you will find this out someday. Then she take hands off. 'Now you looked for last time, now you touched for only time. From now, bother me never and never look at me again!' She leave me in alley."

"Did you stop looking at…at…?"

"I still looking…" He tapped his head.

"Did you ever…um…see her again?"

"That is private. I not can tell you."

Why was that private but everything else was not private?

"Did she come to your bar mitzvah?"

The Cantor's laugh was deep and resonant.

"She is not Jewish, so big trouble for me. We did not have no parties, no invitations. Only a *l'chaim*. And bar mitzvah we do in secret place because Iron Guard is attacking Jews. Enough with my stories. You call girlfriend on telephone?"

"Maybe."

"Adam?"

"Okay." Maybe. Not.

"Now, you sing Amidah. I want you should concentrate."

"Now?"

"Why no?"

That girl and her soft breasts and now prayers?

But it must have had some effect, because Adam's Amidah felt exultant, until the Cantor cut him off.

"You are thinking of sister in alley, not about Amidah. Start again or no sock hockey."

CHAPTER 17

Valerie slid into the seat next to Adam in Science Lab.

"They'll be in a car," Valerie said, as if continuing a conversation, although Valerie and Adam had never spoken before. "Probably Tommy's blue Pontiac Firebird with racing stripes. They painted the stripes pretty good."

Valerie was an atypical SP girl, with her sleeveless jean jacket dotted with metal studs. She could cut to the basket past anyone and never missed a layup, was the only girl in the boys' games in gym class, and since Adam had become persona non grata, Valerie was routinely chosen ahead of him for three-on-three. She was not from Adam's elementary school, and she hadn't cried when the Beatles split up. Valerie had high cheekbones, purple eyes a little bit off to the side, giving her a horsey look that could be almost beautiful when they didn't make her seem slightly mad.

"They're gonna be waiting for you after school."

Any girl (except Sharon) sitting that close would have made Adam nervous, and Valerie would have made him fluttery even if her message hadn't been terrifying.

"Who?" A minuscule amount of oxygen was entering his lungs.

"The Hill. That's the big hitter gang. You know. Hair slicked back. Italian, jean jackets with studs? That's who's waiting outside."

Valerie was Italian and she was wearing a jeans jacket with studs. Adam wanted to ask if she was a hitter, if they were called hitters because they hit people.

"You mean the gang that stole my watch? I mean my brother's watch, a diver's watch, it glows in the dark. It's bigger than my watch."

Why am I talking so much?

"I didn't hear about that. That sucks."

Adam had assumed the whole school knew about the watch.

"I got it back."

"Oh good. Is that why you brought the cops?"

So she did know about *that*. Adam wanted to scream that the police came on their own to stop a feeder gang for criminals and he did what the police told him to do and he did the right thing and nobody should be afraid they'll be mugged when they go to school. He told Valerie all this in a psychic whisper, but his telepathic powers proved immature, so he summarized:

"I didn't..." This stymied her for a minute. "Bring the cops."

"They *think* you brought the cops," Valerie proclaimed, "so it doesn't matter what you did or didn't do, or think you did or didn't do." And then the coda: "Nobody's cool with that."

"No."

They sat in silence.

"Does the Hill have black kids in it?"

"Are you crazy?" she jumped. "That's who they beat up on. Black kids stole your watch?"

"And white kids. Together. A gang."

"Hitters and black kids? The Hill better not find out. You know what I mean?"

He had no idea what she meant. "Yeah, I guess," he said, falling into her rhythms.

She glanced right, caught Adam's eye, but quickly looked down to check the table where his brown bag lay, glanced left, flicked her hair around to look behind her. Her profile was striking, distracting, but who was she checking for? She moved closer to Adam, conspirators. Summoning a solitary grain of Michael Mason cool, he asked, "What should I do?"

She answered in the flat tone of deep knowledge and absolute truth. "They won't jump you in the schoolyard. They'll stare you down through the fence, step after step. That's to freak you out."

Your description is freaking me out.

Adam imagined hundreds of hitters pressed against the chain link fence, the metal strands of the chain links impressing diamonds into their foreheads, all eyes on Adam, accusing, jangling nunchucks against the fence, Adam's death rattle.

He was freaking himself out.

"I don't want to get beat up," Adam confessed before he could stop his mouth.

"Nobody *wants* to get beat up, Adam."

Valerie said his name. *That* made him jump.

"They won't jump you when you get past the gates either."

"Why not?" he squeaked.

"They'll wait till you start to run, then they'll chase you. They like chasing people."

His first hope.

"I'm pretty fast."

"So listen to me, what I'm telling you. Even if you're Speedy Gonzalez, whatever you do, *don't run!* Running is the worst thing."

"Okay. So I should…um…take my lumps?"

She twisted up her mouth and turned to face him. *Take my lumps* was the wrong expression.

"I meant, get the shit kicked out of me?"

"If you have to, you have to. Maybe you won't have to. I don't know. I'll see if I can do anything…. I'm not sure…. You know what I mean?"

She seems to know much more than I do about everything. She probably likes me, at least a little teeny tiny bit, if she's trying to help. She's not Jewish, but if she saves me, falling in love with her would be the least I could do.

"What if I don't go home? What if I never walk out the gates?"

"You gonna sleep here with the test tubes?"

No, that was an imbecilic suggestion. Mouth, say nothing.

"Just don't run away. That's what gets them going. Shit, I gotta go. I'm not in this lab."

It seemed to be Adam's fate to be targeted by every gang in New York City.

Jesus, I've turned into Dennis.

When the day ended and Adam exited the building, it was almost exactly as Valerie had prophesied, except it was a red Pontiac, not blue, with two hitters in studded jeans jackets sitting on the hood, smoking, plus two more inside the car, not hundreds, not pressed against the chain links, no weapons visible. They seemed relaxed, which made them more menacing.

He would face them and fight. He would get hit, punched, kicked.

I wouldn't mind losing a tooth, so long as it's not a front tooth.

If they were in the Watch Gang, they'd be violating probation.

It might be worth getting beaten up once, to send them to juvenile detention. (Nipping and budding. Or snitching and ratting.)

But they didn't look familiar, didn't summon up anyone he'd seen on the corner or at the precinct.

Running would be the worst thing to do.

Adam decided to walk slowly, casually, leisurely, as if he had no idea that they were waiting for him, whistling a happy tune, except he couldn't whistle, so *humming* a happy tune. The instant he was beyond the gate, he would make a mad dash to the buses and police on Main Street while they chased him in their car, caught him at Union Street and Bowne, cracked his skull with a bottle, broke it open on the curb of Roosevelt Avenue, and laughed while his brains leaked into the storm drain. The police would ask him who assaulted him, but the talking part of his frontal lobe would already be in the drain with his teeth and his left eye.

Maybe it was not Tommy's car, and maybe it was not the Hill. Maybe this car was there by completely by chance. Then they pointed at Adam.

Not a coincidence.

Adam pulled himself up and glared defiantly.

I can wait you out. You won't attack me on school grounds. I'll stand here until Dr. Lefkowitz comes out.

Adam heard footsteps behind him. He couldn't break eye contact, so he prayed quietly that it would be Valerie. She could give the Hill the *all's cool* signal, and Adam and Valerie would stroll past them with nonchalance to the Q17 bus stop. If not Valerie, then Mr. Selenko or Mr. Beck, or better yet, Mr. Vogel.

It was Suvan Chakrabarti.

Suvan had appeared in their class two weeks before, dark-skinned, short, skinny, with unnaturally straight black hair, and a faint mustache. Mrs. Bell assigned the new boy the place next to Adam, moving the tower who had replaced Jason Boyer in home room as well as science to the back row. Suvan wore a school uniform that baffled his classmates, had a British accent, called teachers *ma'am* and *sir*, was fussy and proper, and took detailed notes in the kind of old-fashioned pressed-cardboard notebooks with black-and-white Jackson Pollock covers that Adam had abandoned in fifth grade.

Their SP classmates kept their distance, polite and indifferent to this odd duck, but Adam recruited him to the DP squad where, despite his badge, Suvan was targeted by the change hustlers. "Hey, brown boy, buy us some lunch"—although Suvan was less *brown* than they were. Suvan offered to check "what he could spare," which fueled more demands. Adam couldn't stomach watching Suvan's pockets emptying and showed him how to fend them off—"Got no money, man"—but Suvan would slip and begin to reach in his pocket, and the game was lost. Then one of them asked him his name.

"Suvan."

"A boy named Sue?"

Suvan was serenaded with terrible Johnny Cash impressions at every meal. Adam told him he would be bothered less if he dressed normally, and Suvan told Adam his parents had come to England from India before moving to America and this was how "one was attired for school." Adam didn't know enough history to question the multiple migrations or the dress code.

"Can I join you?" Suvan asked Adam, stranded in the courtyard.

"Umm."

Adam intuited that a freshly arrived dark-skinned immigrant with a funny accent would be subject to particular abuse; he had to warn Suvan for his own good to go home, but Adam was desperate not to be alone. Minutes passed, perhaps an hour. Finally, Adam spoke.

"Those guys are waiting to beat the crap out of me."

Crap was as far as Adam would go with Suvan.

"I see. How do you know?"

Because Valerie told me.

"I just know."

Suvan waved at them. Adam yanked his arm down hard.

"What the hell you doing?"

"Testing your theory. Ah, they're waving back. I think you're right. They're big. How long have you been here?"

He didn't know. Forever. "What time is it?"

"One thirty-nine."

"Nine minutes."

"Are you having a staring contest?"

"A glaring contest," Adam quipped without thinking. There was a pause, then a titter that built into a bray, so odd and endearing, it distracted Adam from the red Pontiac.

"How long, if I might inquire, are you planning to stay here?"

"Till they leave."

Suvan pondered the implications.

"That could be a long time."

"I know."

Suvan checked his watch again. Adam expected him to make an excuse, to explain that he had to get home, but Suvan surprised him.

"You cannot remain staring at would-be attackers all day. This is not a productive use of your time."

"If I run, it'll be worse. Running is what they want."

"I didn't say anything about running."

No, you didn't.

They glared together at their executioners.

"You don't have to stay here with me."

"I don't mind," Suvan answered. "Let's change the subject. Listen to this and tell me if you think this is a reasonable facsimile. *You lucky bastards!*" Suvan cleared his throat, approximating their science teacher Mr. Beck's disturbingly loud attempts to relocate phlegm. "*You kids are going to live long enough to land on Mars!*"

Adam was too surprised to laugh, then he laughed so hard, he forgot to glare at the ambush. Suvan had Beck's Brooklyn accent down, with no trace of his British. How did he do that?

"Do it again."

"*Write to the government and tell them, 'I'm twelve years old and I want to go where no man has gone before!'*" Suvan followed this with a mouth-and-cupped-hands rendition of *Star Trek* theme music.

"Brilliant!" Adam said.

Suvan had been working up a routine, and Adam was most likely—*most definitely*—the first audience.

"Perhaps if we walk out together, they will not trouble you."

That might happen. Or they might stuff us both in the trunk of their car, dump me bleeding and unconscious in the Shea Stadium parking lot, where'd I get run over by a maintenance truck, and throw you off the Empire State Building.

"Or they'll beat us both up," Adam said to his new but loyal friend.

"Or they'll beat us both up," echoed Suvan.

Loyal friend with timing and a sense of humor. Adam was not alone.

"Or we could wait for a teacher to walk us out," Adam suggested.

"I think they've departed through the faculty door on the other side of the building."

"I didn't know there was one."

Or I could call Detective Riley. If only I had a two-way wristwatch radio.

"You say we are not supposed to run. Why not disarm them?"

"How?"

Suvan suggested a plan that didn't involve taking away any hidden knives and did involve running, but not running away. It sounded slightly more promising than waiting to be rescued.

They used one of their leather book straps to create a finish line next to the flagpole in the middle of the yard. Next came their most daring move—heading straight toward the red Pontiac. The car door opened, two young men exited, watching the boys watching them, tamping down their excitement as cigarettes were extinguished.

Adam and Suvan stopped ten feet before the gate and placed the second leather strap down to serve as the starting line. They were within a few steps of four members of the Hill.

Memorize their faces to identify them later—bad acne, zit cream dried up in splotches, black sideburns that curve like daggers toward his mouth—that's all Adam had time for. They were older, larger, but did not seem as monumental as they had from a distance.

And now, their most dangerous gambit: turning their backs on them.

"On your mark," Adam said, but it came out soggy, as if his throat was clogged with Mr. Beck's phlegm. They each got down on one knee.

Adam stared straight ahead but saw nothing, blinded by the voice telling him Suvan's plan was insane. *Don't run! Get shit kicked out of me.*

"Get set!" Adam continued, rallying confidence, until he yelled, "GO!"

They took off, racing toward the flagpole. Clever he was, but Suvan was not fast. Adam had been running sprints since third grade and beat Suvan by four strides.

They waited, took their time turning around to see if their audience was still in position.

They were.

They walked back to the gate. Adam turned to them and in his best Michael Mason asked, "You want to race?"

"Don't think so," one answered.

The others called their friend *asshole, dickwad, douchebag* for talking to Adam.

"He asked me a question," he protested.

"You seem quite interested in our races," Suvan said.

"You talk funny."

"You'll probably win," Suvan said. "You're all bigger than us."

"We know," answered the second one, which brought on a barrage of insults from his partners.

"I heard you like chasing people," Adam added, trying to distract them from Suvan.

"Heard from who?"

Damn.

Adam had screwed up and had to change the subject.

"Anybody else want to race?" Adam asked.

"Heard from *who*?"

"Gotta run," Adam said, "marksgetsetgo!" and Suvan and Adam took off again toward the flagpole. They waited to catch their breaths, then lined up again, starting at the flagpole. Opposite direction.

"This time, touch and back," Adam called.

Suvan did the starting call.

"Ready, steady, go!"

Steady?

They sped toward the gate, adrenaline pumping their breath and blood into static in their ears. Adam slowed as he approached the end line, making a wide turn to avoid running through the gate, tapped the strap with the toe of his right sneaker, and sped back to the flagpole. He noticed the absence of footsteps only upon crossing the finish line. He spun around and saw precisely what he feared.

Suvan had not stopped in time and had run into their arms.

Pockmarks strolled through the gate and picked up the leather strap, snapping it twice against the ground, and once against itself, three loud sharp cracks that resounded through the yard. Adam snatched up the strap at his feet in disgust, having no idea what to do with it. He walked toward the gate quickly—he would not abandon a teammate again—*whatever you do, don't run!*—wishing, praying Mr. Vogel would materialize or Valerie or Detective Riley or Seth or Dad.

The fear on Suvan's face as they pushed him from one to the other made Adam so furious, he unrolled the strap, wrapped the leather end around his wrist, so the end with the metal clasp hung free. He had a weapon. He stood at the entrance to the school gate, only the sidewalk separating them.

"Leave him alone!" Adam yelled.

"Don't like his looks."

"Blame his parents," Adam answered. Suvan frowned.

"*Who* said we like chasing people?"

"Word gets around," Adam said to the ground. He would not reveal Valerie's name. "If it's not true, let us go home and don't chase us."

"You run, and let's see if we catch you. We'll give you a head start."

You can chase me, Adam almost said, but refrained. It was clear how that noble, pointless, painful gesture would end up.

"You want to race, fine," Adam said. "You want to chase us, we're not running. We're done running."

This stumped them. They didn't know what to do exactly.

"That's his strap," Adam said to the acne boy.

"Why does he talk so funny, this—?" He used the N-word.

"He's not a…not a…" Adam couldn't, wouldn't say that word aloud. "But he can imitate our teachers. Hey, do Mr. Beck for them."

"What?" Suvan mouthed.

"Go ahead," Adam urged. "Show them."

"That mother failed me," one of them said. "Let's hear you."

Suvan cleared his throat, tried to speak, couldn't get a sound out, then cleared it again. He was too nervous. He was trembling. Suvan tried a third time. To get his voice back, he coughed up a chunk of phlegm, which he spit on the ground.

"Hey," said the tall one. "That's pretty good."

Suvan and Adam laughed, a laugh of nerves, of absurdity. The gang was confused.

"*You lucky bastards will land on Mars someday*," Suvan spat out in his best Brooklynese.

"That's him!" the tall one cried. "That's Beck! What a scumbag!"

"*Science is your future!*" Suvan said.

"What's your name, kid?"

"Suvan," he mumbled.

"What?"

"A boy named Sue," Adam said, helpfully, grasping for distractions.

Suvan glowered again, but this set them singing, all of them instantly doing Johnny Cash.

Adam took Suvan's strap from the acne boy's hands so gently he didn't resist.

As they made their way through the ballad, Adam stepped into the circle, took hold of Suvan, and pushed him forward, marching ahead but in tandem toward Roosevelt Avenue, as the Hill got caught up in the ear-biting violence described between father and son.

"Keep walking," Adam hissed. "Don't look back."

Muscles rigid as they strolled toward Giunta's Pizza, they discovered there's nothing harder than pretending to walk casually.

"We left our books at the flagpole," Suvan said, slowing down. "My mother will be furious," Adam grabbed his arm, marched him forward faster.

"We're not going back for our goddamned books," Adam hissed.

"I think we got away," Suvan said.

Adam wished Suvan hadn't said it aloud. Bad luck.

"I will receive quite a talking-to," Suvan said, in his funny way.

"My mom will call your mom if you get in trouble."

Adam said nothing for a long time. He was listening for footsteps, for a red Pontiac. There was silence.

They had done it. What an incredible surprise, to have escaped, and for each boy to be part of a "they" again.

CHAPTER 18

"Those of you who have not yet surprised us are hereby put on notice." Selenko's head swiveled above his turtleneck, tilted down, his nose forming a sharp beak. He spoke in his soft, sonorous voice of gravitas and conspiracy. "The Surprise Challenge deadline approaches. You have been warned."

Selenko switched instantly to his bright tone of excitement. "We now move on to the major assignment for the year. Your mission, should you decide to accept it—although, unlike Mr. Phelps, you have no choice—your mission is to adapt a novel for the stage."

Mumbles and murmuring about this *Mission: Impossible*.

"Now, *which* novels should you consider? you ask, or you should have asked, but I will answer since you didn't, no doubt so captivated by the challenge that you've been stunned into silence. I don't mean the Hardy Boys or Nancy Drew. It must be a work of literature that enriches our souls and has drama and conflict. Think *Of Mice and Men* or *A Separate Peace*."

Murmuring of fear, excitement, confusion.

"You will each work on one project. You will form your own groups, and once your group chooses its novel, you will write the script, stage it, costume it, create the set, light it, and perform it. You have one week to choose your source material and find your cast and receive my approval, after which time I will assign parts to anyone still searching for a project. Remember! You don't want to end up with your picture hanging in the post office like Adam Miller. Regrettably, Adam, the machine gun didn't do you justice."

Every time Mr. Selenko spoke his name, Adam's body twitched and tingled, the recurring joke reinventing him as an outlaw.

Adam knew what his project would be in a heartbeat. Elie Wiesel's *Dawn*. The book Seth had given Adam in their basement was short, suspenseful, and mesmerizing. Seth told him it was a book every Jew ought to read, and Seth had read so very many Jewish books.

The plot was simple. It's 1946. The Jews are trying to drive the British out of Palestine to take control of the country before the Arabs do. To stop the Jewish underground from ambushing British soldiers and blowing up their headquarters, the Brits capture three Jewish underground fighters and threaten to hang them at dawn. In retaliation, the Jewish underground captures a British Army captain, John Dawson, whom they also threaten to execute at dawn. A teenage Holocaust survivor, Elisha, haunted by the ghosts of his murdered family, is assigned to guard the prisoner through the long night, and shoot him at sunrise if he doesn't get a message that their comrades have been released. Throughout the long night, Captain Dawson tries to convince Elisha to let him live.

Mr. Selenko met with each of the "directors" after class the following week, one at a time, to hear their pitch. Adam was last. When his turn came, Mr. Selenko rose and stretched his arms, but instead of returning to the two chairs, he walked over to the edge of the stage, let his feet dangle over the ledge, and looked up at the lights.

"I need to stretch my back," Mr. Selenko said. "You don't mind, do you? Have a seat."

Adam mimicked Selenko, feet hanging over, lying back, and looking directly into the blinding orbs above. Adam closed his eyes.

Mr. Selenko had never heard of Elie Wiesel. He asked to borrow the novel when Adam was done with it. Adam gulped—it was Seth's book—but promised to bring it soon.

"How many characters will there be?"

"I don't know. There's the British captain and the Jewish kid who's supposed to kill him and the other underground members and Elisha's murdered family who are haunting him."

For one brief moment, Adam thought to cast his old friends—Ryan might be weaseled away—but Jason had locked him up, recruited *all* of them to his own production.

"Hmm. Can I give you some advice? Focus on the protagonists, the two of them."

Mr. Selenko was right. He didn't really need the other underground fighters or the rest of the characters.

"What about the ghosts?"

"I haven't read the book yet. You say they're haunting this young fellow. You can show that in the acting. Putting ghosts on stage usually ends up pretty hokey."

Selenko's idea would help solve his biggest problem—finding enough actors, *any* actors, who'd work with ostracized Adam.

"Hmm. Tell me what excites you about *Dawn*."

He tried to explain that Elisha was standing up not just for himself but for all Jews. Elisha knew Captain Dawson didn't deserve to die—he was no Nazi—but he might have to be killed for the cause of creating a Jewish country. Was Elisha courageous enough to become an executioner on behalf of his people?

"So Elisha can't avoid making a life-and-death decision," Mr. Selenko summarized.

"If he's man enough to kill him."

"Do you think that's the message of the book?"

Adam didn't answer. He closed his eyes, saw the ghost glares from the lights drilling down into his retinas. The meaning of the tale, the question of whether the book meant to praise or condemn a Jew who—unlike so many passive victims of the Holocaust—kills to guarantee the creation of a country for his people, was not central in Adam's mind. Adam was drawn to the Elisha who fought back, who was not afraid to sully himself with a weapon, with killing—*was it murder?*—who was not going to be scared any longer. Elisha was brave, steadfast, choosing to act decisively, facing down his moral quandary. Yes, yes, there's a sort of dilemma there, but it's resolved. The truth was that Adam was more intrigued by shuffling images of how to stage the confrontation between Elisha and Captain Dawson.

"I'll think about it."

"Elisha sounds like the perfect part for you," Selenko said. "Who have you cast to play Captain Dawson?"

Eyes still shut, the image appeared in outline but with clarity.

"Suvan."

"The new boy? That's kind of you."

Adam sat up, enthused. "Suvan's accent is real, and I think he's a good actor." Suvan's imitation of Mr. Beck had been *spot on*, as Suvan had taught Adam to say. Adam was eager to show his teacher this was his casting preference, not charity (and not for lack of alternatives).

"Genius."

Adam didn't need to hear more. He worked madly on his script, rereading *Dawn* four times, underlining the best lines of dialogue in different-colored pencils. He would stage only the long night between the kidnapped British Army officer fighting for his life and the teenage Elisha assigned to execute him. The audience would watch, judging, rooting—but for what ending?

Adam discovered the most striking element in their first rehearsal: Suvan could stand very still, like a teacher. Perfect for Captain Dawson. Suvan was slight in build, a toothpick like Adam, but Suvan's ramrod posture and his authentic British accent radiated authority. Suvan's London school uniform was recalled from the closet. Its epaulettes gave Suvan shoulders.

For Elisha, Adam mixed and matched what he remembered from his family's Israel trip with his own outdoor hiking gear—Israeli leather sandals, khaki pants, and a lumberjack shirt—a New England pioneer of Palestine. He wanted his Elisha jumpy, nervous, and if he could figure out how to act it, he wanted Elisha to seem haunted.

Rather than lighting the entire stage in the conventional manner, with spots following the main actors, Adam kept the lighting deliberately low, tried a single spotlight from above—but he didn't have a third person to operate the light—and then settled on placing the spot on the floor to the side, creating long, monster-movie shadows and large patches of darkness on stage. He hoped characters appearing suddenly from the blackness would create suspense.

For the climax, just as the gunshot was heard, the spotlight would go out—he'd need another pair of hands after all—Adam planned for Dawson to cry, "Elisha!"

It might work. It might be devastating.

CHAPTER 19

"These are crazy times," Jeremy Miller pondered. "I don't know what's going on."

Adam had his own theories to explain the dripping red graffiti—*Jews Out of Flushing!*—painted on the front door of the new synagogue building. The Watch Gang taking revenge for their probation, the Hill, the gang on the subway (*no, that was impossible*).

"No matter what," his mother added, "Jews get it in the neck."

"Everybody's angry at everybody," his father surmised. "It's the War, Abbie Hoffman—"

"The Black Panthers."

"We're getting caught in the crossfire, Helen, It's not about us."

"Of course it's about us," Adam's mother insisted. "It's always about us."

Seth mumbled something incomprehensible.

"Did you boys know your father's been pushing the Temple board to put in an alarm system all year?"

"They've already said yes," his father reported.

Seth's incredulity gave way to disgust. "Broken windows! Nazi graffiti! You want us to defend ourselves with an alarm system!"

"The police don't think they're connected," Adam offered.

"Who made you an expert?" Seth snapped.

"I...found them both." He'd met the Cantor Shabbat morning before services to practice, an ungodly early hour, and they were the first to see the message on the door. The Cantor grew red, furious, had cursed in multiple languages.

"The police said they think kids threw the bricks. Because the two buildings are around the corner from each other, they wouldn't know it's the same place."

"We are not surrounded by anti-Semites," Mr. Miller intoned.

"You're not a principal anymore because you're Jewish!" Seth shouted.

"That's not your business, and that was my decision."

"Like hell it was! Isn't that why you went on strike?"

"Calm down, Seth, right now." Helen Miller stepped in to set the record straight. "We went on strike to protect our dignity, for teachers to get respect and safety, to get decent pay for doing our job, which is already almost impossible without being afraid you'll get mugged in your own classroom."

"That's a fairy tale you tell yourself, Mom! They fired Jewish teachers so the Black Panthers of Ocean Hill–Brownsville could take over the school system!"

Adam was trying to follow the argument.

"Seth, if you'll stop yelling for one minute."

"I'm not yelling!" Seth screamed. Adam found it funny that Seth was yelling about not yelling. Seth rounded on his younger brother.

"What are *you* laughing at?"

"Don't take it out on Adam!" Mr. Miller called, his voice rising now. "Listen to me. Every day those kids get told that they're not welcome—not in the classroom, not in the school, not in this city, not on this earth."

"You told me, Dad."

"All they wanted were teachers and principals who would not make the students feel worthless."

"I've heard this lecture a thousand times. You can't see what's right in front of you, Dad. They wanted black teachers and black principals."

But Adam hadn't heard it, and it was fascinating.

Seth continued his indictment. "Is that why the gang attacked Adam on the subway, why the gang tried to steal his watch, because they felt worthless? Shouldn't they feel worthless if they're beating up *kids*?"

"He's not wrong, Jem."

"Helen?"

Is that why Michael Mason was following me?

"Your father's heart never stops bleeding, boys."

Their mother never went against their father in front of them. Never.

"They asked for me specifically to be the principal, right? How does that fit your puzzle, Seth? Helen?"

"That's a point, Jem. Boys, your father risked losing a lot of union buddies by taking that job," Helen added, playing both sides. Adam was relieved to see his parents back in alignment.

"Proves *my* point," Seth said triumphantly. "You sold out your union buddies to make black militants happy."

"I did what I thought was right. But I was on the picket line every day. And since when did you start sounding like William Buckley?"

"Listen to me for once! I organized the anti-war rally at Stuyvesant—"

"You're starting this again? You didn't have enough trouble at Andrew Jackson?"

"That's not the point. The point is the Afro-American Society plasters the stage with posters against Israel!" Seth yelled. "I was almost expelled for protesting cops killing black kids in Georgia, and now, I mean, what the hell? What does Israel have to do with the Vietnam War? They're effing backstabbers."

"Language, Seth."

"I said *effing.*"

"Blacks are not the oppressors of the Jewish People!"

The vein pulsing in Jeremy's forehead gave their father away despite the measured demeanor that came from years of trying to keep the lid from flying off in high schools. "They don't have the power to oppress us. They're oppressed too. A hundred times worse than what we have to deal with."

"So why'd they say those poems on the Julius Lester show?" Adam chimed in.

"Don't say that name in this house." Helen hissed in a quiet voice, and she spat three times.

Jeremy Miller's surprise was as much that his youngest son had entered the fray as that he knew about that incident. He was tired but did not want to miss a teaching moment. "So here's what I'm wondering, Adam. Why did a labor struggle for dignity—or, let's go so far as to say a fight for control of schools—get twisted out of shape into blacks against Jews? We were always allies. I'm thinking it serves someone's interest to turn us against each other."

"The Russians?"

The Russians seemed to be behind everything bad.

"I was thinking Republicans."

"Lindsay was laughing in his limo all the way to the country club," Adam's mother said.

"We're the minorities, outsiders in this country...."

"I'm not an outsider," Adam said, then immediately realized that he did feel like one, but because of Jason, not because he was Jewish. Unless it had everything to do with being Jewish.

"We got to watch out for each other, Jews and blacks."

"Do they hate us?" Adam asked.

"Of course not!"

"Really, Dad?" Seth broke in. "How do you not see it?"

"That's not been my experience."

"Mine either," Adam said, thinking of Gracie, of Curtis, of Connie, of Ellie, happily siding with his father, but wary of showing up Seth.

"You don't know anything!" Seth blasted Adam, infuriated that his twelve-year-old brother had political views.

"And that full-page ad they took out in the *New York Times* against Israel?" their mother quipped. "That must have cost a pretty penny."

Her husband was shocked. "You too?"

"I'm just saying," she said firmly. "A full page in the *New York Times*."

"They're beating up old Jews in Brooklyn and now they're attacking our own shul!" Seth yelled so loud his voice cracked.

"What in God's name makes you think the two things are connected?" his father yelled. "These are vandals. Who said they were black, whoever did this?"

"They might be connected," Mrs. Miller said.

"Since when did you start fearing black people?"

"Since they mugged my son on the subway."

"It's your ghetto mentality," Seth declared. "That's why we delude ourselves, that's why we don't fight back! Brooklyn is a war zone. They're beating up Hassidim for fun."

"The Cantor lives with the rest of the Orthodox in Brooklyn," their father said. "Ask him if he's afraid of black people."

"Is the Cantor Orthodox?" Adam asked.

"What a genius," Seth cracked, then understood Adam was in earnest. "That's why his family won't come to our shul. That's why he never comes here for dinner."

"We'd love to have him," Mr. Miller murmured.

"He wouldn't eat in our house," Mrs. Miller explained. "We're not kosher."

"If Jews don't fight back, it will only get worse."

"Enough, Seth," their mother said. "Let's eat in peace."

The teachers' strike was about blacks and Jews, or it wasn't, but old Jews are getting beaten up in Brooklyn. The Cantor's Orthodox and is alone every Shabbat, and Dad feels guilty that we can't host him because our house isn't kosher. And Seth and Dad are each convinced the other is wrong.

No wonder everyone's angry.

CHAPTER 20

Adam took Suvan to the parking lot to teach him stickball. The bat was from Haben's, a jazzed-up broomstick with tape pre-wrapped around one end for a better grip. A Spalding rubber ball was preferable to a Pensie Pinkie—the Pensie Pinkie was too smooth for throwing curveballs. Anything cheaper would split in half upon contact.

Adam chalked up the pitching box on the wall, the exterior wall of the adjacent indoor parking garage. If the batter didn't swing and the ball hit the box, the chalk would come off on the ball and you could prove you had thrown a strike. The batter stood in front of the box, the pitcher behind a line chalked on the ground thirty feet away.

The second time they played stickball, Suvan showed up with a cricket bat. Adam immediately fell in love with its wide flat face, which made hitting so easy it felt like cheating.

Adam heard a buzzing sound. A remote-controlled model plane was zooming low over their game. Adam followed the swoops and dives of the buzzing bird, tracking the miniature aircraft to its eventual landing on the lawn fronting the building next door. Only when Michael Mason picked up the plane did Adam spot him in his green army jacket, unbuttoned, rips on a pocket and sleeve. Was it pro-military or anti-war to dress like that?

This marked the second time Adam and Suvan had bumped into Michael Mason outside of school. The first was at a Clint Eastwood double feature of *The Good, the Bad, and the Ugly* and *Hang 'Em High*.

Is Michael Mason following me?

Suvan waited for Adam's cue.

"I'd let you try it," Michael Mason said, "but you'd probably crash and burn."

"Probably would," Adam agreed, answering for both of them. *And you would charge me $100 if I broke your plane.*

"That thing get run over by a steamroller?"

"It's a cricket bat," Suvan explained. "I'd let you try it, but you'll probably...in truth, there's no reason for you not to try it. Would you like to try it?"

Michael walked directly to their chalk box without speaking, withdrew a package of tissues from his pocket and erased their box.

"Hey!"

Without turning around to face them, Michael put a hand up, *Stop!* He pulled out three thick pieces of chalk from his pocket and redrew the box, creating several different colored zones by using either one piece of chalk or blending them. This action took seven minutes, during which time Adam bounced the ball to himself, anxious and mesmerized.

"See, an inside pitch will come off red, outside green, high pitch blue, or low pitch yellow. The outer box, the orange, is outside but shows you're getting close."

Michael Mason is an artist of the strike zone. Is he also anti-Semitic, as Seth claimed? Doesn't seem like it.

"Tom Seaver uses this to practice his control," Michael Mason offered.

"And Jerry Koosman and Nolan Ryan," Suvan volunteered. "I read about it the *New York Times.*"

"The *New York Times,*" Michael repeated with disdain.

"I'm a Mets fan too," Suvan announced.

"You are?" Adam didn't know Suvan followed baseball.

"'Course," Michael Mason declared. "This is Flushing."

"Adam's a Yankees fan."

"Yankee fan," Adam corrected.

"What the hell, man?" Michael Mason challenged. "That's...not cool."

"I'm not cool then," Adam said. "I'm uncool."

"He's so uncool, it's cool," Suvan added.

But Michael was on to the next topic. "You'll be too busy chasing my home runs to get any chalk on your ball."

Suvan pitched, Michael Mason never missed. Adam chased, working up a sweat following the bounces after the ball came down, and it was a long time between pitches. Every time he swung, Michael Mason's army jacket flew up in the back, another element of cool. Suddenly, Michael Mason was bored with batting.

"I like your plane," Adam said.

"It's radio-controlled but gasoline-powered. I built it. Move back there to the pitcher's mound, both of you. You like movies so much, I'll show you something."

Michael Mason manipulated the controls of the plane with decisive but delicate movements. The plane took off, and once above their heads, did a loop-de-loop. Suvan and Adam cheered. Michael sent it sky-high, the boys squinting into the sun to track it, and a moment later, Michael yelled, "Car!" the universal parking lot signal to *scatter*. The boys jumped to the side of the road bisecting the parking lot, but there was no car in sight. They turned back to see Michael's plane diving down at them, which was exciting until it came so close, they hit the ground flat on their stomachs.

Michael Mason laughed.

"*North by Northwest*," he said cryptically, before walking away.

Following me, Adam thought, *and trying to kill me*.

CHAPTER 21

Adam could hardly concentrate as he watched scene after scene put on by his classmates, the final day of the three-day in-class showcase. He and Suvan were scheduled last. He pointed his face at the other productions but only partly took them in. Jason had staged *Jonathan Livingston Seagull*, a book everyone in his class adored—except Adam, who found it preachy and tedious—and was glorying in its positive reception. There were embarrassing seagull "caws" that brought laughs in the wrong places, but Jason had done a clever job forgoing bird costumes for occasional bird-like movements, and staging flight by having several actors adopting slightly different body and arm positions in succession. Damn Jason! *Harriet the Spy* wasn't bad, but neither *The Hobbit* nor the singularly unoriginal idea to stage *A Separate Peace* had worked at all. And neither would *Dawn*.

Adam's feeble spark of optimism was doused with a quiet hiss.

It's 1971. The fight for Israel is a historical bore. How can I convince anyone I'm Elisha? There's so little lighting, they won't be able to see us. Jason will lead the boos!

Mr. Selenko instructed them to go backstage and get ready, the final performance of the day. The class was so restless, Adam prayed for the period bell to grant them a stay of execution.

Focus!

By the time he walked out on stage, Adam's knees were trembling. He heard Jason's rat-tat-tat laugh and Buddy's sycophantic whispering.

Adam's voice went vibrato.

He explained that the British were running the show in Palestine ("Boring!" he heard Jason say the word aloud, heard Selenko's "Shhhh"); that the Jews wanted their own country (*Snoring!* Jason, Buddy, and Stu, then a "Shut up!" from Ryan); that three Jewish underground fighters had been sentenced to die at dawn and a British Army captain named John Dawson had been captured in retaliation and would be executed at dawn if their comrades were not freed (Huh?).

That was too much, too long, too mindbogglingly boring.

Adam slipped backstage. Snickering rippled down Jason's row. Adam heard giggles, then, "Shut up, assholes!" Valerie this time from the side of the stage, "Quiet please!" from Selenko. Suvan took his place.

"Quiet!" Selenko ordered.

Forget about Jason! Think only of Dawn!

Adam waited for Valerie's steady curtain pull to reveal the single cot lying on the floor, with Captain John Dawson lit from the side. The audience saw only his back, a giant shadow of danger projected across the stage.

The set and lights were so distinct from the pieces that preceded them that they snatched back the class's attention.

Maybe we have a chance.

Suvan was no longer a thirteen-year-old immigrant to the United States but a British Army officer. Adam was a hyped-up Jewish survivor, stalking his prey. Neither the audience nor Captain Dawson knew where Elisha was whenever he retreated from the light into the greater pool of onstage darkness. They did not forget any lines, and the lighting fed the tension. The scene built to its mighty climax. John Dawson cried, "Elisha!" into the darkness the second before Valerie killed the light and the shot rang out.

The applause was strong, the loudest of the day. The class adored the play, loved Suvan as the officer, Adam as Elisha. And that flipped the switch. As their many small decisions of staging, lighting, costuming, writing, were proven right, his doubts were extinguished as if they had never been.

During the curtain call, there were no boos, but Jason was talking, Buddy as well. Adam thought he'd seen Ryan clapping, and maybe heard Ryan say, "It *was not* boring!" before being silenced by Buddy. The contrast between the lit stage and the dark house made it hard to tell. Were they jeering or cheering?

Someone asked whether Elisha had killed John Dawson or not, meaning a) they had been paying attention, and b) that the applause had come in so quickly, it drowned out the gunshot.

Damn!

The following class, Selenko announced that "it would be a crime if no one else saw the amazing work we are doing." He had convinced Dr. Lefkowitz to organize several assemblies for other classes, but given the time limitations—a single class period—he had been forced to pick only a sampling of plays. And so—*drumroll*—the production teams of *Harriet the Spy*, *Jonathan Livingston Seagull*, and *Dawn* would resume rehearsals. And that would be the order of the show.

Next time the gunshot will work! And maybe Valerie will shoot that goddamned seagull.

CHAPTER 22

A dam was treating Suvan to his first chocolate egg cream at the Cove Luncheonette, spinning on their barstools at the counter while they waited. The racks for the morning newspapers were empty, the afternoon racks thinning out. Three tiny tables with round marble tops and heavy chairs sat empty, their backs intricate metalwork, their weight ensuring they didn't walk off with the clientele. The lunch specials had already been erased from the blackboard. Mid-afternoon was only kids trudging home from school, but the boys had stayed late to rehearse and were alone for the Cove's last hurrah of the day.

"I don't like eggs," Suvan declared.

These moments made Adam miss Jason desperately. During the teachers' strike, Jason and Adam had Adam's old house—his real house—to themselves all day, unlimited television, Nerf ball basketball, Yahtzee, electric football, touch football. That's when their friendship turned *best* and *forever*. Mrs. Boyer was recovering from a miscarriage, and Adam's parents walked the picket line by day and joined smokey union strategy meetings at night, including a couple in their living room. And that's when Adam and Jason established their tradition of egg creams at the Cove before after-school Hebrew School—which was not canceled even when there was no school to come after.

"What did you want to show me?" Suvan asked.

Adam revealed the facsimile *WANTED!* poster of John Dillinger that came as the centerfold inside a one-off comic book about gangsters. It unfolded to eight times the size of the page and was dominated by two mugshots, one head-on and one profile. The crimes that made Dillinger *Public Enemy Number One* were listed—Bank Robbery, Murder, Racketeering. A reward of ten thousand dollars was offered, or five thousand dollars for information leading to his capture (or his death).

"We'll paste in photos of Selenko, put his name over Dillinger's, and I'll rewrite the crimes as jokes about Selenko."

But how to get the photos? At first, Adam thought to ask the Official Yearbook Photographer to take the Selenko mugshots, but he was a ninth-grade Martian with a tiny beatnik beard and hippie hair parted down the middle in a ruler-straight furrow, and Adam was afraid to talk to him. Instead, he'd replicated the laminated card the photographer wore around his neck, stenciling the initials *OYP* in yellow in bold caps on the diagonal. He punched a hole in the card and put it on a string.

His friend's reserved response to the *WANTED!* poster was disappointing, but it was balanced by another Suvan surprise.

"I'll develop the film and size the pictures on my father's enlarger in our bathroom darkroom. My Appa fancies himself a photographer, very good at street scenes, buildings at odd angles, that sort of thing. Appa lives in fear of a chemical catastrophe destroying our carpets, which are precious, so I'll do it when no one is home."

"Perfect!"

They would need a real camera, Suvan insisted—his father wouldn't lend his. Adam explained how they would have to recruit someone Selenko didn't know to pretend to be the Official Yearbook Photographer, the OYP. He brought out the OYP card and told Suvan he would have to get it laminated. Lamination was done at Haben's, and Adam wanted Mr. Haben to forget he existed. Adam would also give him money for the latest issue of *Green Lantern/Green Arrow*.

"A comic book? What will the shopkeeper think of me?"

And back to exasperating.

Adam decided to make one pitch. "Most comic books are about cartoon crime, okay, but *Green Lantern/Green Arrow* shows real life, the problems in our society," Adam gushed.

"Just like Charles Dickens."

Adam took this on faith.

"Denny O'Neill writes about racist white landlords exploiting black tenants and poor people stealing food, and the terrible things the white man did to Indians besides cheating them out of Manhattan for twenty-four dollars."

"I'm Indian," Suvan said.

Adam's train of thought derailed and went down the side of the mountain.

"Umm," he said after a moment, "you're a different kind of Indian."

"And you're the white man," Suvan replied.

"I'm Jewish. It's not the same."

"I don't see why."

"Because we...we help black people. My parents do. We fight for civil rights, equality."

"Very noble. Why do you do that?"

"Because...that's...the right thing to do? Because of racism. Because of anti-Semitism."

Adam told Suvan about his grandparents fleeing pogroms to come to America and about the Holocaust.

"Six million? Is that possible? How do you know?"

"The Nazis counted everything."

"Hmm. We came to America to escape racist class snobbery, but they won't let me in the white bathroom at school."

"That's the hitters' bathroom," Adam objected. "There's no white bathroom."

"But you can go in, or you could, if the Hill wasn't after us."

This had never occurred to Adam before. He *was* white, and in desperation he could wade through the smoke for a quick piss in the hitters' bathroom, although lately he felt safer going to the black bathroom with Curtis.

"Okay, but I'm Jewish so we're not regular whites. We were slaves."

"When?"

"Four thousand years ago."

"That's a long time."

"We still talk about it."

Their egg creams arrived in tall ice cream glasses, topped by hillocks of foam. Suvan fingered the glass but didn't take a sip. A long silver spoon stuck out of each glass.

"Try it," Adam suggested. When Suvan didn't move, Adam explained that the foam was from the seltzer mixing with the chocolate milk. Suvan nudged the spoon to the side of the glass, took a tentative sip.

"Very fizzy and sweet."

"It's chocolate. You could get vanilla instead if you want."

Adam took a few long sips. Suvan stared at his glass.

"I'm not white or black," Suvan explained. "That's why people look at me."

"Not because of your accent?"

"What accent?"

They were quiet.

"Are you going to finish that?"

"I've had my fill." Suvan shoved it over. Adam slurped it down. His plan was off track. "I was called Paki in London," Suvan said, "which is funny because India and Pakistan are enemies."

"They are?"

"Of course. What do you call people from India?"

"Um, we don't call them anything. But Jews are called," Adam lowered his voice, "kikes, Hymies, sheenies, cheap Jews, dirty Jews, and um…and Jew-ball bastards."

"That's a lot of insulting names. Do you get called those things?"

"Not a lot. Um…let's talk about Neal Adams. He draws *Green Lantern/Green Arrow*."

Adam wanted to say, "You can feel the grime and filth and fear and hate reaching into to seize your eyeballs," but he didn't know how, so he summarized:

"Nobody draws suffering better than Neal Adams. You'll see."

"Not even Michelangelo?"

Adam knew no more of Michelangelo than of Dickens. He changed tactics.

"You have to buy this one comic book for me if you really are my best friend."

Suvan twitched, silenced.

"*Am* I your best friend?"

"Come on."

Having said it aloud, it became true. Suvan was his best and *only* friend. Adam noticed Suvan's embarrassment and busied himself digging out change for the egg creams. Suvan's eyes grew wide.

"What?"

"Behind you."

Jason was at one of the wrought iron tables with Buddy and Stu. Adam and Jason had always sat at the counter.

"Look, it's Johnny Quest and Hadji," Stu proclaimed, playing up to Jason.

I wouldn't mind being Johnny Quest, but Suvan must find it insulting. Is it insulting? It is.

"He brought his servant from the mansion," Buddy said.

Mansion?

"Ignore them," Adam and Suvan said simultaneously.

"You owe me a Coke!" Suvan said first, triumphant.

"Yeah," Adam agreed, too distracted to respond properly.

Does he know where I live? Why would he call my house a mansion? He's burning into the back of my neck, my hair is on fire. I will ignore him. I will say the putdown of all putdowns, a putdown that cannot be refuted. I will ask him flat out why he's doing this, but no, not in front of his henchmen.

Suvan leaned in close. "Let's get out of here. He's a nasty boy, Jason."

Nasty boy. That's exactly right. Was Jason always a nasty boy? I have to speak to him.

"Goodbye, Jason," Adam said, as they left. "It kind of sucks that you're so...so...so nasty."

Stu and Buddy started hooting, but Jason said nothing. Adam and Suvan walked in silence for two blocks, but neither one could pretend Adam was thinking about anything else.

"Was that dumb, what I said?"

"I don't think it will be recorded in the annals of insults, but I believe you spoke from the heart."

"My brain froze. It was so stupid."

Hadn't they ever seen a goddamned ranch house before? It looks big because it's all on one floor.

When they reached Haben's, Suvan tried desperate measures to snap Adam free.

"Tell me why Mr. Haben doesn't like you."

Adam kept it brief, and he edited.

"Mr. Haben *thought* I tried to steal a comic book [*not seven comic books*] when all I wanted to do was take it outside to show it to my cousin [*not my real cousin*], who paid for it [*and stole a* Playboy]. Mr. Haben threatened to call my parents and tell the police."

Adam hated twisting truth into a wiry mess.

"Is that why you wanted me to come with you today? You can tell me."

Why didn't I simply lie?

Adam nodded yes, coming clean, in part. "And because we're best friends."

Adam couldn't always see which way Suvan's wheels were spinning.

If you're pissed off, let me have it.

"I'm glad you asked me," Suvan said at last, "rather than someone else."

Adam chewed his lip.

"And I don't want you to die at this tender age. What do you want if they don't have *Green Lantern/Green Arrow*?"

"They'll have it." He handed Suvan a dollar—fifteen cents for the comic book, the rest he guessed would cover the lamination. "Make sure it's issue eighty-five. I already read eighty-four. And here's another twenty-five cents. I think they sell Cokes from a little refrigerator."

Suvan returned a few minutes later, sipping from a plastic straw that stuck out of his glass bottle.

Who drinks Coke with a straw in the street?

"The comic now costs twenty-five cents, although it claims to be bigger and better."

"Twenty-five cents? Really?"

Comics had cost twelve cents for most of Adam's life, then jumped to fifteen cents. A quarter was for eighty-page giants, or more recently, the sixty-four-page substitutes. Before he could send Suvan to double-check, Mr. Haben appeared, pushing back his thinning hair into the three distinct waves that rippled straight back across the top of his skull.

"Don't tell me this kid is your cousin too."

"No…" Adam stammered. "He's my friend."

"Yes, sir," Suvan affirmed with pride, "we're best friends."

"Very nice. Mrs. Bernstein usually sends over the school's lamination and pays for it on account."

Adam froze.

"My mistake, sir," Suvan jumped in. "I was supposed to ask for a receipt, so they would refund me the money. I'm an amateur photographer, and I was asked to join the Yearbook Photography Squad. The faculty advisor believes it will help with my social integration, sir."

Mr. Haben eyeballed Suvan. "Are you razzing me?"

"No, sir."

Suvan said *sir* so naturally with his refined accent, Mr. Haben let his suspicion melt, and instantly revised his assessment of Adam. Adam was appalled and thrilled that Suvan could lie so easily, to improvise for the sake of their friendship.

"Okay. Save your seventy-five cents. I'll put it on the school tab."

Mr. Haben looked at Adam screwy. "That cousin of yours? He's trouble."

"Okay," Adam mumbled.

Are you saying that because he's black? Or because he's done something?

Mr. Haben held up *Green Lantern/Green Arrow*. "This is pretty grown-up stuff."

Adam gave Mr. Haben a cockeyed once-over. "You read comic books?"

"It was mentioned in the *Times*, so I had a look."

"Mr. Dickens would not have been embarrassed by the writing, sir," Suvan said, extremely pleased with himself, "nor would Michelangelo by the pictorial impressions of human despair."

"You're a piece of work."

Mr. Haben turned to Adam. "Listen, you. You don't need to send your proxies in to do your shopping. You made a mistake, but you're a good kid."

"Thank you," Adam said. "I mean, I am."

"I'll set aside a copy of this *literature* for you when they come in. Come get your laminated card, Mr. Yearbook Photographer."

Adam was so happy he insisted on paying for Suvan's malted milk balls, naturally, the weirdest candy on the rack.

At home, Adam read the new, *bigger and better* issue of *Green Lantern/Green Arrow*, which mercilessly blew his mind. The two-page finale was the first image Adam had ever seen of someone taking drugs—*how could a human being stick a needle into his own arm?* More shocking was that it was not a criminal lowlife but Green Arrow's teenage sidekick, his adopted ward, Speedy, who'd become an addict because Green Arrow neglected him while he was off fighting crime.

Adam worried into the night that Michael Mason might be like Speedy, stealing watches to pay for drugs, smoking cigarettes while he waited for a fix. Did Michael Mason's father neglect him while he was off doing God knows what? Was Michael Mason a criminal? A drug addict?

Poor Michael Mason! I will befriend him.

CHAPTER 23

Selenko pulled Adam aside after class.

"You have such talent!"

The heat raced from Adam's stomach to his face, sent shimmers to his fingertips, made him want to clap hands and leap over tall buildings in a single bound. It also made Adam temporarily deaf, and he didn't hear what followed.

He asked Selenko to repeat it.

"I said she's a jurist, and she watched our shows and chose *Dawn*. 189 is going to compete for the very first time in the Citywide Junior High School Theater Competition."

"But we didn't try out…"

"It's invitation only. And *Dawn* has been invited!"

"Not *Jonathan Livingston Seagull*?"

"Only *Dawn*."

Adam was still on fire from "talent." Now he was burning up.

The Citywide Drama Competition. All of New York. No Jason. He had to tell Suvan.

"One word of warning: the performing arts schools always win. I'm sorry. I shouldn't have told you that, but I don't want you to be disappointed. And that doesn't mean you won't do your absolute best. It will be a fantastic challenge, and you'll make the school proud. And I'm going to help you with extra coaching."

We'll be…famous—not famous *famous—but in-school famous.*

If by some miracle they won—Selenko had just told him that couldn't happen—but if it did, that would surely transform Adam's life in a thousand ways, the most urgent of which would be that not only Jason, but Adam's old friends would be desperate to restore their friendship with Adam, to sit with him at lunch, to make him captain of the football team again, and would fight to be closest to Adam on his bar mitzvah dais.

While Adam was imagining his glorious future, Selenko continued talking until an odd comment penetrated Adam's dream.

"I didn't have the chops."

Was Selenko talking about food? Was he inviting Adam to lunch?

"It's ferociously competitive."

Adam arranged his face to maximum attention until he could grab a thread.

"You have to want it more than anything else in life, because ninety-nine times out of a hundred, you get rejected. And not just rejection—humiliation. You feel worthless, as if every decision you've made in your life was the wrong decision." He put one hand on Adam's shoulder. "You're too young to know what it feels like to be rejected."

"I'm not." Jason Boyer had made him an expert. Ryan, Stu, Buddy, Peter.

"Really?" Selenko said. "Have you been auditioning?"

"What?"

They paused to absorb the absence of communication.

"It wouldn't have surprised me if you were doing theater outside of class," Selenko said, "because you're so comfortable on stage. That's what the jurist saw in you. I thought you meant that you were auditioning."

"I'm not auditioning," Adam said.

They were quiet and it struck Adam suddenly that Selenko hadn't cracked a single joke. He was talking to Adam as if he were a person, an adult, and Adam found the release from the role of student exhilarating. Silence would wipe it all away. Adam had to keep the conversation going. He took a chance.

"Are *you* auditioning?" Adam asked.

"Yes," Selenko said. "Yes, I am."

"For the school play?"

Selenko's laugh was like a cascade of glorious sound finally dying down but then morphing into such a hard guffaw that he started to cry. He slapped Adam on the back.

"That's fantastic!" he spit out, "'For the school play...'" before hurtling into another uncontrollable laugh.

Adam began laughing too, proud of inadvertently making such a fine joke. It took Selenko some time to synchronize his breathing and speaking.

"Huyyy boy," he said, exhaling a huge dialogue bubble. "Glad to get that off my chest."

He had told Adam a secret.

But what was it?

Adam geared up to hypervigilance.

"I was called back twice, and now I have final callbacks on Thursday."

"Callbacks?"

"Off-Broadway," Selenko explained. "This is as close as I've ever gotten."

A show!

"Wow!"

"This could be my big chance at last."

"For what?"

"For what indeed. Seven years ago, I took a teaching job to pay some bills, and here I am, seven years later. 'The school play!'" Selenko's laugh went staccato this time, trilled up to giddiness, where it levitated around Adam's head until it died. "That was a good one. The only thing I'll miss—if I get the part, which is a big *if*, a gargantuan *if*—the only thing I'll miss is our class."

Within this barrage of information, Adam understood that Mr. Selenko, his favorite teacher and his sole source of comfort in 189, wanted to be an actor and not a teacher, and if his dream was fulfilled, he would disappear just when Adam needed him most for the Citywides.

"Miss Nadel will cover my classes if we get that far."

Miss Nadel? From the Opportunity Class? Teaching us? On our stage?

"Wouldn't it be something to be off-Broadway? The play takes place in an insane asylum, but it's really a protest against Vietnam. I served proudly at the time, but *I Ain't Marching Anymore!*"

"That's Phil Ochs," Adam blurted out. Seth played Phil Ochs incessantly.

"A hundred points for Adam Miller."

"You were in Vietnam?"

"I was a little early for draft dodging. I was loyal to my buddies, and that saved me. But…so many didn't come back. Sorry. I shouldn't be burdening you with this. It wasn't like Mr. Beck's war."

"He was also in Vietnam?"

"He's an old man. World War Two. No, no, that war was nonnegotiable. And what do you make of Vietnam, Adam?"

The thing with teachers is that every step can be the wrong move.

Adam had never thought to take a position on the Vietnam War, but he did at this moment.

"I'm against."

They were quiet again. Adam never knew when they were finished, couldn't know that Selenko was reassessing Adam, his student acting star, and contemplating his own postponed paternity.

"Adam," Selenko said at last, emerging from his reverie, "you're so much more aware of the world than most of the kids in your class."

The world had become more aware of Adam, it seemed, but Adam didn't want to contradict his teacher.

"I'm feeling lucky," Selenko said, when Adam didn't speak. "You remind me so much of myself at your age. You're my good luck charm."

"I hope you get the part."

"Thank you. I know you mean that. Have no fear, I won't abandon you."

Maybe Selenko wouldn't get the part and he'd stay, maybe he'd go and come back. But without Selenko, they'd have no chance at the Citywides.

CHAPTER 24

"Miller!" Mr. Beck snorted, startling Adam rigid. "Stay after class. Nothing to be afraid of, goddammit!" Which did nothing to calm Adam down.

"Liked your play. Very nice job."

"You saw it?"

"The best thing? You're not afraid to be Jewish. The faculty, count 'em up, *more* than half are Jewish."

"They are?"

"Sure. Wouldn't know it, all these chickenhearts. Selenko lent me your book."

"He did?"

Would Seth be *glad*? Spreading the word.

"This fellow Wiesel, I found his other books at Haben's. *Night*, terrible story, a doozy. I've read the lot. Powerful stuff. You doing your play again?"

"For the Opportunity Classes."

"The ghetto kids? They'll eat you for lunch."

Adam gulped.

"Oh, I get it. Your boy Selenko's got his eye on the OC lady." Adam gulped again. "Can't teach her way out of a paper bag, but she's a looker, I'll give her that. Another do-gooder helping underprivileged underachievers stay underachievers. Too bad. Listen, Miller. Nobody remembers about World War Two, what they did to the Jews."

"I do," Adam said, but Mr. Beck didn't breathe between sentences.

"That's why I'm talking to you. I liberated the camps, Buchenwald, you know. I was there."

Mr. Beck had freed the survivors?

"You can't believe these things happened till you see 'em with your own eyes. That play of yours gave me an idea. What about a Jewish Heritage Club?"

"Like the Afro-American Club?"

"Exactly. The thing is, the club, any club, has to be initiated by a student. So you will have to take the lead here."

"I need to start a club?"

"That's right. Jews are forgetting, and if we forget, everybody forgets. It's twenty-five years since the camps, twenty-two years there's a Jewish country."

"Israel?"

"What do you think, Miami Beach?"

"My brother's in Betar."

"What's that?"

"A Zionist youth movement. He's seventeen."

"So he'll go fight in Israel instead of Vietnam. Smart boy. This war's not like my war. We had no choice back then."

Of course! That must be what Seth's planning!

"I read a lot of Jewish history books. Ask me anything you want to know."

Adam couldn't think of anything but then remembered *Jew-ball bastard* and the graffiti and broken windows at the Temple.

"Mr. Beck, do black people hate Jews?"

"They don't love us, but we're not that lovable. But they don't hate us any more than they hate anybody else who's white."

"But in the teachers' strike—"

"Get wise, kid! Don't listen to that crap."

"Why is there anti-Semitism?"

"Very big question. It's a mental disorder. People always want a scapegoat. Christianity didn't help, saying we killed Jesus."

"Who did?"

"They say we killed their God, their Messiah, their son of God. They're not sure themselves who he is, but they say we did him in. We say the Romans did it."

"What do the Romans say?"

"The Romans are dead and buried. But back then, they ran the show. And why would *we* kill Jesus? He was Jewish."

"Jesus was Jewish?"

"What'd you think, he was Christian?"

"Umm...yeah."

"You got a lot to catch up on, and you know ten times as much as the rest of these ignoramuses. Here are the registration forms. You explain why you want to start the Jewish Heritage Club, put me down and Selenko as faculty sponsors."

"Is he Jewish?"

"He's got a *Yiddishe kopf* all right. God knows how his mother let him go into acting. I bet some of those actresses led him a dance in his theater days. I'll take care of Selenko. I don't see how Lefkowitz can say no."

"Separation of Church and State?"

"Sharp, Miller! I like that. Heritage, kiddo. Not religion. Heritage. History. Legacy. Values. That sort of thing. You know, Miller, you remind me of myself when I was your age.

"Umm...thanks."

Adam didn't mind that teachers saw him in themselves but wished it didn't always come with an action plan.

"I knew I could count on you."

Settled, except for Adam's stomach, now a jumping bean on a trampoline.

"I took pictures at Buchenwald. I'd show them to you, but they'd turn your hair white."

Night and Fog had given Adam nightmares, with its basket of heads.

"Tell me when you file the forms."

Adam thought of Mr. Beck liberating the camps.

How could he disappoint a hero? Starting a club was the least Adam could do.

And then another image began to haunt Adam. A student from 189 was shot and killed, although not at school. A giant blow-up of a boy, spruced up, tied and jacketed, his dark hair slicked to the side, his freckles still dotting his cheeks, was propped on an easel just inside the great heavy doors of the main entrance to 189. His confirmation picture, maybe, or his last photo ever. He didn't seem familiar, wasn't in the Watch Gang, and Adam could not remember ever having seen him.

Adam's school tried to pay tribute to the dead boy. The parents sat next to Dr. Lefkowitz, but the teachers couldn't come up with much to say, and the dead boy's father, choking up, spoke briefly, a rapid staccato, flinching the whole time.

During the memorial assembly, Adam felt sad for a stranger, moved as much by the scale of the tragedy as the ache of his own emotion. But more overwhelming was that this was not an acting scene, that this kid no longer existed, that a boy with freckles could die. *But how could a kid be shot to death?*

That boy's image haunted Adam for weeks, visited him at night when he tried to sleep. His mass, his stuff—was it converted into energy, as Mr. Beck had taught them, or did it just become garbage?

CHAPTER 25

"You get two more trial runs before the Citywides," Selenko said to start their private rehearsal. There were additional performances scheduled for the Opportunity Classes and at the assembly preceding parent-teacher conferences. "We'll sharpen your actions in each beat of the scene, to make sure your characters know exactly what he's going for at every minute." Moment-to-moment acting. That's what Selenko preached.

Selenko followed the boys across the stage as they ran their scene, whispering instructions in real time. He called it "side-coaching," but when Selenko's mustache and eyebrows flapped about as he crouched behind Suvan, it made Adam think of Jiminy Cricket, and he cracked up.

"Get your giggles out now," Selenko commanded, his voice a saber. "This is a duel to the death. Ready to work?"

Adam was embarrassed, tight, choked as Selenko hovered behind Suvan, leaning down into his friend's ear. He tried not to overhear him, but they were too close.

"Up to now, Captain Dawson, you were hiding in plain sight, you wanted Elisha to forget you are here. But now you must make Elisha see you as another human being. Try to get Elisha to shake your hand— that's your action in this beat, in this tiny moment of the scene. Easy now, not too aggressive—you don't want to startle him into shooting you, but look for your moment. Get him to shake your hand."

Footsteps, Selenko behind Adam's left ear.

"And you, Elisha. You see what he's up to. Don't let him get close to you—don't talk to him—that's *your* action in this beat. Make it clear that if he approaches you, you'll kill him on the spot. He's a monster," Selenko's voice softened into a rough-edged hum, a voice inside your head. "He's the Nazi who killed your father."

Adam tried to find that hate, that rage, to want to kill Suvan/John Dawson, but he had not been in the Holocaust, no one had killed Adam's father, and Suvan didn't scare him.

"Do you feel it?"

"No," Adam spat between his teeth, as he swung his rifle in Suvan/Dawson's direction.

"Picture someone you hate. You hate their guts. Is there such a person?"

The list would have been empty the year before, but this was no longer the case.

"Um, yes," Adam confessed.

"Really? All right then. That's who you should be thinking of."

As Adam circled Suvan/Dawson, he imagined the gang on the subway, Jew-ball with his close-shaved haircut, the Watch Gang daring him to challenge them from his place on the ground, Car Coat taking off down the street. But with Selenko so close, he forgot his lines, tripped over the mattress, and smashed his elbow on the wooden floor. Selenko did not move to comfort him or his throbbing elbow, and perhaps because of that, Adam flashed on Jason.

The anger came quickly. Adam leapt up with a surge of pain-fueled energy.

"Stay with me," Selenko hissed down Adam's neck. "Don't let him touch you. He's laughing at you." Adam imagined Jason's sneer, and as if on cue, Suvan's nerves gave way to a whinny.

"No!" Selenko's bark smacked Suvan into stillness.

"Get your anger back in focus," he ordered Adam. "Here it comes. You will not take his hand. You will take your revenge."

Adam raised the gun and aimed.

"That's it…." Selenko's God-voice spoke to Adam from inside his skull, and for that split of a second, Adam saw Jason issuing orders and laughing at him. "You're there!"

The crack was so loud, Adam leapt in the air.

"What happened?" Selenko asked, rattled, no longer divine.

It was Gracie. She had snuck in to watch their rehearsal and snapped Adam's postman's strap.

Perfect. From now on, Gracie on gunshots.

CHAPTER 26

T he night before the performance for the Opportunity Classes, Adam's every dream was "nipped in the bud" by the Watch Gang ripping his arms off or Michael Mason flying airplanes into his head. The first few hours of school, the images continued to assault Adam, until at 10 a.m., Adam watched the sixty OC students enter the auditorium from the wings. The dread trickled down his arms, creating sweat bumps and chills, tremors of jittery electric currents. Adam spotted Michael Mason and Car Coat, watched them and the other OC students settle into the back rows of the auditorium, a hundred miles from the stage. They would recognize Adam and Suvan as the lunchroom door monitors, the one with the funny accent, hassled five days a week, and Adam, Public Enemy Number One for those *in the know. Ratting. Fingering. Jew-ball bastard.* They would hate *Dawn*, rush the stage, and kill them both.

The young OC teacher, Miss Nadel, cajoled her students to move to the front of the auditorium. She was delicate, lovely, fragile in her flowery orange pantsuit, gigantic bell bottoms swishing when she walked. They ignored her. Her back arched and her tone became brisk, harsh, commanding, "Get up this minute! All of you down now to row number two and to row number three, center section." This was followed by a softer instruction. "And let's respect the actors."

Respect the actors! In case they hadn't hated the SP kids enough before. Her charges grumbled as they trudged toward the stage.

Miss Nadel sidled up to Selenko in the first row. Adam knew this was a catastrophic blunder because her students would be behind her and she wouldn't be able to control them.

Harriet the Spy and *Jonathan Livingston Seagull* would suffer, but *Dawn*, which was extremely quiet and required the tension to be constant, had no chance in hell against the heckling to come, with Miss Nadel twisting around too late to silence her brood.

Adam tried to get Selenko's attention, but Selenko was laughing unnaturally loudly, sitting, standing, jumping around. Adam had never seen Selenko like this.

What was wrong with him?

Ohmigod. Mr. Beck was right. Selenko's in love with Miss Nadel!

During *Harriet the Spy*, whispering gave way to talking, which gave way to a coughing epidemic throughout *Jonathan Livingston Seagull*, and eventually even booing, which was silenced instantly and made Adam feel sorry for his former friends. At last, Adam and Suvan's turn came to be sacrificed.

Adam set their lights, Suvan positioned the mattress and the rifle. No one else had introduced their play, and Adam was sure the audience would unleash their restlessness on his talk about the British Mandate (*Boring!*) and the Holocaust. (*Who cares? Kill them all!*)

But the OC kids didn't interrupt Adam once. Once the show began, Adam could feel them sucked into the scene, no coughs, no fidgeting. He could hear them listening. Each time Adam/Elisha emerged from the darkness at a different spot near Suvan/Captain Dawson, the silent stillness was pierced by another sharp and sudden gasp, until his final appearance behind the Captain with his pistol raised evoked an actual scream.

Fueled by terror, the boys gave a terrific performance. And when it was done, the OC kids stood and cheered. They hooted. They pounded their feet. Adam had never heard noises like these in any school auditorium. And it was for him, for Suvan, for their play. It filled Adam in a way he'd never known. He felt powerful, like a giant. He gulped and his eyes teared, which he masked by blowing his nose.

Miss Nadel announced a Q&A, a surprise, and the actors from all three scenes were summoned back to the stage. Near the end, Michael

Mason rose to ask a question. Adam's heart stopped, sank, inflated, then started pumping like mad, expecting a nasty comment that would wipe away the joy of the previous moments.

"Your character, Miller. What happened to the ghosts he was talking to? Were they happy he might kill the British guy?"

These were good questions, although it meant it had not been clear that Elisha had pulled the trigger.

Adam said Elisha's family, who had been murdered by the Nazis, were with him through the long night, watching to see what he would do.

"You have to stand up for yourself or you'll get pushed around forever," Adam explained, feeling the strength to say more, to say anything. "And then you'll get murdered. Elisha, he's not helpless anymore, he can finally fight, and he has something to fight for and people to fight with. John Dawson paid the price for standing in their way."

"I would say it a bit differently," Suvan demurred. "Captain John Dawson is not a Nazi. His government had put him in a hopeless position between two warring groups."

Adam was thrown by this tiny crack in their united front.

"Not much choice for that poor sucker," Michael Mason said, agreeing with Suvan and sitting down, ending the debate.

Long into the night, Adam heard the stomping applause and the cheers, tainted only by his frustration that the audience had missed the gunshot. *Damn.*

In that darkness, Adam found himself puzzled.

How could the OC be our best audience?

Maybe the life-and-death stakes in Dawn *came as a relief after snooping girls and philosophizing birds. Was that it? Maybe this isn't a history lesson for them. Maybe they know what it's like to feel threatened, to face a gun. And why is Michael Mason in the OC? He asks good questions and builds remote-controlled gasoline-powered airplanes. He might be strange, a thief, unpredictable, and dangerous, but he's not stupid.*

CHAPTER 27

They set the rendezvous with Michael Mason in the parking lot of Temple Gates of Hope, a safe site for Adam. Days were winter brief, and it was already dark fifteen minutes before Adam's four o'clock bar mitzvah lesson.

"There's Dennis!" Suvan said with excitement. "Hey—"

Adam yanked his arm down hard. "I don't want him to see us!" Dennis just might recognize Michael Mason.

"Do you all come to this place?"

"Who all?"

Adam knew Suvan meant Jews, but he didn't like it when an outsider did the grouping. He didn't know if religion mattered to his friend, and Adam's ignorance of Hinduism was total.

"You want me to buy you comic books or *Playboy*," Michael Mason said, "it'll be five bucks plus the cover price." He had materialized behind them.

Suvan blanched twice, first at Michael's voice, then at the mention of *Playboy*. Michael offered Suvan a cigarette, startling him so much Suvan's face couldn't function. Michael Mason lit one for himself, returned the pack to his pocket.

"This is something else," Adam said, motioning to come closer. Instead, Michael jumped back behind a ten-foot circle.

"Please stop doing that."

Michael inched closer, closing the distance halfway. Adam told Michael Mason about the Surprise Challenge, showed him the *WANTED!* poster and explained his plan for Michael to pretend to be the Official Yearbook Photographer. Suvan handed Michal Mason the laminated OYP card on its string. Michael fingered the card, tucked it into his front pocket.

"You'll need to take mugshots of Mr. Selenko, the drama teacher."

"The mustache guy?"

"That's him." He explained the need for unsmiling close-ups and profiles.

Michael Mason blew a smoke ring, irresistible magic to the other boys. "We're cool."

You are, Adam thought.

"But I don't have a camera."

"That's why Adam is giving you his brother's reflex camera. His brother doesn't know we've borrowed it, so you must be extremely careful with it."

Adam hesitated, suddenly unsure, then handed Michael Mason Seth's Canon in its black leather case, and its wide black strap with a red racing stripe. It was Seth's bar mitzvah splurge, the big-ticket item he'd bought with his gift money.

Working fast, Adam showed Michael the focus, the zoom, the shutter button, rushing lest Dennis return with one of the Greens.

"This job requires…" Michael Mason considered, then blew a smoke ring for emphasis. "Savoir faire. Six bucks."

"Three."

"Four fifty."

"I've only got four left. Payable on delivery."

"Yeah, all right."

"I happen to know that Adam doesn't have four dollars," Suvan protested. "We are asking you to join us in a great adventure, not hiring you for a bank job."

Michael Mason twirled the camera on its strap. "That's different."

"Sharing credit in our mutual success will have to suffice."

"Will you do it?" Adam asked anxiously, ready to offer payment again to speed things up.

Too late. The door opened and the Cantor stood silhouetted against the corridor back light. Adam jumped a foot in the air.

"They tell me you are out here smoking. You boys too young for that."

Dennis.

"I wasn't smoking," Adam said, offended. "Smoking's disgusting."

The Cantor sniffed. "Oh, you the one." Michael Mason was cupping the cigarette in his hand, twisting his arm so the lit end faced backward.

"You want to make something out of it?" Michael Mason said. He considered taking one last puff but flicked his butt away.

"Tough guy," retorted the Cantor.

They eyed each other, neither cowed in the slightest. Adam wondered if Michael Mason could have written the graffiti on the synagogue door, berated himself for his suspicion, wondered again.

"What your parents think?"

"I get my cartons from my father."

So Michael Mason has a father.

"Your father give you smokes?"

"I borrow them."

"Yours only funeral, my friend."

And that was it. The Cantor didn't threaten to call Michael's parents or the rabbi or the police. "You are late for your lesson," he said to Adam.

"I'll get this back to you when the mission is accomplished," Michael said, swinging the camera up into position and pretending to take a photo of the three of them. "We'll talk money again later."

"Wait," the Cantor said. "What is going on here really?"

Adam felt the heat of the Cantor's suspicion and couldn't speak.

"We are here to take pictures for the school yearbook," Suvan improvised. "Adam has told us how much he loves his lessons, so we want action photos of Adam with his singing coach."

"I am not singing coach. I am teaching Adam to lead services, to sing from down here, to wake up people, wake up God."

"We'd like to capture Adam waking up God on film," Suvan said.

"You talk very nice," the Cantor said. "Come. This is a good idea."

It is?

"We make pictures for lobby, and for sign outside. Pictures will sell seats for High Holidays. Smart boys. You will see."

Adam gave Suvan and Michael Mason each a white nylon yarmulke from the wooden box inside the door, clipped on his precious thick woolen Sharon-knitted purple special. Michael twanged its pom-pom.

"Boys. Quick, quick."

They followed the Cantor down the corridor past the coat room, the office Greens and the rabbi's study through the central lobby into the main sanctuary.

"Adam, go bring a tallis and a siddur."

By the time Adam made it back to the sanctuary, the Cantor was decked in white High Holiday kittel robes and his white cantorial box hat. Michael Mason was on the stage, snapping shots of him, *wasting film*.

"Stop!" Adam yelled. "You have to attach the flash!"

The Cantor eyed Michael Mason. "You are photographer?"

"Still learning the ropes."

Flash in place, Michael shot the Cantor from below, *flash*, side-view, *flash*, running behind him, *flash, flash, flash*. Adam tried to stop Michael, but only when the Cantor raised his hand did Michael obey.

"Your photographer is excited-over, boychik," the Cantor said.

My photographer is using up my thirty-six exposures.

"We have enough," Adam said, but the Cantor ignored him.

"You stand there…" the Cantor directed Michael to the edge of the *bimah* and pulled Adam close.

"First, we put on tallis, but we don't say no blessing because this not for real, and we not take God's name in vain."

The Cantor swept his great white tallit high over his head, and let it land on his broad square shoulders. Adam could not manage the same panache.

"I sing, then you sing after me. We show how we do it."

"We don't need to show them," Adam said, teeth clamped.

"Then we do for make fun."

For make fun.

"Now you take pictures," the Cantor ordered Michael Mason.

The Cantor let loose.

"*Shochen ad Marom v'Kadosh Shmo!*"

The Cantor's voice roared out so suddenly Michael Mason forgot to snap.

"Jesus!" Michael Mason said. "That's loud!"

"Now you," the Cantor said to Adam.

"Ready whenever you are, SFB," Michael Mason said.

"SFB?" Suvan inquired.

"He knows," Michael replied.

Adam didn't, but he knew he did not want to sing in front of Michael Mason. Adam cleared his throat, cleared it again. Adam's singing didn't have the resonance or the timbre of the Cantor's, but he stayed on key.

"That's enough," Adam said.

"Not yet," the Cantor said. "We will sing together." He whispered, "This time, I want you should enjoy." Adam started to object, but the Cantor shushed him and patted his own stomach.

"From this place, with me."

Adam closed his eyes. There was nothing to lose. He might as well show his friends this other kind of performance and please his teacher at the same time. Instead of lagging after the Cantor, he let his voice disappear into the Cantor's thunder. The Cantor continued, so Adam kept going, eyes still shut. They sang the entire first prayer in the morning service. By the end, was Adam was singing alone and was dazed to open his eyes into a flash. He could hardly see for the blaze.

"Wow!" said Suvan.

"Today we find your voice I am looking for all this time!" announced the elated Cantor. He clapped Adam on the shoulder with his great bear paw. "This is a great day, Adam! Important day! Mazal tov!"

The Cantor swung open the doors to the ark, yanked a cord in a side crevice of the inner ark, and the gauzy curtain parted.

"Now, boys, watch."

The five scrolls that made up the treasure of Temple Gates of Hope were revealed, most wrapped in velvet jackets, protected by sculpted silver breastplates and topped with glorious silver crowns. It felt naked to Adam for the Torahs to be exposed with no fanfare, without hundreds of people singing.

What is the Cantor doing? A known thief is now taking a photographic record of my synagogue's valuables.

"They have to go," Adam announced.

"In one minute, yes. First, a story."

"I don't think my friends can stay."

"I'm rather intrigued," Suvan said.

"Let's hear the man." Michael lowered the camera.

"Adam, I want for you to hear this too. Boys, this Torah is very special, so valuable it has no price."

"Invaluable," Suvan volunteered.

Relenting, Adam joked, "He's a dictionary," which made Suvan and Michael smile, one in pride, one in mockery.

"Come close and touch with your hands the Torah, this one."

The Torah's cover was brown, faded, worn, and unlike its brothers, it had no velvet, had never had velvet.

"You are twelve years old. I was twelve years old once too."

"I'm thirteen," Suvan said.

"I'm fifteen almost, man," Michael Mason protested.

Fifteen?

"I was in Bucharest. It is 1943. The Nazis are not there. They went around Bucharest because Romania has Iron Guard. They are like Nazis, only Romanian. I got beat every day, on the way to school, on the way back from school. So I learned to fight. To be not afraid of no one."

"This is during the war. Things were running out. There is no soap, no sugar, no salt. In Romania we heard stories about what Nazis are doing in Germany, Poland. Not just breaking up synagogues, also they are burning Torahs. We decide we will rescue our Torah. It was not hard to borrow Torah from synagogue; people were afraid to go there. But where to hide it? And then we see signs that soap has arrived in apothecary windows."

"Drugstores," Suvan translated.

"Yes, drugstores. But we hear that this soap is not soap. They are not only burning synagogues, the Nazis, they are burning people, sending Jews in trains and murdering them and making them into soap. There are long lines to buy soap. The Bucharest people are washing in dead Jewish bodies."

"So we make another plan. We break in at night into back door where they take shipment. We steal the soap, and then we decide we will put soap with the Torah in a place where nobody looks. Where is nobody not going to look? In the Jewish cemetery. Yankel's uncle digs the holes. He's a…"

"Gravedigger," Suvan supplied.

"That is right. He shows us how to dig holes. One for soap, one for Torah. Is not winter, so ground not frozen, but is dark and cold. If Romanian police catch us, if Iron Guard catch us, they will shoot us, and we will be in the graves already that we dig for ourselves. We dig all night until the sun comes out. We bury soap in wood box—coffin and Torah is in second coffin. We filled in the holes. And we sang 'El Maleh Rachamim' and we said Kaddish for the dead Jews although we not have minyan."

"Wow," Suvan said again.

"After war, you know what they are doing in Bucharest?"

"What? Who?"

"Still killing Jews there."

"But the Nazis were defeated," Adam said.

"They don't need no Nazis to murder people who are starving, people they hate. I came out of hiding and I go back to Bucharest."

"That sounds suicidal," Suvan said.

"You boys. You live in a nice world. After what I see, I was not afraid of nobody. I don't find no family in Bucharest. I found my parents later, thank God, but not yet. So now, I go to cemetery. Remember coffins I tell you about? I dig them up at night, just me, so nobody sees. I leave soap in the grave, leave dead Jews in peace. But I took the Torah. I took it with me, across Europe, across the world. I tell the rabbi this story, and when I see he was so excited, I donate the Torah to this synagogue. We can't read from it. It's no good anymore. But the rabbi put it in the ark so we don't forget."

"That's very symbolic and courageous," Suvan said.

"That's crazy brave, man," Michael corrected. "You're, like, a hero."

At this moment, Adam liked Michael for the first time.

"Hey there, Cantor. What are these boys doing in here?"

Floyd's entrance severed them from Romania. Floyd was the synagogue custodian, a tall black man who lived in a small apartment adjacent to the banquet hall.

"They take pictures for Temple lobby," the Cantor said.

"That one was loitering outside for the past two hours, smoking behind the building."

Michael flinched, turned away. Adam had never heard anyone say the word *loitering* aloud. It was a word on signs.

"They're my friends," Adam explained. "You can trust them."

Later, after his friends had left, when he finished his delayed bar mitzvah lesson, Floyd was waiting for Adam in the hall.

"You shouldn't be hanging around that boy, loitering all afternoon." Floyd had a gentle, formal way of speaking. He'd once told Adam he'd grown up in South Carolina. "You listen to Floyd."

Why had Michael Mason come so early? And why is everyone so suspicious (including me)?

CHAPTER 28

Seth rode low over the ram's-horn handlebars of his English racer, wearing his dark blue Betar shirt, his knapsack festooned with his Jewish buttons, his breath forming puffs in the late winter cold. Adam trailed behind his brother, out of sight on his golden Stingray, as they crossed Flushing, pedaled down 164th Street past the Italian Ices and Vinnie's candy-striped barbershop pole, the tiny tidy front yards of row houses narrower even than their own former home, past Peter's Florist—a greenhouse on a traffic island—skirting Kissena Park, and splitting off to Main Street and Seventy-Second, which Adam immediately recognized as the location of Speedway.

Speedway housed the most intricate slot car track in Queens, famous for the Death Drop that fed into a hairpin turn notorious for flinging cars off the table. The track was decorated with scale-model Flushing landmarks—the library, the post office with its Doric columns, the grand RKO Keith movie theater, the Unisphere and the New York City Pavilion—relics from the World's Fair six years before.

From across Main Street, Adam watched Seth press a door buzzer for the entrance adjacent to Speedway. A head popped out of the second-floor window, a hand appeared which dropped a set of keys down to Seth.

Not Speedway, but the jackpot! The B House, Betar headquarters!

Astonishingly, Seth took his bicycle chain and lock with him, leaving his English racer tottering on the kickstand, unprotected.

Two youths in Red Ravens jackets came out of Speedway, a little young for such an established gang, one cupping both hands protectively around his finicky and fragile slot car. He walked smack into Seth's bicycle, knocked it over, and fell on all fours as his car went flying. Adam heard him cursing over the traffic.

Instead of helping his friend or retrieving the car, the second boy raised Seth's bike from the ground, ran his fingers along the downward curve of its handlebars, flipped up the kickstand, lifted his leg to straddle the crossbar, and got ready to ride off.

Without thinking, Adam pedaled madly across Main Street, standing in the stirrups for maximum forward thrust, eyes on the racer, ignoring the drawn-out car horns. He skidded to a halt within inches of the thieves, blocking their exit.

"That's my brother's bike!" Adam yelled.

"Get him out of the way," said the boy straddling Seth's racer.

The friend carefully placed his damaged slot car on top of a parked green Dodge Charger. It was two against one, and Adam had to decide fast whether to fight or flee. Adam backed up, spun as if he were about to escape, but instead zipped around the pair in a tight circle to the door buzzer, which he pressed for one long ring, then several staccato beeps. The second Raven threw Adam down, his body slamming into the concrete with one leg under the bike. The window screeched open.

"Why the hell you buzzing…hey, what are you doing to that kid?"

"Seth! Seth!" Adam screamed.

"That's my brother!" A pause, then footsteps trooping down the stairs. Adam was still on the ground when the door flew open. Seth stepped out first and was coldcocked by a fist to his face. A grizzly bear in navy blue emerged next, waving his arms and roaring like a madman. "*Sto-o-o-o-p!*"

That was enough to freeze the two boys. Behind the bear came normal-sized high schoolers. There were five, ten, a dozen of them.

"That's my bike," Seth moaned from the ground.

The bear grabbed the boy on the bike with both hands.

"Let go of me…"

"What do you think you're doing?" the bear growled at them.

The bear finished dislodging the teen from the bike, placed him down on the ground. The would-be thieves split fast, leaving only the slot car still perched on the roof of the Charger.

Seth clutched his eye, Adam his leg.

"What're you doing here?"

"They were about to steal your English racer. Why didn't you chain it up?"

"That's my business."

"Bring your brother inside," the bear said. "And take your bikes."

Seth carried his bicycle awkwardly up the narrow staircase. He was in pain, wanted to rub his face, but needed both hands to manage his racer. Adam followed behind, struggling with his Stingray on the steep steps, the front wheel flapping loose, slapping the wall.

"Let me help you," said a teenager with stringy-brown hair and glasses. He took the bike from Adam. "I'm Greg."

"Adam. Thanks," he said. "Wait, I forgot something." Adam ran outside, retrieved the slot car, a beautiful blue Ferrari, its wheel badly bent.

Safely upstairs, Seth held a bag of ice on his eye, which was swelling shut. He grumbled to Adam to sit on the floor against the wall and not make a sound.

Adam was too surprised and delighted to complain. He was in the secret sanctum.

The B House bulletin boards were laden with Betar photos and colorful posters with fists flying upward, manacles shattered, and Jewish stars aplenty, some familiar from Seth's basement cave.

"We just saw why Jews must train for self-defense," the bear declared. "Pay attention. Ari has come from National to brief us."

Although he wondered what a thwarted bike theft had to do with the Jewish People, Adam wisely kept silent.

"What I'm about to tell you is confidential," said a fellow with long sideburns, the only one not in navy blue. He nodded questioningly toward Adam.

"He's okay," Seth said.

Adam had been forgiven.

Greg slid his back down the wall to settle next to Adam on the floor. He took the damaged Ferrari in his hands like an injured bird.

"I can fix this."

Greg pulled out a case with a minuscule screwdriver from his pocket and fiddled with the car while Ari addressed the group. Ari's tone was even but urgent, sharing secrets.

"One month ago, sixteen Russian Jews asked to emigrate from the Soviet Union to Israel. The Soviet overlords label all would-be émigrés enemies of the state, since the desire to leave shows that Russia is not a paradise. Like all Jews refused permission to move to Israel from the USSR, they immediately lost their jobs and were kicked out of the university."

"But these sixteen Jews devised a desperate plan to reach the Jewish homeland. They claimed to be flying to a wedding, then tried to hijack their small plane to leave Soviet airspace and touch down in Sweden. They were ratted out, arrested before takeoff by the KGB."

Sweat trickled down Ari's forehead. He removed his glasses, wiped his lenses and his face with a handkerchief. Whether planned or impromptu, the pause built the tension.

"Friends, all sixteen were tried in Leningrad, and now, some of our Jewish brothers have been given the death sentence. They are prisoners of conscience!" Ari thundered with a suddenness that froze the room. "They're going be executed for wanting to go home!"

Adam immediately thought of *Dawn*, of the underground fighters sentenced to death by the British for wanting to establish a Jewish country. It all connected.

"It's 1971, not 1941. As American Jews, we are free. We have to take action now. Never again!"

They all yelled, "Never again!" Adam joined in quietly, unsure if the silence rule applied.

At Ari's cue, the Betarees recited the names of the prisoners, a mantra of Jewish resistance.

"Mark Dymshits, age forty-three, sentenced to death. Eduard Kuznetsov, age thirty-one, sentenced to death. Yosef Mendelevitch, age twenty-three..."

Adam mouthed the names silently.

Ari's plan was for the Betar members to chain themselves to the fence outside the Russian Mission in Manhattan.

Why should the Russians care that Jewish teenagers are chained to their gates? Won't they just leave them there to freeze to death?

If the *New York Times* covered their protest, Ari explained, as if reading Adam's mind, it would embarrass the Soviet authorities. It could generate enough pressure to commute the death sentences, creating a chance the Leningrad Sixteen would someday be freed.

Why would the New York Times *care?*

(Adam was wrong about the *Times*. His brother made page five.)

"We have to be vigilant at home as well," Seth said, his gravitas enhanced by his black eye. "First, bricks were thrown through the windows of my shul, Temple Gates of Hope, then they painted 'Jews Out of Flushing' on the door."

"I found them both," Adam offered. Adam remembered he wasn't allowed to speak and reddened.

"That's right," Seth affirmed. Adam was tingling.

("Don't let it go to your head," Seth told him later. "You still can't join.")

Just as Greg deposited the repaired Ferrari back in Adam's palms, the buzzing started. Greg leapt up, raised the window, turned to the group inside.

"We got company!"

Adam, Seth, and the closest Betarees crowded around Greg at the window, heads colliding as they jostled to catch a glimpse of the gathering storm below. Adam counted a flock of fifteen Red Ravens in their leather jackets, all older than the thwarted bike thieves.

"Send down the kid who punched my little brother."

"He means you," Seth and Adam said at the same time.

"Nunchucks ready," Shlomo the Bear commanded. "Let's meet our neighbors."

Shlomo led them down the narrow staircase, footsteps thudding as they descended in disorderly quickstep. He put up his hand to halt the march behind, opened the street door cautiously in case of an ambush, but the Ravens had kept their distance.

The Betarees paraded outside. It was cold, but uniforms required uniforms in return. A few of the Ravens had sticks and two had bottles. Shlomo counted aloud in Hebrew, "*Ehat! Shtayim! Shalosh!*"

and the Betarees extended their nunchucks horizontally in front of their chests.

Ari and Adam alone were unarmed.

Let's rip the Raven logos off their backs and take revenge on the Hill-Watch-Subway-Jason Gang.

"On *Shalosh*," Shlomo called. "*Ehat! Shtayim! Shalosh!!*" The Betarees swung their nunchucks in a figure eight, a whirring blur of wind with a low and steady hum. The Ravens took a step back. They were not familiar with nunchucks or these dark blue uniforms.

"We are Betar," Shlomo said. "You've made a serious mistake, but we don't want to rumble."

The Ravens' leader turned to his gang. "They don't want to rumble!"

"This ain't *West Side Story*," another called, provoking laughter down their row.

Adam dug into his pocket for Detective Riley's card with its NYPD emblem and waved it in the air. "We're the Jewish police," Adam said.

"Put that away," Seth jeered, mortified.

But the Ravens' swagger dropped a notch, and they took another half step backward.

"At ease!" Shlomo called. The nunchucks slapped back into armpits, then were brought out front for show. Adam was impressed by their synchronicity, their discipline.

"That cop kid," the little guy screamed pointing at Adam, "he ran me over with his Stingray. And that guy punched me," pointing at Shlomo.

"What Stingray?" Adam asked.

They swiveled their heads.

"What Stingray, Dougie?" the Ravens' leader repeated to his younger brother.

"He was riding a Stingray!"

Someone is going to get hurt, and with my lack of luck, that someone is me. I will talk fast.

"If I had run over you with my bicycle," Adam said, "a) there would be tire marks on your face, and b) my brother would not have a black eye from when you punched him after you tried to steal *his* bicycle, which was leaning against the building but is now inside. Which goes to prove that c) nobody hit you. So if anybody deserves an apology, it's my brother, who was minding his own business and did absolutely nothing to you."

"Dougie, did you try to steal his bicycle?" the Ravens' leader asked.

"What bicycle?" Dougie asked, smirking at Adam. But Adam had an answer.

"The blue English racer that's upstairs now," Adam said. "You dropped your slot car when you tripped over the bike that your friend tried to steal. All I did was keep you from riding away."

"I saw it all from up there," Seth said. They looked up to heaven. "That's what happened."

Seth backed me up!

But the Ravens' leader did not back up his younger brother.

"Where's my Ferrari, Dougie?"

Dougie deflated. "I left it on the hood of a car."

"What car?"

"A green Dodge Charger," Adam helpfully supplied.

"I don't see a green Dodge Charger. Do you see a green Dodge Charger?"

"It must have…driven away," Dougie answered. "That kid made me drop it. He broke it."

Adam continued from behind his fraternal shield. "I couldn't have made you drop your Ferrari because I was across the street when you banged into the bicycle, which wasn't chained to the wall because everybody was upstairs practicing chaining themselves to the Russian mission to stop the Russians from executing Jews for going to a wedding."

The Ravens' leader got jumpy. His teeth were grinding, biting each word.

"What. The. Hell. Is. He. Talking. About?"

"Russian bastards have sentenced to death Jews who wanted to go to Israel," Shlomo explained. "We're going to get them freed."

"I really don't give a shit," the Ravens' leader replied, moving forward, his gang in lockstep behind him.

But the battle did not start, because Michael Mason walked out of Speedway carrying a canary-yellow Buick LeSabre.

He is following me.

"What's happening, Adam my man?"

Michael stood between the two gangs. He handed Adam his car and calmly lit a cigarette.

"Who's this guy?" Raven Team Leader asked.

Seth repeated the question. "Who's this guy?"

"He's...he's my friend?" Adam answered.

Michael kept smiling. "I am the best slot car racer in Flushing. And yo, there's the badass who raced that Ferrari down Death Drop at full speed. Ugly wipeout, man."

Michael held up his palm toward Dougie for a high five, but Dougie's blood was racing from his face to his feet, so Michael patted his Afro, as if that was what he had intended all along.

How do you get that slick?

The Ravens' leader turned on his brother. "You broke my Ferrari, *and* you left it on a car that drove away. I'm going to kick your ass to Astoria."

"Before you kill him," Adam said, "wait a minute." He handed Michael back his LeSabre, raced up the B House stairs and came down with the Ferrari.

"Our engineer repaired the wheel."

The Ravens' leader examined the car from several angles. That's when they heard the police siren.

"I think we're done here," Shlomo said definitively. "Everything cool?"

"All right, big man," the chief of the Ravens said softly. "I don't care what you do up there. But this is our street. Don't get in our faces again. *Capish?*"

"We're not looking for trouble, but we're not afraid of a fight," Shlomo replied. "*Capish?*"

They glared, then backed off. Nunchucks were concealed, bottles discarded, and the groups dispersed.

Seth didn't thank Adam for saving his English racer, but Adam was content that he didn't blame him for his black eye.

"Good timing," Adam said to Michael. "You just prevented World War Three."

"It'll only cost you four bucks." Michael jumped away.

"You're kidding."

"Four bucks, tomorrow, Miller. Or should I tell your brother to look for his camera? *Capish?*"

Adam's good feeling popped. Every time he liked Michael Mason, things went sideways.

"I don't get you at all," Adam confessed.

Michael smiled. "I like it that way. I'm kidding about the money, my man." Michael strode off, leaving Adam to retrieve his Stingray alone.

You like to see me sweat.

Adam replayed the events of the afternoon during his long bike ride home. Ever since *West Side Story* had been on television, Adam's universe was peopled by Sharks and Jets, like summer camp color war, arbitrarily dividing campers into Blues against Reds. The artificial tribes squared off for fun competition, but within hours it devolved into hatred and Adam came to despise it.

In the dangerous real world, you needed to belong for protection and loyalty. Until Adam was old enough to join Betar, he would defend the Jewish People—and himself—with his brother's nunchucks. Whenever Seth left them home, Adam took his brother's weapons, concealing the two sticks, as he had learned from the baffling Michael Mason, in the sleeve of his coat.

CHAPTER 29

Michael Mason walked on to the stage, the laminated OYP card and Seth's Canon Reflex dangling around his collar, his plaid shirt buttoned up to the neck, as close as he could come to simulating a science geek.

"I gotta take your picture," Michael announced, too loudly.

Selenko stared at him in amazement. "Can't you see that we're in the middle of a scene?" Selenko's face changed suddenly. "Oh oh oh… the Yearbook Photographer."

Lamination!

"You'll have more lively compositions if you shoot the actors rehearsing their scenes."

"Just you. That's my mission."

Selenko announced a five-minute break. Suvan and Adam pretended to be running lines, watching in astonishment as Michael Mason positioned Mr. Selenko.

"Can you please stand still and look straight at me." *Flash.*

"Aren't you too close?" Selenko asked.

"Very, very close. It's our new concept. And this time, no smiling." *Flash.*

"That was right in my eyes."

"I'm very sorry about that, sir. I will discuss the new concept with my editors. And now turn to your left." *Flash.* "Remember please, no smiling." *Flash.* "You should blink a few times, so your eyes will go back to normal. And turn to your right." *Flash, Flash.* "We are done here, sir, and I thank you for your time and your cooperation, and I regret any inconvenience I may have caused to your rehearsal."

Adam and Suvan were dumbfounded and goggle-eyed. Michael Mason was brilliant!

But Michael didn't show up to the rendezvous with Suvan at the end of the day to return the camera and film and renegotiate the fee, if any. Adam also couldn't find Michael on Tuesday, Wednesday, Thursday, or Friday.

He must have fenced Seth's camera. Seth will demand all my bar mitzvah money. And I brought Michael Mason into the synagogue—to photograph *the joint! The Temple will have me arrested as an accessory. I am so stupid! I could lie and claim Michael Mason stole the camera. Everyone will believe me. Except Suvan. And the Cantor. And me. And it would be wrong. Morally. But practically?*

By Monday, it had been seven days of hell. Adam staked out the OC. Miss Nadel rushed past him before he could ask her a thing.

Miss Nadel poked her head out. "Why are you haunting my classroom door?"

"I'm looking for Michael Mason."

"He's been absent all week."

"Is he sick?" Adam asked.

"I don't know. What's your name?"

"Adam Miller."

"Richard's boy!" she said, her lovely green eyes lighting up, inquisitive but supportive. "I mean, you're Mr. Selenko's student." Adam could see why Selenko liked her. "Do you want to come in and ask his pals before we begin?"

Another police lineup. "No thanks. I'll check back tomorrow."
Selenko talks about me!

This made Adam skip down the hall three times.
I am an actor.

Adam straightened up and walked head held high, but he caught himself.

It's only a matter of time until Seth finds out and murders me. How long can Michael Mason live on the money from fencing a camera? A year? Twenty years?

Adam returned to his defensive posture, which is when it hit him. *SFB. Shit For Brains.*

Michael Mason is laughing his head off at me, the stupidest kid ever in the SP.

Adam's thought of the card in his back pocket.

Yes, Detective Riley, I handed my brother's Canon Reflex to a known thief, along with a fake photographer's badge that I made and had laminated at Haben's, where they charged my school for my fraud, and I'm also carrying a concealed weapon.

Instead of that terrible idea, Valerie offered to find Michael Mason's address—not through the Hill this time; her mother worked in the school office—in exchange for being included in their Surprise Challenge. Suvan and Adam agreed. While Valerie studied the *WANTED!* poster, Adam imagined how, Selenko's mouth would open into such an oversized circle, you could shove a basketball inside when Adam unfolded it in front of him. Adam caught himself studying how Valerie's hair peaked at her side part and crossed her forehead in a gentle cascade. Valerie's imagination and her face flushed.

"The poster's—you know—fantastic and all, but we need a full-scale extravaganza!"

We need our film back.

"Like what?"

"Think of something."

How could he make an extravaganza out of a poster?

When the Cantor asked if his photos for the Temple bulletin board were ready, Adam's resolve collapsed and he told the Cantor about the missing Michael Mason. He didn't relate how Mr. Selenko had pulled Adam aside after his class, confided that he'd been cast in that off-Broadway play and would soon be leaving, how Selenko called Adam his *good luck charm* again, gave him a hug, and failed to notice Adam's despair.

"You sure he is stealing camera?" the Cantor interrogated. "Maybe he is borrowing."

"Yes. No. Maybe. I thought I could trust him."

"No or yes? *Maybe*—this not an answer."

Adam wasn't sure of anything.

"Borrowing…I hope…I don't know, but we need the film."

"Go to his house and get camera back from your friend. You know where he is living?"

Adam produced Michael's address in South Jamaica.

"I don't know this place exactly, but we can find it," the Cantor said. "Skip haftarah today. Read me the third aliyah."

Adam made mistakes on all twelve verses but was not corrected once. The Cantor slammed the volume shut.

"Let's go get pictures."

They crossed Flushing in the Cantor's 1965 Pontiac Ventura. In South Jamaica, the cold blue afternoon sunlight was choked off by the elevated subway tracks. The train rumbled on top of their brains, covering them with a churning grid of noise and flickering light. When a sunbeam sliced through, it was blinding.

Except for two cops, almost everyone on the street was black. In Adam's old neighborhood, there were some black families, but there were mostly Jews, Italians, Irish, Greeks, and a few Chinese and Japanese. His new neighborhood seemed mostly white, as far as he could tell from the pedestrian-free streets, closed front doors, and unwelcoming, imposing lawns.

"Are we still in Queens?"

Geography had meant survival for the Cantor, and he marveled at the ignorance of Jewish boys who never explored their own borough.

"Jamaica is still Queens, yes, of course, south part."

The low-rise storefronts looked familiar, but the stores seemed off. Woolworth's with an ancient sign, a phony Kentucky Fried Chicken outlet with a weird name, and businesses Adam had never seen: *Dream Nails, Everything One Dollar or Less, Bail Bonds.*

"What's a pawnbroker?" Adam asked.

"Is a hockshop. You hock things. You don't know? You give them things, like your watch, they give you money. You can buy your watch back, but after some time, thirty days, if you don't buy your watch back, they sell it for probably more money."

He asked the Cantor if they should check the pawnshops for Seth's camera.

"Your imagination is running away."

They parked at a meter, but the Cantor didn't put coins in. Adam dug in his pockets for a quarter. "There's police right there. You'll get a ticket."

"Don't worry, boychik," the Cantor said with ease. "Nobody is checking in this kind of place."

The Cantor was right. The police paid the car no mind.

"We will find this address better if we are walking."

They passed a young man with a pointy beard in a red, green, and black striped robe and knitted cap, who dropped newspapers into the hands of anyone he could reach with his long arms. Large reflector sunglasses covered his eyes, despite the dark.

"He is selling drugs," the Cantor announced with the same bluster with which he made all of his pronouncements.

It didn't seem likely, not within sight of the cops. Why would the Cantor think the man was selling drugs? Because he was black? The Cantor asked directions, was pointed down an alley. On the other side, they found the building, trudged up three flights, in the dark after the first floor. The Cantor removed his black hat, wiped his forehead with his handkerchief, placed Adam in front of him to make the duo less threatening, and knocked on the door above Adam's head.

An elderly black woman cracked the door, peered up at the Cantor over her glasses, and through them, down at Adam.

"Who are you?"

The Cantor nudged Adam from behind.

"We're looking for Michael Mason."

"I live by my lonesome." The crack began to close.

"We apologize for bothering your time," the Cantor said.

"No bother," the woman smiled, not correcting him, charmed, as people were when they weren't put off by the Cantor's exuberance.

"We thought the Mason family lived here," Adam said.

"They used to, but, oh no, they moved up in the world."

Adam sagged but rallied quickly.

"Do you know where they went?"

"I put the address somewhere. I don't know where. Oh, I'm sorry about the name mix-up. Look at this." She held up a strip of adhesive paper, wax paper backing still in place, with the name *Farrar* printed in wobbly capitals. "That's me. My fingers are too stiff to put the sticker in that little slot next to the bell."

"I can do that for you," Adam volunteered.

"Oh, honey, would you?"

"I'll do it on the way out."

Downstairs, Adam peeled off the backing and covered Mason with Farrar, finalizing their loss. No film. No *WANTED!* poster. No extravaganza with Suvan and Valerie. Soon no Selenko.

Maybe I should call the police, before Seth does.

They were in the alley when Mrs. Farrar stuck her head out the window above them.

"I found their address!" she yelled. "Here goes nothing."

The paper fluttered down, wafting left, sailing right. Adam tracked its progress, until he snatched it out of the air.

"Thank you!"

"Good luck, gentlemen."

Mrs. Farrar's handwriting was all zig and zags, as if the letters were trembling. Adam was shaken by more than her penmanship. He knew exactly where Michael Mason lived because it was Adam's old house.

CHAPTER 30

A dam shriveled into his seat when they reached the tree-christened side streets of his old neighborhood—Oak, Cherry, Elm—onto Poplar, a one-way single-block stretch with detached row houses on one side, but on Adam's side, connected, with minuscule grass fronts surrounding fancy stoops—a *shtikel* lawn, his father called it. His father had put up a basketball hoop for Seth, earning at first the opprobrium of the Schiffmans across the street and later their friendship. The childless couple became Adam's babysitters in the early grades of public school.

It was a union street, and except for those on night shifts, by 6 p.m. the teachers, nurses, social workers, garbagemen were home tucking in for early dinners, their parked cars lining both sides of the street, leaving an unforgivingly narrow blacktop for exiting onto the major thoroughfare, Kissena Boulevard. Antsy drivers began to test their horns behind the Cantor, so he paused only long enough for Adam's soul to lurch back through his old front door to the rapidly receding world of last year.

From the corner of Poplar and Kissena, Adam could see the field of skyscrapers, a meadow filled in during Adam's dozen years there, each four-building complex distinguished by a slight variation in orange brick, two or three floors taller than the last, like a bar graph of adolescents reaching adulthood, and near the top of the B building of Carlyle Towers, Jason's seventeenth-floor bedroom. Adam and Jason had played one-on-one kickball with a Spalding in the hallways for hours, the ball ricocheting off the neighbors' entrances, and raced each other from end to end, trying not to get waylaid by the recessed doorways. They pushed all the buttons in the elevators before jumping out and doing staircase endurance climbs to avoid suspicion.

"Parking is not simple here," the Cantor summed up.

"Make a right at the corner, and I'll show you where."

"This part of Queens you know?"

I used to… He couldn't get out the words.

Adam directed the Cantor to Maple Park, a concrete rectangle with handball walls and metal monkey bars behind chain-link fences.

"There," Adam pointed. No Parking signs bookended a stretch of curb, but closer inspection revealed that the limits were only during school hours. Neighborhood residents avoided these spots until late-night parking desperation set in.

They walked back in silence, until they turned onto Poplar. Ten-year-old Eddie Weiss ran down his stoop steps, made like he was going to spit on Adam, had second thoughts, then ran back in the house. "Eddie!" but the door had slammed.

"This boy you know?" the Cantor mumbled, perturbed.

"I did," Adam mumbled in response.

A For Sale sign on the lawn half a block up mangled Adam's soul. How many times had Adam dreamt of destroying the For Sale sign when it was piercing their front yard, its red letters the blood of children huddling together. Ryan stole the sign once—a gesture of friendship now unimaginable—but that failed to keep the Millers in place. Eventually, Mr. Dueno—Ryan's father—returned the sign, and pounded it back into the ground with a massive mallet. A second For Sale sign further down Poplar ripped Adam's heart.

And then they were standing in front of Adam's home. Adam had not returned since they had moved, at first because he didn't know the way from his new neighborhood, later, to prevent homesickness and Jason encounters.

Adam put a foot on the first step leading up the stoop to the front door. He grew cold. A toppled bicycle and a tricycle speckled the tiny front lawn.

"I'll wait here," Adam said, turning to face the Schiffmans across the street. *Let's visit them instead.* Adam thought he saw Mr. Schiffman in the front window for a second. It *was* Mr. Schiffman—he turned away, but that was impossible, since he surely would have come out to greet him.

The Cantor seized Adam, a firm hand but a gentle grip, as if he were cradling a fragile egg. "Remind me of tough guy's name?" the Cantor said.

"Michael Mason."

The Cantor pressed the buzzer, heard a muffled two-note chime. The door opened part way. The Cantor nudged Adam. He had been prepared to speak, but not to a nine-year-old child with enormous eyes.

"Is Michael home?" Adam asked, kicking himself for not being more polite.

"Maaa!" the boy called. "Some kid wants Mike! And there's a man."

The door slammed shut. Adam shifted from foot to foot, tapping haftarah trope, humming the notes to calm himself.

"Sing always with big voice!" the Cantor declared. Adam hadn't realized he'd been doing it aloud. The Cantor sang out several notes.

"Not here!" Adam squeaked.

"Adam!" called Mr. Shamowitz from a few yards away, walking toward them on the sidewalk but not coming up the steps. He was the principal at Seth's old high school before Seth transferred out, who lived three houses to the left. "I thought that was you."

Adam remembered Mr. Shamowitz leading the chants on the teachers' strike picket line, screaming into the bullhorn with his clear cadence and incomprehensible words, his voice so hoarse it sandpapered Adam's throat to listen.

"Hello, Mr. Shamowitz. How are you?"

"I'm fine, Adam. Would you give your parents a message for me?"

"Okay."

"It's true I don't like seeing in the *Long Island Press* students occupying my office, but I would never have hurt your brother's college prospects. You didn't have to move like thieves in the night. Tell your parents that. Will you remember?"

"I will."

Mr. Shamowitz stalked off before Adam could formulate a question. *We moved so Seth wouldn't get in trouble from protesting?*

The Masons' door opened.

Adam's door. Adam's home. But Mrs. Mason filled the doorway, a squat black version of his own mother.

"Yes?"

Adam's confusion mingled with fear. The Cantor cleared his throat.

"We are from junior high school."

"Okay, Michael's missing school on account of his father took him on a trip."

So Michael didn't go off to fence my camera! I'm so judgmental.

"Not no problem. We come for camera, not for boy. Michael is Official Yearbook Photographer, but he did not return the equipment." The Cantor was proud to have remembered Michael's title.

"I think I would know if my son was any kind of photographer. What's he talking about?" Mrs. Mason asked Adam.

"Michael borrowed my camera and didn't bring it back."

"That's Mike. Nadine, go see if there's a camera in Mike's room."

They could hear her taking the steps two at a time.

"Robert won't open the door!"

"ROBERT! Let your sister in!"

"You have many children," the Cantor said. "I have six, ages seven to seventeen and one half. Very much life with many children. Very much laughter and much tears."

Adam cringed, sure the Cantor's combination of bad English and sentimental pap would turn Mrs. Mason against them, but it had the opposite effect.

"You can say that again. We've got five," she said, "We're fostering two, one is giving us fits, and another will be gone next week. Always a sad time."

Michael was going to *lose* one of his brothers or sisters? How terrible!

"I don't see a camera," came a cry from within the house, above.

"You better look yourselves. Nadine! Show them Mike's room."

"It's okay," Adam said, "we'll come back."

"We are here already," the Cantor reasoned.

"You might as well have a look-see." Mrs. Mason echoed. "Nadine!"

Nadine appeared, fifteen or sixteen, black hair braided in a thousand rattails, huge eyes, and a tight sweatshirt.

"Coming?" Nadine asked.

Nadine pivoted, submitting to her mother but expending not a single gesture more than necessary.

The living room wallpaper that had wrapped Adam's childhood, the orange plush carpeting that had inspired barefoot treks to feel the individual curls slip through his toes, still there. But the furniture was wrong—beds in the TV room!—the residents were wrong, not to mention that the Cantor didn't fit in Adam's memories and the neighbors turned away or wanted to spit on him. Was Adam on Earth-Two?

Nadine skipped down to the landing, teetered with balletic balance. *He's taken over my home. He lives in our bedroom.*

"I know the…" Adam caught himself. "I know Michael won't mind."

The first words he uttered in his new-old home were false. Adam knew bad luck would result from this lie.

Seth's old sign to ward off trespassers was still on their bedroom door—*Access Restricted to Residents Under 20!*—now embellished with a skull and crossbones and a blunt *Keep Out!*

Nadine turned the knob, then leaned in with her shoulder when the door didn't give. They heard someone tumble.

"Don't mind Robbie."

A plump ten-year-old boy had been flung into the corner. He was lighter skinned than the ebony teen. *Could he be the foster child?*

Their white walls had been repainted orange and blue—Mets colors!—and the ceiling light was gone. But, remarkably, their double-decker beds—separated when Seth reached junior high—had been reassembled! Shoes, sneakers, boots of various sizes were neatly arranged along one wall, and a rolled-up mattress sat in the corner. Did three boys share Adam's old room?

"Where's Mike's stuff?" Nadine asked.

Robbie motioned toward the wall closet with the sliding door. Nadine struggled to move the door, and Adam lurched forward, adjusted the door slightly so it would slide better on its track, then regretted revealing this forehand furniture knowledge.

"Thanks," Nadine muttered, before wading in. "Christ almighty."

Nadine threw out blankets, socks, notebooks, *Mechanix Illustrated* magazines, a *Sports Illustrated*, a stickball bat, a Mets batting helmet, a Mets shaky-head doll, four Mets yearbooks, Michael Mason's bright-yellow Buick slot car, six metal wings from radio planes, a box of colored chalk, cans of red and blue house paint.

Robbie stepped carefully around Adam and the Cantor, speeding off once he crossed the threshold.

"I don't see a camera," the goddess mumbled. "We done here?"

"Wait…" Adam stumbled. An intuition, a revelation, had flown into his brain, and he knew where Michael would hide the camera.

"Can I go in the closet for a minute?"

Nadine twisted her mouth in a way that made Adam woozy for reasons he couldn't yet decipher but which amused the Cantor, then squinted with such suspicion, it wiped away Adam's intoxication.

"It stinks in there, but be my guest."

"Do you have a flashlight?"

"What would I be doing with—"

"Try here." The Cantor produced a penlight from some inner pocket. Cantor boy scout.

Adam pushed through the paddy field of hanging coats. He removed the panel that Seth had inserted to hide the passageway the boys had created, handed it out to Nadine, then crouched down and entered the dank crawl space that undergirded the entire house.

Adam went down on all fours, the flashlight pen clutched tightly in his right hand, moved forward through the hole that he and Seth had created by accident, then covered up and kept mum, his head scraped against the ceiling, the crawl space lower and colder than he remembered. Seth used the crawl space for his secret storage, but Adam never liked being in there, fearing he'd meet some wildlife, that he'd get stuck inside. The familiar odor of damp concrete was now mixed with dead cigarettes.

Of course, what better place for Michael to smoke!

Adam's laser beam landed on objects distanced from the entrance so they would not be visible to someone peering in. Cartons of Marlboros and loose packs, five, six, ten, and then a stack of *Playboys*, no doubt pilfered from Haben's one at a time by the master thief.

Was that his old diorama from the Science Fair? And there, stacked in low piles, in freezer bags, were Adam's missing comic books! They'd been left behind. On purpose? Adam wanted them, but how could he explain that he was retrieving his own property to Nadine, to the Cantor, to Mrs. Mason?

And then a stripe of red.

The camera strap!

He reeled it in, clutched the camera to his chest, his precious baby. He exhaled, pirouetted slowly on his knees, until he pointed the flashlight back toward the entrance. Two eyes met his! Adam became ice.

Was he dead? Entombed by mistake?

"M-m-m-Michael?"

"Don't point that thing in my eyes!" Nadine hissed.

Adam struggled to find a sound to make with his voice.

"I…I…I found the camera."

"Mike's going to get it for not telling me about this. But how'd you—"

"Um… A lot of these old houses… Let's go out…."

"Yeah. This place gives me the creeps."

Adam inched forward, but Nadine didn't move and her face came so close to his, her braided rattails fell back in Adam's face. A waft of springtime shampoo fragrance made Adam woozy.

"Let me outta here first! Jeez."

She retreated, to Adam's relief, without surveying the treasures.

"So who are you again?" Mrs. Mason asked at the door.

"The Yearbook Committee," Adam said.

"Mom, you know there's a whole nother room running under this entire house?"

"Please tell Michael we were on deadline and we couldn't wait."

"Look what I found in Mike's closet." As the door closed, she dropped a stack of *Playboys* and Marlboros on the floor.

Shit.

In the car, Adam opened the camera case and checked the counter. He felt giddy. They had done it.

"The film's inside."

"Boychik, you going to make me nice big pictures for lobby and for the sign on lawn."

They got stuck in a traffic jam, and the Cantor put on a station in Yiddish. Adam's laughter subsided into exhaustion, confusion, and guilt.

Adam knew they shouldn't have come, gone into his old room, his closet, now Michael's closet, the crawl space. They should have waited for Michael Mason.

But damn him! He must have known who I was all along, from back when he was dancing down the corridor, following me to Haben's, to the movies, to stickball. His father had to be the man Dad talked to at the precinct, and what had come of that little chat? Probation. The ten-foot rule. And now, this. Michael's got my bed, my crawl space, my comic books. Selenko and Miss Nadel want to merge the SP and the OC for drama class. How long till Michael takes my place onstage and becomes Jason's new best friend? And the neighbors. They've all been podified.

And Seth! We moved because of Seth?

No. My imagination is "running away." Or is it?

"Do you really have six kids?" Adam asked.

"Seven," the Cantor said. "But I do not want to scare her."

CHAPTER 31

A few days later, Cousin Harry, a police captain at a downtown Manhattan precinct, showed up at Adam's house.

"I heard you've met some of my colleagues. Parading you in front of every thug in the school was third-class police work. Fortunately, your father anticipated what would happen. Tell me how I can make it up to you."

"You don't have to…"

"One of the benefits of carrying a badge is that I don't have to do anything I don't want to do. But I'd like to make things square."

"Twenty-four-hour protection?"

"I like this boy." Cousin Harry's grin made his cheeks rosy and Adam's parents' laugh, reminding Adam that Harry was a prankster. At their Passover Seder two years before, Adam had opened the door for the prophet Elijah and a life-size dummy swung down and knocked him back five feet. Cousin Harry had fixed it up and the adults had been in on the joke. The moment Adam understood they were not laughing at him, he allowed himself to be amazed by the mechanics of the rigging.

"I told them to send you," Cousin Harry had confided, "because I knew you could take a joke."

And then, all at once, Adam knew how he would transform his Surprise Challenge into an "extravaganza," and he knew what he needed from Cousin Harry. He asked if it would be all right if he showed Cousin Harry something in his bedroom. Harry winked at Jeremy and Helen over Adam's head as he followed the boy down the hall.

Adam's hands were jittery as he unfolded the completed *Selenko WANTED!* poster. Suvan had sized the prints to fit just over the frontal and profile views of Dillinger, Adam had written the text, and Valerie had done the lettering. Cousin Harry handled it with great care, read it silently, finally laughing out loud.

"This is a fine facsimile you've created."

To Adam's surprise, when he explained what he'd envisioned, it came out fully formed, although it had occurred to him for the first time only moments before in the kitchen. Cousin Harry gave Adam several specific tips about setting the crime scene, and suggested they keep it secret from Adam's parents "and spill the beans, so to speak, only after the fact."

Adam folded the poster as carefully as a flag, and Cousin Harry slid it carefully inside his jacket. Adam watched him retrieve his service revolver from the upper shelf in the front closet and return it to the holster strapped across his shoulder, hooking it under his armpit. He wanted to handle the gun—research to play Elisha—but he knew better than to ask. Cousin Harry withdrew a card and handed it to Adam.

"Take this so you can reach me. We're on for C-lenko Day."

Adam slid the card into his back pocket, next to Detective Riley's.

CHAPTER 32

t was Suvan's idea to distract the audience with the soundtrack from *2001: A Space Odyssey.* Valerie cranked the pounding drums of *Thus Spake Zarathustra* up to full volume, dimmed the stage lights to make it look like the accident occurred while rehearsing *Dawn.* She rigged the crime scene tape, three yellow tape measures braided into a lanyard.

Adam lay facedown inside a chalk outline of his crumpled body. Suvan knelt beside Adam, at the edge of a radiating bloodstain of Hershey's syrup mixed with strawberry jam that Valerie had used to make a glistening trail of crimson splotches and smears.

The bell rang for third-period drama class.

Only now did it occur to Adam that lying on his stomach, he would not see Selenko's reaction.

"Pssssssssttt!!!"

Suvan's hard shoes click-clacked on the wooden stage as he crawled toward Adam. Their heads were touching.

"I should be facing up so I can see."

"The bullet hole's in your back."

"Let's switch places."

"You're already bloody."

"They're coming!" Valerie yelled.

"Sorry. Too late!" *Click-clack click-clack.* Suvan retreated on his rabbit knees.

Adam heard the door slam, footsteps, intakes of breath, "Ohmigod!"

Adam wished he could see who'd been startled.

"An accident," Suvan mumbled under the music.

A woman's voice.

"Oh no! What happened?"

Miss Nadel! Where's Selenko? He's left already? This is a disaster!

"It was an accident," Suvan babbled, "an accident…"

"Go to the office right now and call an ambulance! Now. NOW!"

"The detective said not to touch the body till he returned."

Brilliant, Valerie!

"The body?" cried Miss Nadel. "Detective?"

Adam heard shrieks, squeals, cries, eking through the blasting drums. *Who was bawling?*

"Shot in the back!" someone yelled.

It was unfolding too fast.

Footsteps approaching, retreating, *dammit*, Adam couldn't see anything. *If Selenko missed the Surprise, it would all be for nothing.*

"Someone turn off that music!" Miss Nadel cried, but no one did.

"An accident…"

Come on, Suvan! Next line! Oh, I get it. You're holding for Selenko, just the way Selenko taught us to hold on laugh lines! Bloody genius!

Adam heard the slam of the stage door, running footsteps behind the curtains.

"Sorry I'm late, thespians."

Thank God!

The drumbeat was building, *bom-bom, bom-bom, bom-bom*, perfect! Heels clacking across the stage, Miss Nadel, drumbeats, and horns.

"Richard, something terrible…"

"It was an accident…an accident…"

Go for it, Suvan!

"An accident…an accident…"

Suvan isn't holding. He forgot the damned script!

"An accident!"

Say the next line!!! Make something up!

"Not supposed to be a real gun."

There we go!

"Not supposed to be loaded…"

Selenko bellowed at poor Suvan. "What did you do? Oh no! Not Adam!!! No no no!"

A wailing, keening, broken sound just as the music exploded.

My cheeks are going to explode! Tell him how the gun went off when Captain Dawson tried to take it from Elisha.

Suvan's weeping stopped, he gulped, a long pause, then childish crying, very pained, very real.

"Are you the teacher in charge?"

Dammit...too late—

"Speak up!" Cousin Harry was abrupt and commanding, in full voice over the crowd.

"Y-Y-Yes," Selenko blubbered. "Why...do you have a badge?"

"Would one of you lads or ladies turn off that music!" Harry ordered at the climactic *daDah*! Zarathustra spake no more.

The absence of music came as a shock. Adam had to clench every muscle in his face.

"I'm Captain Harry Licht, Ninth Precinct, Homicide. Son, give me that revolver, please."

"Homicide?" Selenko peeped.

Brilliant!

"The revolver, please. It's evidence."

Adam tried to keep still as Suvan retrieved the gun.

The buzz of the auditorium lights, girls sobbing, boys mumbling. "So screwed up... don't believe this..."

Plastic rattling. *An evidence bag!*

"Are you Richard Selenko, the teacher and actor? Speak up!"

"Ye...yes. I am."

"Richard Selenko, you are a Wanted Man!"

"Richard?" piped Miss Nadel.

Adam heard the poster unfolding. The crowning glory! No, no, he couldn't miss this, had to turn his head ever so slightly, but he couldn't risk it. He listened so hard he could hear eyes straining toward the poster.

"Wanted," Cousin Harry pronounced in his official tone, "for five counts of impersonating a teacher, four counts of making lame jokes, two counts of giving tests of excessive difficulty, and one count of pursuing an acting career on school time. I will add one count of beguiling a colleague. A twenty-five-thousand-dollar reward has been offered for your capture. I have only one thing to say to you, Richard Selenko."

"Wh-what?"

"This is your picture from the post office, but the machine gun doesn't do you justice."

A hoot went up from Peter and Jason, Adam's former friends, schooled in Adam's humor.

"You mean..." Selenko's voice was cracking. "Adam's not...?"

"Surprise!" Adam yelled, as he leapt to his feet and smashed into Selenko's chin.

"Ow! Ow! Ow!"

"Surprise!" Suvan peeped in British.

"Surprise!" Valerie called out.

The class exploded in laughter, which broke down to "fooled me... not me...no way...totally convinced..."

Selenko worked his jaw manually to relieve the sting and shock. His face was full of wonder, but his mustache and eyebrows were twitching.

"You...you...you..."

I went too far, mentioning his plans to abandon us. And Cousin Harry went too far.

"Fooled me." Selenko took several deep breaths. "ACTORS," Selenko called, regaining himself. "Surprise is the essence of theater! And I was—we were—surprised! And shocked and terrified and mortified! Applause!"

Applause meant he would tear up, and Adam had to blow his nose to cover it.

"And you two, my friends," Selenko said to Adam and Suvan, "are exempt from the final exam."

Adam had not imagined any such immediate reward, had not imagined any reward, beyond Selenko's pleasure.

"It was all Adam's idea," Suvan piped up.

"No," Adam said, "we did this together, with Valerie and Michael Mason."

Valerie curtsied and received a round of applause.

"Exempt?" Adam asked.

"Yes, yes," Selenko affirmed. "Valerie too."

"I will tell Michael Mason he is exempt from our exam as well," Miss Nadel added.

Adam wanted to celebrate his success, wanted to jump up and down with Suvan, with Valerie, and despite himself, wanted his old gang to gather round. But Jason was smirking with Buddy and Stu, twisting history to prove he had not been fooled for a minute.

"May I have that?"

Selenko snatched the poster from Cousin Harry, read the charges half aloud, smiled, grimaced.

Cousin Harry clapped Selenko on the shoulder. "You must be quite a teacher to inspire these young people to such lengths. No hard feelings?"

Selenko *hmmed* and cleared his throat but didn't reply.

Cousin Harry turned Selenko away from his class. "Let's go someplace quiet and discuss a few details."

At their next lesson, the *Selenko WANTED!* poster was hanging, framed, backstage, with a small museum plaque on the wall with the names of the four students, the date, the year, and the title "Crime Scene—Best Surprise Challenge. Ever."

That night Adam redid the dais plan. He moved Jason to the far-left end with his attack dog Buddy, where they might fall off the platform, seating Peter and Stu with Ryan at the opposite end. Divide and conquer.

MY BAR MITZVAH DAIS (3)

Jason	Buddy	Karsh	Albert	Barry Camp Friend	Eddie Camp Friend	Marla Camp Friend	Sharon Camp Girl-friend!!!	ADAM	Suvan	Valerie	Ryan	Peter	Stu

CHAPTER 33

The tiny RSVP cards from Adam's summer camp friends came all at once. Eddie Mandel had checked off, "Regrettably, I will *not* be able to attend," with "really sucks!!!" inscribed by hand. A curlicued "So So So SORRY that I can't make it!!!" in red pen from Marla. Similar cards came from Alan, Joel, and Julie. He envisioned them together, glowing in the hyper-vivid colors of the summer, crisp mountain greenery, wood smells, crickets chirping and frogs croaking, deciding as a group not to come to his bar mitzvah.

Sharon's reply arrived a few days after the others.

"Regrettably, I will *not* be able to be attend."

It was a very small envelope, but Adam searched it several times. He studied the card from every possible angle. He put the card back in the envelope and took it out again, hoping it would change, like the magic coin trick.

Could she have accidentally checked the wrong box?

Regrettably

I will not have my girlfriend at my bar mitzvah.

not

My Bear Mountain Love will not sit next to me and be my surprise.

be able

I cannot show her off to my friends.

to

Sharon is not my girlfriend.

attend.

I do not have a girlfriend.

No Sharon. No camp friends. Adam *regrettably* wouldn't need a dais at his party. Suvan and Adam could sit at a card table with the ventriloquist and his goddamned dummy.

The next day, a bulky envelope arrived, adorned with Adam's name in calligraphy.

Adam Miller was cordially invited to Barry Rosenblum's bar mitzvah at 8:30 a.m. on Saturday, June 5, 1971 at the Beth El Synagogue in New Rochelle.

It took many minutes for Adam's brain to defrost from this invitation almost identical to his own, with an alias in place of his name and set in the wrong location. He was being replicated again.

Adam told the Cantor at his next lesson that Sharon couldn't come to his bar mitzvah.

"I remember. Girlfriend you never talk to, girlfriend you not see, don't write, don't call?"

"That one, yeah." He explained that his summer camp friends and bus-ride girlfriend were going to Barry Rosenblum's bar mitzvah instead of his.

The world sucks and friends always abandon you. (Except Suvan.)

"You want we should learn a new Torah reading for different Shabbes so girlfriend will come?"

"No."

"I was kidding."

"She made me this kippah." Adam twanged the pom-pom, thought about tossing it into the garbage, but he couldn't bear the synagogue's nylon flyaways. He twanged the pom-pom three times, trying to channel his hurt into the ball of fluff.

"Probably the last present I'll ever get from a girl."

"Probably you going to get a lot more, I bet."

"Everything sucks."

"Yes. Yes. You feel this way today, and tomorrow you also going to feel this way."

"Thanks."

"Also next day."

"Great."

"But not for always. Better you find girl you can talk to right here in the shul."

"Maybe."

Adam thought of Seth's friend's youngest sister with her pixie cut and porcelain skin. But Hebrew School wasn't summer camp. The rules were different in the real world, and he didn't know what they were.

"This one, she is now a memory."

"Like the sister in the alley."

The Cantor turned very red, wiped his face with his handkerchief several times, blew his nose, and stuffed it back into his jacket.

"Smart-alex."

Adam remembered he hadn't given the Cantor his photos yet. No reason they both should sink into misery.

"Close your eyes!" Adam said. He laid out the three eight-by-tens on the table: one of the Cantor in his full regalia, one of him singing with the five glorious Torahs behind him in the open *Aron HaKodesh*, and one of Adam and the Cantor wrapped in tallitot, mouths open in full song. "Now you can look!"

The Cantor jumped out of his chair. His eyes teared and he reached for his handkerchief. He pulled Adam into a tight hug.

"She make a mistake, that Sharon."

CHAPTER 34

Charter Application for New Club – J.H.S. 189
Date <u>April 23, 1971</u>
Name of Club <u>Jewish Heritage Club</u>
Applicant (Student) <u>Adam Miller</u>, Grade <u>7</u>
Home Room Teacher – <u>Mrs. Bell</u>
Faculty Sponsors – 1. <u>Mr. Beck</u> 2. <u>Mr. Selenko</u>
Reasons for Establishing Club
    1. _____
    2. _____
    3. _____

Club Charter Committee Approval Status
    Approved _____
    Denied _____
    If Denied, On what Grounds _____

Expand on your reasons. Please be concise:
The Jews have been around for 4,000 years.

The religion of Judaism—*No, I can't mention religion. Separation of church and state.*

Jews have a long tradition.

Jews have a culture that goes back to the times the ancient Israelites of the Bible. *Who cares about ancient Israelites? I don't care about ancient Israelites.*

The tradition of the legacy of Jewish heritage…the legacy of the Jewish tradition has a long heritage…

Blahbityblablah!

Since Jews are not allowed to be Jewish in the Soviet Union, we Jews who are free have to learn about our culture and history.

That's good. That's Reason #1.

Reason #2—My synagogue was attacked twice already this year, once with bricks and once with graffiti. We have to fight anti-Semitism.

But I don't want to start a club because people hate Jews. There should be positive reasons to start a club, like how much everyone cares about each other at Temple Gates of Hope, like fighting for Russian Jews, like starting our own little country in Israel. Still, it's a good reason.

Reason #3—Jewish kids in 189 deserve to have a bathroom they can go to without an escort. And what about Indian kids who can't go in the *hitters'* bathroom *or* into the *black* bathroom?

They'll think I'm scared to go to school. I am scared to go to school, but I don't hate everybody. It's fine with me that Kevin and Gracie have the Afro-American Club and Ryan and Buddy and Valerie have the Italian-American Club. (Do any of them go? I don't think so.)

Many of the students in JHS 189 are Jewish and Jewish students should explore their unique history and learn about Israel, because being Jewish makes us different. *(Do I want to be different? No. And yes.)*

I want to make Mr. Beck happy. I need a high grade in science class.

Can't say that.

Elisha's story and *Dawn* matter to me. Jews in Russia matter to me. I don't really know why, but they're like my family. I wear *Free Soviet Jewry* buttons and want to save the Refuseniks who are facing the death penalty for trying to go to Israel. We didn't save the Jews of Europe in World War II, so we must save the Russian Jews now.

Reason #3—We are going to fight to free Soviet Jews.

Damn! That was Reason #1.

Being Jewish is very confusing in 1971. *Is that something we could talk about in a Jewish Heritage Club? Maybe.*

Reason #3—To discover how to be Jewish in New York City in 1971.

CHAPTER 35

A school, Adam knew, should hibernate at night. To be *present* in the school building after dark was to be displaced in time and space, but parents were not free in the daytime, so parent-teacher conferences and assemblies were in the dark.

From his perch at the side curtains, Adam watched the SP parents, come to imbibe praise of their offspring, among the vastly larger throng of parents destined for all kinds of mixed reports. Suvan pointed out his mother and father, and Adam was surprised that Mr. Chakrabarti was fat, although not as huge as the very pregnant Mrs. Boyer. He'd forgotten that Jason would soon have another sibling.

"Ready, boys?" Selenko asked, his bright-blue turtleneck raising his head high above his blazer, his face black lines dancing with delight.

"Yessir," Suvan answered.

This would be their final performance of *Dawn* in front of an audience before the Citywides, and they were eager to try out Selenko's refinements. Dr. Lefkowitz had shortened the program, and the other two drama class performances had been cut, including Jason's *Seagull*.

"If there are no questions, we will proceed to our show," the principal said.

But Mrs. Silver had something to say. She wanted all of the boys in the Two-Year SP transferred into the Three-Year SP at the end of the year, "Because every year we keep them in 189 gives us more time to stop the War and save their lives."

"But this school isn't safe!" yelled another parent, which brought on a chorus of agreement.

"It's safer than Vietnam!" Mrs. Silver persisted.

"Pray for the soldiers," a man called out.

"Baby-killers."

They want me to stay here another year?!

"Are they moving us into the Three-Year SP?"

"A nervous mother, that's all," Selenko reassured them. "The war will be over long before you finish high school."

The anti-war movement skirted Adam's awareness due to Seth's protest activities. Adam asked Suvan if he was scared of going to Vietnam.

"I won't be drafted," Suvan surprised Adam. "I'm not an American citizen."

Adam considered this. "But you will be by then, won't you?"

Suvan shrugged.

Or will Suvan be whisked off to England—or India—or, like Takashi, to Japan?

The boys were quiet. Adam's confidence that America would always be victorious and glorious came from watching *Combat!* wearing his father's fatigues, his air rifle aimed at the TV screen, but the idea of going to war without Suvan was impossible. Suvan pondered pointless death on distant foreign shores. They paused their parallel dreaming to listen for Dr. Lefkowitz's introduction.

"What about the gangs?" yelled out an unidentified voice from the darkness.

"In light of the incidents near the school in the fall," Dr. Lefkowitz said with confidence, "we are working very closely with Detective Riley and Detective Fein at Precinct Fourteen to ensure the safety of our students."

"What about the gangs in the school?"

"Please, let's not get sidetracked."

Dr. Lefkowitz sighed loudly into the microphone, begging for silence. This time no one called out.

"We have a treat in store for you tonight. An encore performance of a play performed by the students in Mr. Selenko's drama class. I think you will be delighted."

Only when Adam stepped out onstage to set the historical scene did he take in the magnitude of the audience. His voice fluttered, his skin fluttered, the hairs on his arm fluttered. Once backstage, he told Suvan to project at the top of his lungs as loud as possible, which Suvan said "is obvious to any experienced actor. You must calm down."

Yes, yes, all right.

The performance went well, despite Adam's adrenaline. The applause was solid but brief, and again came in before the final gunshot. Most of the six hundred parents were eager to petition their children's teachers before heading home to eat dinner and collapse at the end of their very long day.

The boys made their way to the foyer outside the auditorium.

"You are the famous Adam," a petite woman said with a pronounced British accent.

"Yes, Mama," Suvan affirmed.

"So nice to meet you. You delivered a marvelous performance."

"Thank you," Adam said. "Nice to meet you. Suvan did a great job too."

"Yes, he did. Suvan's father has started on ahead to the classrooms. Must catch up. We hope we'll see you again."

Taking her cue, Mrs. Boyer chided, "But *we* don't see you anymore, Adam," as if it was Adam's fault. "As you can see, I'm almost ready to pop."

"Yeah, I…congratulations!" *Is that the right thing to say?* "I've been really busy…the play and my bar mitzvah…" *and Jason is ruining my life…*

"Come, Adam, put your hand here. You might feel him move. It's all right, really."

Adam wasn't frightened but was tentative. He slowly, gently placed his open palm on her bulge. It was like a drum. Something moved, and Adam jumped back.

"You felt him kick, Adam, isn't that wonderful? I don't really know if it's a boy, but I'm carrying high, so that's what they say, but it could be an old wives' tale. Think of it, Adam. There's a little person in there."

"In there…" he mumbled. *Another Jason forming inside your pod, a good one to replace the evil one, or perhaps, one even worse.* Adam's shiver ran head to toe. He hoped she hadn't noticed, was glad to be interrupted.

"Wasn't he great, Mom? Adam's the best actor in our class, by far."

Wait…that was Jason praising me.

"I would have brought you some cookies," Mrs. Boyer said, "if I'd realized we were going to see a performance. Why didn't you tell me, Jason?"

"I wanted it to be a surprise."

"Jason was also supposed to—"

"That doesn't matter, Millsy. I was sick of our show. But I really loved the way you popped in and out of the light and vanished into the darkness. And when your character is seeing ghosts? That gave me chills. I watched it twice, Mom, and I was still in suspense, like, the whole time.

What's going on?

"We all think Adam is extremely talented."

Not now, Selenko! Jason's on a roll! And he understood my lighting design perfectly.

"I always said Adam was smart and polite," Mrs. Boyer added, "and it turns out he's a born actor."

Adults have commandeered our conversation. Is the ban over?

"Your son might have a career onstage, Mrs. Miller," gushed Selenko.

"I'm not Mrs. Miller."

"I think he has other ambitions," Adam's father interjected. "But we're very proud of him. Both of you boys were terrific." Mr. Miller hugged Adam while his mother smooched him.

I have other ambitions? What other ambitions?

"Sorry to break up the cheerleading, folks," Mr. Vogel interrupted. "Conferences are beginning."

Driving home, Adam's parents seemed more interested in *Dawn* than his stellar academic reports.

"It takes guts to put on a show about Israel," his father said, "and you did it magnificently."

"We're very proud that you're such a proud Jew," his mother agreed. "And a terrific actor."

Adam wanted to ask his father about the "other ambitions" he was supposed to have but asked instead if Seth would have to go to Vietnam.

"It depends on what Seth wants to do. We'll explore all the options during the next year."

Is Seth going to evade the draft? He'll go fight for Israel! Trading nunchucks for an Uzi. And that's what I'll do, if Vietnam drags on for six more years. But what will Suvan do?

These thoughts were overwhelmed by a much cheerier thought.

"I was happy to see you and Jason together," Mrs. Miller remarked.

Don't say it out loud, Mom, but you're right, my old life is back.

MY BAR MITZVAH DAIS (4)

Buddy	Stu	Peter	Ryan	Jason	ADAM	Suvan	Valerie	Albert	Karsh

Jason was absent for several days after Parents Night, and his entourage—Buddy, Stu, Peter—ignored Adam as usual. Ryan reached the verge; his neck, jaw, vocal cords geared up to speak to Adam, but Buddy stopped him cold, and Ryan's face collapsed like a basset hound's.

They haven't been told yet.

Adam called Jason to see how he was feeling. He was too ill the first time, couldn't come to the phone the second. Strike three came when Mrs. Boyer confided that Jason was better but wasn't available.

Not available?

When Jason returned to school, it was as if Parents Night had never happened.

"It was all a show for his mother," Suvan opined at their next rehearsal.

"What?"

Adam had never confided to Suvan about being shunned. The girls must have told him. The girls liked talking to Suvan.

"So she wouldn't know what he's been doing."

No wonder Jason had exaggerated so much. What a stinker! Nasty nasty nasty. God, I wish he was in another country! In another dimension! I wish he was dead!

He could see the outer nunchuck smashing into Jason's grin, scattering his teeth across science class, until Mr. Beck summoned him back to the basic laws of physics.

CHAPTER 36

Adam had only to sing out the first three words, *Etz Hayyim Hee*, "It's a Tree of Life," and the Junior Congregation rushed in to swell the song to its rousing final note. Once the ark was closed, Adam was done with his part. He joined the kids below in the old wooden pews, reading the Amidah in silence, then slipped to the back to use the bathroom, where he met Karsh, on one of his extended bathroom breaks.

"Shhh!" Karsh hushed.

Karsh was counting the days to his own bar mitzvah, after which he'd be free at last on Saturday mornings. Adam had recruited Karsh to play lineman for the Carlyle Towers, and Karsh became unexpectedly protective of Adam off the field as well when Jason booted him off his own football team. Although he could have skipped the occasional service, Karsh quit the team when the games were moved to Saturday mornings, out of loyalty to Adam.

"You hear that?" Karsh asked.

Thump. Long pause. *Thump*. Longer pause. *Thump*.

Something was hitting the wall.

Karsh told Adam that he'd seen suspicious types on the steps leading into the old synagogue when he'd gone outside for air. Going outside for air was another of Karsh's survival tricks to get through services.

"What'd they look like?"

"You know, suspicious." *Thwack. Thwack.* "Sounds like eggs."

They listened hard.

"No splatting" Adam ruled.

"A battering ram."

A Roman legion was unlikely. "Don't think so."

"Think they're trying to break in?"

"The doors aren't locked."

But damn, anti-Semites could be defacing the synagogue again. Would they look like the Russians threatening to execute the Leningrad Sixteen? Or would they look like Jew-ball Bastard?

"We better check," Adam said. "Let me get my coat."

"It's not cold."

"I know, but I need it."

Whenever Seth went to Shabbat morning youth services in the new building, Adam took Seth's nunchucks to Junior Congregation. Adam, Karsh, nunchucks—this trio would scare the perpetrators away.

Adam leapt out onto the landing, nunchucks held taut across his body, approximating the stance the Betarees had used. A projectile flew past his head. Adam jumped back and crashed into Karsh. Karsh pushed past him, ready to sacrifice his body as Adam's offensive tackle, but the blow never came.

Michael Mason was standing on the flat ground at the bottom of the steps, going into his pitching windup to a boy with a stickball bat on the top step standing three feet from Adam and Karsh.

"Wait!" Adam yelled, scrambling to his feet.

Michael Mason reared back and fired a red rubber Spalding at Adam. Adam ducked and the ball thudded off the door and bounced away. While Michael's compatriot chased the ball, Michael pulled out another ball from inside a large green duffel bag sitting at his feet and went into his windup again.

"All dressed up and nowhere to go, Adam Miller?" he quipped, as he snapped a quick pitch over Karsh's head that also thudded off the door.

"You know this guy?" Karsh bellowed.

"Nowhere to go except my closet!"

Michael fired at Adam again. Adam tried to swing the nunchucks at the ball but only succeeded in hitting himself in the side.

"To get my camera!" he screamed between yelps. "And Nadine went in your closet!" Nadine wafting springtime.

"That's not what I heard. Makes no difference anyway. You didn't wait for me. Partners in a great adventure my ass!"

Michael bent down, but instead of taking out another Spalding, he unzipped the duffel bag, splitting it open like a pea pod, lifted it over his head with one mighty yank.

"You like my fucking closet so much, you can have it!"

The boys jumped back, thinking Michael Mason was going to hurl the duffel bag at them, but Michael poured out the contents on the synagogue steps: dirty clothes, torn T-shirts; white socks, some so caked with mud they stood like tiny sculptures; Michael's green army jacket; a box of chalk; a carton of cigarettes, two of the packs bleeding individual cigarettes like pick-up-sticks. And magazines—to Adam's horror, six, eight, ten *Playboy* magazines, blowing open on the synagogue steps!—and Adam's fourth-grade reports on Greek mythology and Madagascar, and two packages of his comic books in plastic bags. The crawl space had come to shul.

Michael lit a cigarette, picked up the duffel bag, called to his pal, "Outta here," and strolled off down Roosevelt Avenue.

"What was that all about?" Karsh demanded.

"He's crazy."

"Crazy is right. What are those sticks you're waving around?"

"My brother's…they're nunchucks."

"Oh, like Kato! Hai Karate!"

"Come on! We've got to hide this stuff!"

Adam needed a giant garbage pail, but there was no garbage pail. There was nothing. This was much worse than Michael dropping the centerfold on the post office steps.

"Hurry up," Adam urged. "We'll stash it in the bathroom."

"Mr. Levin always uses the *terlet* before he goes home," Karsh said. Mr. Levin was the young replacement for Mr. Rockowitz.

"Then where?"

"The balcony."

"It's locked."

"I can get in."

"You can?"

"I go up there sometimes," Karsh said.

201

"You do?" Another strategy. "Let's pick this crap up. You get the *Playboys!*" Adam rasped, whispering the last word, afraid it would contaminate him, pollute the building's sanctity, mark him as a deviant. Adam grabbed the copies of *Sports Illustrated* and his comic books, then fingered the cigarettes delicately, as if they'd leave a stain. They were softer than he expected. "Let me," Karsh said, as he swept up the loose cigarettes in two quick swipes, smashed them back into the open pack, and stacked the cartons on top of the magazines and the packs on top of the clothes.

"Open the door, quick. Keep real quiet on the steps. Take your shoes off."

They crept upstairs in their stocking feet, stopping their breath each time a board creaked to swallow back the sound. Karsh balanced his bundle against the banister, dug out a plastic card from his pocket, slid it into the crack next to the doorknob. With a few swipes, he released the bolt. The boys crawled into the balcony, staying low and out of sight. Dust mushroomed up in their faces, fluttered in the colored sunbeams of the stained-glass windows. Just beyond the balcony floated the massive, ancient chandelier, a cake of crystal both weighty and delicate that Adam had been looking up at for six years.

The *Aleinu* ascended from below. Closing prayers. They had to hurry.

Next to Adam were cardboard boxes of old *Shilo* prayer books, their spines spitting fibers, the hardcovers worn through, exposing their dark, dense Hebrew text. Adam emptied the cartons, filled them with magazines, leaving the *siddurim* on the pew. Adam kept the comics out. Those he'd take home.

Goddamned Michael Mason. We should have waited for him.

Karsh shoved a *Playboy* inside his pants.

"For my father." Karsh mouthed.

"Your father reads *Playboy*?"

"Everybody's father reads *Playboy*."

"Not mine."

"You just haven't found them yet."

Adam tried to picture it but couldn't.

Back downstairs, the boys heard voices outside. Adam readied his nunchucks, cracked the door open, and found Floyd with the rabbi, two of the ancients, and embarrassingly, his father.

Adam slammed the door shut, fumbled the nunchucks back into the sleeve of his coat.

"Adam?"

Hid dad had spotted him. He stepped outside.

"Where's your coat?" his father asked. "It's chilly."

"No respect for holy places," Floyd said.

Holy places? Adam had just profaned the building with filthy laundry and naked women. Mr. Gelfand pointed at the door. "Look what those bastards painted on our synagogue!"

"What do the colors mean?"

"A flag? The John Birch Society? The Klan?"

"Maybe it's some kind of warning."

"Adam, did you see anybody suspicious?"

"I'll get the cops," Floyd summarized.

"Don't call the police," Adam said. "It's not a warning. And it's not a flag. It's a stickball box. Red is a strike. Green is a ball. Blue is borderline. That's all. It's chalk. We can wash it off. The rain will wash it off. But you're right. No respect."

CHAPTER 37

nstead of igniting the blazing overhead lights in the boys' bedroom to wake him for school, Helen Miller sat on the edge of Adam's bed, and shook her son's shoulder gently.

What's the matter?

She told him that something terrible had happened, that Jason Boyer's mother had died in childbirth.

Adam dug deep under his pillow to turn off this bizarre nightmare. His mind flipped channels, words and images skipping by, but his mother's voice was low and steady, appearing in every dream.

Mr. Boyer had called to tell Adam's parents. He had wept on the phone.

Jason's father crying about Jason's mother with her Laura Petrie flip and cookies. How can she be dead?

Adam's mother was crying.

"Those poor people, poor children, poor Stan. What a tragedy."

Adam sat up and hugged his mother, and for the first time in his life, Adam felt one of his parents holding him to hold on.

"It happened this morning around dawn." His mother said, her voice cracking. "They were in the hospital. That poor woman. And the baby gone too."

The baby had died. I felt that baby kick my hand. She was sure it was a boy. They died at dawn.

Adam's mother began to puzzle out Adam's expression through her own tears.

"I know," she snuffled, "you're not friends like you were. Sylvia and I were both unhappy about that. I thought it was getting better."

Their mothers had discussed it? And Mrs. Boyer was named Sylvia. A name that no one would answer to anymore. How was this possible?

Mr. Miller appeared in the doorway; his face clenched tight in sorrow.

"It's awful for you to have to do this, but Mr. Boyer asked and you can't say no."

"Do what?"

Mr. Boyer wanted Adam to tell their teachers and the principal the terrible news. Adam's father had agreed.

"The poor man is shattered," Mrs. Miller said. "He couldn't make the calls himself."

Don't you know Jason's my enemy? You must say no. You must call him back to tell him to ask Stu or Ryan or Buddy, Jason's new best friends. Call Jason's mother. She'll underst—ohmigod!

"But why me?"

His parents looked at each other. Adam had been chosen, rightly or wrongly, and in such a special, terrible situation, you can't say no. *And won't Jason feel bad when he finds out who—*no, Jason must be feeling bad in a way that Adam *never* wanted to imagine.

What does our fight matter? His mother is dead.

"What should I say?"

"Just tell them what happened."

"Okay." Adam would deliver the message. This horrific information was now Adam's, and Adam had to pass on it on to get rid of it.

Adam's parents drove Adam to school together, another first, and he hoped they'd tell Dr. Lefkowitz themselves, but no, Adam's mother had canceled her remedial reading instruction for the entire day and was heading to Temple Gates of Hope to make funeral arrangements. Adam's father was going in late to his own school.

Entrusted with death, Adam felt invulnerable to routine dangers as he walked through the yard, past the smokers and the hitters and change hustlers. Adam rehearsed twenty different formulations, settling on: "Jason Boyer will not be in school today because his mother died."

He started with Mrs. Bell in home room. She called Jason's name taking attendance, Adam shuddered, but nobody said a word, which meant nobody knew. Adam fidgeted until the chimes rang, slowing his pace as he walked up to Mrs. Bell. Adam was terrified he would laugh from nerves. She would think he was a horrible, inexcusable human being.

"Yes, Miller, what is it?"

"I have to tell you something sad." *That was a good way to start.* "Jason Boyer won't be in school today. His mother died."

"Oh no!" She paled.

"She died giving birth, and the baby died too." He hadn't intended to add this, but once he started, he felt he must share the full awfulness.

Mrs. Bell's face collapsed as if the muscles holding her cheeks and eyebrows in place had gone to sleep all at once, a sight Adam saw only for an instant because she seized him. "That's terrible…so terrible… terrible." Three times "terrible," then, "dreadful."

Adam was sad and horrified and scared to death, and still petrified that he might have smiled out of excitement. Whatever he felt about Jason, he loved Mrs. Boyer.

"They asked me to tell you."

"That poor boy. Terrible. Terrible. Thank you for letting me know…oh that poor child."

Adam worried all day his features would realign on their own, but the teachers were wise, and no one mistook his intent. Nor was Mrs. Bell the last teacher who grabbed hold of Adam as he shared the evil tidings. The women teared up. The men used the voice they reserved for meaningful pronouncements. Mr. Beck took the news stoically, said it was "a darned shame. Does he have brothers and sisters?"

"One younger brother. He was supposed to have another."

"It's a cruel world, my boy. Poor kids. No child should have to endure such a thing." He told Adam he was "a fine young man and a good friend."

I am not Jason's friend. But what does that matter?

It was after algebra, the fourth class of the day, that Suvan ambushed him in the corridor.

"What's going on? You're moving, aren't you? Where to? To California? Is that where one goes from New York? Or Florida? Don't tell me you're moving to Florida."

"That's not it."

Adam had no instructions about telling friends. Was it supposed to be kept from them?

"I'll tell you, but we have to keep this secret."

"Loose lips sink ships," Suvan said, drawing a zipper across his mouth in another inexplicable reference. Adam told Suvan what had happened.

"Jason is not a nice boy, but this is extremely sad."

Adam had an urge to hurt Suvan, to remind him that Jason didn't have an accent, that he loved science fiction and comic books, rooted for the Yankees not the Mets, that he'd had fun with Jason, truth be told, more fun sometimes than with Suvan. Jason was, nasty, yes, but now they could no longer hate him, because his mom was dead.

At lunch, Debra, Valerie, Gracie, and Ryan sat at the Door Patrol table with Suvan and Adam. This configuration was extraordinary— Debra talking to Gracie, whom she'd been ignoring for seven years, and above all, Ryan next to Adam, with no sidelong glances toward the absent Jason. (Poor Jason! *Motherless.*)

What had Suvan done?

"We know something bad happened."

Adam was shocked at Suvan's betrayal.

Gracie said, "I was watching you…"

"She's always watching you," Debbie said, but Gracie ignored this.

Valerie socked Debbie in the shoulder.

"Ow," Debra said. "Gracie followed you."

"She's always following you."

Gracie? Gracie liked him?

Ryan jerked up. "And I saw Mrs. Glixon cry after you talked to her."

"Suvan knows what's up," Valerie announced, "but he won't crack."

No betrayal after all.

"Okay," Adam said. "Come closer."

In this huddle, Adam shared the death of Mrs. Boyer, and then, after a pause, the baby. He hadn't intended any dramatic effect, only to catch his breath and to try to control his body, which was starting to shake, and to force his face, using both his hands to hide his mouth, not, at any cost, to form a smile. Valerie, who had just punched Debra so hard she'd made her cry, Valerie went waterworks.

"I'm so sorry," they said, the girls hugging each other, then each one hugging Adam in lieu of Jason, as if Adam had become an orphan, as if Jason and Adam were not sworn enemies. It was warm and strange and exciting to be held close by girl after girl, and above all, confusing. The girls hugged each other and cried again.

Girls, Adam thought, *do that.*

Adam couldn't speak when they ushered him inside Dr. Lefkowitz's office. Dr. Lefkowitz remembered Adam from the watch theft. The principal sat perfectly still, made no sound or movement, wondering what was about to befall him. After Adam said his lines, Dr. Lefkowitz was silent for a long time.

"When did this happen?"

"Early this morning, around dawn, my mother said."

Jason doesn't have a mother.

Then Dr. Lefkowitz put a hand on Adam's shoulder.

"Thank you for telling me, Adam," he said, giving Adam a familiar half-grimace half-smile. "They entrusted the right messenger, but I'm sure it was hard for you."

That's when it hit Adam.

Dawn.

Mrs. Boyer had died at *dawn. That could not be a coincidence.*

The cosmic equation was simple: Adam had wished that Jason was dead, although he never meant *dead* dead, and somehow those wishes had missed their target and hit Mrs. Boyer instead.

I killed Mrs. Boyer.

Adam knew this made no sense. Bad wishes couldn't kill, couldn't be rerouted by mistake and strike the wrong target, but…but…but…He began to tear up, smile, and shake all at once, but Dr. Lefkowitz slapped Adam on the back, as if to stop a choking fit, and Adam's body realigned to normal.

The bell had rung before he left Lefkowitz, making Adam late for Selenko's class, but what did that matter? As he stumbled slowly down the forever long and hollow hallway, Adam dealt with God. (Agnostic on the question of belief, Adam talked to God when he needed to.)

Cancel this day! I promise to be good for the rest of my life! Give her back her life and her baby! Let me change places with Mrs. Boyer!

"Hey, Jewboy!"

Jewboy?

Adam recognized him, wished he could remember his name. It was Car Coat, from the Watch Gang. Red hair slicked over to the side. On this of all days!

"Talking to you, Jewboy!"

Not Jew-*ball*. Jew*boy*! Not a boy who is Jewish but a boy who is not a man, a Jew who is helpless, who can't fight, won't defend himself. *Was that what Jew-ball Bastard called me on the subway?*

Car Coat came like a gunfighter, but Adam wasn't afraid, not of his glare or his freckles. Adam was the bearer of death, he was Elisha. Mr. Selenko believed in him, Mr. Selenko, who'd been in Vietnam and probably killed half a battalion. No backing down.

Adam got ready to slug Car Coat.

Gracie stepped out from nowhere, from the wall it seemed—*she is following me*—but Adam froze, and while distracted with Gracie, Car Coat punched Adam in the stomach, then three quick rabbit punches to Adam's back when he tried to stand up. Car Coat took off running. Adam was still down when Ryan zoomed past—*following me too? No, following Gracie*—and chased down Car Coat, catching up to him at the stairwell. They disappeared through the door. A thud, a scream, a crash, a whimper.

Ryan emerged from the doorway, strolled up the corridor, helped Adam up.

"I threw him down the stairs."

"Good," Adam said, then grew afraid. "Is he okay?"

"He didn't break his neck."

"Okay," Adam said. He didn't want another death on his hands.

"Too bad, though," Ryan said. "Friends stick together."

"We should," Adam answered.

Gracie is following me. Gracie must like me. She's black. Black is beautiful. Do I like Gracie? Now I see it. Ryan likes Gracie. He's my friend. He was. He is. I can't get in his way.

Mr. Selenko stepped out of the teachers' bathroom.

"Won't your teacher be angry you're late?"

Selenko's joke fell flat.

Selenko doesn't know yet. Not his fault.

Still, speech eluded Adam.

"Wait. Adam, what's going on? Ryan, Gracie, go on ahead. What's wrong?"

Should he tell him about Car Coat—No!—but he had to deliver his message.

Adam said there was bad news. He told Selenko about Mrs. Boyer dying without fighting his smile because there was no smile, and without rushing his words because he was too worn down to rush. He told him about the baby. They started to walk together, and Adam told him how Jason had turned his friends against him all year and his only friend was Suvan because he was new, and the other kids thought Suvan was weird, and how it was crazy that Mr. Boyer had asked Adam of all the kids to share the news instead of one of Jason's traitorous new friends, not Ryan, he was okay, but you can't say no in a special situation to someone who is grieving so bad, and it was so, so sad. He had told all the teachers already and Dr. Lefkowitz.

Selenko was the first of the male teachers to hug Adam, and the only one who cried. And instead of laughing, Adam cried too, sobbing for Jason and for his lovely mother who looked like Laura Petrie, and for himself.

Adam felt a handkerchief appear in his hands and blew his nose and wiped his eyes and handed it back. His eyes were red.

"Does the class know?"

"Some of them. At lunch."

"We'll tell them together."

Those weren't Adam's instructions. Selenko saw Adam's hesitation.

"By now, rumors must be flying. We should be sad as a group. And you and I will discuss the rest of what you told me later."

Adam's fear came through his eyes. Adam nodded in agreement.

"Amy, Karen." Selenko spoke over Adam's head. "Come out, please."

There were more girls? And they heard everything I said? But what does it matter compared to Mrs. Boyer's death?

"We were following Ryan following Gracie following Adam," Amy said.

"Let's not discuss that right now," Selenko said.

No, let's not.

"Please ask the class to assemble onstage. You already know what we've got to say."

CHAPTER 38

All night, the terror that something would happen to his mother shook Adam awake, and in the morning, he had a burning, soaring fever. His body, with no explicit instructions from his conscious brain, had reorganized internally to demand that his mother stay by his side. It was during these three days that Mr. Selenko left JHS 189, turning over his classes to the OC teacher, Miss Nadel, a changing of the guard, an absence that in Adam's fever became confused with the greater void of Mrs. Boyer's death. On the fourth day after Mrs. Boyer died, Adam's fever retreated, and his parents told him they were going to pay a shiva call together.

Adam's grandfather had died when Adam was ten, in the middle of the teachers' strike, and for seven days their house had been transformed: mirrors covered because vanity is nullified by death; low chairs in the living room intended to remind them how low they felt, which made it appear they were hosting small children; the front door left open by extruding the bolt outside its socket—so friends, neighbors, relatives, labor buddies, and work colleagues—only some of whom had seen the inside of Adam's house before—could comfort the family in its most fragile hour. Adam had ventured from his bedroom only to raid the gargantuan platters of delicatessen or the white cardboard boxes of bakery cookies. On each circuit through the living room, it seemed the visitor in the hot seat next to his father morphed into someone else: his bald uncle grew hair; Mr. Schiffman became Mrs. Chilten with her pointy glitter glasses and her latest chihuahua; the Board of Ed district supervisor smoking the cigar transformed into the young neighbors his mother had helped find a kindergarten for their child the year before.

Adam couldn't go to Mrs. Boyer's shiva. Not possible, no way, non-negotiable. It didn't matter that Adam's mother was cooking holiday dishes—fried chicken and steak marengo—to bring to the Boyers. His mother grasped neither how fully Adam hated Jason, a feeling no longer permitted, nor that Mrs. Boyer's death was Adam's fault. These thoughts were too tenuous and outlandish to survive the glare of his parents' common sense, so Adam dared not speak them aloud.

She died at dawn. My fault my fault my fault my fault.

He tried to tell Seth.

"That's crazy. Who do you think you are? God?"

"No, but—"

"But nothing. You don't believe that. Period." Seth put his arm around Adam, gave him a squeeze, then pushed him down on his bed. "It's super sad, but you know, it's nobody's fault."

Adam didn't believe it and he did. He needed to stew in his guilt a little longer.

"I can't." He announced it plain and simple to his parents. "I'm still feeling sick."

"We put off visiting for four days, and Dr. Saffrin says you're fine."

"What am I going to say?"

"You're going to tell Jason how sorry you are," his mother advised. "It's normal to be nervous. Grown-ups also don't know what to say. And Adam, I'm healthy as a horse, so you can stop worrying about your mother."

"I wasn't—well, a little."

"What's going on in that head of yours?"

I wished Jason dead and it misfired.

"Nothing."

"Something." A softer key replaced his mother's omniscient teacher's tone in anything connected to Mrs. Boyer.

Can't tell you.

"We're not friends."

"We're not blind, Adam. Friends fall out and then they fall in again. Especially in times of need. This is one of those times."

Not answering the call was something his parents would never excuse. Adam would do the right thing, but how could he face Jason Boyer?

"Is there anything else you want to tell me?"

"No."

Adults can't understand true thoughts that make no sense. They want to solve feelings as if they are problems, overeager to erase them. I won't be like that when I grow up.

Adam practiced his lines as he peered out furtively from the back seat. To Mr. Boyer he would say, *I'm so sorry for your loss.* To Jason, simply, *I'm really sorry about your mom. I really liked her so much.* He would not be able to say the words "mother" and "died" in the same sentence.

Adam prayed his father would not drive down their old block, but Mr. Miller ignored Adam's silent prayer. On this day when he *needed* Poplar Street to be packed, a parking space appeared in front of the Schiffmans' house. All three Millers stared across the street at their old home. *Our* real *home,* Adam thought, *except Michael Mason is in my bed, climbing through our secret entrance to the crawl space, plotting to kill me.*

Recalling their mission, the Millers forcibly realigned their collective gaze across Kissena Boulevard up at the towering apartment buildings where Jason had ruled until—Adam could not finish this thought, could not add finality to finality.

But how could she be telling Adam she missed his visits, and the next minute, she's nothing, vanished from this earth, a ghost?

Would Jason think he had come to gloat (as if he could ever gloat over such a loss)? Would Jason blame Adam somehow?

His father's social calm would be seen as gravitas, tailored perfectly to situations in which his surehanded managerial tone was comforting, but Adam's mother would do the talking. She was never shy, always direct, would figure out exactly what to say.

They could still turn around, retrace their steps to the car, escape in their Bonneville before any Boyers or old neighbors spotted them or Eddie Weiss returned to spit on them. But parental momentum carried Adam to Carlyle Towers. Entering the lobby felt like visiting a lost life. Ten years old, the building no longer felt freshly unwrapped, but the exterior wall was glass and filled the lobby with sunlight. There was the double elevator bank, the ground floor corridor that led to Adam's dentist. He would gladly get a cavity filled rather than fly up to see Jason Boyer.

"I always wanted to live in this building," Adam's mother said when they got in the elevator. "Let somebody else shovel the snow."

So why did we move to another planet instead of crossing the street to go up in the world? Down the hall from Jason, our friendship would never have crumbled.

How can I be feeling sorry for myself now?

"Apartments are little boxes," Mr. Miller said dismissively.

"And houses have leaves to rake and basement leaks to fix."

"We'll have enough time in a box...well...today's not the day for that."

"Hold it!" they heard, a split second before the elevator door shut. Mrs. Miller attacked the Open Door button, her courtesy overruling her judgement, as Mrs. Paul, a Poplar Street gossip, slipped inside the cabin.

"Oh Greta," his mother said. "We've missed you."

"Not as much as we've missed you."

"It's a terrible thing about Mrs. Boyer."

"Who?"

"Sorry," his father replied. "We thought you were going up to the Boyers on seventeen."

"I'm going home. I live on fourteen. I'll let you in a little secret. It's really the thirteenth floor, but there is no thirteen because it's bad luck. It would hurt my resale value."

I should have skipped from twelve to fourteen years old. That's what I should have done.

"When did you move?"

"In September. You got out before things went to hell, but you saw which way the neighborhood was going. I always wanted a room with a view, and now I have one. So thank you for giving me the courage."

The elevator stopped once, twice, three times, each glimpse of another orthodontically straight corridor made Adam start, thinking they had arrived. It was stopping on every floor. A prank, no doubt, by kids in the building. Adam and Jason had always been careful not to get out on Jason's floor, so it wouldn't be traced back to them.

"What happened to your friend?"

"She died in childbirth."

"Oh my! That pregnant woman? I know who you're talking about. She's a darling. *Was*...oh my...how awful. Are there children?"

"Adam's best friend. And a younger boy."

Not...my best friend.

"Fathers are well and good, but children without a mother... they're orphans now."

Orphans crushed the Millers, and the elevator became a cell. It stopped on two more floors.

"I'll have to stop by," Greta said as she exited on fourteen. "Tell me, Helen, do you know if they're planning to sell?"

Adam's mother rammed the Close Door button with her out-stretched accusing index finger.

"Horrid awful woman," she said, when the elevator resumed its ascent. "I saw those For Sale signs, Jem. What did she mean?"

"Later."

"You can talk in front of me," Adam said, eager to hear, but they reached seventeen with no additional stops or words spoken.

The Boyers' apartment was at the end of the long, dark hermetically sealed green hall. They did a forced march, his parents pushing Adam ahead to be their guide, to pierce the ice. The door was unlocked, but the Boyers' house was not set up for shiva. There were no special chairs, no platters of food, and no relatives came to greet them.

The adults milling about couldn't remain still. One couple perched on the edge of the sofa, popped up from their seats, wandered a few steps, backed up, sat again. Several men paced and smoked, the cloud making the room airless and foul, musical chairs gone wrong.

Adam spotted Mr. Boyer circling through the connected kitchen, dining area, and living room, briefly disappearing on each circuit, his head down, getting progressively lower. Adam had never seen an adult so miserable. A man who resembled Mr. Boyer—his brother?—trailed behind him.

Adam's parents did not manage to get Mr. Boyer's attention for their own rehearsed condolences. Helen delivered her tightly wrapped food parcels to the dining room table—there was no one to hand them off to—and then joined Jeremy in scanning the room for two adjacent seats. Adam appealed to his mother for instructions and was sent off to Jason's room.

As Adam slid along the smooth hallway paneling, Mr. Boyer shot out of the kitchen, yanked Adam to his chest briefly, gave a staccato bark of "Jason," a shake of water from his face—sweat, tears, Adam wasn't sure which. Adam's vocal cords were still warming up—"I'm so sorry for—" when Mr. Boyer grabbed his shoulders and stared into Adam's eyes, looking at him directly for the very first time.

"What am I going to do, Adam?"

Adam was too terrified and guilty to respond.

Mr. Boyer set Adam aside and pulled Jason's younger brother Kenny to his chest, then spun him around so Kenny's back was against his stomach. "Look at him!"

Adam looked at Kenny. He'd seen Kenny a million times.

"Every time I look at him, I see her!" Mr. Boyer screamed, and then he sobbed.

He was right. Kenny and Mrs. Boyer had the same face. Kenny *was* Mrs. Boyer's replica, their duck mouths identical.

Mr. Boyer dropped down to the floor. He pulled Kenny onto his lap. "What am I going to do?"

Adam felt his father's hands on his shoulders, momentarily expected to be pulled down onto his lap. But Mr. Miller turned Adam away, aiming him down the hall.

"Go find Jason."

As the adults crowded near Mr. Boyer, Adam moved as slowly as possible, his apology jumping in his brain, failing to formulate—*so, so sorry for wishing you were in Japan, wishing you were dead*—wanting to confess his crime, to reverse time, to undo death, bring her back, to take Mrs. Boyer's death upon himself and offer his life in her place—*on condition, God, that you make it as if I never existed, so my parents won't suffer losing me. God, why are you always so goddamned quiet?*

"Hi," Adam said.

217

"My mom's dead."

"I know. I'm really sorry." That wasn't enough. "Really, really," Adam said, trying to load the *really* with the depths of pity he felt for Jason and the sadness he felt about Mrs. Boyer. "It's so sad," he added, meaning, that he was sad, and guilty, and frightened.

"The baby died too."

Adam had stopped thinking about the baby and didn't take responsibility for this doubled tragedy. He had touched the baby, almost, and he would never have wished a baby dead—of course, he had never wished any harm to Mrs. Boyer either. It was all Jason's fault really—what had Adam ever done to Jason? But it had gone horribly wrong.

"That's even sadder. Or also sad. It's very, very sad."

Adam didn't know what else to say. Jason said nothing so they were silent for a long time.

This was the room where Adam and Jason had played Stratego, All-Star Baseball, Electric Football, Careers, Life, Yahtzee. And there was the black dial phone from which they made phony phone calls with intricate and elaborate scripts, with music and sound effects, some to gullible Ryan, but mostly to strangers, to stores or churches or synagogues. Jason had his own TV, and they had watched *Get Smart*, *Creature Feature*, and *The Dick Van Dyke Show* when they were feeling uncreative. They'd also thrown dead baseball cards out the window, watched them set sail on air currents, always falling but moving horizontally in all directions, crisscrossing the parking lot and front lawns, sometimes flying across the street. It could take ten or twelve minutes before a card reached the ground, sometimes with gangs of young boys chasing it to and fro, and it provided a great show. And while Adam and Jason did their mischief, Mrs. Boyer baked cookies. There would be no more care packages.

Then these words came out of Adam's mouth:

"Your mom was so nice, like Laura Petrie."

Jason looked at him like he was crazy.

"I mean, she was pretty like Laura Petrie. I mean, I really liked your mom."

Jason's lips fluted into a funnel as if he was going to speak, then murmured "Yeah, she was."

Kenny came into the room.

"Want to see my turtle?"

"Sure," Adam replied, happy to focus his attention elsewhere.

Kenny was probing his turtle with a sewing needle. Adam thought he was trying to clean off the turtle's shell, but he saw that Kenny was poking the turtle repeatedly in its underbelly. The turtle's legs were flailing. Adam put his hand on Kenny's hand to still his motion and pulled the needle out.

"No," Adam said. Adam lifted Kenny's arm to examine the turtle, which didn't seem to be bleeding. He didn't know if turtles had blood. Kenny looked at Adam fiercely.

"I want to," Kenny blurted through gritted teeth.

"You don't," Adam said. Adam was stronger than an eight-year-old and held him fast.

"Stop stabbing your stupid turtle!" Jason yelled at Kenny. Jason removed the turtle from Adam's hand and put it in an empty fishbowl, perhaps the turtle's home. Adam released Kenny, who sprang away in tears.

"It's *my* turtle," Kenny whimpered, rubbing his arm hard before stalking out when he was ignored.

"Sorry," Adam said. "I didn't mean to hurt him."

"Doesn't matter," Jason said.

Jason held out a pile of comic books.

"These are for you."

"What?"

"I…um…saved them."

There were six issues of *The Flash* and *Green Lantern/Green Arrow* and the entire three-part *Justice League of America* "Crisis on Earth-Two" saga, *The Phantom Stranger*, and both Jack Kirby's *The Forever People* and *Tales of the New Gods*.

It was an astonishing, unexpected gift. And Adam could carry these comic books openly, not smuggled inside his clothes. His parents couldn't refuse an offering made in a house of mourning.

Questions were fighting to escape Adam's mouth—*Why did you dump me? Why did you turn our friends against me? Were you planning for us to be friends again?* But Jason's mother was dead, and Adam couldn't ask him. He wanted to comfort Jason, and he wanted to run, not to be contaminated by death, and not to let his guilt show or his anger leak out. One leg started to go to the door, but his mouth formed the words that he'd been rehearsing for seven months.

"Jason? This year…was it because…you thought I snitched on the gang that stole watches?"

"You snitched?"

Why did I say that out loud? Dammit!

"The subway? Those guys who—"

"That? No. Like…that wasn't really your fault…"

Adam had never thought it was his fault.

So, why? *Was Jason angry about something? Jealous? Insulted?*

"I could…" Jason's voice dropped an octave and stayed there. "Damn. The doctor says my voice is changing. I'm not supposed to talk. Sorry."

Was that "sorry" an apology? "I could." Was that the reason? You did it because you "could"? Did you do this on purpose?

"You started to say it wasn't really my fault. Was it my girlfriend?"

"What girlfriend?"

"I told you. In camp. But she's not my girlfriend anymore."

What made me tell him I'm a loser?

"What're you talking about? There it goes again. I'm not really supposed to talk."

"Wow!" Adam said. "It *is* changing. That is so weird."

And a relief to discuss.

They were silent. Adam was not going to get an answer, and it was wrong to be looking for one in Jason's time of grief.

"You're not mad?" Jason asked.

Mad? I want to kill you. You're a selfish shit who gets pleasure from causing pain. But your mother is dead, and you have your father's voice.

"Your mom. It's so sad. It doesn't matter."

Adam flipped the pages of the comics, but he couldn't focus. There was a long silence before Jason spoke.

"You shouldn't have been the spelling bee champion."

Spelling bees belonged to elementary school, which felt to Adam like distant and unreachable childhood.

"In fifth grade. I got out on a word that wasn't on the list."

"I didn't know that."

"I told you. So you did know. You should have told Mrs. Ruggiero that I should be champion and not you because it wasn't fair."

The spelling bee? That's what this was about?

"I thought you were mad that we moved…or the football game maybe…when we got beat up or when we got mugged…"

"You should have told Mrs. Ruggiero."

"Okay. Sorry."

I can't get mad at you because your mother is dead, and that's too terrible, and you gave me comic books, which is amazing and inexplicable. It can't be about the spelling bee. It can't. I don't believe it was, even if that's what Jason thinks. But as much as I'm sad and guilty and sorry for you, I guess, I know, we're not going to be friends anymore.

"It's not the spelling bee. It's every single time…in school…in Hebrew School—"

"You hate Hebrew School."

"So why don't you hate it?"

"Because—"

"It's so ugly there, so stupid. I had to go because my mom thought you were—you're not better—my mom…" But Jason never finished his sentence, because he choked on the word "mom" just as Rabbi Ellenbaum's voice infiltrated the bedroom and the rabbi's stentorian "time of grief…" was erased by a blast from Mr. Boyer.

"Take your God, and go to hell!"

"You don't mean that, Stan…"

"Have a drink of water, Stan!"

"Sit here, Stan!"

"Stan, don't…"

They heard the thud of bodies, a gasp, grown-up grunts, then the Cantor's big voice, "What you are doing?! Don't do that thing!"

Adam grabbed his comic books and reached the living room ahead of Jason.

Adults were standing, huddled together, blocking Adam's view across the smoky living room haze. The rabbi was on the floor. A few feet away the Cantor was sloppily pinning stubby Mr. Boyer to the carpet. The wisps of Mr. Boyer's curly hair were glued to his huge fore-head, and he was breathing hard, fast, sock hockey breaths.

"Get off my brother!" Jason's uncle yelled, pulling ineffectually on the Cantor's arms.

Adam's father untangled the three men like a wrestling referee. The Cantor scooted up to a squat, then to standing, in two athletic moves.

"My wife is *dead*!" Mr. Boyer spat out as he sat up.

It was the same hatred Adam had seen in Kenny.

"It's a terrible thing. I am very sorry for you," the Cantor said.

The rabbi pushed his glasses back into place, struggling for com-posure as he was helped off the floor.

"I don't take it personally, Mr. Boyer," the rabbi said solemnly, rub-bing the side of his head. "I'll come back when you're—"

"Don't you dare!" hollered Mr. Boyer.

"That's right," echoed his brother.

The Cantor took the rabbi's arm in his grip. "We going now. We are sorry for your loss. Rabbi and I, we are leaving."

They exited the apartment, defeated. Mr. Boyer slammed the door after them, but the unsheathed bolt preventing any satisfying finality as the door clanged and bounced.

The room became silent for a full minute. Adam's father placed a comforting hand on Mr. Boyer's shoulder. Suddenly, Mr. Boyer leapt up past him, lunged for the front door, hurled it open so hard the brass knob left a crevice in the plaster, then bellowed down the hall-way of the seventeenth floor, "And there's gonna be no goddamned bar mitzvah!"

Except the Cantor was in the doorway, in his goalie quarter-crouch, alert, ready for attack.

"The rabbi went."

Mr. Boyer was spent. "I don't want your God," he said wearily.

"I'm here for boy, not for God," the Cantor said. On his grace-ful Babe Ruth feet, the Cantor stepped delicately around the mis-erable man.

Before Mr. Boyer or his brother could intervene, the Cantor swooped Jason up into a hug, pinning one of his arms while his free arm flailed, not connecting with its target.

"We are very sad," the Cantor said.

The Cantor let out a noise like a goose and cried big tears. Startled, Jason stopped struggling. The Cantor rocked back and forth, davening with Jason attached to him.

"My mother is dead also," the Cantor wailed. "This summer."

Jason peeped out, "Did the doctors kill her too?"

The Cantor sobbed again, and Adam began to cry. Jason cried and tried to hide it. Adam turned away so Jason wouldn't see him trying to not see him. Adam's parents teared up, as did the other visitors.

"I was so sad and angry the day I meet you coming from shiva for my mother on the train with those hooligans." The Cantor put Jason down.

I knew it!

"I saw you get scared, and then you come to shul, and I made you sing, which you hate because you are—the truth—not such good singer but you are not so bad as Karsh. He sound like a frog someone is stepping on."

"Adam said it was you, but I told him he was wrong."

"So you are wrong. So what? And you were not friends since then. So what? And now. You have to be brave, more brave than anything hooligans can do to you."

"Okay."

"I will help you get ready for the bar mitzvah, like I help Adam, but we will do haftarah only."

"There's not going to be any bar mitzvah," Mr. Boyer's brother said.

"That's right," Mr. Boyer said, down on the floor, muttering again, "That's right."

"I think he means it," Jason whispered to the Cantor, just loud enough that Adam could hear. It was the first hint ever that Jason wanted his bar mitzvah.

"We will do it for mother," the Cantor said, and hugged Jason again.

CHAPTER 39

As the doors opened into the lobby, their old neighbor Mr. Shamowitz, Seth's former high school principal, stepped in, blocking their exit.

"Jeremy! Helen!"

"Phil! What are you doing here?"

"Same as you, I imagine. Terrible thing. Young woman like that. He's a nice fella. Joined our bowling team last year. Very good on spares. You should join the league, Jeremy."

"Let's hope we'll meet on happier occasions," Mrs. Miller said, as she stepped out of the elevator. Shamowitz placed his hand on Mr. Miller's arm.

"Do me a favor, take a ride with me."

Shamowitz's hand was not resting on his father's arm, Adam saw, but holding it tight.

"I'll let you go when we reach seventeen. For old time's sake."

"We have to get home. Adam has homework, and so do I, so does my wife."

"We're all slaves to the school bell. Hello, Adam." Adam had never passed on the message from Mr. Shamowitz after meeting him outside their old house—how could he have explained what he was doing there?—and was glad Mr. Shamowitz didn't mention it now.

"How are you, Mr. Shamowitz?"

Bells rang in rapid succession, signaling they'd been holding the elevator too long, Adam's mother released the door, remaining in the lobby, but neither Mr. Miller nor Adam stepped out. Adam rustled against Mr. Shamowitz's perennial rough tweed jacket, trying to get near the control buttons as the elevator took off.

"How am I, Adam? I'm confused. I'm wondering how such a fine family took the money and ran."

"Phil, the union got everyone reinstated—except me—but I took not one penny in compensation, so there was no money," Adam's father answered, rescuing Adam from the need to reply to the baffling comment.

"I'm not talking about UFT combat pay. You wanted to get your kid out of my school so he could have a clean slate."

"Seth transferred to Stuyvesant without even telling us. That's what's bothering you?"

"What bothers me is that you left like thieves in the night."

Mr. Miller explained that his father had left them some money, they'd found a bigger house they liked, and that was all there was to it. "And my brother-in-law did us a favor and got a crew to do the move for us after hours because it was ninety-eight degrees, so we moved at nine o'clock. It was not the middle of the night."

"Our street was a nice community, Jeremy. You sold above market value while you saddled the rest of us with a colored family who brought our property values down by forty percent. You deny it?"

The door opened on the ninth floor. A young woman stood poised to climb aboard.

"Come on, Adam. We'll take the stairs."

Shamowitz put his arm across the door. "We'll send it down for you in two secs, honey." The door closed and the ascent continued.

"This was a very painful shiva call and we're all exhausted. Jason is Adam's best friend."

Was. Was. Now he's…what? Not friends?

"Don't play holier than thou."

"I'm not playing anything," Mr. Miller insisted. "I know Gretta Paul sold her place."

"That awful woman? Good riddance to bad rubbish."

"Okay, then. If by chance we integrated the street—and I think that's a good thing—and if you have a problem with that, then that's… that's…that's your problem."

"One black family is all it takes."

"He's a teacher, just like us. He's on the principal track."

Michael Mason's father is a teacher?

"I'll admit. They seem like nice people, not *vilde chayas*. But it makes no difference. *The Negroes are coming! The Negroes are coming!* Did you see that movie? *The Russians Are Coming, the Russians Are Coming.* Now that was funny. Wasn't that funny?"

"Alan Arkin is funny," Mr. Miller agreed, hoping the conversation had changed course for good, but no such luck.

"It was a hot August morning, if I remember correctly, so a lot of us were outside looking for air. And you were gone and your boy Andrew Meyer was there at the crack of dawn, buttonholing anybody who'd listen on their front steps to tell us our homes had lost almost half their value when the Washingtons moved in, but he'd pay seventy percent on the dollar. Then he'll ratchet them up to one hundred twenty percent for colored families, who will pay top dollar to get into our street, and make himself a pretty penny. Now half the block wants to clear out at discount prices, before they hit rock bottom. That's blockbusting, Jeremy my friend. Don't tell me that was a coincidence. Did he pay you off, your Andrew Meyer?"

"I never heard of Andrew Meyer. It was a direct sale, Phil, for exactly the market value, no markup, no discount. And I honestly have no idea where you got this from."

"From the goddamned horse's mouth. Andrew Meyer himself. You gave Andrew Meyer his winning Negro ticket, the Washingtons of South Jamaica, drug capital of Queens."

Adam spoke up. "Their name is Mason."

"Adam!" they said at once, startled to rediscover his presence.

"What about the other half of the block?" Adam asked. Mr. Shamowitz scrunched his eyes closed. "You said—"

"I did say that. Well, Adam, seeing as we're among the tribe, I'd say half the Jews will stay on principle because they're good people—"

"Thank God for small favors," Mr. Miller quipped.

"But the other half are as rattled as the Italians, who are already on the way out, unless they um…find another way…well…let's not speculate."

"This is the floor, Mr. Shamowitz." Adam said. "The Boyers are the last door at the end of the hall on the right. We were just there."

"Thank you, Adam. Very helpful. Keep pressing that Open button for one more minute." Mr. Shamowitz turned back to Mr. Miller.

Adam pressed Lobby, let the button go in protest, the doors slid shut, the descent began. Neither of the men noticed.

"I don't care what you believe, Phil. If this Andrew Meyer character found out we sold to a black family—"

"Hey, we're going down."

"My finger slipped."

"I bet it did," Shamowitz snarled at Adam before wheeling on Mr. Miller again. "Riddle me this. How come it's okay for blacks to be anti-Semitic, but we can't be racists, not that we are?"

"You just told me that half of Poplar Street wants to join the Klan," Mr. Miller said.

"I didn't say anything like that. That's against everything I believe in. You tell your father, Adam. You know we're not racist. Right?"

"I know," Adam said.

Did Adam know that? Why would people move out if black people moved in? That made no sense. Could you be against racism and still be racist? There were black people in Jason's building, but he'd seen no black people in his new neighborhood. And why did black people live by themselves in Michael Mason's old neighborhood?

They reached the lobby.

"I was going to send the police after you, Jem. Phil! You forgot to get off on seventeen."

"Phil never forgets anything," Mr. Miller said.

Mr. Miller pressed seventeen then Close Door and almost yanked Adam's arm out of his socket exiting the elevator. Mr. Shamowitz yelled after them as the doors shut.

"You know what my house is worth now?"

"I don't know, and I don't care."

"Of course not. You got your—"

And he was gone.

"What happened to you?"

"You wouldn't believe it."

"Dad was great," Adam said.

"I was?"

"You're always great."

"Thanks, Adam," his mother said. "That's why we hired you."

They walked in silence. Adam could see his father's lips moving, rehashing the conversation, formulating zingers that would have left Phil Shamowitz begging for mercy. But this was not their last encounter of the day. A parking ticket was tucked under the windshield wiper. Adam's father started cursing, which he never did in front of his children. Adam ran ahead.

"Dad, it's not a ticket."

Someone had left a note. "Please stop by when you come back." They didn't have to guess who wrote it because Mrs. Schiffman's door opened and she skittered down the front steps.

"I saw the Department of Education satchel through the window, and I knew it had to be your car."

"It's lovely to see you, Shirley," Mrs. Miller began. "We're in a bit of a rush. We just made a very sad shiva call."

"I won't take a minute. I wanted to explain about Edwin being so angry. I'm afraid he insulted poor Adam."

"It's all right," Adam answered, remembering Mr. Schiffman turning away instead of responding to his wave.

"When did Edwin see Adam?" Mrs. Miller asked.

"When he came to visit the Masons with that Hassidic fellow."

"What?"

"I was here with the Cantor. We had to pick up something from… Hebrew School…"

"Phil Shamowitz thinks we made a deal with the NAACP," Mrs. Miller deadpanned to her old neighbor.

"The NAACP is a fine organization," Mrs. Schiffman said. "We give them fifteen dollars every year."

"And we didn't sell our house through Andrew Meyer," Mr. Miller declared a bit too stridently, as if he was still in the elevator.

"That huckster, riling everybody up over nothing. That's not what got into Edwin's bonnet."

"Was he upset because we didn't say goodbye? It all happened so suddenly."

"That too. You took our Adam away from us. We raised that boy."

Mr. Miller froze.

"You…babysat for him."

"Jeremy!" Adam's mother snapped.

"Babysat five days a week sometimes."

Adam remembered those afternoons among the Schiffmans' overstuffed old-fashioned furniture and its orderly grandeur, doing homework, politely and impatiently waiting for his mother or Seth to liberate him.

"I am so sorry," Mrs. Miller jumped in.

"No warning, whisked him off to summer camp, and then poof, the Millers have disappeared."

"We should have brought Adam over, but Adam was already in camp when we finalized arrangements."

"That's water under the bridge. Edwin's not been right, not for quite a while. But I see you're in a rush and this is not for the street. Promise me, Helen, you'll come back here soon so I can tell you some things."

"I will, for a long talk. I'm so sorry."

Mr. Miller unlocked the car doors on both sides. His mother and Mrs. Schiffman shook hands, leading to a tight squeeze. Mrs. Miller pulled Adam in, and Mrs. Schiffman kissed Adam on top of his head. Ordinarily Adam despised being used as a prop, and particularly hated adults kissing him, but he was emotionally ragged, all of them were, and a group hug in the street in front of his old house felt welcome.

CHAPTER 40

M r. Selenko was gone, and Miss Nadel had taken over his drama class. She'd shifted the focus from acting to deciphering Shakespeare with the SP and the OC, only rarely bringing them together.

Adam was confused when she asked him to stay after class.

"I've had a visit from Mr. Chakrabarti." Miss Nadel fidgeted. "Suvan's father is very unhappy with your play."

"But Suvan's acting, his posture, his accent, they're *spot on!*"

Adam's attempt to speak with Suvan's vocabulary and clipped intonation to lighten the mood had no effect.

"Mr. Chakrabarti objects to the way the British officer is portrayed. I told him it's based on a book, and Richard told me the author is highly regarded. I don't completely understand the politics, but Mr. Chakrabarti says it's unacceptable. He strikes me as very proud of his British heritage."

Miss Nadel strolled away from Adam. Adam thought the weight of history, managing Selenko's drama class, all these unfamiliar demands coming in concert, had exhausted her, but she doubled back on him with fire in her voice, behind her eyes.

"Mr. Selenko really believes in you."

"He does?"

"Yes, he does. We both do."

It was impossible to hate her because she was so sincere and had that fire.

Adam calculated what changes he would have to make in the play to satisfy Suvan's father—an escape attempt by Captain Dawson? Hand-to-hand combat?

"Mr. Chakrabarti was quite insistent that Suvan cannot be in the play. He won't budge. I am so sorry. I know how hard you two prepared for the Citywides. Richard had such good intentions."

Adam could not speak.

"Richard—Mr, Selenko—says that when an actor can't appear in his show, his understudy goes in his place."

"There's no understudy," Adam mumbled.

"I know. But you have three weeks. When the going gets tough…"

She didn't finish her sentence.

"What?" Adam asked.

"The tough get going."

They do? No, the Citywides are going.

"Does Suvan know?"

"I believe he'll be told when he gets home. Good luck," she concluded, pulling herself up. "You'll figure it out."

CHAPTER 41

I t had been exciting to Adam to carry picket signs during the teachers' strike emblazoned with slogans: *Dignity for All Teachers, Stop
Teaching Race Hatred to Children, End Mob Rule in the Schools*, all
emblazoned with the logo of the United Federation of Teachers. His
parents had explained the fundamental right to protest, that it was a
privilege to take part in a demonstration—an exercise in freedom, in
democracy. Adam had felt grown-up marching next to his father and
his parents' colleagues whom he recognized from union caucuses in
their living room, mounted police high above them, occasionally pulling their horses back.

But marching in an oval in the same counterclockwise direction
quickly became boring. What was the difference if you picketed for
one hour or eight hours? Why not thirty minutes? What was it supposed to accomplish? To call attention to the justice of the teachers'
cause, it would have to get someone's attention, and who exactly, Adam
wondered, was paying attention?

The teachers' strike succeeded, his mother argued.

Some victories cause so much bad blood, they're self-defeating, his
father philosophized.

Now it was Seth's cause, freeing Jews from a country that wouldn't
let them live as Jews and wouldn't let them leave. Adam had imagined
the Russian Mission as a grand mansion with Russian minarets—a
Czar's castle—but it was a nondescript building surrounded by a metal
fence of tall, spikey posts. Why would the Russians care about a bunch
of teenagers?

A man in a black fedora not unlike the Cantor's conducted the group in fits and starts, his gray spring car coat sweeping up behind him each time he raised his arms in sudden arrhythmic jerks, his voice amplified and distorted by the bullhorn like Mr. Shamowitz's had been.

"*Am Yisrael Chai!*" The people of Israel Live! Or "Free Them Now!" The group took up the chant, "Let My People Go!" but the bullhorn blared so much louder, the unamplified human voices were no more than a wash behind his screeching.

"Let My People Go!"

The Betarees were bedecked in their dark blue Betar shirts, almost the same color as the cops' uniforms, uniformly uniformed, an observation Adam would have shared with Seth had he not feared his disdain.

"Arrest the Russian Murderers!" they called.

Enraged adults made Adam nervous, but they didn't seem to ruffle the two police officers standing nearby, perhaps used to protests against the Russians.

"Break Their Chains! Break Their Chains!"

This chant was picked up by the group, and was apparently a signal, because all at once the Betarees withdrew their bicycle chains and locks from pockets, pants, shirts, and jackets and began to chain each other to the fence. Chainless, Adam had been warned by Seth that he would let him tag along but would not allow him to take part in their "action."

One cop went directly to the man with the bullhorn, the other spoke into his walkie-talkie. Adam eavesdropped.

"Rabbi—"

He was a rabbi!

"Tell your boys to put away their chains."

The rabbi screamed through the bullhorn.

"He wants us to put away our chains! Are we going to put away our chains?"

"Break Their Chains!" the boys and men yelled. "Let My People Go!"

Adam couldn't picture Rabbi Ellenbaum screaming at a police officer, but this rabbi had no reservations.

"I can't let you chain yourselves to private property," the police officer said. "You're going to have to disperse."

"He wants us to disperse!!!" the rabbi roared through the bullhorn. "Are we going to disperse?"

Not well rehearsed, the three chants coincided—"Break Their Chains! Let My People Go! Free the Leningrad Sixteen!"—but out of step. The rabbi pointed the mouthpiece of the bullhorn toward the protesters, but their voices were too insignificant to rise above the ambient ocean of taxi horns and bus rumblings. Vapors steamed out of the ground in the Manhattan twilight, sucking up all sound.

The rabbi felt his power slipping and began to scream at the cop, then into the bullhorn.

"Never again! They're killing Jews! We won't be moved! Ignore the police."

"Pig! Pig! Pig!" the youths cried, half of whom had managed to chain themselves.

"Stop that!" the rabbi screamed into the bullhorn. "Not *pigs*! No *pigs*! Never again! Never again!"

Was the rabbi furious because they were calling the cops unkosher animals or because anti-war language got mixed into the Soviet Jewry protest?

"I'm just doing my job, Rabbi," the officer protested in an even tone.

"Your job is to protect us, to protect free people, not fascist murderers."

"I'm not here to debate you. You can't chain yourselves to the fence. That's the law."

"There's a higher law!"

"We'll arrest the lot of you. Last chance, Rabbi!"

"Arrest the Russians! They're the criminals! Never Again!"

"We need a bus," the officer said into his walkie-talkie.

"For shame!" the rabbi cried. "For shame!"

Would the police turn them over to the Russians to be shipped to the Gulag and put on trial with the Leningrad Sixteen?

Adam hurried back to Seth.

"They're going to arrest you!" Adam said, alert now to the immediate family danger.

"That's the point!"

"What?"

Adam turned to flash bulbs popping. Half an hour passed before the police bus arrived. The contingent of cops still seemed more annoyed than outraged. The officer with chain cutters moved up the line one protestor at a time—*crack*, squeal of metal on metal, sometimes breaking through on the first cut. On thicker chains, the shears would slip sideways, requiring several tries. They took out their annoyance by seizing each unchained protestor roughly, snapping his arms behind his back to be handcuffed, leading him onto the bus to be carted away.

"Listen, Adam, quick, pull my left boot off."

"What?"

"Now!"

Adam crouched down, began to pull.

"Unzip it first, idiot! Come on! Now!"

But the boot didn't budge.

"How'm I going to get home?"

"Take the 4 train. This is Sixty-Seventh Street. It's on Sixty-Eighth. It's one block. You can't get lost."

Adam was still struggling with the boot, which finally moved, almost getting past the heel, while trying to listen to Seth.

"I take the 4 train to Main Street?"

"The 4 to Grand Central. Don't you know anything?"

"I don't go to school in the city."

"At Grand Central switch to the 7 and take it to the end, to Main Street. From there—"

"I know my way home from Main Street."

"Never mind! You gotta get outta here. Don't tell Mom and Dad you were here! Whatever you do! Swear!"

"I swear!"

"Go, go, go! You're fast, show your speed!"

"Hey, kid, what are you doing?"

So Adam ran from the police, leaving Seth and the boot dangling, as he had run from the Watch Gang. He sped across Lexington Avenue, grazing a woman with a shopping bag, heard the paper tear, taxi horns blared, a bus horn lifted him from his feet. He didn't dare look back, certain cops were in pursuit, guns drawn, ready to arrest him for aiding and abetting the destruction of Russian property!

Adam ran straight to Park Avenue, and having no sense of Manhattan, turned left, and kept running all the way to Sixty-Third Street, until he was stopped by a wall of pedestrians blocking the curb, waiting for the light to change.

No footsteps.

He turned his head slowly to glance back.

No one.

Where the hell am I?

Ordinarily, Adam would ask a policeman, but he couldn't now because they were looking for him. He asked a woman in a purple coat where the subway was—*women were safer*—and she offered to walk him to the station. Fifty-Ninth Street. Not where Seth had told him to go.

Did he have a token?

No.

He could buy one at the booth downstairs. She would show him.

They went down the steps into the station.

Did he have any money?

He handed her his only dollar.

"Good," she said, and bought a token, but instead of handing the coins to Adam, she put the token in the slot, went through the turnstile herself, and kept the seventy cents change.

"That's how you do it," she called back, as she disappeared into the terminal crowds.

It took Adam several seconds to absorb that he had been scammed. He had no more money. He couldn't buy a token or even make a phone call.

I can sneak under the turnstile, but the token lady will match my description with the runaway from the Russian Mission, and I'll be shipped to the Gulag.

Spare a dime? That's what they always said to him in the lunchroom. *Got any loose change?*

Adam scanned the passengers going through the turnstile for friendly faces, but found only harried, tense adults, intensely focused on avoiding eye contact with the other commuters. He began to approach a woman, shied away at the last second, tried a teenage couple. "I need to buy a token," was all he could get out of his mouth. The boy dug into his pocket, but his girlfriend stopped him.

"You don't look poor."

"I'm not, but I was…" *What? Was about to get arrested at the Russian Mission? Was ripped off by a woman in purple?*

"Poor baby," she said, and gave Adam a dime. "Go call Mommy for help. Come on, Brad." They disappeared.

He had a dime. There was a pay phone. He dropped the dime in the slot, heard it tinkle into place, the dial tone appeared. He couldn't call his parents, couldn't tell them where he was. He hung up, rescued his dime, stuck his hand in his pockets, and found the business cards.

Officer Riley. *No*

Cousin Harry. *Yes.*

He called the precinct, asked for Captain Licht, waited for a very, very long time, and finally Harry came on the line.

"Cousin Harry? It's Adam. Seth was arrested because he chained himself to the Russian Mission to free Jews from Leningrad—"

The Operator said, "Please deposit ten cents for the next five minutes." Adam only had time to say, "I wasn't—" before the dial tone returned. He was broke again. Now what?

Adam returned to the turnstile, approached six more adults. "Spare change?" "Do you have a dime?" but they determinedly ignored him, heads down.

This is what the bused-in kids do in the lunchroom, and it sucks! This is hard. And they do it because…because they have no money!

Adam felt guilty for stiffing them.

Suvan isn't afraid of them. He's just generous. No…he's afraid of them.

"Boy in the army shirt, come here right now!" The female voice came through the raspy speaker, originating, Adam realized after a moment, from the token booth. "I mean you, young man. Come to the front."

Adam thought about dashing up the stairs, but the line shifted ever so slightly, and reluctantly, to let Adam squeeze ahead to the booth. He wasn't tall enough to look through the partition.

"What are you harassing these people for? You can't scrounge for money here."

"I'm sorry," Adam said, felt his stomach convulse, tears coming, turned away. "The lady in the purple coat...she took my money."

"She wasn't your mother?"

"She said she would buy the token for me...it was my dollar...I need to...go home..."

"Where's home?"

"Flushing."

A woman in a red zip jacket opened her purse.

"I'll buy him a token. Here." She handed Adam a quarter and a nickel.

"That's all right," the intercom said. "Young man, go over by that door. When you hear the buzzer, go through. Do you need a bus transfer?"

"Umm. Yes."

"Here." She slid it under the grating. "Don't beg for change."

"Of course not."

"And don't trust anyone."

"I won't."

"And go right home."

"Thank you."

He had been rescued again.

Adam followed Seth's subway protocol. He squeezed into the packed conductor's car, the middle car, although it meant standing the entire way. He was wary, agitated, kept his eyes open for any flash of purple. Only around Elmhurst Avenue did Adam release his fear, and his wandering mind wondered first, why Seth wanted his boot off— *the nunchucks! Of course! Idiot!*—and second, what if Michael Mason needed a subway token.

Michael would never have been scammed. And Michael would never have been rescued.

Having exhausted his quota of misadventures, Adam reached home to find his mother frantic about Seth. She already knew Seth had *made a* shonde *for the Goyim, destroyed his entire future, and thank God for—Cousin Harry who had gotten Seth released and was bringing him home* (and had not ratted on Adam).

Adam's father arrived ragged. He huddled with Adam's mother in their bedroom behind closed doors, but only briefly, before moving into the boys' room, which he searched, before descending to the basement.

His mother offered Adam Fudgetown cookies and milk, had an entire conversation with herself, then offered Adam the same cookies and milk again. Mr. Miller entered the kitchen with an unwieldy pile, pamphlets, booklets turning every which way, with the photos of Betar heroes ripped off the basement wall. His father and his brother were on course for a smack-up. Cousin Harry rang the bell, and the time was now.

Adam wanted to signal his brother that his parents didn't know that Adam had been at the Russian Mission, to tell him about the purple lady, but Seth was churning from Cousin Harry's quiet harangue. Seth expected to be welcomed as a hero, but when no one rushed to embrace him, he froze, recognized his parents' fury, and seethed, mumbling Arabic curses he'd learned in Betar camp as he took a seat at the kitchen table.

Cousin Harry produced a brown paper parcel, whispered something to Mr. Miller. Adam's mother begged Harry to stay for dinner, hoping his charms would derail the collision, but Harry had already given Seth an earful on the drive from the city, and duty called. He winked at Adam on the way out.

Mr. Miller's rage was bubbling in a different pot than his wife's.

"Go to your room," his mother told Adam.

"Stay, Adam," his father barked, as he turned to Seth. "I want him to hear this. Seth, take off that uniform!"

Seth was confused by this directive, but he undid the buttons and wriggled out of his long-sleeved official Betar shirt, sweaty from his long day. He draped it across his chair and leaned back in defiance, despite being bare-chested.

His father lifted the shirt up, Exhibit A.

"A Jew in Blackshirt!"

"It's dark blue," Seth protested.

"Marching around like…like…*them!*"

Mr. Miller carried the shirt to the kitchen cabinet, reached down and removed garden shears from the lower drawer. They were smaller than the chain cutters the police had used, but Adam couldn't help comparing them.

"What are you doing?" Seth cried.

"Don't you dare get up!" their mother commanded.

Mr. Miller stabbed at the shirt in frustration, until he caught hold of the flap and cut straight across the chest, then cut in another direction. He continued cutting and slashing until the Betar shirt was party streamers.

"Bring your brother an undershirt."

Adam was back in a flash. He slunk into the kitchen chair so his mother would have to fuss if she wanted to evict him. She didn't. Adam looked away from Seth, lest they inadvertently reveal Adam's involvement in the day.

Their father held up the papers, Exhibit B.

"I never want to see this fascist garbage in our house again!"

Rip went the Betar newsletters. *Rip* went Seth's photos of Menachem Begin and Josef Trumpeldor. *Rip* went the underground fighters executed by the British in Acre Prison, the real-life models for Elisha's comrades in *Dawn*.

Their father unrolled a poster of a giant fist pushing up through the points of the star of the Magen David, bursting through chains. He had torn it off the wall. A corner was missing.

"This isn't strength!" their father roared, denying the words emblazoned across the fist while letting out the huge voice usually tucked under his calm. "It's sickness!" He ripped the poster down the middle. "We are not bullies! We do not act like animals!" He tore the poster into shreds, getting the satisfaction that had eluded him with the shirt.

"That's for Soviet Jews!" his brother yelled back.

But his father had more in his arsenal. He took the brown paper parcel that Cousin Harry had brought from the police station. The clincher. Exhibit C.

Seth's nunchucks.

"Your son has been carrying weapons."

"Ohmigod!"

"Give me your boots!" their father ordered.

Seth didn't move.

"Now, Seth," their mother insisted.

His brother reached down, battled with his boot zippers—*so it's hard for him too!*—finally yanked them off, and threw them down, thudding one after the other.

Shoes on the dining room table and Mom not screaming bloody murder. Another first.

"Look at this!" spat Mr. Miller, exposing the lining of the boots. Adam popped up to peek at the pocket sewn inside before his parents barked in unison, "Sit down!"

How did Seth learn to sew?

"You've armed yourself with sticks?"

"Nunchucks!" his brother yelled. "For self-defense."

"Have you been taking those to school?" their mother asked, imagining suspension, expulsion, college canceled, career denied.

"You'll get yourself killed," his father countered. "And if not for Harry, you'd be in jail right now!"

"We're going to free the Leningrad Sixteen the way the Stern Gang got the British out of Palestine!"

"Where do you get this *mishegoss* from?" Mrs. Miller asked.

"The Stern Gang were killers!" Mr. Miller blared. "There almost was no Israel because of them."

Twenty-five-year-old politics, as if they still mattered.

Of course, they do *matter. It's Elisha's story.*

"*I'm* defending our people. The police don't do a damn thing when old Jews are mugged by gangs in Borough Park!"

"And you're going to protect them by destroying public property with your fascist thugs?"

"Wake up! They're attacking our shul and *you're* putting in alarm systems!"

Mr. Miller gushed out a comic book *arghhh*! "Cousin Harry risks his life every day so you won't have to! Ask him how many times he's fired his gun! Call him and ask him. Helen, call Harry right now."

"He's still driving back to the city."

"Never once! He's never fired that gun once in his career, and his greatest hope is that he'll never have to!"

"But your parents ran guns to Palestine!"

"To the Haganah, before there was a country. It's 1971. Israel has an army, one of the best in the world."

Their father lifted the nunchucks as if they were a Torah scroll commanding communal devotion. He took up the garden shears, and in one swift motion, before Seth could begin to plead, he severed the short cord that connected the wooden batons.

Seth sank into circumcised shame. Even Mr. Miller was stunned by what he had done.

"You are through with those thugs," he said quietly.

Now Seth was bubbling.

"I'm seventeen years old. I'll do what I want!"

"Not while you live in this house!"

"Then I won't live in this house!"

Seth marched as dramatically as possible with no shoes out of the kitchen to his room, grabbed his sneakers, tromped to the front entrance, and slammed the door behind him.

Mr. Miller was breathing hard. His hands were shaking. Mrs. Miller made him sit down, fretted over him, made him take deep breaths. They stayed like that for three minutes, five minutes, seven minutes. Adam was afraid to break the spell.

Suddenly, his father popped up.

"I should have thrown his shirt away, but I shouldn't have cut it up."

"He won't get far barefoot," his mother said.

"He took his sneakers," Adam said.

Mr. Miller hurried to the front door, opened it wide to the street, and called, "Seth! Seth! Seth!"

There was no response. He yelled a few more times. They waited a few minutes for Seth to come back, but Seth was long gone.

"I'll find him. I'll take the car."

"Go with your father," Adam's mother ordered. "You'll know where to look."

So Adam and his father drove together, Mr. Miller smoking in anger, debating in his head the justice of his rage and the tactical errors of his behavior. They crisscrossed the neighborhood, at first randomly, then, once his father calmed down, systematically, street by street.

"I don't want you to misunderstand," his father told Adam. "We are fiercely proud Jews."

These were the first words he spoke aloud. Adam tried to pick up on them, telling his father about the Jewish Heritage Club.

"That's fine, Adam."

Adam went on, in part to distract his father, sharing how he felt a responsibility to Mr. Beck and to Soviet Jews and to the Leningrad Sixteen.

"If you want to start this club, that's great. But what about your friend?"

"Jason? We're not…friends anymore."

"I meant Suvan. How will you explain to him that you're starting a club that he can't join?"

Adam was as surprised by his father's awareness of Suvan's name as he was by his attitude. The Jewish Heritage Club was negotiable after all.

"Where the hell is he? We'll keep driving. We'll find him."

"Dad," Adam asked after they'd circled their local pocket park three times and Adam suggested they shift to fast food joints. "Why did they attack the shul?"

"I don't think it's an anti-Semitic…you know…organized…thing. I've never encountered the slightest anti-Semitism in Flushing. So I'm hoping someone's trying to scare us out because the synagogue property has become very valuable."

"Blockbusters?"

"Whoever it is, we have to stand up for ourselves."

"Isn't that what…Seth's saying?"

"Yes, but—and this is a big *but*—never stoop to their level! Stand up to them like you did when they tried to steal your watch."

"Like the Cantor did on the subway."

"And neither of you had weapons."

"But he has a big voice."

It was a relief to hear his father laugh.

"Seth said during the teachers' strike, anti-Semitism came out of the woodwork, like, especially from black people."

"Seth doesn't know what he's talking about."

"But they read an anti-Semitic poem on the radio."

"Yes, that was horrible, and it's awful that kids can think such things. And we have real enemies in the world. But the union blew it out of proportion to scare the Jewish teachers."

"I thought the whole union's Jewish."

"It just seems that way. And Albert Shanker is Jewish, and he's the head and he's a tough cookie and a manipulative sonnuvabitch, excuse my French. I've tried to explain this to your brother. When the black community got control of their schools and there were some radicals—"

"The ones who hate Israel?"

"I work with plenty of black people in the school system. They don't hate Israel. They don't even think about Israel. We obsess about Israel because it's ours."

"But Julius Lester—"

"I was on the Julius Lester show. He's not anti-Semitic."

"You were on the radio?"

"I brought someone from the city's Human Rights Commission to Andrew Jackson—he was a judge—to hear the teachers' grievances and explain what the community activists wanted. I thought I understood both sides. Instead, I got it from both sides."

"So black people don't hate Jews?"

"Adam, where a lot of black people live in the city, those used to be Jewish neighborhoods, so even though the Jews have left, some people who live there have Jewish landlords and store owners, and some of them rip them off. So they're angry. And education has not been the ticket to the middle class for black people as much as it has for Jews. So they're frustrated."

"But the black leaders fired all the Jewish teachers, right?"

"It looked that way, but in actuality, they replaced them mostly with other Jewish teachers. That's how I became a principal. They asked for me because they knew I believed in their kids' potential."

"So why were you fired?"

"Things got so…out of hand…loaded, symbolic, I couldn't do my job. I *asked* to be reinstated to my previous position. Another symbolic gesture that fell flat. We all went back to start."

"Dad, if you got to be a principal, why were *you* on strike?"

"I'm a union man even when the union lets me down, so I walked the picket line every day, and you walked with me. Jewish teachers, non-Jewish teachers, white, black—all of us together."

"Mom said—"

"Your mother's disappointed because our salaries are…disappointing, and it's insane that we don't feel safe in our own schools. But we still believe that education can lift all boats. Adam, I've applied to be the principal of a different school in the Bronx."

Adam froze. "Are we going to move again?"

"No no no. Your Mom has applied to replace Mr. Beiner as principal at the Hebrew School, so we'll stay right here. He's retiring."

"Mom? What? Hebrew School?"

"She's tired of all the commuting. And the stress."

Adam sighed. His father sighed. His mother was going to take over Hebrew School. Thank God he was about to graduate.

His father lit his third cigarette, Adam told him about Jew-ball on the subway, told him the whole story for the very first time. Jeremy Miller's impulse was to get on the 7 train to find that gang and smash their heads against the shatterproof windows.

"I shouldn't have told you." Adam said.

His father expelled his anger with three quick sighs and looked for a teaching point as they drove to Wetsons, White Castle, the Cove, the kosher deli. At each stop, Adam was dispatched to run inside, as their conversation moved on in staccato fits and starts.

"Adam, listen to me closely. The mugging was a terrible—but what that mindless punk said to you—that's stupidity, that's ignorance. How many times in your life have you been called an anti-Semitic name?"

"Umm…once…no, twice…"

"So there are two ignorant prejudiced idiots in a city of eight million people. You can't hate an entire group of people because of two stupid comments."

"I don't hate anybody. I won't."

"Black people are not our enemy. They don't oppress us. They don't have the power to oppress us."

"Are we still oppressed?"

"We're…insecure. You have black friends on your football team."

"They quit. They joined the All-Blacks of Corona. And Jason kicked me off the team."

"Aren't you the captain? Oh. Oh! I see now. Jason…and Mrs. Boyer…that gang and your watch. What a year for you…"

"Yeah. I mean, yes."

"You're still in one piece, and I couldn't be prouder of you."

"Thanks, Dad."

"Look for a phone booth. I have to call your mother. Maybe your brother's home already."

All the pay phones in Queens seemed to have vanished. Adam's father made a course correction toward Marchal's, the Millers' favorite diner. Adam tried to piece together his father's story and finally asked his real question.

"Why *did* we move?"

His father reached for the door, then sat back. The phone call would wait another minute.

"You know I grew up in a much bigger house in the country in New Jersey. Zeydie died and left us a little money. I wanted us to have a real backyard we could enjoy as a family. Throw a ball around. Plant a garden."

"But we don't do any of that."

"We've been too busy. But I love the crickets."

"It wasn't to get Seth away from Mr. Shamowitz?"

"Seth got himself out of Andrew Jackson."

"A backyard. That was the only reason?"

His father didn't answer immediately.

"Dad?

Several sighs.

"There were some…threats, Adam."

"Black radicals?"

"You sound like your mother. Listen, Adam. Some people were angry that I'd accepted that principal position in the Bronx—felt I'd betrayed the union—and there were some activists who didn't want a white principal—"

"A white *Jewish* principal!"

"A *white* principal. I've worked in those neighborhoods for years… you can't imagine…being black in this country. Violence is not the answer, but we need change all right."

The Jewish Underground used violence to get rid of the British. That's how they brought change in Palestine.

"Who were the threats from?"

"Let's find your brother."

"Dad!"

"Your mother and I have different theories. We didn't know. We don't know. The police…well…the car was vandalized over and over, seven times in all, and they left some notes."

"What did the notes say?"

"Stupid stuff."

"Dad!"

"The notes said they knew where we lived. The car was right in front of the house. So obviously they knew where we lived. So we thought…well…we thought the family was in danger. That you were in danger. And your brother."

"You moved to protect us?"

"We had been thinking about moving a long time, and that pushed us over. And now that's enough. I have to call your mother."

Mr. Miller walked across the parking lot to the pay phone.

We moved to protect us.

Adam spun the radio dial.

My life was ruined to save my life.

Adam watched his father in the greenish ghost light of the phone booth. Mr. Miller's face, his body, slumped, as he lit another cigarette and the booth filled with haze. Adam saw him bang his head against the glass.

Our parents are as afraid of losing us as we were of losing them. That's what Elisha's ghosts are telling him, that they were losing Elisha. They're being forgotten. What they believed in was being forgotten. That's what Selenko had been getting at.

Poor Jason. Poor Mrs. Boyer.

Adam felt it for an instant. Her ghostly presence, his memory of Mrs. Boyer. He heard the noise, a very slight syncopated, tap-tapping. Adam turned on the car light to see where it was coming from.

His own fingers were tapping the trope.

"I know where he is," Adam told his father, as Mr. Miller slid behind the steering wheel.

They drove to Temple Gates of Hope. Adam took the flashlight from the glove compartment. Mr. Miller started toward the new building's back entrance to ring for Floyd, but Adam led his father to the old synagogue instead, to the three windows that had been smashed, replaced now with wooden slats. As Adam suspected, nobody had fixed the window latches. He jimmied the window halfway open, slithered inside.

"How do you know about this?"

"You know…Hebrew School is not always…fascinating."

"We need an alarm system for this building too," his father said, choosing not to investigate Adam's truancy.

"Dad, keep watch so they don't arrest me for breaking and entering."

The window led to a small room behind the *bimah* in the sanctuary, which connected to the Hebrew School passageway.

Complete darkness.

"Do you see your brother?"

"Seth?" Adam's voice was timid.

"Nobody's going to hear that," his father said. Mr. Miller got down on his hands and knees, wedged his head sideways through the window, and yelled, "Seth!" full blast.

Nothing.

But Adam knew sound didn't carry from behind the *bimah*. His flashlight beam created shadows, and his bravado dried up. He was glad his father couldn't see him hesitate at each squeak and scrape as he moved gingerly to the front of the stage, the sanctuary in front of him, ghosts in the darkness.

"Seth?" Adam tried. "Seth?"

Adam cleared his throat but couldn't muster his voice. He inched forward and there was no floor. He didn't fall, but his legs went wobbly.

"Do you see him?!"

His father's voice made him jump. Adam summoned up sufficient sound to tell him no.

Adam aimed the flashlight at the pews, scanned from side to side, thought he saw a figure—Mrs. Boyer—*ridiculous.* He was scaring himself. It wasn't her; it wasn't anyone. Maybe Seth wasn't here.

"Hello?"

"What's going on?" his father yelled.

"Nothing!" Adam yelled back.

Adam swallowed several times. He hopped on both feet to get the blood moving, another of the Cantor's tricks, then planted his feet, but instead of "*Shochen Ad Marom!*" he sang out, "Seth Miller!" with his full cantorial trill.

"What's the yelling?" Mr. Miller called.

And then Adam heard his brother's voice, from high up, in the far end of the old sanctuary. He walked tentatively down toward the center aisle, pointed the flashlight up, and leapt when it highlighted Seth in the balcony.

"Found him!" Adam cried with all his might.

"What the hell are you doing here?" Seth bellowed down from celestial heights.

"I came for Junior Congregation," Adam quipped.

"There's no—"

"I'm looking for you! What do you think I'm doing here?"

"Oh," Seth mumbled, deflating. "How'd you know?"

"I…uh…old synagogues…you…I mean…where else would you go?" neglecting to mention the fifteen places they had searched first. "You coming down already?"

"Okay, okay."

Adam heard Seth descending the stairs slowly, carefully. When he appeared at the door, Seth had magazines tucked under his arm. Adam felt his stomach drop.

And one count of procuring pornography.

"You'll never believe what I found up there."

"*Playboys.*"

"How the hell did you know? These are going home with me," he said, shoving two magazines into his pants. "I threw the rest in the garbage so no one will find them."

Does every man read them?

"But look at what else."

"What?"

Seth held up a copy of *Dawn*, by Elie Wiesel.

Where did that come from? Michael Mason must have bought it, left it with the magazines.

"Gimme your flashlight." Seth snatched it out of Adam's hand.

Adam changed the subject as quickly as he could. "Dad's shitting in his pants." *And you've got* Playboys *in yours.*

"Serves him right!" Seth said, the anger flaring. "He should never—"

"No!" Adam cut him off. "He's really worried about you!"

Adam went motormouth, confessed how they'd searched all over Flushing, describing every stop in detail. He couldn't stop talking, which was unusual, because Seth did the monologues when they were together. Seth softened, let his rage flutter away. The brothers helped each other through the window.

Mr. Miller hugged Seth in a tight clinch and wouldn't let go. They both started crying, and Adam saw for the first time that Seth had grown taller than their father.

On the car radio going home, James Taylor sang his cover of "You've Got a Friend."

Won't that song ever go away?

But I do have *a friend! My co-star, who can't be in the Citywides. Maybe more than one. Valerie. Gracie. Karsh. Ryan? And not likely, but maybe the mystery man also known as Michael Mason.*

CHAPTER 42

Three weeks before Adam's bar mitzvah, the Cantor took him onto the *bimah* of the main sanctuary of Temple Gates of Hope. He bent down under the *Aron HaKodesh*, the Holy Ark. "I will stop the alarm."

Thanks to Adam's father, the ark was now wired with an alarm system, as were the doors and windows. The Cantor swung open the doors of the sacred armoire, revealing the Temple's five Torah scrolls, huddled together like brothers.

A Torah is an awkward object—two bulky rolls of the same connected heavy parchment, each one wrapped tightly around a wooden dowel. The rolls fall away from one another inside their velvet sack, threatening to split apart.

Adam knew if he dropped the Torah while he was carrying it, he would have to fast—to starve!—for forty days. Adam did not know the punishment if the parchment of the Torah tore, but he imagined it to be celestial and terrifying.

The Cantor braced his back, settled into a squat, heaved a Torah onto his chest, straightened up, carried it to the reader's table, and tilted it down softly onto its surface. A grand silver crown adorned the knobs at the top end of the scroll's two rollers, and a hammered silver chest protector dangled down from fine silver chains suspended over the handles. Together, The Cantor and Adam removed the coverings, setting each one tenderly aside. The Cantor opened the scrolls to reveal the three columns of handwritten calligraphy that Adam was supposed to sing. He handed Adam a pointer, a skinny silver finger to keep his place, since it was forbidden to touch the scroll itself.

"Here!"

This was the first time Adam tried to read from the actual Torah, but the words looked nothing like what was printed in his practice book, his Readers' Tikkun. He didn't recognize anything. His panic was complete, instant, overwhelming. He would not allow the tears to leak out.

"It looks different," Adam squeaked.

"What's different?"

"The writing. The letters."

"Exactly same."

But it was not *exactly same*. These words were wildly irregular. The letters wore tiny crowns, which cluttered things up. Adam pointed to one letter, stretched out into taffy to the width of several words, reaching for the edge of the parchment.

"What's that?"

"That is nothing," the Cantor said dismissively. "The sofer was making words fit in column. This word he make a little wide, that one he squeeze. That's all."

The scribe had done so much *making words fit*, they morphed into animal shapes.

"It looks really strange."

"That's why we are here," he said. "So it won't look strange when you make your bar mitzvah."

The Cantor told Adam to start.

Adam sang the first few words from memory, stuttered, got stuck, continued. Once the music in his singing took over, he was fine, but when he stumbled, Adam couldn't board the train again. The Cantor had to restart him every time.

"Stop now and breathe."

Adam tried to calm himself but couldn't.

"Breathe like a person, not like tractor. Do not hyperventilate, please."

Okay. Breathe. Calm. These verses are etched in my brain.

Adam stared hard, trying to imprint the layout, the columns and distorted taffy letters, in his memory corridors, so at his bar mitzvah, he could open his mouth and let the sound flow by itself. He tested himself—glancing at the scroll, looking away, looking back again. Each time the pattern seemed brand spanking new, unseen in human history.

I'm concentrating too hard.

Adam attempted to distract himself by thinking about the Citywides, Mrs. Boyer, remembering he had never apologized to Michael Mason!

I am making myself crazy.

"You should not be feeling so much nerves," the Cantor said.

Adam changed the subject.

"Are people going to be talking to their friends when I'm leading the service, like they were on Shabbat?"

At the Cantor's orders, Adam had accompanied his parents to the adult service the week before, to "familiar yourself." Adam feared he had overstepped again with an adult trying to help him.

"So now you know secret. Grown-ups are not better at praying than kids."

"Maybe they get bored saying the same words, over and over."

"The words are not so important like you think."

Adam reminded the Cantor that he had drilled him to be word-perfect.

"Yes, yes, you will read it all perfect." The Cantor took his time. "Inside the singing is the prayer. Being with everyone, that also is prayer. But don't worry. When the bar mitzvah boy sings, the grown-ups do not talk, they listen. God is listening too."

Adam fessed up in his quiet voice, not to amplify potential blasphemy, that he didn't know if he believed in God.

"You ask questions. You come to bar mitzvah lessons. Maybe you talk to God sometimes."

I negotiate, but God never answers.

"You will sing best you can sing. That also…believing."

"You're Orthodox. It's easy for you."

"No. People think so, but it's not easy, not one bit. When I sing, I feel underneath, something. You will feel that too."

"Is that God?"

"I'm not no expert. Enough talk."

Adam wasn't sure if God mattered not at all or mattered more than anything. But he had a pure and glassy feeling when he was onstage, moving an audience with *Dawn*, or hearing the Junior Congregation thunder back the line he had just sung. He loved performing. And if Adam was sure of anything, it was that he didn't want to disappoint the Cantor.

"You know, Adam. I see in you...um..."

"I know," Adam answered, "you see yourself in me." *Everybody does.*

"That's not what I am going to say. You are *not* like me."

Oh?

"You have a *Yiddishe kopf*, like your father and mother, but your life is *not* like mine. You are free. You are a fine boy, with big heart, bright head, big voice that nobody ever hear that come out to play on your special day, and you will make a beautiful bar mitzvah."

When they finished, Adam asked if he could do it again, and then a third time. Adam was scared his song would disappear as soon as they disappeared from the sanctuary.

"Why the worry?" the Cantor said. "You have found voice."

Adam found his voice that day with Michael and Suvan taking photos in the synagogue, and it hadn't left him. Adam wanted— needed—one more look, one more run-through. Maybe three more.

"All right," the Cantor said, "we stay here as you long as you want. Today we don't rush. But you know your *parsha*. The fifth one not so good as the first four, but pretty okay. Seven is also fine. You don't worry about talking people or nothing else. You ready. Trust me."

"Okay."

The next day, Adam told Mr. Beck that while he was a proud Jew and would join, he couldn't be the founder of Mr. Beck's Jewish Heritage Club. His bar mitzvah was coming up. His Jewish heritage was in place.

Ready or not, I'm ready.

CHAPTER 43

They hurled themselves into Times Square as if freed from subway prison, the SP drama class joined by the OC in two separate loose and wobbly packs, roaring and howling at the sizzling neon and Olympian billboards. Miss Nadel was now teaching both classes and had relayed the dual invitation to watch Mr. Selenko in an evening rehearsal for his show.

For the nine blocks to the theater, they leapt and jumped on each other in spasms of exuberance—Adam, Suvan, Ryan, Peter, Stu—back together, as if nothing had happened, as if Adam had not been discarded like yesterday's sandwich for most of the year. Jason had stayed home, still in mourning. Valerie joined in, racing and attacking with her mean shoulder punch before retreating to Gracie and the other girls. Ryan drifted off to talk to Gracie from time to time, working up his courage to tell her he liked her.

Thrilled to be running with his reconfigured pack of new and old friends, Adam was distracted from his other agenda—to apologize to Michael Mason, to explain, to make his peace offering. Michael clung to his OC classmate bodyguards—friends? brothers? gang members?— while Adam's half-hearted, quarter-hearted, minimalist to the point of non-existent efforts to get Michael's attention produced nothing.

The neon of Broadway dazzled Adam. When he spotted *One Flew Over the Cuckoo's Nest* on the theater marquee so brightly lit against the night sky even off-Broadway, he felt a glimmer of promise that Selenko would know the magic solution to avert a Citywides catastrophe.

They followed Miss Nadel into the glass atrium that fronted the theater, thrusting onto the sidewalk, their single file dissolving into a pile-up inside the glass box. The heavy lobby doors opened, and Mr. Selenko appeared, transformed, angelic, glowing, all in white, his arms spread wide to welcome his acolytes to heaven. His eyebrows and mustache danced, full of magic, as his students swarmed around him.

Adam felt the surge of Selenko's love, but it was a generalized warmth, not directed specifically at him. He slithered in close and secreted his bar mitzvah invitation for Mr. Richard Selenko (*and guest*—Miss Nadel?) into Selenko's pocket, then worried that it would fall out during the scene or disappear during a wardrobe change. Adam tried to catch Selenko's eye, but there were too many hungry hands and faces.

"Isn't this wonderful!" Selenko proclaimed, without a tinge of sarcasm, his beatific gaze directed at all of them, but not, Adam trembled again, specifically at himself.

A voice rumbled through the PA system, summoning Selenko back to the stage. He hustled the crowd through the lobby and into the empty and grand auditorium with its ornate red velvet seats, the worn edges invisible in the dim lighting. Mid-rehearsal, the actors' voices curled back toward the students as Selenko corralled them down to the front rows, where he abandoned them, leaping gracefully onto the stage in a single bound to join the cast, his new family, then sidled offstage to the wings. The actors broke character to allow the kids to take their seats, and then at the director's command, reset their places to take the scene from the top. At Selenko's first entrance, a whoop brought stern looks from Miss Nadel. Adam caught a grin skip across Selenko's face before he dove into the scene.

Selenko was playing a vicious orderly at an insane asylum. He taunted, robbed, and beat the inmates. While Adam knew Selenko was an actor, he had never seen him perform more than a line of free-floating dialogue as an in-class demonstration. It shook him to see his touchstone being *not* Selenko. Adam hated Selenko's character, and should have credited his acting, but was feeling too much pride, envy, longing, anxiety, anger and excitement to sort out his thoughts.

At the same time, it was exhilarating to watch a professional rehearsal. There were no discipline problems. Everyone knew their lines. The director was a lithe man who moved with a dancer's grace, with close-cropped hair in a black T-shirt, who seemed older than Selenko. He did not have to badger the actors to pay attention. He popped on and off the stage during the scene—*side-coaching!*—and again after the scene to quietly give each actor a few words during his onstage stroll. They did the same scene repeatedly, tiny differences appearing in how it was played each time through. Adam was relieved when they finally moved on and he did not have to watch Selenko's character inflicting so much pain. Time didn't matter. Minutes became an hour, then nearly two, the actors seemingly tireless, the director instructing with surgical precision. Adam tried to catch the thread of the plot, but gave up to bask instead in this magical place.

Adam had never thought much about the director's role, but it was clear, the director was God. Adam was mesmerized and would have stayed all night, except he knew Suvan's father was driving into the City to take them home at 10 p.m. Adam was marveling at how smooth and practiced it seemed, when the director grumbled, "We're going backwards."

The actors froze, as if deactivated by the director's displeasure, stranded until he chose to revive them.

"Let's take our last fifteen-minute union break of the night and give teacher-man a few moments with his charges."

Four actors trooped down with Selenko to the edge of the stage as the others receded into the wings. The house lights remained off, leaving the stage brightly lit and the students in the dark. Selenko emceed, introducing each of the actors by name—the students didn't recognize them but applauded mightily—then introduced the guests as his "wonderful, favorite two classes."

How could he lump us together with the OC?

Selenko asked the actors to share their process of developing characters. This discussion had only begun when the star of the show marched on from backstage.

"Make way, you ragtag band of amateurs!" he proclaimed.

Everyone laughed. The hierarchy of leading roles took over, Selenko ceded the center spot, and the cast members became arrows pointing toward the star's square-jawed magnificence.

"McMurphy is the rebel against injustice," the star proclaimed, "the one man who can stand up to those who would abuse the weak and helpless. This character, my character, will shake the earth."

Adam liked his message but was pained that the star's luster dimmed Selenko's. The star answered all the questions, and some that no one had asked, as if he were alone onstage.

Could there be only one star?

Adam turned away and noticed Michael Mason heading up the aisle toward the exit. This was Adam's chance, to explain and apologize, to make his offering, to make things right.

Adam scooted to the end of his row and slipped out to go after Michael. The exit doors were curtained to keep light out, and Adam lost sight of his quarry. The lobby was also darkened, barely visible under the dull yellow service bulbs. Michael's silhouette crossed in front of the illuminated sign pointing downstairs to the Gentleman's Lounge.

The perfect place, quiet and private.

The smell reached Adam before the bank of cigarette smoke engulfed his mouth and nostrils.

"There's your boy!" one of them yelled, a cigarette in the corner of his mouth. They came at Adam out of a fog. Michael's gang.

If I hadn't stopped carrying Seth's nunchucks, I would fight them here and now, but no, not alone, not out of earshot, not one-on-five. I will remember every face in detail, but I will never tell the police or anybody else what happened. I am not running away, only finding a better place for our finale.

Michael was behind them, then raced past his classmates toward Adam.

"Wait up!" Michael called, but Adam was committed to escape, assuming Michael meant him harm. Hearing more footsteps pad up the carpeted stairs after him, Adam moved faster, headed back toward the safety of the auditorium, pictured himself flying down the aisle pursued by the Mason boys and their cigarettes, and knew Selenko would be undone. The other way then, out of the theater.

Adam shouldered through the lobby exit doors back into the atrium, under street lights so bright it felt like afternoon. The glass walls intensified the glare.

A swarm of New Yorkers were outside, not passersby but people waiting for something to happen, as if they had known in advance Adam would make his entrance. The parents stood in small clusters, leaning on their cars, which were parked hodge-podge, riding the curb. Two fathers checked their watches, several mothers smoked, paced, chatted. Adam recognized Ryan's dad and Peter's mom. Spaced along the other side of the glass wall, they seemed to be on display but left a clearly defined force field around a bowery bum sitting on the ground in his bubble, his back against the glass, drinking from a brown paper bag, so his world wouldn't contaminate theirs.

Upon sighting him, the parents surged in Adam's direction, reaching the outer door to the atrium when Adam did on his side. They discovered simultaneously that it was locked. The parents crushed together, waved in dumb show, their voices stifled to almost nothing by the soundproof glass. Those closest to the opening pressed their mouths to the crack, their calls reduced to tiny chirps. They begged for information, wanted their children so they could go home. Adam yelled through the fissure that *they weren't finished yet.*

Adam turned to go back into the theater, but the heavy lobby doors had clicked shut and locked behind him. He returned to the crack facing onto the street, but before he could yell to the parents to get help, Michael Mason flew through the lobby door. Adam reacted too late to stop it from closing.

"We're locked in."

"What?"

Adam motioned toward the adults outside. "Say hello to everybody's parents!" Adam waved.

Michael tried the lobby door, rattling the horizontal push bar.

"What the hell?"

"Where's your gang?" Adam asked.

"I don't need them."

All at once, like monkeys washing coconuts, the parents grasped the situation. Desperate for entertainment, they pointed, started laughing.

"They're watching, so you can't beat the crap out of me. They can't hear us."

"That true?"

"Soundproof."

Michael tested the technology. "Fuck you, Mom and Dad!"

Michael laughed as he tracked Adam circling away from him. "They really can't hear me." Michael knocked on the glass. He took a bow, enjoyed the silent applause from parents. "Why'd you think I was going to beat the crap out of you?"

"Isn't that why you chased me?"

"You followed *me*."

Michael offered Adam a cigarette, triggering panic.

"Put that away!"

Michael lit his cigarette calmly. "My parents know I smoke."

How is that possible?

"Are they here?" Adam began to scan the crowd.

"I take the subway, man. I'm fifteen."

Michael's hands were occupied. This was Adam's chance. "I wanted to explain why—"

"What kind of asshole goes into somebody's closet in front of their sister?"

Adam's acknowledgement was rushed, half swallowed. "That was wrong, but—"

"You didn't wait for me 'cause you didn't trust me!"

Precise and stinging.

"You disappeared with my brother's camera."

"You *gave* me the camera, shithead."

"I thought you fenced it."

"*Fenced* it? What the fuck?"

Adam cursed his uncontrollable urge to voice his thoughts.

"You came to my shul with all your garbage—and my stuff—and your, your…magazines…"

"You didn't like the *Playboys*?" Michael taunted. "You looked at them in the temple, didn't you! God will get you for that."

"That's none of your business." Adam was already deeply in lust with Miss May without understanding why.

"You like my jacket, I see."

"You got my room, my bed, everything, so I took a jacket that you threw out."

Adam forgot he was wearing Michael's army jacket as an olive branch.

"You blaming me for moving into your house?" Adam watched Michael crush his cigarette under his heel, knowing he would be next.

"No..." *I mean yes. For moving into my life.*

"You got me in deep shit with my mom, you know that? Come here. Stand right there."

"Can't. The ten-foot rule." Adam jumped back to demonstrate.

"Listen, shit-for-brains," Michael barked. "I have to keep ten feet away from you. You don't have to keep ten feet away from me."

This stopped Adam cold.

"Is that true?"

"Jesus. How did you get in the smart class? Come here. I've got to hit you, just to get it over with."

Adam approached Michael, exploring his new freedom, imagining himself not flinching in the face of nunchucks.

"I got to do this for your own good," Michael warned, then quickly punched Adam in the face, catching his cheek and the side of his head.

Adam went down. The parents pounded on the glass with fury.

"Ow...ow...ow..." Adam rolled over, rocked onto his knees, breathing hard, rubbing his face, still in shock from Michael's punch. He saw the appalled expressions of parents trying to smash through the glass to rescue him, and was surprised to feel fear for Michael's safety. Adam stood up quickly, raised both hands to signal the parents to *Stop!* tapped his chest and mouthed the words "I'm okay!"

Michael had backed into his corner while the invisible referee continued the count.

"Gonna call the cops?"

"No. Ow." Adam's face was on fire, but he tried to ignore the pain in the glare of the lights, of Michael's gaze, and the parents' fury. "What the hell did you do that for?"

"That's what you've been afraid would happen all year. Am I right?"

Adam didn't answer. He intended never to speak to Michael Mason again.

I've been hit before.

He thought of the Cantor fighting his way to school and back and resisted rubbing his throbbing cheek.

Michael Mason watched him. "I was having some fun with you."

Fun?

The word set Adam off.

"It wasn't fun for me," Adam screamed, as the entire torturous year launched his skinny body into a missile of anger, attacking Michael for real with his fists and his words. "I didn't do anything to you, and you made seventh grade hell." The pounding on the glass began again, rapid, muffled, rhythmic thumps. Michael covered up with both arms, instincts Adam lacked, as Adam swung wildly, ramming Michael with every charge and question. "Why'd you ambush me with sticks and bottles?"

Michael waited out Adam's frenzy, got Adam in a hold, immobilizing him. The parents' drumming immediately went heavy metal, a stifled riff inside the glass box.

"You called the cops!" Michael accused.

"The cops called *me!*"

"We just wanted to scare you."

"*You* made me scared to come to school all year. *You* followed me up and down the halls, to the movies, to the parking lot. *You* know what that feels like?"

"*You* got me on probation! You know what *that* feels like?"

"It's not the same!"

"It's fucking worse!"

Equating the punishment with the victim? Was he insane?

Adam struggled, broke free from the clinch just as Michael pushed him away. Again, Adam signaled to the parents that he was all right. The frenzied pounding died down. To hell with stoicism. Adam rubbed his cheek and his eye hard.

Michael's rage, which Adam couldn't imagine, was as vast and complex as his own, similar in part that it was fueled by the powerlessness of youth but also so much more. It made Michael focused, colder. But Adam wasn't done.

"You put graffiti on my synagogue!"

"A fucking stickball box!"

"'Jews Out of Flushing!' Sound familiar?"

"What?"

"On the door to the synagogue."

"What are you talking about man?"

"You didn't?"

Michael's sincerity froze Adam.

Maybe Michael had nothing to do with the graffiti or the broken windows.

"Why'd you follow me in school?"

"No reason."

"Yeah, there was a reason, and I want to know what it was."

Michael lit a cigarette, puffed. Adam watched, waiting for an answer.

The violence apparently over, the parental percussion died away. The parents lit their own cigarettes. The mob broke into small groups. Adam made eye contact with one or two, saw their concern, turned away from their pity. *Were they trying to protect both boys*, Adam would later wonder, *or only him?*

"You know why," Michael said.

"I don't."

"I'm living in your fucking room. *My* room. All that stuff you left on the other side of the wall under the house."

"That's the crawl space. That's what it's called."

"Good name. Like Tom and fucking Huck finding treasure. I wanted to know what the fuck was up with you…"

"Why didn't you just say so?!"

"Just say what? You were the same guy getting me on fucking probation. And look at you, man, in my jacket, like a different version of me, like a pod person, a *body snatcher*."

"That's *my* movie!"

"I was curious."

Michael Mason was curious about me. Was that it?

"Why'd you tell me your sister was in *Playboy*?"

"And you're calling *me* stupid?"

"I never called you stupid."

"You—"

"Never!"

Michael considered this, accepted it, ground out his cigarette. The smoke was choking, but familiar to Adam from home. They had an audience, waiting to see which way things would go, but the boys didn't know themselves.

They stalled, stymied. Finally, Adam spoke.

"Selenko was about to quit. That's why I couldn't wait for you to come back to finish the Surprise Challenge."

"How'd you know?"

"He told me. And he put your name on the Crime Scene plaque backstage."

"Really? I bet all the teachers like you."

"Some of them. A lot of them."

"I hate quitters."

"Me too."

"I found nine bucks inside a *World's Finest* from 1943."

"You what?"

"In the crawl space. That's why I didn't charge you for taking the pictures. We're even."

"Even?"

"Yeah!"

"Yeah?"

"Okay."

"I brought you something," Adam said to Michael Mason. "But fucking hell, I don't know if I want to give it to you." Adam took a baseball out of his jacket pocket, held it up. "It's signed by the Mets championship team."

"What the—?"

"My dad knows the third-base coach. He got one for me and one for my brother, but I'm a Yankee fan. I hate the Mets."

"For me?"

Michael walked away from Adam, to the far end of the atrium, studied the ball.

"That's like...valuable. Naah. You're going to take it back. Is it for me?"

"No backsies."

"What are you, in third grade?"

"Sorry I went in your closet, my closet." This time no *buts*.

"This is cool. Kranepool. Swoboda. There's my man, Cleon Jones. I can read their names. The fucking jacket, Adam Miller, that was a fucking present, man. You were always looking at it, so I gave it to you."

The inner door connecting the atrium with the theater lobby opened and Suvan appeared.

"Don't let the door—" both boys called, but too late.

"Here's your Romeo," Michael said.

"I wanted to let you know—" Suvan stopped short as the parents surged forward. "There's my Appa!" Suvan waved at his father, who waved back with passion through the glass. "So many parents. That reduces the embarrassment factor over getting a ride."

Adam had the very same anxieties about appearing coddled in front of his classmates.

"Your...associates told me you were out here," Suvan continued. "I came to tell you we're finishing."

"Now you're trapped in here with us."

"What?" Suvan spun, pushed against the unforgiving lobby door.

"That's...unexpected."

The boys were quiet.

"We have an audience," Suvan offered.

"A restless audience," Adam said.

"Well, chaps, let's put on a show."

"Spot on!" Adam agreed, whirling on Michael. "They don't know if it was for real when you punched me in the face. We can pretend it was just part of our Broadway debut."

"He punched you in the face?" Suvan said, backing away from Michael, lest he lash out again. "Oh yes. You have a purple patch."

"I got an idea," Michael Mason said. "Take off your watches, put them down here in the corner."

"You going to steal them?" Suvan needled.

"I'm putting mine in too," Michael answered. "See? Adam, you play yourself. Little man, you stand here and you play my brother. I'll tell you what to say."

Michael whispered in Suvan's ear, "Got that?"

"Crystal clear."

> *(Adam Miller, Suvan Chakrabarti, and Michael Mason are locked in a glass atrium outside an off-Broadway theater.)*

> *(Michael Mason is fifteen, a light-skinned black teen with a full Afro. He's a bit gangly, as if he's just completed a growth spurt. He has a jeans jacket and is wearing black shoes. He carries himself in a more aggressive and challenging manner than the younger boys. He has a pack of cigarettes in his breast pocket and a wallet in his back pocket.)*

MICHAEL MASON
Action!

SUVAN
I'm going to kill that mother. (*Suvan breaks character.*) What mother? I don't see any mother.

MICHAEL MASON
I'm talking about Adam. He comes on in a second.

SUVAN
I'm going to kill that mother. Let's roll this kid.

(Suvan Chakrabarti is thirteen, wearing brown slacks, a light blue button-down shirt with a string tie, black high-top Converse sneakers, and a lightweight New York Mets jacket. All of his clothes seem very new. Suvan's natural pose is straight-backed, and he moves somewhat stiffly. When he acts the part under Michael's direction, his physicality changes entirely.)

MICHAEL MASON
(Michael grabs Suvan, playing his brother, and shouts close into his face.) You're already on the edge, man! Dad is going to kill you!

(The pounding on the glass intensifies.)

Those people banging on the glass, they're my brother's gang, and they're saying…here's what they're saying: "Beat the shit out of him!" *(Michael lifts his arms to egg on the crowd.)* They want you messed up.

SUVAN
I don't believe the parents would genuinely desire me to get a beating. Or Adam.

MICHAEL MASON
(To Suvan) We're acting here. Use your imagination, man. In scene. Ready? Action! Listen, bro. You're going to get sent away. This kid's the first one all day who fought back, you know, deserves some respect. *(To Adam)* Now you come in and fight me like you did.

(Adam is about to turn thirteen, a slender boy, short for his age, with long dark hair, parted on the side but

hanging past his ears down to his neck. He wears white Converse All Star high-tops and a loose-fitting army jacket over a button-down striped shirt and brown pants. He has several Save Soviet Jewry and Peace buttons pinned to his chest. Adam has the presence of a deer, staring at a fixed point with intensity, lost in his dreams, but darting suddenly when startled.)

ADAM
I really don't want…

MICHAEL MASON
Come on man! Trust me! Come now. Get your watch back.

ADAM
Okay. *(Adam launches himself at Michael Mason.)* Give it back! That's my brother's diving watch.

MICHAEL MASON
(Breaks character.) A diving watch. Damn, that's what it was! I've been trying to remember that all year. *(Back in character.)* Get out of here.

(Adam shoves Michael Mason, and Michael thrusts his open hand hard into Adam's chest, then pushes him down toward the corner where the watches have been placed.)

(Pounding on the glass resumes but does not reach maximum volume.)

MICHAEL MASON
Grab your watch, Miller, and run away, you know, out of the scene. *(Adam moves to the opposite corner. Michael whispers further instructions to Suvan.)*

SUVAN
You gave him his watch back! You piece of...You're dead.

MICHAEL MASON
Man, I just saved your life and you're too stupid to know it. You'll be lucky as hell if that kid doesn't remember your face. You gotta wise up, but I guess that's not gonna happen. End Scene! *(Spins, facing Adam.)* You see now, Smart Boy? *(Pause.)* Do you see?

ADAM
See? Yeah, I see. I saw.

MICHAEL MASON
What'd you see?

ADAM
You...you were protecting me.

MICHAEL MASON
Nooo! Shit-for-brains. *(Pause.)* I was protecting my brother. *(Pause.)* You want to fucking know where I went when you came looking for your fucking camera?

ADAM
I want to fucking know.

SUVAN
Me...fucking too.

MICHAEL MASON
My father and I took him to a fucking Last Chance
program in a closed facility.

ADAM
He's in prison? For stealing my watch? I got it back!

MICHAEL MASON
For breaking and entering, that total fucking asshole.
Nothing to do with you. That's where I was. It's not
prison, but it's not playtime.

SUVAN
Because you are the good Samaritan who showers his
wayward sibling with love.

MICHAEL MASON
(Eyes Suvan with suspicion, not sure how to answer.)
He's a head case, my brother. But Dad didn't want to
drive back alone. That's what happened. Believe me?
Do you?

SUVAN
Wait, is he supposed to not believe you?

ADAM
I can't figure you out.

MICHAEL MASON
Stop trying, man.

ADAM
But you tried to figure me out.

MICHAEL MASON
That's different.

ADAM
What's different about it?

MICHAEL MASON
Now you're pissing me off.

(Their classmates appear outside the glass, having exited through the stage door, then Miss Nadel pushes through the crowd. She bangs on the glass. Adam ignores her.)

ADAM
I did figure something out. You're a good actor. Suvan's father won't let him be in the Citywides. But you could do his part. You can be Captain John Dawson.

MICHAEL MASON
Don't bullshit me.

SUVAN
(Distracted by something going on behind the glass.)
Adam?

ADAM
I'm serious.

MICHAEL MASON
I'll think about it.

SUVAN
That derelict has removed a walkie-talkie from his brown paper bag.

MICHAEL MASON
(*Adam and Michael turn around and see the wino, an undercover cop, calling in to the station that three boys are trapped in the theater atrium.*) Cops are everywhere, for Chrissake. Okay.

ADAM
What?

MICHAEL MASON
I'll do it. I'll act in fucking Dawn.

(*Adam's face stretches into a broad smile, until he catches Suvan's accusing look of abandonment and betrayal.*)

CHAPTER 44

"I have parked in the Hippodrome," Mr. Chakrabarti said. "Let us not tarry, boys. There are a thousand evils in this foul neighborhood."

"Yessir," said Suvan.

Sir. Adam would remember to *Sir* him. Adam felt invincible after the atrium, certain he could win Mr. Chakrabarti over to his brainstorm and make things right with his best friend.

They skirted Times Square, past frightening drunks and half-undressed adults. Street dealers offered nickel bags, but Mr. Chakrabarti waved them off to make way for his ducklings. "Eyes straight ahead, boys!" he ordered, trying unsuccessfully to keep them from seeing the triple-X marquees. Adam knew that inside those buildings something *sordid* took place, but what? It caused ripples along Adam's scalp, but not as much as seeing a dark shape materialize into a full-size rat, skirting off into the shadows before Adam could point it out. Had he really seen it?

A car ride was the perfect time and the place for serious conversations with adults. Adam waited for the car to be in motion, out of the garage, past the Times Square squalor.

"Mr. Chakrabarti, sir," Adam asked from the back seat. "Why can't Suvan be in the Citywides? I don't think it's fair."

Suvan froze, pulled on Adam's arm. Mr. Chakrabarti drove ramrod straight, tightly clutching at ten and two, the opposite of Adam's father, who was at his most relaxed behind the wheel.

"I'm afraid it's impossible. But nonetheless, please explain yourself."

They made a series of right turns until they were pointed south, then finally turned left toward the Midtown Tunnel. The *thrum* of the tunnel gave Adam courage to speak.

"I get it that you think that we're not doing it right," Adam started. "Mr. Chakrabarti, sir, Miss Nadel said…I know you think John Dawson wouldn't wait around instead of escaping or fighting, that that's not the way a British officer behaves."

"Go on. To understand how children think is of great interest to me."

"It's too late," Suvan whined. "It doesn't matter."

"It matters to me," Adam said.

"Never mind, Appa."

"We don't say 'Appa,' Suvan. We are in America now."

"Sorry, Papa."

We don't say "Papa" in America either.

"Adam, I am afraid you have the wrong end of the stick, my boy. I did not object because Captain Dawson was insufficiently courageous or resourceful."

Adam expected that Mr. Chakrabarti would tell him what he did object to, but Suvan's father left the boys dangling in silence as he concentrated on the tunnel, then for fifteen minutes more before pulling off the Long Island Expressway into a parking lot facing the Jib Lanes bowling alley.

"This isn't where Adam lives."

"I'm aware of that, and I apologize for the long delay in responding to your question. It takes my full attention to drive on the right side of the road and ensure that we do not crash into a lorry."

"No problem, sir."

"But there is a problem, dear Adam."

Mr. Chakrabarti turned around. In the passing headlights, the purple patches under his eyes became ink, with depths Adam could not fathom. He wondered if it resembled his Michael Mason-inflicted badge of courage, if Suvan would get these patches when he was older.

"Your Captain Dawson is reasonable, a man of empathy and intel-lectual rigor."

"Okay." These sounded like positive attributes.

"But you see, the British dispatched hooligans to police their colonies."

Hooligans again.

"They were gussied up in uniforms and posh club memberships, but that polished exterior did not restrain their brutality. My father fought them and paid dearly, a gruesome story for another day. But if you are interested, I will tell you sometime."

Suvan leaned forward. "Why did we move to England if you hate them so much?"

"Because Mr. Churchill alone stood up to Mr. Hitler and saved the world from the Nazi barbarians." He said Nozzie, and it took Adam a beat to translate. "And the British told us they had the finest schools in the world, and I believed them."

"So why did we come to America?"

"The British may have lost their empire, but, as you know, they did not lose their snobbery. I wanted you to have a new start in a country that allows anyone to join its accursed club. And that's enough chatter for one evening."

Mr. Chakrabarti aimed for the Grand Central Parkway, the long way to Adam's house, so Adam explained how to get on the Van Wyck to the Whitestone Expressway.

"Thank you," he said. "That sounds faster than what I had mapped out."

Only a few minutes remained. Adam would have one last chance.

"Mr. Chakrabarti, sir, would you object if Suvan acted in *Dawn* but didn't play Captain Dawson?"

"Go on."

"How about if Suvan plays Elisha, the young Jew who executes the British officer? Would that be a capital idea?"

Mr. Chakrabarti burst into laughter. "*A capital idea.* Where did you get that from? I don't talk like a toff, and Suvan speaks American."

"I do?" Suvan asked.

"Would you let Suvan play Elisha, sir?"

"You cannot use my revolver again."

"No, Papa, that was a bad idea. Can I play Elisha, Papa?"

"That would be…capital!" Mr. Chakrabarti said with delight.

I am brilliant, but what have I done?

CHAPTER 45

Michael Mason—dancer, Haben's thief and savior, phony Official Yearbook Photographer—had protected Adam, and it was Adam's fault Michael was on probation. As Adam crossed the threshold of the 109th Precinct, he felt himself a tiny, inconsequential child, but he found the courage to ask the desk sergeant to see Detective Riley.

"Why?"

Adam's voice yipped when he said, "I have new information." The sergeant didn't react. He asked Adam's name, didn't listen when Adam answered, asked and ignored him again, and when Adam finally volunteered his name a third time, told him to stop being a pest and sit and wait like a good dog on that same unforgiving perpendicular bench where Adam had waited with his father in the fall, the seat so deep Adam's feet dangled in air.

He didn't write my name down. He's already forgotten I'm here. I'll still be waiting long after Detectives Fein and Riley retire. I'll miss my bar mitzvah, I'll grow old and die on this bench.

Adam found Detective Riley's card, went into the phone booth, closed its accordion door, put in his dime, and dialed his number. He watched the desk sergeant reach for the phone.

"109th Precinct."

Adam froze, afraid his voice would be recognized, but just before the sergeant replaced the receiver, he mimicked Suvan.

"May I have the pleasure of speaking with Detective Riley?"

"Hold on." The sergeant punched some buttons.

"Riley."

Adam was startled, unprepared again. "I'm um...um...Adam Miller from 189 who broke up the watch gang. I need to speak to you in person. I'm here outside in the lobby."

"What lobby?" Adam hung up. Detective Riley swept into the middle of the waiting room, trench coat aloft like a cape, hands on his hips. He motioned for Adam to follow him.

"Hey, you!" the sergeant yelled at Adam with malevolence.

"S'all right, Sarge," Riley called out, and in the same breath, "Fein!" The three of them squeezed into Riley's office.

"Do I remember this kid?" Fein asked.

"The gang at 189."

"Right. And the synagogue. Oh yeah."

"And he blabbed to that Jew lieutenant from the City, and the Captain put our nuts in a vice."

"That guy had a mick mug just like yours."

"One of your tribe, Fein, I'm sure of it."

"You're right," Adam gulped, butting in for the first time. "He's my cousin. And he's a captain."

"Cousin?" Fein exploded into a gigantic smile, showing his gums and all his teeth. "It was family talk."

"I'm the one who told you this kid was square!"

"Family talk, that's right," Adam said. "I didn't snitch on anybody."

Adam reminded himself why he'd come, tried to speak, couldn't, tapped out a few beats on his thigh, and finally told the detectives he wanted to change his story.

"You don't stand behind your complaint?"

"I thought one of the boys was trying to hurt me, but he was trying to keep me from getting beat up."

"And how did you figure that out?"

"I saw what really happened."

"Somebody filmed it?"

"It was acted out."

"In a play? On Broadway?"

"Yes, kind of."

"An instant replay?"

"Just like that!" Adam answered excitedly. "Only not instant."

"Adam," Detective Fein said in a friendly voice, "is someone pressuring you?"

Adam *was* pressured, by his guilt. As for the story, the gang had incriminated themselves and the police had written it out. And it was their story more than Adam's.

"You're not sure?"

"No one is pressuring me."

"And let me guess. The name you want to change is Michael Mason."

"I… I… That's right."

"That's interesting because Michael Mason was also in here a few weeks ago. Somehow he got the impression that you'd been shot dead at school."

"That was a…for my teacher…the Surprise Challenge."

"It was a surprise for us too, see, 'cause we didn't hear about a shooting, but we did hear about a teacher being fired because of a weapon onstage. Maybe that's the information you came to tell us about."

A teacher was fired?

"What teacher?"

"Stinko?"

"Selenko?"

"So you *do* know what I'm talking about."

My best ever Surprise Challenge cost Selenko his job?

"Do you want to tell us about the Webley service revolver?"

Suvan's father's gun!

"That was a prop," Adam said. "And there were no bullets. We wouldn't even know how to load it. Listen. You have to cancel Michael's probation."

"The probation's over, kid," Detective Fein revealed. "It was for six months."

"Adam. These junior gangs, they feed into the grown-up gangs, real criminal activity. One of the Mason kids got in trouble—"

"In real trouble."

"But we haven't had any complaints about muggings outside 189 since November."

Adam was trying to understand the implications.

"But the Hill still runs the schoolyard," Adam protested, "and the bathrooms downstairs, and the second-floor bathroom is for black kids only."

"Here's the score, kid," Detective Riley explained. "The I-talians stay with the hitter gangs and the Negroes stay with the Negroes, and they do not start mixing together."

"We can't be everywhere, Adam," Detective Fein said. "So we limit the damage."

But I came here to limit the damage!

"You did good, Adam. Didn't he do good, Riley?"

"It was a good day's work, kid."

"Thanks," Adam said, out of politeness, *thanks*, as he wandered out, dazed.

The police wanted to keep black and white gangs separate so they were easier to manage. Adam was too late to help Michael Mason. Everyone's probation was over, and it was open season on Adam Miller. And Adam's favorite teacher *ever!* had lost his job because of Adam's Surprise Challenge—Cousin Harry must have reported him—and would never forgive Adam. Turned out it wasn't Adam who had new information.

CHAPTER 46

Adam was Jewish like Elisha, and Suvan had his British accent, but would the audience believe that Michael was Captain Dawson and that Suvan was Elisha? Yes, if the acting is good enough, if Michael can stop looking all around, and if Suvan can loosen up, but would that be enough?

Seth found his brother's dilemma hysterically funny.

"You're all kids!" Seth laughed. "Hasn't bothered your audience up to now. It's cool that you got a black kid in *Dawn*. We should learn to understand each other better."

"But you said black people hate Jews."

"I never said that. I don't believe that."

Adam knew better than to challenge his brother's declarations.

"We're usually on the same side," Seth went on, "so I get pissed when we're not. That's all there is to it. Anyway, you're just kids doing a play."

We're kids from Flushing in 1971 playing a British Army captain and a Holocaust survivor in pre-state Palestine. And no, this fact hasn't bothered anyone and it won't.

This helped Adam grope toward another insight: "Theater is about the imagination of the actor as much as the imagination of the audience." *Thus spake Richard Selenko.*

And toward his new cast member's attitude:

"What the fuck do we care what the fucking audience thinks?" *Thus spake Michael Mason.*

And Mr. Chakrabarti informed the boys that, contrary to Adam's assumptions, there had been many Indian troops in Palestine—"the

British sent us where they would"—but he thought that Suvan "approximated a very fine Jew."

Adam's anxiety about pairing Suvan and Michael was off base. Michael had nothing against Suvan, and Suvan had nothing against Michael. Suvan was Suvan, and Michael behaved with the same fuck-you attitude toward Suvan as he did to everyone else.

The boys went to work. At their first rehearsal, Suvan mimicked Adam's movements with ruthless accuracy in his attempt to reproduce their original performance, but it came off peculiar. By the second try, Suvan shed his accent and his reserve. He let loose, stalking the stage like a hunter. He found a guttural, Brooklyn growl, starting with his Mr. Beck impersonation until it became something different, from inside.

They were improving, but his actors didn't have the flow, the ability to anticipate and feed off each other, that Suvan and Adam had developed. That might come with time, but there was no time.

They discussed the play—the fact that both Elisha and Captain Dawson were far from home, but Dawson had a home to return to while Elisha's world had been destroyed and he was forced to create a new one from scratch. Suvan told them a little about London, "which my Papa," Suvan sighed dramatically, "decided we must abandon. He thought we'd make a better life here."

"My father made us move too," Adam said. "I guess for the same reason."

"My dad, yeah," Michael grunted in affirmation, "it's his fault we're in Flushing. He kept saying the neighborhood would be better for us."

Fathers who couldn't sit still, who were looking for something, who uprooted their families, who were striving upward to the limit of where they were welcome and what they could afford. Why did these restless men make their sons miserable? The three boys considered their parallel homesickness.

"My house is cool, but I hate my new neighborhood," Adam said, a bit more forcefully than intended.

"I guess we'll be moving there next."

There was a pause, followed by an explosive laugh. The surprise of Michael Mason cracking a joke was as funny as the joke itself.

Were their lives proof texts of social mobility? Was Adam's new house a step up for the Millers, or had they lost their way? And where did Suvan's family fit in? Adam wasn't sure of any of it.

"I rather like our new surroundings," Suvan demurred. "I have grown very fond of Flushing and the Amazing Mets!" At that, to Adam's astonishment, Suvan launched into the Mets theme song, "Meet the Mets." By the end, Michael had joined in and Adam, reluctantly, as well.

Adam experimented. He asked Michael to stand perfectly still for an entire run-through. That was no good. Then he turned on the stage lights to eliminate the darkness, but that made both actors self-conscious. At one of their last rehearsals, Adam tried the opposite, performing in total darkness. He couldn't see Michael or Suvan, and they couldn't see each other. Sound became everything.

The darkness unlocked Michael Mason. His voice dropped an octave, his invisibility gave him confidence, and Captain Dawson became the hunter, baiting his jailer, taunting him, testing him. Suvan became a cat, listening, his Elisha sensing where Dawson was, ready for an assault, but not afraid.

And there it was. Michael was a British Officer, older than his captor, radiating authority despite Elisha's rifle. He stopped looking around all the time, perhaps less afraid of collision, but more, it seemed to Adam, because he was feeling his power. His accent made no difference.

Adam began to speak, thought better of it, let go of the blocking that he and Suvan had so carefully choreographed. He told them very quietly that he was going to turn on the side spotlight but to ignore him and continue in scene and start again when they finished.

Michael circled, Suvan prowled. The boys were convincing, unpredictable, for the first time entirely in sync. In place of the gunshot, Adam extinguished the black light, returning them to subterranean darkness. Their breathing becoming collective breath. Adam was moved by the success of his project.

Why aren't the Citywide judges here right now?

Two days before the Citywides, Suvan changed how he was playing Elisha. His posture altered, his cadence, his accent. But it was only at the last rehearsal that Adam recognized that Suvan had modeled himself on the Cantor, one immigrant impersonating another, which was *spot on* and All-American.

The night before, Adam heard from Mr. Selenko. Adam was sure that Selenko would blast him for ruining his career, but he had called to thank Adam for the bar mitzvah invitation—*no guarantee, but he'd see what he could do*—and to tell him to "break a leg" at the Citywides.

"But you lost your job. I'm sorry my cousin..."

"It was the best thing that ever happened to me, and your cousin never said a word. I opened my big mouth to Dr. Lefkowitz, so he had no choice."

Adam breathed deeply.

"I'm proud of you, Adam, for finding such a generous solution to your casting problem. The director is the visionary, and this play is your vision of a great novel. And remember, Adam, actors are fragile souls in need of encouragement."

"Okay."

Fragile souls in need of encouragement.

CHAPTER 47

The morning of the Citywides, the Millers took yet another morning off and drove Adam to their old house to pick up Michael Mason and drive together into the city. Michael's parents would be leaving work to meet them there.

Adam rang his bell—Michael Mason's bell!—and Nadine told him Michael wasn't ready yet, as she traipsed past him down the steps off to high school. By the time Adam had aligned his brain to say hello to Michael's sister, she was gone, and Mrs. Schiffman was calling his name from across the street. The Millers, protective of their son's artistic sensitivities, emerged from the car to intercept their old neighbor.

"Adam's going to be in a Citywide Drama Competition today."

"Oh, an actor! Adam, good luck to you. Let me give you a kiss. I know you'll make us proud." She turned to Mr. Miller, who exited the car to stretch his legs. "And, Jeremy, I'm sorry about Edwin. The truth is, Edwin has not been himself this past couple of years. He should never have done that to your car."

There was silence, the group disentangled, each solitary again.

"Done what?" Mr. Miller asked.

"I think he might have slashed your tires once. And broken the window. I know he tried to take the radio and make it look like a burglary. Vandalism, I told him, pure and simple. I'm sorry about that. It was wrong."

"Obviously it was wrong," Mrs. Miller said. "Was Edwin having a nervous breakdown?"

"He's *fertummelt*. His brain. *Famisht*. And those notes he put on your dashboard. I told him that was outrageous."

"What notes?"

"Last year."

"The ones that said, '*We know where you live.*'?"

"That's right."

"Edwin put those there?"

Mr. Miller started laughing.

"I'm glad you think it's funny, Jeremy. I didn't think it was funny. I wanted to divorce the idiot."

"You didn't divorce him, did you?"

"Do I look divorced?" This question she turned on Helen.

"I don't know. What does—?"

"Do you know," Mr. Miller interrupted, broke into laughter, calmed down, continued. "Do you know I reported it to the police and took the car in to have the radio replaced for the third time and they said, 'Buddy, your radio is still there.' I had just assumed. Did Edwin steal the radio the other times?"

"Of course not, but that's what gave him the idea. He wasn't thinking straight."

"I couldn't think straight either. 'We know where you live.' I thought it was a threat."

"Of course we knew where you lived. You lived across the street."

"And all that because we were planning to move and take Adam away from you?"

"Oh no, that was because of the judge. That Nazi you brought to the high school."

"He was from the City's Human Rights Commission."

"And teachers don't have human rights?"

"Of course we do. And I don't think the Nazis would have a black commissioner."

"Edwin didn't tell me he was colored. Oh my."

Dad in the middle again, getting hit from all sides.

"Keep your voices down," Mrs. Miller warned quietly.

"Well, that's what Edwin was angry about. But it got all mixed up."

"Shhh…"

That means…we moved because of the Schiffmans.

Michael emerged from the house.

"Who's that?" Michael asked.

"Your neighbor," Mrs. Miller offered. "Mrs. Schiffman, Michael Mason."

"Nice to meet you," Mrs. Schiffman said. "Break a leg, boys!"

"Don't say one more word, Jeremy. We are leaving right now. Adam, Michael, get in the car. These boys have to put on a show. Goodbye, Mrs. Schiffman. Goodbye, and goodbye."

CHAPTER 48

Groups from performing arts middle schools arrived with professional costumes, collapsible sets, and elaborate lighting designs. They delivered polished renditions of short plays. Like the others, the boys from 189 were given seven minutes to set the stage for *Dawn*. Adam positioned the spotlight, which he would control, and placed the leather strap to make the gunshot within reach, which he would time perfectly in Gracie's absence. Adam checked one last time that Suvan and Michael were on their marks.

His first thought was, *we're going to lose, but we knew that going in*, and his second was, *this is a terrible mistake. Suvan is not Elisha. I'm Elisha! And what is Michael Mason doing on stage? We could switch everything in sixty seconds and Suvan and I can perform Dawn as it's meant to be. Michael will do the gunshot and the blackout. He'll understand.*

The bell rang time, and Adam's fantasy was throttled.

Adam moved downstage center to introduce the play, his nerves jangled as before every performance. Spurred by adrenaline, pride, and grievance, Adam ad-libbed an epilogue to his British Mandate history:

"I want to dedicate our performance to Eduard Kuznetzov, Mark Dymshitz, and Yosef Mendelovich, three Jewish freedom-seekers imprisoned by the Soviet authorities this year. Like the underground fighters in our play, they have been sentenced to death because they wanted to live in a free Israel. Please tell your congressmen to fight for their lives."

This garnered a few isolated claps. Some in the audience of parents and jurists nodded in assent, others sat up a bit straighter. Adam stepped off the stage. He felt woozy, nauseous. He was losing Elisha, would never play Elisha again.

Lights dimmed, spotlight on, footsteps, the opening lines.

Adam tried to force his attention to the stage, but his feelings were swooping and soaring, and he couldn't watch. He zoomed out and up, looking down at the stage from the Apollo mission far above. Way down on earth were spirits, muffled voices, movement, heads bobbing in a student theater, two figures darting in and out of a harsh and horizontal beam of light. There were the Masons, and Adam's and Suvan's parents sitting together, their fathers beaming. Mr. Miller's eyes met Adam's, and with a tiny headshake, he tried to redirect Adam's eyes to the stage. But it was a moment later, when the audience pitched forward, and in that one shift of position, Adam knew they were hooked, that Adam was reeled back in.

His reentry was instant. In this true black-box stage, the lighting and shadows were more effective than at school. In fast-motion flip-book, he saw the nine thousand decisions he'd made with Suvan, then the changes when Michael joined, and parts reassigned. He watched *Dawn* as if for the first time.

Suvan embodied the Cantor, embodied Elisha, sliding in and out of the light. And Michael was magnetic, vanishing and reappearing, radiating authority. Adam's mind worked at triple speed in multiple dimensions, acting, feeling, remembering, moving with the actors, directing them, observing them, observing himself observing them.

Ghosts. Suvan's arm motions—simple, repetitive gestures—summoning and fending off his parents, his uncles, his brothers, all gone, all dead, not just dead to him but extinguished. In that struggle, the ghosts were not hovering but flickering past in lighting zaps—Elisha wrestling with ghosts, Adam wrestling with ghosts. Mrs. Boyer beckoning Jason, offering Adam a brownie, "he can't come to the phone just now"—*zap*—the dead boy in the picture pasting back his hair as the bullet strikes him—*zap*—Adam's grandfather falling asleep on the couch; "no sweetie, I'm not dead, just asleep"—*zap*—Takashi's mother,

quiet, polite, afraid to speak English, and then…gone…replaced—
zap—Takashi, Jason, ghosts.

Adam's gasp swiveled heads across the back row.

He'd misunderstood the entire year. Elisha's ghosts were not fearful
of losing Elisha. They had come to judge him, condemning Elisha for
becoming an executioner.

Adam snapped out of his reverie as the plea "Elisha!" left Captain
Dawson's mouth, Adam's hands jerked the leather strap, the hang-
man's rope, the pistol finger, to simulate the gunshot, and then, a hair's
breadth after the sound registered, he killed the spotlight.

Dawn was over.

The applause was steady, lengthy, and genuine, not thunderous, no
standing ovation.

The boys didn't win for best actor or for best play or for best directing, but they were called up for an Honorable Mention for Adaptation,
reason for Adam to join them to take their second bows to respect-
ful applause, a "Bravo!" from Adam's mother, whistles from Michael's
father, and a gentle cheer of "Well played, lads!" from Suvan's father,
which brought tears to Adam's eyes.

Afterward, Adam accepted the hugs of his parents, the congratu-
lations of Suvan's and Michael's parents. Michael allowed himself to be
hugged, Suvan as well. The Masons didn't mention the encounter with
the Cantor, and nobody mentioned the watch incident or Michael's
probation or the atrium.

"Earth to Adam…. He's still flying."

"He deserves it."

Dazed, happy to have succeeded, Adam was glad to let the parents
imagine he was too elated to focus.

Michael's father asked Mr. Miller what a bar mitzvah was all
about, Mr. Chakrabarti said he was also eager to know, and that set
the parents off.

Suvan and Michael and Adam stole away to relive their par-
tial victory.

Adam was amazed by Michael and Suvan's thirst to be told how
well they had performed, and told again, and told one more time, but

he remembered Selenko's description of actors, and heaped on the praise, all deserved.

Mrs. Mason and Adam's mother were comparing bar mitzvahs and confirmations when the boys rejoined them. Everyone fell silent again. Adam was struck by how difficult it was for adults to sustain a conversation.

During this awkward pause, a Citywide official who had been crisscrossing the hall finally delivered a telegram that had been sent to the "JHS 189 Production Team for *Dawn*." It was from Mr. Selenko, who could not join them because he was performing the Wednesday matinee. This is what he wrote:

1. *Break a leg.*
2. *Bravo. I knew you could do it.*
3. *I saw your picture in the post office. The machine gun didn't do you justice.*

Before they went home, Adam gladly invited Michael Mason to his bar mitzvah. What choice did he have? His parents hadn't stopped talking about it.

CHAPTER 49

MY BAR MITZVAH DAIS (5)

Cousin Kay	Cousin Harvey	Dennis	Albert	Karsh	Michael Mason	Suvan	**ADAM**	Valerie	Gracie	Ryan	Peter	Stu	Jason	Buddy

It was done.

CHAPTER 50

Adam was with his parents, greeting friends and unidentified flying relatives at the main entrance, close hugs, lipstick kisses, wiping, smearing, perfume, warm air, coming up for breath. Adam was relieved when it was time to go in. He sat next to Seth, the brothers wedged between their parents in the second row, Adam's father in full smile, the gap in his front teeth showing as he tried to suppress the wild surges of paternal pride rippling from his heart to his cheeks. With no errands possible for the next three hours, Mrs. Miller became calmer. At the end of services, the assembly would move as a protozoan mass next door into the ballroom for the party.

Adam removed his new silk tallit from its velvet bag, read the blessing imprinted in shimmer across the collar, and swept the prayer shawl around his shoulders, covering completely the electric-blue bar mitzvah jacket that had cost Adam and his father many days of searching and frustration, and that his mother had finally found on her own.

Rabbi Ellenbaum, in his silver hair and silver aviators, scanned the crowd from his seat. The Cantor, by his side, looked down at Adam from the three-step elevation of the *bimah* stage. Adam needed to align his brain for liftoff, but his heart was jumping, speeding up as the pages counted down. He couldn't get his eyes or his brain to focus on the words. He turned each page mechanically, following the motions of his brother. His mother, determined that Adam wouldn't miss his cue, leaned across Seth four separate times to tell Adam to "get ready."

In the end, it was the Cantor who gave Adam the nod to ascend the wide *bimah* steps and take his place at the lectern. Once set, the Cantor twirled his finger, signaling Adam to turn around and face away from the congregation. For most of the service, Adam would be looking at the doors of polished silver behind which the Torah scrolls huddled. He lay his *siddur* on the stand, and sang out five words in Hebrew:

"*Shochen Ad, Marom, v'Kadosh Shmo!*"

Adam's voice had never before been answered by a full throng of adults, and the bombardment of sound startled him. This didn't last long. By the third time he felt their rousing response, he had settled in, and it gave him strength and courage. When the congregation stood, their cushioned folding seats snapped up to close, pitter-patting around the grand room. When they sat, their bodies hit all at once in a terrific thud, making the *bimah* floor bounce. Up and down, prayer and response, silence and bowing, timing his cues.

His brother told Adam later the Cantor was mouthing every word in case Adam screwed up.

No, the Cantor was lending me his big voice.

At last, they reached the Torah service.

Rabbi Ellenbaum stood by his side as Adam approached the Ark and opened its doors. The Cantor placed the Torah in Adam's arms, the scrolls bulky, heavier than he expected. Encumbered by his suit, his tie, his tie clasp, his tallit, Adam grabbed at the wooden dowels emerging from the bottom, speeding his hands down to get a better grip.

If I drop the Torah, I will starve for forty days.

It was time to face the congregation.

There were more people than Adam had ever seen in the synagogue, far more people than he knew. His cousins Harry and Frances sat directly behind his parents, one of their sons back from Vietnam, the other with long hair fighting his formal outfit. Michael Mason was in the fourth row, spiffed up with a sports jacket, Suvan by his side, decked out in a checkered suit.

The synagogue's *gabbai*, the sergeant-at-arms, had plopped an electric-blue silk kippah on each of the boys' heads. The color matched Adam's suit. His name and the date of his bar mitzvah were imprinted on the cotton lining inside. Suvan alone, out of all his non-Jewish friends, was also wearing a tallit. Valerie was there in a stunning green dress, Gracie next to her in brilliant red, and when she stood, he saw, in high heels, Ryan canoodling with her a bit—*he must have declared his love, brave boy*. Next to Ryan sat Karsh, bulging out of his blue jacket, his tie already askew.

Costumed characters from a surreal play about Adam Miller.

His old pals had shown up, three rows further back, Jason whispering to Buddy, a sight that brought a twinge of the anger that had dogged Adam all year but without its potency, weak enough that Adam brushed it aside with only the slightest regret. There were no summer camp friends, no secret girlfriend, no last-minute "Fooled you!" Sharon surprise.

The Cantor's hand clamped down on Adam's shoulder, almost knocking them both over.

"*Shma!*" the Cantor coughed at Adam.

Muscle memory took over and Adam's mouth sang, "*Shma Yisrael, Adonai Eloheinu, Adonai Echad!*" "Listen Israel! The Lord is our God, God is One!" the credo that Jews repeat morning and night, on their lips when they die. A thrilling reverberation as three hundred people sang the declaration back.

Adam joined the procession through the sanctuary, carrying the massive, clumsy Torah. The rabbi, directly in front of Adam, stopped repeatedly without warning, and Adam bumped into him every time. Congregants leaned in to tap the Torah with the corner of their prayer shawl, then touching the corner to their lips in a vicarious kiss, nudging Adam in their motion, some of them missing the Torah entirely and touching down on Adam's head. Others reached across Adam to shake the rabbi's hand, the Cantor's hand, the president's hand.

Adam's arms were weary, his palms slick. He released slightly his grip on the Torah handles, snapping them lower to get a better hold, the Torah dropping down an inch or two on each attempt. It was going to fall. He was not going to make it back to the stage. Shame awaited.

Will they really make me fast?

The Junior Congregation kids sitting in the back saved Adam, singing the double-time melody they used every Saturday morning, a tune Adam knew in his bones. The rabbi and his entourage picked up speed to match the melody, leaving outstretched hands hanging as they returned to the *bimah*. At last, the colossal Torah was taken from

Adam's arms and placed on the table to be uncovered and unrolled. Adam's muscles trembled, twitched. His face was on fire.

It was time for the Torah reading.

Adam didn't have a chance to start because one of the floor-to-ceiling stained-glass windows behind the *bimah* shattered. Shards of blue, red, yellow, and green glass cut through the air, their colors flashing across Adam's tallit, replaced in the same instant by the startlingly bright morning light of the world outside pouring through the wound in the wall. There was a pause, an intake of breath as if the oxygen in the airy sanctuary had been sucked out by a giant.

Then voices, all at once: "What was that?… Police…!"

Congregants started to move, some stumbling over the legs of their seated neighbors, struggling to escape their row and the sanctuary, while others sped toward the *bimah* as if to ward off further danger or find an explanation in those slivers of shattered glass. The center aisle immediately became a bottleneck.

The rabbi was at the microphone. "Please stay calm! Please stay in your seats! Everyone!"

Most of the congregants, including the Millers, already on their feet, rallied to the rabbi's call, collected themselves, eager and thankful to follow a leader, but too many were overcome with dread to allow an orderly exodus.

There's something burning.

Adam ran toward the object on the *bimah* floor, a bottle on fire, but the Cantor barreled past him, his grace defying his bulk. He stomped on the end of the bottle while trying to take off his jacket, got tangled in the sleeves, jumping about on a hot foot. Adam pulled on the cuff to free the jacket, as the Cantor yelled, "Go from *bimah*!" His jacket finally off, the Cantor swung it like an axe straight down, over and over to extinguish the fuse. Michael and Suvan were next to Adam on the *bimah*, then Michael darted to the shattered window.

"Kids, please get off the *bimah* right now!" the rabbi commanded over the microphone. "Please go right out of the building! Everyone please stay calm. I'd like to ask the first three rows—please, Mr. Heckelman, be careful—listen to me, we don't want to make this worse than it already is—please, everyone, please be quiet—we need your cooperation, we want you all to file out the back and wait for us outside. Everyone else, stay in your places. Rows four through six, please go now."

Seth was at his side, pulling on Adam and Suvan, "Get off the *bimah*, idiots!"

"Rabbi, take Torahs," the Cantor cried.

"They're invaluable!" Suvan added.

Michael was leaning out through the broken window, Adam squeezing next to him to see what Michael was looking at. Michael turned and ran down from the *bimah*, up the wall aisle, edging sideways past the slow-footed adults. When Adam spun to follow him, he caught his electric-blue bar mitzvah jacket on the glass, felt it shear.

"All right, please, no running, please, now rows seven to nine, please file out, and I need four strong fellows to carry the Torahs."

Adam's friends were the first ones up as Seth distributed the scrolls. Seth, Valerie, Karsh, and Albert, each outside with a Torah, could be recognized most easily in the photo in the next day's *Long Island Press*, the fact that a girl, a *gentile*, was holding a Torah went unremarked by the reporter, but would not by the congregants.

Adam hesitated, then made his decision to pursue Michael Mason. The center aisle was filled in with people, so Adam opted instead to hug the side wall to reach the lobby as Michael had done. Adam sped out the main entrance and left his own bar mitzvah.

Michael was standing in the intersection of Parsons and Roosevelt Avenue, scanning in all four directions.

"They broke the God window!" Floyd yelled to Adam. "That boy, he knows who did it."

Michael made a mad dash east up Roosevelt Avenue, and in that instant, Adam knew Michael was involved.

I should never have trusted him. Floyd was right! And I'll go to prison for helping him case the joint. A family of thieves and, it turns out, anti-Semites after all.

Adam chased Michael. He wanted to arrest him, to kill him! But when they got close, instead of running away, Michael ran toward Adam, having thought they'd been running together.

"Come on, Miller; hurry up Sue-boy!"

Suvan was trotting after them.

"Look for a baseball hat. Blue. Come on, man!"

Adam cursed his suspicions, apologized to Michael in his heart, wondered again if Michael had a connection since he'd recognized the perpetrator, dismissed this thought, apologized again, as the three boys continued past the Watch Gang corner with all speed but no finish line, searching for a blue hat, any kind of hat, but it was late spring, nobody was wearing a hat. They ran for three blocks, spacing apart, then clumping up again as they passed the five- and eight-story apartment buildings that lined Roosevelt Avenue.

Michael stopped, bent over to catch his breath, straightened up. Suvan and Adam followed suit.

"Damn, Miller, what was that thing?"

"A Molotov cocktail," Suvan explained. "A gasoline-powered incendiary device used to attack Soviet Foreign Minister Molotov for signing a pact with Hitler. It should have exploded."

Gasoline? Michael would know how to build one. Stop that, Adam!

"And the Cantor," Michael said, "jumping up and down on it…"

"The man in the baseball hat…?" Adam probed.

Michael didn't respond. Adam regretted speaking, wrecking the friendship yet again before it could happen.

"Did you recognize him?" Suvan asked.

"Suvan!" Adam yelled, furious Suvan had voiced his own suspicions.

"No, asshole. Thought we'd catch him, that's all."

The boys circled around themselves, energy seeking purpose, looking inward, outward, for a glimpse of blue, but nothing.

"As pleasing as it might be to play the conquering heroes," Suvan said, "a rather large audience is waiting for the star to return."

They walked back in silence. Adam was waiting until the last possible moment to tell Michael that he couldn't smoke inside the Temple on Shabbat, but when they came in sight of the shul, Michael ground out his cigarette without being asked.

"I saw somebody looking, a Mets hat. He started running, I thought, 'what the fuck?' man."

"But he might have been running for some other reason."

"Might have. Dunno."

The Cantor was standing sentry when they reached the synagogue corner, huddling with Floyd, hurrying back to the crowd outside before he saw the boys approach.

"That guy again..." grumbled Michael.

"The Cantor comes from the old country," Adam jumped in protectively. "So he sometimes acts...you know..."

"The Cantor's cool. That guy from down south..."

"Floyd?"

"He came out three times to the parking lot to shoo me away that day. Didn't stop giving me the hairy eyeball all morning. I know what he's thinking now."

Adam remembered Floyd's warning about Michael Mason *loitering* outside.

Suvan said, puzzled, "But he's..."

"They're the worst. And Mr. Haben. Man, that *look*. And three-quarters of our teachers. You don't know what I mean."

"I receive..." Suvan stuttered, "I believe...a different look."

"That must be right," Michael agreed.

They didn't ask Adam. They knew Adam didn't get any looks. But his shul had been attacked and his bar mitzvah ruined. Only now, in the last few steps before rejoining his family, did the full desolation seep in. Adam's strength for words was finished.

The evacuated congregation had reassembled outside in clumps and clusters across the front concourse, in their tallitot and nylon yarmulkes. The men looked old and wrong outdoors, as if the building had vanished around them mid-prayer. A fire truck was parked on the curb. Adam heard the disturbing rattle of adults crying.

"There you are!" Adam's father roared, churning with anger and worry. "What were you thinking? You don't go near those things. And running off like that? You ripped your jacket. Don't let your mother see."

Adam's blue jacket was shredded. Adam tugged his tallit to cover it as best he could. But what did it matter? Adam saw his mother consoling someone.

"We'll fix it up," she was saying, "Don't worry."

"A shul burning... I thought I would never see it again..."

"It's a little bit of damage, that's all, Vera. But we're safe. Don't worry."

"I think you're right, Dad," Adam said, "about trying to get us out of the building,"

"We're not going anywhere," his father declared. "This is our home."

Cousin Harry had taken command after the attack but ceded his place to Detectives Riley and Fein, to Mr. Miller and the rabbi, to men Adam recognized but whose names he'd never registered.

"I'm sorry, we'll have to cordon off the building for an hour or two."

"It's a crime scene now." Cousin Harry winked at Adam.

"My son thinks somebody's trying to force us out, to sell the building for cheap."

"We'll investigate all possibilities, but I'm afraid your event will have to be canceled."

"We're in the middle of his bar mitzvah."

I have to learn another Torah reading? No, no...

"Hey, Riley, it's your boy Adam."

"It's *your* bar mitzvah?"

"Yeah."

"Tough break, kid."

"Mazel tov, Adam. You're a trooper. You'll be all right."

Adam was pulled away from the detectives by the Cantor, who lectured him on how stupid and dangerous but also brave he was for helping with the Molotov cocktail.

"Give us a minute to discuss the options," said the rabbi.

Congregants drifted toward their small committee, as Adam awaited his fate.

"We'll move it," Mr. Miller announced.

It took almost an hour for Adam's bar mitzvah to be relocated to the Junior Congregation sanctuary in the old synagogue building. The congregants rescued their belongings and trekked around the corner.

Mr. Selenko arrived after his morning rehearsal holding hands with Miss Nadel, too late for the fireworks but in time to join the procession to the old sanctuary for the rest of the service.

"You never cease to surprise," he said, his eyebrows and mustache jumping about like slashing swords. They both gave Adam a hug.

The Junior Congregation was banished to the dusty balcony, unlocked for the first time in Adam's life so the kids could sit up with the chandeliers.

Thank you, God, the Playboys *are gone.*

Everyone else crowded into the pews. The electric charge of upheaval offset the dim light and dark mahogany gloom. Adam was back on his own *bimah*, from which he'd led services so many times, ready for the Torah reading.

As they unrolled the scroll, Adam recognized it was not the right Torah, not the scroll he'd practiced on! If he had to read from a scroll he'd never seen, he was going to make mistakes on every verse. He clutched the pointer, squeezing it with all his dread. Adam's energy dribbled into his socks. The Cantor saw his terror.

"Is fine," he said.

But it wasn't fine. The calligraphy was from Mars, the alignment of the columns was bizarre, the crooked letters were hopping around with weirdly shaped antennae.

The Cantor lifted a hand to stop the proceedings, conferred with the rabbi, their heads bobbing in harmony while Adam shuddered. The rabbi made an impromptu speech, explaining that "in light of the morning's events" they were going to read from the Torah scroll that the Cantor had rescued from the Holocaust. He repeated the story of how, at the age of thirteen, the Cantor had buried the scroll in the cemetery at risk to his own life to save it from the Iron Guard, and how the Cantor returned after World War II to dig it up when there were still plenty of anti-Semites murdering the few Jewish survivors who had returned.

"And just as the Cantor refused to be intimidated, no one is going to scare us out of our neighborhood!"

Applause reverberated through the congregation, which the rabbi silenced. But Adam's stomach churned because the rescued Torah was also *not the right scroll.* Adam's relief was incalculable when the Cantor laid on the table not the rescued Torah from Romania but their practice Torah. The Cantor said into his ear, "We needed good story. We don't tell no one."

The Cantor squeezed Adam's shoulder again.

It was do or die. If Adam sang the first note wrong, he would be lost. If he fell into the musical trope for the haftarah instead of for the Torah, he would never recover.

But this was *Adam's* Torah scroll. The words were lined up properly, the calligraphy an old friend, the tiny crowns on top of the letters waved him on. The musical section of Adam's brain took command.

Adam's father was called up by name to chant the blessing before Adam began to read the next section. He hugged Adam tight, kissed him, and Adam surfed the third aliyah all the way home.

Adam was so worried about the fifth section, his weakest, that he made a mistake on a simple verse. The ancients were merciless, all of row six correcting Adam aloud at once, each singing out the proper way differently. Adam survived this onslaught because he knew what he'd done wrong, needed no assistance to correct himself. He blocked out the clamor, repeated the verse he had muffed, inhaled deeply, and let it ride.

When Seth was called to say the blessing for the sixth aliyah, the rabbi interrupted, talked about their family, two brothers making the Temple proud. Adam thought Seth was going to make a joke, but he said, "I know you've been taking my nunchucks." Adam blanched. "I got you your own."

"It's all right. I don't want—"

"You're doing good, almost done."

On the very last section, the maftir, Adam, took one last visual swallow of the black ink he had been singing, drilling, memorizing. He rolled the Torah scrolls closed, chanted a blessing, the scroll was lifted, the congregation stood, the scroll was covered up, the silver crown and cover restored. The people sat.

It was behind him.

Time for the haftarah. The light green stapled booklet with a drawing of a bar mitzvah boy that he'd been carrying for ten months opened to the right page from overuse.

"*Baruch...*" the Cantor's deep voice, sang the first word of the blessing before the haftarah.

"*Baruch...*" Adam sang slowly and clearly. The haftarah was embedded in his sinew and ligament and heart, its minor-key trope tapped on Adam's fingers through classes, bus rides, and every waiting moment. The closing blessings were the victory lap, accelerating, speeding up and down the roller coaster until the finale, up and up and up to the last words.

And Adam was done.

There was a mass of shuffling, cries of "*Yashe koi-ech!*" "May you have strength to do it again!" A short burst of clapping from guests who didn't know not to applaud in synagogue, quickly silenced by the regulars.

The rabbi spoke about what a terrible and wonderful day this had been, terrible because "our home has been attacked," and wonderful "to see a young person, our future, perform so magnificently despite the circumstances."

The Cantor nudged Adam toward the rabbi. The rabbi laid his hands on Adam's shoulders and bent down close to give him his "charge."

"Keep nodding as if I am blessing you," Rabbi Ellenbaum said.

"What?"

"I have three things to tell you, and I need you to keep nodding as if I am explaining to you your life's purpose. First, the box I'm giving you is empty. It's supposed to be a new Tanakh, but the Bible we inscribed got destroyed by the firemen. I promise we will get you a new one next week. Is that okay? Nod your head."

"It's fine. I understand."

"You don't need to speak. Considering what we've been through today, I don't think an empty box or the next thing I'm going to tell you should matter so much, if you can keep it in perspective. Can you promise me that you'll try to keep it in perspective? Nod your head."

"I promise."

"Just nod. We can't use the ballroom today, so your party is being set up in the auxiliary hall."

"The bingo room?"

"Exactly. And there are two tiny changes in the party that I hope won't upset you or make this day anything less than it ought to be for you. The first one, your parents have informed me, is that we are so far behind schedule that the ventriloquist had to leave to get to his next bar mitzvah in Great Neck."

"Thank God."

"Oh! Very good. I'm so pleased you're not upset. But there is one more thing. Unfortunately, we only have round tables in the auxiliary room. I told Mr. Heimovic last year to store the long tables, not to trash them, but he didn't listen to me. So unfortunately, and I am so very, very sorry about this because I understand you put a great deal of thought into the seating plan, but unfortunately there will be no dais."

Adam's mouth dropped open.

"Try to keep it in perspective."

Adam was so happy, he hugged the rabbi with all his strength. Adam felt the rabbi's hands settle down on his back. The congregation, moved by the sight of their embrace, emitted a swelling sigh.

Adam raised his head to look at the rabbi.

"I don't care about the party."

"Really?"

"Don't tell my parents."

"No, I won't. What a surprise you are."

Adam asked the rabbi to announce that he wanted to dedicate his bar mitzvah to Eduard Kuznetzov, Mark Dymshitz, and Yosef Mendelovich. Adam started to explain about the Leningrad Sixteen but the rabbi stopped him.

"I know who they are."

Adam asked the rabbi for one more favor.

"Can you thank my friends Valerie and Gracie and Albert and Karsh—Jamie Karsh—and Michael and Suvan for...you know...taking the Torahs and looking for...you know..."

"Your friends? Jamie Karsh I know. Tell me the other names again."

The rabbi called Adam's friends up to the *bimah* to thank them publicly for rescuing the Torahs. They each shook the rabbi's hand, and Michael Mason almost gave Adam a hug but thought better of it and punched him in the shoulder. Suvan did give Adam a hug. Gracie patted his shoulder, but Valerie leaned over and kissed him on the mouth. Adam felt faint.

"Bravo!" Selenko yelled out, which evoked a mix of laughter and murmuring, "Jewish?… Not Jewish?…" which the rabbi cut short by saying that in this one case, applause would be allowed.

Adam's friends went back to their seats, and Adam started to leave the *bimah*, dazed and dazzled, but came awake in time to pivot back to the Cantor.

"Thank you for everything."

Adam held out his hand, but the Cantor leaned forward, grabbed him by his shoulders, and pulled him into a tight squeeze. Adam hugged him back. The Cantor kissed Adam on both cheeks. Adam turned red.

"You make me proud, so proud, boychik. You never forget. I never forget."

Back in the first row, Adam didn't resist being tugged, hugged, kissed by parents, brother, grandmother, aunts. Seth started to pull the box out of Adam's hands, but Adam yanked it back. "Not now!"

"Who's that girl?" he whispered.

"Later!"

It was over.

A good show, but not a show, about becoming a man, but not in the way people think. Not about boys doing what men do, but about doing what only Adam could do better than Adam believed he could, with three hundred people joining in, a community, and no prizes awarded. Adam sang and lost his place and lost his friends and found his friends and found his place and found his voice.

ACKNOWLEDGMENTS

My unbounded thanks and love to my wife Shira, for tirelessly reading draft after draft with a loving and critical eye, and insisting that it was always a pleasure. And to my other earliest readers, my sons Yaniv and Nimrod, who gave me extensive comments and insights on multiple drafts and also led me to the title, and to my daughter Maayan, who caught up at the finish line. Equally important, my family inspired me to write the novel in the first place and never ceased to lead the cheerleading.

My deepest appreciation to my publisher and editor, Adam Bellow, and to David Hazony, Aleigha Kely, Jim Villaflores, Ashlyn Inman, John Mitchell, and everyone at Wicked Son Press for believing in this novel and for their thoughtful and constructive guidance in its revision.

My profound gratitude to Gideon Stein and Mary Ann Stein at the Moriah Fund, whose generosity, support, and forbearance enabled me to pursue the completion of this novel.

My thanks also to friends who read early or late drafts and provided crucial feedback, encouragement and fact checking: Gil Troy, Galina Vromen, Steve Greenberg, Bill Slot, Marshall Brinn, Len Levitt and Larry Derfner. Many thanks also to Julie Gray and her three fabulous readers, who gave essential coverage to an early draft of the manuscript, and to my meticulous proofreader, Greg John.

My appreciation and admiration to the members of the New Tel Aviv Writers Group, who provided incisive and insightful feedback, creative and precise suggestions, and unlimited encouragement:

Galina Vromen, Anna Levine, Miryam Sivan, Judy Colp Rubin, Michelle Orelle, Michal O'Dwyer, Eli Jacobs, and Keren Zehavi.

My thanks also to writers who I knew a lot, a little, or not at all, but who extended themselves to move this novel forward and into the hands of readers: Gil Troy, Colum McCann, Yossi Klein Halevi, Joshua Henkin, Eeta Prince Gibson, and Haim Watzman.

I continue to be amazed by the generosity of spirit of so many.